ONE

AN IMPRINT OF PUSHKIN PRESS

BAD ASIANS

'The four friends at the center of *Bad Asians* are bonded by the brutal pressures of their immigrant parents, racist schoolyard bullies, their crushing expectations of themselves, and their jealousy of local "it girl" and parent dream-come-true Grace, who seems incapable of doing any wrong . . . The ugly underbelly of internet notoriety—and whether or not it's survivable—is the riveting question *Bad Asians* explores'

SUSAN CHOI
author of *Flashlight*

'A smart, engrossing, beautifully observed examination of millennial friendship, social media and generational differences—I loved it'

FRANCESCA HORNAK
author of *So Good to See You*

'Li's masterful prose crackles with humor and insight, exploring the language of belonging—between cultures, generations, and the people we call friends. *Bad Asians* is a novel about the stories we tell ourselves and the ones we can never quite escape'

WEIKE WANG
author of *Rental House*

'Li captures the tenderness and mess of youth. A book that reminds us how little we know about the people we treasure most. It made me want to call my oldest friends!'

ROWAN HISAYO BUCHANAN
author of *Starling Days*

'A delightful dose of nostalgia and an affecting interrogation of the personas we put on, both online and in real life. . . These characters are messy in the best way; reading this novel was like catching up on the gossip of old classmates'

KATIE YEE
author of *Maggie: Or, A Man and a Woman Walk into a Bar*

'A wild, propulsive ride of a novel that explores the damaging spiral of social media fame with razor sharp observations and dialogue. *Bad Asians* is also a touching coming of age story about old friends who are trying to find their place in the world as they navigate the pressures of parental expectations, changing values in a close-knit multi-generation Asian immigrant community, identity and trying to hold onto their bonds as they are tested in every way'

EMMA NANAMI STRENNER
author of *The Other Heart*

'A richly drawn and emotionally honest novel that explores the complex entanglements between friendship and family, ambition and happiness, and childhood and adulthood. Lillian Li's writing is poignant, funny, and filled with keen observations—in short, a perfect read for anyone trying to make sense of our unsettled times'

ANGIE KIM
author of *Happiness Falls*

'Li's reflections on the experiences of immigrant families were heartbreaking, and her observations on internet culture were as hilarious as they were existentially depressing. The characters were so immediate and real, I felt for them so deeply from the first page'

CIARA BRODERICK
author of *Catfish*

© Margarita Corporan

LILLIAN LI is the author of *Number One Chinese Restaurant*, which was longlisted for the Women's Prize for Fiction and the Center for Fiction First Novel Prize. Her work has been featured in *The New York Times*, *Granta*, and *Travel + Leisure*. She is from the DC metro area and lives in Ann Arbor, Michigan.

BAD ASIANS

LILLIAN LI

ONE

AN IMPRINT OF PUSHKIN PRESS

ONE

An imprint of Pushkin Press

Somerset House, Strand

London WC2R 1LA

Copyright © Lillian Li, 2026

First published by Pushkin Press in 2026

Hardback ISBN 13: 978-1-80533-777-5
Trade Paperback ISBN 13: 978-1-80533-814-7

Map by Laura Hartman Maestro
Designed by Meryl Sussman Levavi

A CIP catalogue record for this title is available from the British Library

The authorised representative in the EEA is eucomply OÜ,
Pärnu mnt. 139b-14, 11317, Tallinn, Estonia,
hello@eucompliancepartner.com, +33757690241

Offset by Tetragon, London
Printed and bound in the United Kingdom by Clays Ltd, Elcograf S.p.A.

Pushkin Press is committed to a sustainable future for our
business, our readers and our planet. This book is made from
paper from forests that support responsible forestry.

FSC
www.fsc.org

MIX
Paper | Supporting
responsible forestry
FSC® C018072

www.pushkinpress.com

1 3 5 7 9 8 6 4 2

For Amanda and Anita,
the next generation of bad Asians

Bad Asians Locations
Presented by MeMe Productions

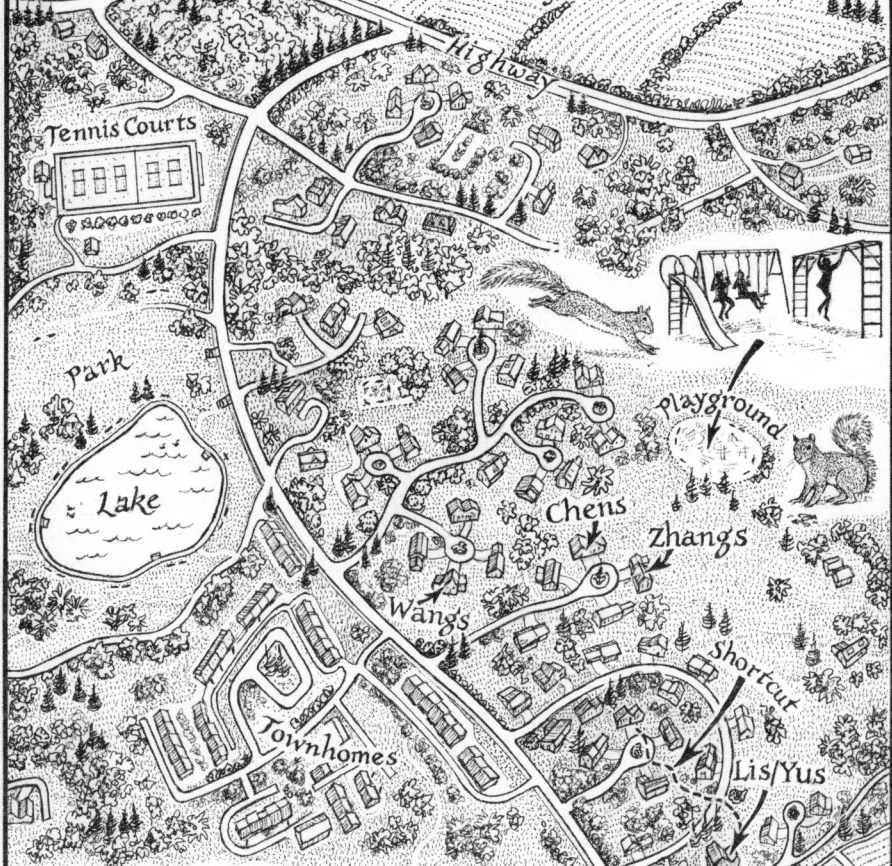

Highway

Tennis Courts

Park

Lake

Playground

Chens

Zhangs

Wangs

Shortcut

Townhomes

Lis/Yus

Lincoln Elementary School

THE ZHANGS
Zhang Bowei
Zhang Ming
Diana
Kevin
Tim

THE WANGS
Wang Tian
Wang Dong
Michael
Vivian

THE CHENS
ChenHe, "The Professor"
Chen Yue
Errol
Lucy

THE YUS
Yu Huang
Yu Zhao
Justin

THE LIS
Li Hong
Li Ping
Grace

Illustration by Laura Hartman Maestro ©2023

BAD ASIANS

July 2009

The doorbell rang again—such a familiar sound, but for the first time, the party was Diana's. Coming in from the deck, she checked herself in the hallway mirror. Her parents' kitchen was behind her. The other incoming students had picked over the sushi trays; the potstickers were long gone. In the corner of the mirror, her mother's reflection sank a cleaver into another watermelon. She caught Diana's eye and smiled. Her morning's worth of unspoken worries was now unfounded as well because her daughter had thrown a hell of a party.

The last guest was out on the stoop, wearing a tank top with a big crimson *H*. When Diana opened the door, the girl froze mid-greeting.

"Don't worry, you're in the right place." Diana pulled at the hem of her plain white shirt. "My Harvard swag must've gotten lost in the mail."

"You're Diana?" Her voice was awestruck.

Diana took a longer look and the girl stuck out her hand. She introduced herself as Jennifer Lo. Had Diana known a Jennifer? Perhaps back in high school.

"So great to see you," Diana said, to be safe.

She told Jennifer to leave her shoes on and led her out to the deck. Fifteen soon-to-be Harvard Law students were gathered in a large circle. Someone had taken Diana's spot closest to the screen door where the A/C was the strongest. Gathering her hair back into a ponytail, Diana felt sweat trickle through the strands. Beside her, Jennifer was staring.

"Are you excited?" Diana wiped her hand across her upper lip.

"I can't believe it," Jennifer said. She had a slightly nasal voice, one that vibrated in Diana's ears like a fly. "It's crazy. Like, yeah, Georgetown, Berkeley, Columbia, those weren't a big surprise."

Diana had heard some variation of that list from the other incoming students. After introductions were done, they'd displayed their law school acceptances like baseball cards, trying to sniff out who had the best collection.

"I heard this was the most competitive year to date," a boy had said. "Everyone is going back to school."

Diana had made the mistake of revealing that she'd barely gotten off the waitlist. "Harvard must have known that if I had to live at home for one more year, I'd kill myself and my parents."

No one had laughed, and one girl had apologized, as if on behalf of the university.

In the past hour, Diana had learned that self-deprecation was not a universal currency. These people around her had no interest in making fun of themselves. They were the best, and they expected the best in return. Diana had recovered from her earlier stumble, but inside she was reeling. Was this why her mother had always wanted her to find a more ambitious group of friends?

"It was Harvard or nothing for me," she said to Jennifer, shading her eyes from the sun. Two weeks earlier, she'd been set on Georgetown. Her friends didn't know she'd applied anywhere outside of DC. They thought the four of them would be rooming together in the house in Virginia. "Anywhere else would be a waste of money."

Jennifer's eyes widened and she nodded with religious ferocity.

"That's so true," she said. "Wow, you're exactly how I thought you'd be."

Diana started to ask Jennifer what she meant by that—had the girl been a year younger at the University of Maryland?—but the fly kept buzzing.

"I mean, first, Harvard, like, that's already *so* amazing. I wake up some days and think, *Was I dreaming?*"

Definitely younger, Diana decided. She'd been on the board of multiple clubs at Maryland. She was trying to place Jennifer's name against those club rosters when Jennifer riffled through the little pink purse hanging off her shoulder.

"So when I saw you . . ."

Jennifer pulled out the folded invitation Diana and her mother had sent to every local address on the incoming student list. Seeing the invitation for the first time since they'd been mailed brought back the strangeness of the past two weeks. Her parents were bursting to tell everyone they knew, but each time Diana had seen her friends, she'd acted as if nothing had happened.

The invitation was pushed into Diana's hands, along with a ballpoint pen. Jennifer looked at her expectantly.

"Is there something wrong with the invitation?" Diana said.

Jennifer turned red, as if the sun had dropped behind her head. "I'm sorry." She snatched back the invitation and pen.

"No, I'm sorry, I spaced out for a second." Diana smiled while sweat stung the corners of her eyes. "What were you asking about the invitation?"

"I was joking about the autograph, but you are Diana, right?" Jennifer asked. "From *Bad Asians*? On YouTube?"

A large drop of sweat slid from the top of Diana's head down the length of her back.

"What's *Bad Asians*?"

"Oh my god, this *amazing* short film about these four Asian kids who graduate into the recession. I swear you look just like the Diana who's in it."

Diana's entire face felt underwater. Cutting Jennifer off, she excused herself to check on the food and drinks. In the kitchen, her mother held up a large bowl of cubed watermelon.

"Have you been talking to everyone?" Her mother, crisp and elegant in her sundress and apron, quickly scanned Diana for stains. "Make any new friends?"

"I have to use the bathroom." Diana grabbed the bottom of her shirt and scraped it against her sweaty face.

Instead of yanking Diana's shirt back down and telling her to use a towel, her mother took the watermelon bowl out on the deck. She let the screen door slam shut, her one sign of disapproval. She was staying true to her word so far. Two weeks earlier, when Diana had thrown the heavy Harvard envelope onto the kitchen counter, her mother had burst into tears. She'd declared that her job was done. Whatever Diana did with the rest of her life, no one could say that her mother had failed her.

In her bathroom upstairs, Diana splashed cold water on her face. She opened her laptop, water dripping down her neck. She didn't know how to search for what she wanted because what she wanted was for Jennifer to be wrong. She typed in the words, and the video appeared. The same title, the same website, and the thumbnail picture displayed was unmistakably *them*.

But it was the number that threw her back on her bed. She covered her eyes. Her hands shook. The A/C clicked on and every inch of exposed skin prickled.

1,607,801 views.

She sat up and refreshed the page to make sure.

1,607,889 views.

She slammed her laptop shut, as if those 88 viewers were peering out at her through the screen. Eighty-eight new views in less than a minute. She regretted closing her laptop without studying the video further. Who had posted it? Grace, of course, but under what alias? For what purpose? Why *Bad Asians*? The title gave nothing away. A bad Asian was what you called yourself if you didn't like dim sum, or if you got a B in math. None of this made sense. Grace had been gone for almost nine months. They'd assumed the project had ended with her departure.

Diana's laptop had shut itself down and would not wake up no matter how hard she banged on the keyboard. The feeling of being watched crested over her again. Her laptop pumped hot air out of its sides, burning her legs, and now her mother was knocking on the bedroom door, her silence finally broken. Who had taught Diana to act this way? Her guests were downstairs and here she was hiding. She was going to have a lonely time in law school if she thought she could make friends at twenty-three the way she had when she was nine.

* * *

The deck smelled of hot wood and hot people. Jennifer beelined for Diana and pulled her into a small group of students who fell silent at her presence.

"Doesn't she look *exactly* like the Diana in that YouTube video?" Jennifer held on to Diana's wrist. The way everyone looked at her felt like Jennifer's grip—insistent, and much too intimate.

"It's uncanny," said the boy who'd earlier called Harvard, Yale, and Stanford the Holy Trinity.

"That video was like Wong Fu. Maybe better." This came from the girl who'd responded to Diana's waitlist joke with an apology.

"Who goes on YouTube?" Diana tried to change the subject. "I've used it, like, once for a school project."

Everyone said roughly the same thing. A high school friend had sent the video to them; someone from college had posted it to their Facebook group; a member of the Asian American Student Association had forwarded it to their listserv.

"That was White Hills Mall, right?" Jennifer said. Diana nearly nodded along with everyone else. If they looked to the left, they would see the playground where Grace had shot hours of what she'd called B-roll. "How cool is it that they shot it here?"

"Sounds pretty boring." Diana was hot enough to faint. She grabbed a cube of watermelon and bit down.

"Oh my god, can we watch it now?" Jennifer clapped her hands.

Diana's mouth was too full of fruit to object. Someone pulled out a BlackBerry. Someone else offered their new iPhone with its bigger screen.

"Can we go inside?" Jennifer suggested. "Use a computer?"

"Yes, it's too hot out here!"

"I could rewatch it a hundred times."

Like sharks drawn to blood in the water, the other groups on the deck gathered toward the shouts. Diana swallowed quickly and pulled a face.

"Sorry, guys, my laptop's got a bug. The only computer we could watch it on is in my dad's office, and he's strict about people going in there."

The partygoers drooped with disappointment. Who among them did not have strict parents?

Diana's mother's voice came from behind.

"I'm sure we can make an exception this once." Her mother was holding a near-empty tray of sushi from inside, ready to foist the last pieces onto somebody's plate. Ignorant to Diana's distress, she courted the crowd. "Your father doesn't have to know."

Already people were tramping into the kitchen and kicking off their shoes.

Diana, last in line, tried not to show her anger. Her mother gave her bottom a soft whack.

"Be a good host," she whispered. The screen door shut with a bang.

PART 1

FIRST YEAR POST-GRAD

2008 – 2009

CHAPTER ONE

September 2008

"Be a good host." Her mother took the bottle of wine Diana had been trying to sneak down to her friends in the basement. "Come say hello to the aunties and uncles."

"It's *your* party," Diana said, but she let herself be led away from where her friends were hiding.

Her mother's annual Back to School potluck was one of her larger parties. The house was full of people whose business Diana had known her entire life. In the hallway, Master Yi, with his thin radish of a head, promised to read her fortune later. His partner, Dr. Song, shouted after Diana that the whites of her eyes showed a liver inflammation. Passing through the open kitchen and living room, Diana's mother placed the confiscated bottle on top of the microwave, the only surface not covered with Tupperware. She reminded Diana's younger brothers to let the other kids have a turn at the Wii. Kevin and Tim continued to pummel each other's avatars in the boxing ring.

Entering the formal dining room, where her family never ate, Diana greeted her friends' parents, who were also her parents' longtime friends. Mr. and Mrs. Wang, Dr. and Mrs. Chen. Only Mrs. Yu, Justin's mother, was missing.

Beyond the mandatory questions about how Diana's job search was going, the parents were more likely to talk about her as if she weren't there than direct their conversation to her. Tonight, however, they looked up eagerly.

Her mother explained. "They want to know if you've heard from Grace Li."

"No." Although Diana had heard plenty *of* her. Grace Li was the golden child of their neighborhood. She'd graduated summa cum laude from Harvard this year, and to make matters worse, she was going straight to Harvard Law. The mood of the table, however, was conspiratorial. "Why? Did something happen?"

Her mother pushed her toward the empty seat next to her father. His mouth full of melon, he gave her shoulder a hearty pat.

Across from her, Dr. Chen pointed a toothpick. "These old gossips heard that Grace is back in town this week. They think she's come to deal with her mother's foreclosures while Big Lady Li runs and hides in China."

Dr. Chen was her friend Errol's father, and although he hadn't taught since his PhD program his nickname was "The Professor." He had the waxy pallor of someone perpetually studying under candlelight. Talented at making people feel stupid or immoral, Dr. Chen only looked soft with his wife beside him.

"*Big Lady* my ass," Mrs. Chen said, plump and upright where her husband was thin and stooped. "She couldn't afford to invest in those properties in the first place. What's difficult about staying within your means? At the end of the day, you only have yourself to blame." Mrs. Chen looked at Diana as if she were a rat stuck in a maze. "Look at you kids. You get a few rejections and say there's no jobs? We had the guts to move to a new country. Everyone your age is weak."

The Chens were Diana's next-door neighbors. Since their son Errol had left Microsoft last month, he'd hidden in Diana's basement every day, and not just at these parties.

The parents speculated whether the big mansion in Potomac was the culprit behind Mrs. Li's problems. Diana's mother had heard through her Blüm network that the mansion was worth half a million less than what Mrs. Li had paid in '07. With her equity tied up, she'd had no choice but to foreclose on the properties she'd been flipping. The Wangs, her friend Vivian's parents, polled the room to see if buying the mansion would be tacky. They felt the exchange was fair, given the projects Ms. Li had canceled with their contracting company.

While no one was looking, Diana filled a cup with the Moutai that Mr. Wang had brought. Her cheeks went bright red after her first burning swallow. No wonder everyone at the table was so worked up.

"You little alcoholic." Her mother surprised her from behind with a cool hand to her hot cheek. She grabbed Diana's elbow and scrubbed at a stain Diana hadn't noticed.

Diana yanked her arm away and got up from the table. Her mother followed her into the kitchen. To Diana's surprise, she gave her back the bottle of wine.

"Invite Grace out while she's in town," her mother said. "I don't know why you two didn't stay in touch. She's the kind of friend I wished you would make." She looked meaningfully at the basement door, her voice low in case the other parents overheard.

"If I do, my loser friends are coming too," Diana said loudly. "You want us to find out if her mom lost their money?"

Her mother gave her elbow stain one last hard wipe, her temperate tone cracking. "I want you to go to law school and get out of my house. If you've got any sense left, you'd ask Grace to tutor you."

* * *

Bounding down the basement stairs, Diana tossed the bottle to her friends. "You'll never guess what I heard about Grace Li!"

From the couch, Justin, Vivian, and Errol looked up with alarm, as if she'd announced a ghost or a celebrity. In a way, Grace Li was both. Almost a decade had passed since they'd last seen her in person, and yet days since they'd heard her name used against them.

Diana repeated what she'd heard upstairs. "I can't believe she's going to law school *and* coming down to help her mom. What a perfect daughter."

"As if my parents don't talk about her enough." Vivian stopped fussing with the cowlicks in Errol's hair and pressed her fingers against her temples. Her foxlike prettiness made her gestures as dramatic as an actress's.

Diana had worse news: "We have to get dinner with her. Or I do, so you guys are coming too."

"Does Grace know what's going on with us?" Errol lifted his head off Vivian's lap. In his oversized shirt, he looked thin and jumpy, like a rabbit that had sensed a shift in the wind.

Diana gestured for the wine back and took a sip off the top. "Duh. Everybody talks."

That spring, the four of them had graduated from Maryland's class of '08 only to move back in with their parents. A fate more embarrassing than death, especially given that Diana, Vivian, and Justin had majored in economics and should have seen what was coming. They'd heard rumblings from the year above, and by the final semester, every conversation was around which companies were still hiring. Yet each of them had believed they were the exception, like Errol, who at nineteen was hired by Microsoft. Up until graduation, they were focused on their careers, while everyone else was scrambling for a salary. Although they'd been horrified when Errol had quit his job after three months—like burning a winning lottery ticket!—once he'd moved back from Seattle, they could almost pretend their situation was a choice. The four of them formed a line of defense against the cautionary tales other people hoped to make of them.

"No way am I going just to hear her say"—Vivian made her voice simper—"*The recession has been hard on everyone.* Like, girl, you're at the best law school in the country."

"Where's she staying if everything's been foreclosed?" Errol's attention never lasted long.

"I think she's at her mom's place in Potomac." Justin looked up from his phone, his broad face as blank as an Easter Island statue. Noticing their surprise, he said, "She texted me a few days ago."

"What?" Diana lunged for his phone. Justin held her back easily with one hand. "Why didn't I know that? What kind of psycho doesn't bring that up?"

"I forgot until now." Justin slipped the phone into his pocket. His new shoulder muscles hunched up by his ears. "She wanted to grab dinner, but she didn't say she was going back and forth from Harvard. She said she's here until January."

When it came to Grace even Justin was driven to gossip. They argued about what this discrepancy could mean. Diana was sure it was a money thing. Errol hoped she'd dropped out, but Vivian thought law students could defer for a semester. After decades of falling short to Grace in every measurable race, they yearned to hear that she'd fallen off the track entirely.

Was their glee a simple case of unresolved childhood rivalry? Grace had been the teachers' favorite not only from pre-K to eighth grade, but also at Ann Hua Chinese School on Saturday mornings. While their piano teacher Miss Elena had taped rulers to their wrists, Grace had been allowed to play Chopin freely. Even on the tennis courts with Coach Stevens, Grace was singled out for a serve that seemed to freeze time before moving too fast to see. Their parents often compared their kids, but with Grace the group detected a real longing when they said, "Why couldn't I have had a child like Mrs. Li's?"

After Grace had left for boarding school in ninth grade, the comparisons grew more outlandish. Their parents would report not only her academic wins, but also how her roommate was a princess from Thailand. Vivian winning homecoming queen paled in comparison to Grace dating the heir of a Japanese car company. And while Diana's full ride to the University of Maryland was impressive, did she know that Harvard had offered Grace four years' tuition at full price? This equation also meant that Errol's Microsoft offer was on par with Grace going straight from Harvard undergrad to Harvard Law. As if earning six figures now was the same as potentially making partner in a decade. Not even Justin, whose mother was happy no matter what he did, could shake Grace's shadow. Not when everyone knew that he and his mother had lived in Mrs. Li's basement for two years after his parents had separated and they'd moved back from Iowa.

Yet Diana believed that any sense of competition she felt toward Grace began years before they'd been born. This fight was inherited, the seed planted the day Diana's parents had moved into this neighborhood.

Diana's parents, the Zhangs, had grown up a neurosurgeon's son and a diplomat's daughter. In China, they'd only known people like themselves. Before immigrating to Maryland, they'd asked around for a neighborhood of the right kind of families. Friends had recommended North Potomac. A tract outside Gaithersburg with its own top-ranked elementary school, North Potomac had as many Chinese families as the rest of Montgomery County, but was less affordable, and therefore less . . . messy.

Long and narrow like a peninsula, the community they chose was bisected by one main road, an artery that eventually led to the interstate. On one side were the single-family homes, spread out in roomy cul-de-sacs with names like Snapdragon Circle. On the other were the rentals, smaller townhomes framing shared parking lots, everything packed tight as tiles. Diana's parents had liked that the larger homes could be seen from their townhouse, a tantalizing vision of where they hoped to earn their place.

A vision more urgent when they learned that their neighbor, Mr. Yu, had never finished college. He'd violated his university's morality laws by being engaged to three women at the same time. Mrs. Yu, a salon girl with no education, was the one who'd stuck around. Next door to the Yus, Dr. and Mrs. Chen seemed better positioned, both scientists at the NIH labs, but the entire block could hear them fighting late into the night, and you had to think a divorce was coming. One more house over was Mrs. Li, a farmer's daughter turned scholar turned stay-at-home wife. By some witchcraft, she had persuaded her husband to trade a VP position at his father's company for an accounting master's at UMD. Now Mr. Li was waiting tables to pay for night classes while Mrs. Li lay around and watched movies.

All this had poured out of Mrs. Wang, who'd been the first to welcome the Zhangs with a basket of overripe peaches. She looked too young and pretty to be the mother of the little boy she called Michael clinging to her leg. Diana's parents exchanged a glance when she mentioned she was her husband's secretary. Mrs. Wang said she hoped they wouldn't judge Mr. Wang for being uneducated. He was a "bit" older than them, and everyone remembered how China used to be—the kids sent down to work the fields, and the classrooms shuttered. He'd left to make his own success. Wasn't that why they were all here? People like them had to stick together.

When Diana's parents had shut their door, they'd looked at the walls connecting them to these strange new neighbors, their backgrounds diverse and parentage blurry. Back home, the hierarchies were set in stone, down to which cemetery your loved ones could bury you in. Neighbors were also coworkers, entire apartment complexes owned by one government corporation or another. While they'd known that moving to a new country meant starting over, her parents now understood what it meant to have their pasts wiped clean. In this neighborhood of clear divisions, America required those who looked alike to hold each other as equals.

In no alternate universe across the ocean would the Zhangs have ended up in the same neighborhood with the Wangs, the Yus, the Chens, and the Lis, and yet here they were, throwing parties, raising children, and doing business together. Success was measured by generations. Before Diana's parents became her parents, they'd already conceived of her purpose. She would reestablish, in this new world, their family's rightful rank and order.

"Should I text her back?" Justin asked from the couch.

"I already did." Although she'd upgraded her ancient flip phone last year, she'd found Grace's number easily. "We're getting dinner on Monday, at the CPK. I swear—what would you guys do without me?"

* * *

Despite the exclamation points in her texts, Grace was more nervous than Diana had expected. She'd barely spoken during the drive. Pulling into the mall parking lot, Diana had the urge to put an arm around Grace's shoulders, something she'd never done when they'd been kids.

"Are you sure it's okay?" Grace tucked her long hair behind both ears. "I don't want to intrude on a tradition."

Despite the warm weather, Grace wore an oversized cardigan that she wrapped tight around her body. Growing up, she'd been more nice-looking than pretty, but now that her face was thinner, her eyes had turned large and arresting. Diana was struck by how fragile Grace seemed, as if the weight she'd lost had included her heavy sense of superiority.

Diana said, "Eating at the California Pizza Kitchen is not a tradition." And then, more gently, "You're the guest of honor. They're excited to see you again."

The rest of the group was already seated by the time they arrived. They'd gotten their drink orders in too, and frosty glasses of light beer stood guard over the table.

"I brought Grace." Diana went around the table, hooking her arm around the boys' necks and pressing her cheek against Vivian's. She whispered, "Behave," to each of them.

Justin stood to give Grace a hug. Once the shy one in the group, he now took every chance to show off his new muscles. Grace blinked like she'd never seen someone that bulked out before.

"Don't press too hard," she said, and everyone laughed.

When Grace took her seat at the head of the table, Vivian gave her arm a squeeze and offered her a Pepcid to counteract the flush they all suffered when drinking.

"You're a lifesaver," Grace said.

Vivian, easy to blush, went as red as if she'd already finished her beer.

"Welcome back." Errol bobbed his head.

"Hey there, Errol," Grace replied, and somehow this simple greeting stopped his squirming.

They were all looking at Grace now, who rather than shrinking away was studying each of them in turn. For the first time, Diana wondered if Grace was as fascinated with them as they all were with her.

Hours later, waiting parties kept their table in sight, coveting their good time. They had finished a second round of drinks. Soon a third would be under consideration.

They'd forgotten that beyond Grace's outward markers of success, she also possessed a magnetism that made them eager to impress her. Diana laughed at stories she'd heard so many times that she thought they'd never again amuse her. For once, the group didn't have to hide that they were living with their parents or avoid questions like "What did you do today?" Despite their initial intentions, they focused on their shared pasts, understanding that everyone was at home for an unhappy reason.

"Wait." Grace looked a little awestruck. "I forgot you guys have been friends since fourth grade."

"Well," Diana said. "You remember how we all ended up in Mrs. Strider's class."

She began with the remarkable fact that Errol had skipped two grades to end up in their year at Lincoln Elementary. His new-found celebrity came with certain allowances. To help him adjust to being seven years old in fourth grade, the rest of them, including Grace, had been assigned to sit at his table. Besides Errol, these were not the desk mates Diana would have chosen.

"No offense," Diana said to the group. Until that point she'd had her whole life to befriend Vivian and Grace. In any other suburb in America, simply being Asian and a girl would have been enough to bond them. In North Potomac? They had so many Chinese kids alone that when Justin had arrived that summer, no one noticed.

Diana handed the story over to Errol, who said that, despite his supposed guardians, trouble had found him in the shape of Warren Cho. Rumored to be twelve, Warren had recently emigrated from Korea and his parents had refused to put him in ESL. A private English tutor pulled him out of class every morning. The classroom joke was that Warren was Opposite Errol.

Warren and the posse of boys who followed him around soon made a sport of stranding Errol on an old calisthenics set out of view of the recess aides. One day Warren had instructed his gang to scatter broken glass under the eight-foot bar to ensure Errol could not jump down. Warren had been lifting Errol, shoeless, into the air when Diana, Vivian, and Justin had found them.

At the restaurant, Errol did his impression of Warren, who had curled his face into a sneer. "Babysitters," he'd said to his posse.

Drumming his fingers on the table, Errol grinned. "And when he wasn't paying attention, I released my secret weapon."

"The baby's pissing himself!" One of the boys had pointed and screamed.

Errol's pee ran down his legs and onto Warren's Air Jordans. Warren had flung Errol onto the ground, thankfully beyond the broken glass, where he scrabbled on all fours until he was safe behind Diana and the others.

Vivian took over next. "That made things way worse. Classic Error." She gave him a kiss on the cheek.

Her social standing precarious with the popular girls of their grade, Vivian usually kept her distance from Diana and Errol on their walk home. That afternoon, however, Vivian had pressed right up against Diana, hissing that Warren's gang had been following them for blocks. Soon, the other kids would be safe in their homes, while their own parents wouldn't be back until dinner. With no adults to save them, a wild chase had ensued, rocks raining against their heels. Diana had found a shortcut that brought them to the cul-de-sac across the street from school. They'd still been a hundred yards away from the safety of adults when—

"In here!" Justin shouted, surprising the tables around them. He took over the last lap of their story.

This was Diana's favorite part, and her heart pumped as if she were back in the garage that Justin had jumped out of thirteen years ago. She could see Warren and his friends coming over the hill, the garage door closing with excruciating slowness until the last crack of light disappeared and a hail of rocks smashed against the metal door.

Laughing with Grace, Diana felt an itch in her brain. The story was incomplete. It hadn't ended in the dark garage. In losing touch with Grace over the years, they'd had to leave out the real finale.

Eventually their eyes had adjusted enough to the dark to see the wooden stairs. The four of them had entered a house that Diana hadn't seen since Grace's father had left and Grace's mother had stopped hosting potluck dinners.

"And of course." Diana pointed to Grace. The noisy restaurant faded around them. "You were there too."

Thirteen years ago, their foursome had walked into the Lis' kitchen, where Grace had sat eating a sliced Asian pear. Nine-year-old Grace had put her index finger to her lips, and twenty-two-year-old Grace did the same at the head of their table.

"Justin's mom is cutting hair downstairs," Grace recited. For a moment, her younger self was curled within the larger flower of her face.

Looking through the front windows, Grace had noted that

Warren's group was waiting outside. "You shouldn't have brought them here," she'd said to Justin. She'd climbed the stairs to the second floor, which she'd said was off-limits to everyone. "Warren's crazy. You'll have to hide out here every day after school."

Again, they had come to an end, but for Diana the story kept zooming forward, zooming out, until that moment in the garage was one point among many of frustrated boy fury being spent. She'd not only skipped over Grace in the kitchen, but also the harassment the four of them had faced for the rest of fourth grade. Long after Warren lost interest, there would be another boy trying to get in with that group, another humiliation waiting in their desk or jacket. In this house, however, their foursome had been safe. A safety that had spread beyond Warren's gang. The other kids Diana would grow up with, Grace included, she couldn't help rooting against. Her parents compared her to everyone she knew, and the only way to win was if they were to lose. Diana thought back to those afternoons after school in Grace's and Justin's house, those two years where no adult was watching. How lucky she was to meet her friends without their parents, to see who they really were.

Diana searched for their waiter, ready to put in that next round after all. Seeing this, Grace reached into the pocket of her cardigan. Diana was ready to fight for the check when Grace pulled out an unmarked DVD.

"Before I forget," she said. "Do you remember the movie we made together?"

* * *

While the others took the northbound loop in Justin's car, Diana drove south to deliver Grace to her mother's mansion. Merging onto the highway, Diana counted down the minutes until she could talk with her friends. They must be debriefing about the bombshell Grace had dropped when she'd pulled out that DVD. Diana watched the full moon out of the corner of her eye, pretending to race it the way she had when she was a kid.

Grace leaned over and turned the radio down. Diana braced for another pitch about her documentary of "the recession at a personal scale." As she'd told them at the restaurant, the group would be the stars. She would use the footage she'd shot of them in eighth grade and pair it with new material. She was wasting her breath. None of them wanted the lowest point in their life captured forever.

Instead, Grace said, "It's crazy that you guys have stayed friends all these years." She curled up in the corner of her seat. "My oldest friend is from college. *Junior year* of college."

"You grew up with us too."

"It's not the same." Grace burrowed deeper, pressing her cheek against the cradle of her seat belt. "I wasn't part of the group."

Looking at Grace, squished like a squirrel in a tree hollow, Diana felt as if she'd stepped on a tiny piece of glass. When Grace had confessed at the restaurant that she'd dropped out of Harvard for her documentary project, the foolishness of that decision had delighted them. Now Diana was embarrassed by her breathless desire to rejoin her friends. She should know more than anyone what it felt like to be in a crowd of people whispering about her failure. Even if they hadn't been in touch since they were thirteen, Diana had once seen Grace every day after school. It wasn't Grace's fault that in the intervening years she'd become their impossible standard.

"Trust me, you're not missing much. Do you remember Justin in fourth grade? Tracing those manga characters under his desk?"

Grace laughed. "Mrs. Strider had to call on him three or four times before he'd answer."

"Well, he decided artists didn't make enough money and being a consultant was his real dream. He was obsessed with getting into the Big Three. He thought he was settling for an internship at PWC, and they didn't even hire him after. His new obsession is the gym. He's more ripped than those dudes he used to draw, and he texts his trainer so much they're basically dating."

Having sacrificed Justin, Diana could have stopped there. She was not exactly apologizing. She only wanted to give Grace enough dirt that she might find herself on even ground.

She told Grace that Vivian was still Asian girl basic. Did she remember the milky pens and rolling backpack in elementary school; the orange-streak highlights in seventh grade? In high school Vivian had upgraded to Coach wristlets and digital perms. Her parents threw her a birthday party every year, timed to show off a new home renovation. The rumor was that their company hired workers without papers, which allowed them to set their prices so low.

"That's why my mom used Mr. Wang's contractors to flip her houses," Grace said. "All anyone cares about is money."

"Totally," Diana said. "Vivian's parents have been trying to get her to break up with Errol since he quit Microsoft."

"'Vivian will marry rich.'" Grace perked up, reciting their parents' insistent belief, which had all but sealed Vivian's fate.

"Honestly, I'd do the same if she were my daughter. Who quits a job like that? Even before everything tanked, only a few UMD kids got Microsoft offers. You'll hear him bitch about how bored he was. He could've gotten us hired if he'd stuck it out for longer than three months. Helped refer us to a communications role, or something in marketing. Everyone knows the hardest job to get is the first one."

Diana could rile herself up by thinking about how proud she'd been when Errol had gotten his Microsoft offer. His parents used to call him *retarded* in front of everyone they knew. She alone had believed in his genius. Since they were kids, she'd understood that spacey look in his eyes, and the way his brain whizzed past ideas so fast he seemed slow.

"He's never acted like everyone else. Remember how he'd whip out his thing and pee right there on the playground? Just to get a few more minutes out of recess."

Long after Errol had tested into the 99th percentile for first through third grade, Diana was still fighting kids who called him names. He felt more like a little brother than the two she had. Unlike Kevin and Tim, Errol had needed her protection. Forget Microsoft, he'd have flunked out of school if she hadn't made sure he got to his classes on time. Did this mean he owed her? Of course not, and yet if their positions had been switched, she would have found the hiring managers in software development, taken them out to lunch, and talked Errol up until he was working right there with her. She would have done the same for Vivian and Justin too. That was what made the group different from the other friends they'd made. For them, there was no limit to what she would do.

Diana didn't know how long she'd been talking when Grace pointed up ahead. "Turn right after this light."

They'd reached the street that led to Grace's mother's house. Diana could barely see the *No Outlet* sign from earlier. The community road had no streetlamps. Miserly glass lanterns guarded the serpentine drives. Diana's headlights plowed the darkness off the road and iron gates glimmered like spider webs. Flanking the gates, giant evergreens partially hid the stately mansions, which only accentuated their grandness.

"I can't believe your mom lives in that place by herself." Diana slowed down when she reached the last driveway.

"She likes a lot of space."

Up at the end of the steep curving drive, Grace's mother's house was visible under the full moon. A gleaming obelisk of yellow brick, the mansion looked like it had been airdropped from Spain, with its red-tiled roof and large arch-like windows. Diana had seen pictures when Grace's mother had bought the house last year. No one knew what it looked like inside.

Mrs. Li's house might have been the smallest one in the neighborhood, but up on that hill, it was also the tallest and the brightest. The mansion's big iron gate was propped open by a small pile of bricks. The steepness of the driveway was protection enough.

Diana's beater whined from the effort. She hadn't had to go up the hill earlier. Grace had been waiting by the gate. The longer Diana's car climbed, the stranger this seemed. Why would Grace walk so far down to meet her? What hadn't she wanted Diana to see?

After everything Diana had shared, the amount she knew about Grace felt paltry in comparison. She'd made a movie of them in eighth grade. She'd dropped out of law school. Her mother had given up flipping houses.

Diana's mother always said, "You don't give up more secrets than you get." Diana felt the vertigo of the hill.

At the top, Diana put the car in park and said, "I hate to do this. Can I use your bathroom?"

"Oh." If Diana had actually needed to pee, Grace's tone would've made her feel small for asking.

"I can pee in the bushes if it's easier."

"No, I'm sorry." Grace rubbed a knuckle back and forth under her eye. "You can use the bathroom. It's just . . . well, you'll see."

"Thank you." Diana's curiosity swelled. "My bladder's bursting."

Rather than enter through the front door, Grace led Diana around the back of the house. They walked down a small grassy slope toward what must have been the patio. No motion sensor light clicked on; they had only the moonlight to guide them.

"You'll have to use the basement bathroom," Grace said. "My mom's redoing the rest of the house while she's out of the country. They cut the utilities to fix the pipes and wires."

An obvious lie. No one foreclosed on a bunch of properties and then turned around and planned a renovation. They must be pinching pennies on their electric bill.

The door to the basement wouldn't slide open until Grace put her full weight against the handle. Inside, the air was chilly like a cave.

"You don't have to take off your shoes," Grace said. "The bathroom is back there."

Grace handed Diana a flashlight from the floor. The room shot into view, so glaringly empty that Diana thought her eyes were still catching up. Dust patterns on the terra-cotta tiles revealed where the furniture had been.

While Diana took in the room, Grace went up the stairs, saying that she'd be back with a gallon jug of water, for "flushing purposes." The chill of the basement caught up to Diana. Grace had to be joking. The utilities couldn't be cut. Or maybe Mrs. Li *was* redoing the house with what money she had left to help boost the property value. That made more sense. Diana had let her speculations run too wild. A few seconds later, Grace's footsteps padded overhead, and Diana listened until she could no longer hear them. She shut off her flashlight and crept up the basement stairs. She poked her head through the half-open door. In front of her was a hallway that led into a kitchen. No signs of a renovation. Like the basement, the room was empty.

Her eyes adjusted again. Crumpled McDonald's bags littered the kitchen island. She took a few more steps. A sleeping bag lay unfurled on the ground. All the tiny hairs on her body went straight up when she heard the floor creak under her weight. Sounds echoed without anything to muffle them.

When Diana turned back toward the basement stairs, Grace was right there, holding a plastic jug. Diana shrieked at the sight of her.

"Sorry for scaring you," Grace said.

"I wanted to see what you were hiding." Diana was too shaken to pretend otherwise. "I didn't need to use the bathroom."

Grace put down the jug and took Diana's wrist. Diana let herself be led through the front door she'd been barred from entering.

Outside, the moonlight spilled their shadows against the brick walkway. Diana couldn't find a trace of anger on Grace. She just looked a little tired.

"Is everything okay?" Diana asked.

"Of course." Grace wrapped her cardigan tighter. "LA's an expensive city, but it's where you have to go if you want to make movies."

The story spilled out. What Grace had told them at the restaurant was true: She'd dropped out of law school because she had no intention of becoming a lawyer. The problem was that she could hardly use the tuition money her mother had given her on a dream that her mother would never approve. She had until January to save enough money for the move, when a friend would be subletting his apartment in Koreatown. Not paying rent now would make this deadline possible. She had gotten a job at Best Buy and another one at McDonald's, in part to use the employee discounts. A free trial at the local gym took care of her showers. Compared to Massachusetts, Maryland winters were mild, and worst-case scenario, she'd buy a generator and resell it.

"Aren't you worried you'll get in trouble?" Diana felt childish as soon as she said this.

"My mom lost this house a few weeks ago. There's been so many foreclosures that no one's come by to check. Or change the locks." Grace glanced off to the side. "I read it could be months before the bank tries to sell this place, and it's huge, who'd buy it? I'm pretty lucky to have a free roof over my head."

Diana glanced at the mansion's pitch-black windows. The September night air was like a wet paper towel against her bare skin.

"I want to help," she said.

Grace threw her arms around Diana, a fierce hug that briefly winded her. "You'll be in my movie?"

Diana had meant that Grace could stay with her and her parents.

"Well . . ." Diana looked down at her feet.

"I want to capture what your lives are like right now. Just like I did in eighth grade." Grace pressed her hands together in a plea. "I know this is a huge favor to ask, but I need your help. I'd do anything to make this movie."

Snatches of memory swept past Diana like a conversation distorted by wind. Grace turning up in the first week of eighth grade with a video camera the size of a loaf of bread. Following them around and asking them questions. They'd never gotten to see the final product and Diana had assumed that Grace had lost interest, especially after she'd left for boarding school the next year.

Instead, Grace had not only made this first movie, but she'd also spent her four years at Andover making more. At Harvard, however, she had decided against majoring in film studies. She'd chosen to be practical and study econ like everyone else. When she had started law school she'd considered entertainment law, a path parallel to the one she'd stopped traveling. She'd been happy with this compromise, or so she'd thought, until she'd found the DVD in a box of childhood things her mother had sent her for safekeeping.

"You'll see when you watch it," Grace had said at dinner. She'd waved the plastic case. "We were so much more than what our parents told us we could be. We once had our own dreams. I wouldn't know that if we hadn't made that movie."

While Diana had dismissed the idea at the restaurant, her interest had been piqued. Not about her dreams—who cared what an eighth grader wanted to be—but that she was more than her parents could see. Her entire life she'd been told that she was the selfish one. The one always in trouble for pushing to the front of the line, her loud voice forcing everyone else's into submission.

"Selfish to your core," her mother would say after she'd once again demanded her way.

"If she doesn't start thinking about others," the other parents would add, "she'll turn into a real monster."

Diana had worked hard to reform, but tonight she'd proven the parents right again. She'd orchestrated the dinner and wormed her way into Grace's house to satisfy her own curiosity. She'd thought she'd be happy with what she'd found. For years, Grace's ability to hold herself apart had flooded Diana with envy. She had thought that its absence now would be like the absence of weight. Instead, where her envy had lived was left carved out and cavernous.

She imagined herself years in the future watching the person she was today. She had a choice to make. Stay hollow and empty, or look back proudly at how far she'd come, at how much could change on the face of one selfless decision.

"Alright," she said. "Why don't you come over Saturday? I'll make sure everyone else is there too. You can use my basement to shoot. It'll be a trial. If we're uncomfortable, we stop."

"I promise." Grace gripped Diana's hands. "You won't regret this. Thank you." She stepped back through the darkened threshold. "Have a safe drive."

Cranking up the heat in the car, Diana shook off the last of the chill. The moon had risen, its light cold and remote. The house looked even lonelier up on that hill, shrinking in her rearview mirror.

* * *

In the playground behind Diana's house, Errol waved off her explanation. "Don't tell me you fell for that." He pumped his legs to get his swing higher.

"You weren't there." Diana zipped the hoodie she'd grabbed from her house. Grace wanting her to see the emptied mansion didn't mean what she'd seen was fake. "She's living without any heat, water, or electricity."

"So they did run out of money." Vivian took a seat in the swing next to Errol's. "And she still paid for dinner?"

"Exactly." Diana shot Errol a look. They'd babied him for years and now he assumed everyone was comfortable asking for help. "If—and that's a big if—she wants to feel like she tricked us into being in her movie, I had to let her save a little face."

"I'm in," Justin said to her surprise. He rarely chose sides. "You said she's coming over Saturday? I'll try to get out of the Blüm meeting early."

"I want to help," Vivian said. She turned to Errol. "Is that okay?"

Errol kicked up a spray of woodchips. "Sounds like it's not my decision to make."

Diana pushed Vivian's swing to help her build height, feeling gracious now that she'd won the round. "I can't believe none of our parents know Mrs. Li lost the mansion."

"Leave it alone." Justin climbed up the metal slide. "It's a secret."

Diana jumped and caught herself on the monkey bars. "My mom says that real secrets are the ones you don't tell anyone." She crossed the monkey bars, taking them three at a time, her arms stretching out like wings. "Anything else is fair game."

"That's convenient," Errol said. "Since you've already blabbed to us."

Diana dismounted and picked off the paint chips that had flaked onto her palms. Before she could say what she was thinking, Justin cut in: "An open secret, then. Something we pretend not to know."

"Like Grace's dad," Vivian said. "I heard he's living in China with some other woman while being married to her mom. A second family."

"That's not a second family," Justin said. "That's what Chinese people call a long-distance relationship."

Justin's dad, whom he hadn't heard from since third grade, was rumored to have had a few more kids somewhere near Shanghai. This was the most directly Justin had spoken about him since Diana could remember.

"Bet you wish you'd stuck it out in Seattle now," Diana called to Errol to change the subject.

Errol sailed out of his swing and dismounted with a soft thump at the edge of the playground. He kept going, walking onto the grass, to the top of the hill that separated them from his backyard and Diana's.

Vivian let her swing shudder to a stop, her feet scraping the worn ground. She gave Diana a tired look and jogged after Errol.

"What's his problem?" Diana said. She felt like she'd been slapped on the hand. "I was joking."

"Yeah, well, you guys have been weird since he got back." Justin reclined against the slide, his hands behind his head.

Diana looked out at the hill, where Errol and Vivian were sitting against one of the pines. She could not make out what they were saying about her.

"Why don't you go tell him that instead of putting it all on me?" She pulled Justin off the slide and dragged him over to the hill.

Justin swung his sweaty armpit around her shoulder and leaned his full weight to slow her down. Diana fell onto the grassy incline.

"Get off!" Justin had sunk himself on top of Diana like a sandbag. "You fatass, you're crushing me!"

Giggling came from the hill, and Justin was saying, "You're the one who fell. I'm just trying to get back up."

Diana stretched out her arms. "Help!" Through the shadows of the trees, Vivian and Errol came over to haul Justin off her. Diana dug her elbows into the ground. She was laughing too hard to pull herself up. Everything felt weak. Vivian and Errol reached out their hands to grab hers and Justin wrestled them down too. They kept forgetting how much stronger he'd gotten. Tangled together, they no longer wanted to get free.

A back door slammed, and the sanctimonious sound of Errol's father's voice rose from his backyard. Did they know what time it was? Some people had to work in the morning. The group dispersed like scolded children. Diana ran back to the parents she couldn't help but embarrass and into the bedroom she'd thought she'd outgrown.

Brushing her teeth, however, she pictured her friends back on their playground, banding together for someone else's cause. The streetlamps cast them in pale gold, a light that felt particular to their neighborhood. She'd told Grace at dinner that in a year they would look back, unable to recognize who they'd once been, but what was wrong with who they were now?

Maybe they'd been cruel, lobbying for front-row seats to their childhood star's fall from grace. Yet when the moment came, they had shown themselves as better than the children they'd been. How sweet and easy they were, how quickly they could take in a stray and turn her into a long-lost friend.

CHAPTER TWO

Justin carried the final stack of Blüm boxes up from the basement. His view obstructed, he followed the sound of women chatting. Diana's house was often open to Mrs. Zhang's Blüm sellers. The last Saturday of the month was reserved for her highest performers. The private meeting offered early access to new products in the Swedish beauty line. The women no longer pretended this was why they'd upped their orders. Whether your child needed an internship at NIH, or you wanted to buy a house in a competitive neighborhood, anyone invited would leave with the right connection. Justin's mother was the only one who successfully sold the products. The others would throw or give their surplus away.

This Saturday, however, the women had put their business deals aside. News of Grace dropping out had quickly spread from his friends to their parents. Besides Justin's, none of the other mothers were in touch with Mrs. Li, which meant they could speculate whether she knew what her daughter had done without feeling duty-bound to inform her. From the kitchen, Justin could hear Mrs. Zhang at the center of the conversation. Both mother and daughter naturally took the lead, but while Diana could be as blunt as an alarm bell, her mother was like a wind chime, all sharpness hidden by her delicate manner.

"Your heart can't help hurting for the girl," she said to the circle, not for the first time. Good gossip was repeated, often in the same conversation, to get every bit of flavor out of the story. "Growing up, she never did anything to make her mother worry."

Mrs. Chen's voice slapped the air around her. "Children are supposed to obey their parents. If I had Li Ping's number, I'd tell her she needs to control her daughter. I swear that girl dropped out of Harvard just to be vindictive."

Justin had heard this argument. After Errol had quit Microsoft, Mrs. Chen had taken up a portion of every product meeting to put her son on trial. Convinced his choice was meant to punish her, she would grow so heated that some of the newer invitees reacted with alarm. Justin remembered how he'd been equally bewildered when he'd first started accepting these invitations. His mother worked weekends and could never come herself. She would have been at a loss if she had. Over years of meetings Justin had learned the hopes and pains of these women, and how his friends were the sources of both. His own mother never complained. She had no expectations for him. Everything he'd learned, from what AP classes to take to what jobs were most respectable, came from these Saturday afternoons. He returned home from each meeting ears ringing, windswept, his house more resoundingly empty.

"Justin, over here." Mrs. Zhang directed him away from the corner of the living room where he usually piled the boxes.

He followed her instructions and dropped them by her feet. Mrs. Zhang put her hand on his arm.

"Is it true . . ." She lowered her voice. The women moved their heads closer. Their perfumes made Justin's head swim. He thought Mrs. Zhang had thrown her voice when the question continued rapid-fire from the opposite side of the circle.

Mrs. Wang had taken up the baton: "Is Grace living in one of her mother's foreclosures?"

"I heard the same," Mrs. Chen said.

Justin looked down at his socks. He'd known that his friends would tell their parents about Grace dropping out, but they'd been more careless than he'd expected. Misunderstanding his silence,

Mrs. Wang repeated herself, this time in English. Already the other women were reacting with alarm. A girl on her own in an unsecured house! Something terrible could happen to her and no one would be the wiser. Grace had to stay with one of them. Did Li Ping know what her daughter was doing? They needed to get ahold of that woman.

"My husband might be able to reach Li Ping in China," Mrs. Wang said. "I swear, that woman makes no sense. She wouldn't go back when everyone told her to go, and now she's there when her daughter needs her at home."

"Don't worry," Justin interrupted in halting Chinese. Everyone leaned in his direction and his face went hot. He was never good at lying. The best he could do was a partial truth. "Grace's mom has one house left. Everything works. She is fine."

The women did not look disappointed so much as thwarted. They'd been ready to mobilize on Grace's behalf. Their energy had nowhere to go.

"What a relief." Mrs. Zhang had left the circle to stand by the fireplace behind them. "After what that poor girl has gone through, let's not go around spreading rumors." She picked up the clipboard resting on the mantel. "The recession has caused problems for everyone. Lucky for us, beauty sales go up when the economy goes down. Let's take a look at the upcoming releases."

The rest of them drifted over to the semicircle of chairs, each seat bearing one of Justin's mother's business cards. Duty done, Justin slunk out of the room, taking a handful of almond cookies. Everyone was down in the basement, waiting for him to start the screening. Diana had sworn that at the first sign of discomfort, they would shut this project down. As if the very setup weren't already uncomfortable. Grace filming them while they watched her film *of* them. His head spun imagining the layers. He'd agreed because he felt sorry for Grace. They'd once been close, almost like siblings. Stuffing another cookie into his mouth, he checked his phone, and when he looked up, he bit the inside of his cheek.

Grace was standing in the foyer. Diana had told her to come in through the basement to avoid the Blüm meeting. They were keeping the documentary hidden from their parents. Grace must have taken advantage of the unlocked front door. He didn't bother asking how long she'd been listening. When they'd been younger, they could eavesdrop for hours. From the foyer, he could hear Mrs. Zhang clearly.

"Perfect timing." She ignored the cookie he offered her, her face impassive. "I need help carrying in my equipment." A familiar vein stuck out of her forehead. The one he used to joke pumped molten lava.

"That must've been weird," he mumbled through the crumbs in his mouth. "Everyone talking about you."

She lifted a shoulder and said, "Thanks for covering."

She stood aside to let him through the front door. He brushed his hands on his shorts. He'd eaten every cookie, and his teeth were caked with mush.

Helping Grace unpack the equipment in her car, Justin felt compelled to apologize.

"It's not *your* fault," she said. "I don't know what I was expecting."

Justin wanted to explain, but no one knew better than Grace that in this world information was communal.

"I'll talk to them," he said.

"I think that would make us both unhappy." Grace gave him a sideways glance. "If you want to help, do you mind if I go to your house after this? I want to shoot some B-roll."

He took hold of the projector screen she'd pulled from her back seat. If Grace had no other motive, she wouldn't mind if he told his friends. "What if they ask what I'm doing after?"

"Tell them you're going to the gym," she said over her shoulder, two camera bags hanging from its delicate ledge.

* * *

In the basement, Grace set up a projector screen, and a camera for each side of the sofa. She had a handheld for wider shots. The four of them squeezed onto the sofa, with Vivian on Errol's lap, and Justin between him and Diana. Justin sometimes forgot the proportions of his new body, and Diana shoved him aside to make more room.

"Just pretend the cameras aren't here," Grace said. With a flourish, she pressed the button on her laptop.

The sudden presence of their adolescent faces magically erased the awkwardness of the cameras around them. With their goofy brags and bad hair, the kids in front of them were endearingly pre-teen. Soon Vivian was draped over Errol's shoulders, her laughter muffled against the back of his neck. On-screen, Errol's younger self stared open-mouthed at the ceiling, unaware that the classroom had emptied. "Space Face," they'd forgotten they'd called him. Diana jabbed her elbows into Justin when she saw herself. They screamed when they heard her say, "I've started studying physics on the side."

Then Diana was yelling: "What are you wearing!"

Justin's entrance reminded everyone of his middle school uniform. Oversized basketball shorts that fell below the knee and white gym socks pulled up to his shins.

"Like he's changed at all." Diana seized the mesh fabric of his shorts.

"I'm going to the gym later," he said, which provoked another wave of laughter.

"Show Grace your protein smoothie!" Vivian unearthed the plastic container Justin had stuffed between the cushions. "He used to eat solid food."

Justin took a good-natured slug of his drink. He barely heard their teasing anymore. Instead, he listened to the sound of young Grace laughing off-screen. He loved the way the shot wobbled with her. He'd forgotten this softer side of Grace. Growing up, he was one of the few who got to see it.

Justin, who rarely dwelled on the past, felt he was living parallel to it. Grace had called her eighth-grade footage a "time capsule for the new millennium." More like a time machine. While Grace drove on ahead with her car full of equipment, he walked home accompanied by all the other walks he and Grace had made. The ease with which they fell back into their old friendship felt supernatural. Grace hadn't stepped foot in his house in seven years, not since his mother had bought it from Mrs. Li, and yet the moment she announced, "Home, sweet home!" time compressed, its distance disappearing between them.

He'd been right that Grace's request to film his house was a pretext. What he hadn't guessed was that she'd wanted time alone with him.

"I guess I was afraid to ask," she said. They were sitting in the backyard. She'd brought a bottle of wine, which Justin agreed to split despite the afternoon sun glaring above them. "You're always with your friends."

"They're your friends too," he said.

The sound of her uncorking grew slow and sullen.

"I know they seem clique-y. It's not personal. I mean, we've been friends since fourth grade, we went to the same college, and now that we're back home, all we do is hang out."

The cork popped out and Grace poured them each a glass. They drank from plastic cups stamped with faded superheroes.

"How do you know if you still like each other?" she asked, after they'd had enough to drink that no topic felt off-limits.

Justin chewed on the lip of his cup. "I don't. It kind of doesn't matter. At this point, they're basically family." He stumbled over the last word. "I mean, it's different from us."

Grace smiled with purple teeth. "Thanks, bro."

Sharing a drink in the backyard became part of their routine. After Grace was done shooting for the day, Justin would tell the group he was going to the gym. He would head home and meet Grace to debrief about how filming had gone. He would get her to take a shower, or to eat whatever was in the fridge. Once, she brought a load of laundry.

Outside, Grace liked to pull out her handheld to show him her favorite shots: Errol shooting baskets like a granny while explaining the statistics behind throwing underhand; Diana mouthing along to a story Vivian was telling too slowly.

Once, Grace had shown Justin a close-up of himself. His face was in profile, watching his friends play leapfrog in the background. The shot was shaky, and Justin focused his attention on their blurry movements. "What are those idiots doing?"

Grace refused the bait. "That's not what I'm trying to show you."

Justin combed his hair over his eyes. "I don't like looking at myself."

Grace studied him like a piece of footage. "I'd never make you look bad."

She offered the camera, the video replaying on the display screen. The Justin there looked like he belonged in a movie. The combination of the direct noon sun and the way that he'd folded his arms made his muscles look like canyons.

Sometimes, Grace would turn the camera on him again, insisting that the light was too perfect for her not to try. He found that the easiest way to get her to put the camera down was to ask how the documentary was going. Clearly frustrated by the progress, the most she would say was, "The story will reveal itself eventually." The worst thing would be to force it. A good documentarian focused on forming a relationship with her subjects.

"A bad one, like me, needs help."

After the eavesdropping incident, Justin had been pushing Grace to see his friends and their parents in a more generous light. She was a sharp observer of people's weaknesses and faults—as kids, she'd been the one to coin "Error Chen"—and while she wasn't wrong per se, no one's personality ended after the first impression.

"That dinner at the mall," Grace said. "I thought you'd totally changed. But without the others, you're the Justin I remember."

"What's he like?" Justin joked.

Grace nudged her camera with her toe. "That's what I'm trying to show you."

*   *   *

Including that Saturday afternoon in Diana's basement, Grace had the group do four interviews together spread out over two weeks. Eager to earn their trust, she avoided anything too personal. She asked them about what TV shows they were watching, what celebrities they followed. Like talking heads, they covered Obama and the upcoming election, Tina Fey's impression of Sarah Palin, how Jabbawockeez had proven Asians could dance. They focused more on the lives of Brangelina than on their own. Soon they were letting Grace film them playing Mario Kart, drinking boba, working out. Their attempts to kill time were transformed; they saw themselves as if the movie already existed and they were carefree images on a screen.

At the end of those two weeks, Grace told Justin that she'd figured out what her documentary was missing.

"Individual interviews. I need to see you guys away from the larger group."

A little tipsy in his backyard, Justin said he was happy to go first and persuade the others. He'd thought about canceling all the way up to the shoot, but their interview was no different than the group ones. He was in charge of the conversation, Grace happy to go wherever he wanted. After Grace put the rest of the equipment away, she kept the handheld out to show him how he'd been staged. They'd shot in the guestroom upstairs, which had once been Grace's bedroom. She'd had him sit on the bed by the large picture windows that looked out on their old elementary school. The faint sound of play-screaming had drifted through the glass. The Lis had left some of their furniture when they'd sold the house to Justin's mother seven years ago. The desk and headboard were dotted with star stickers. Grace's computer, once a high-tech machine that had opened their world, looked ancient taking up half the desk.

The camera disappeared under one of the blankets they'd brought outside, replaced by a six-pack of Miller High Life. The air was nippy enough that whenever the clouds covered the sun, they were left shivering in the grass. Neither of them mentioned going inside, only drank their beers a little faster. Justin had spent too much time in basements. He wanted to talk under the open sky and say whatever came to mind. His friends would be shocked by how he chattered on without a filter. Around Grace, he didn't have to consider his words first to make sure they fit in with hers.

Unlike Justin, Grace didn't flush when she drank, and the only sign of the bottles she put away was a slight blurriness that came over her gaze. They'd been watching the squirrels leap across the grass when she pointed to the edge of the yard.

"Remember?" she said, referring to the game she'd had them play when they were kids. Pretending their dads were dead, they would make crosses out of sticks and plant them in the sod.

"You were such a bully," he said. She used to pinch him to make him cry.

He was trying to guess why she'd brought this up when she said, "Do you know why my mom's gone to Beijing?"

Justin said no, although he'd heard a few guesses.

"She's begging my dad for money." Grace looked up at him, her forehead wrinkling. One eye seemed to be opening slower than the other. "It's not the first time either."

"I didn't know they were in touch." Justin remembered an essay contest Grace had won in eighth grade on the topic of personal heroes. The principal had invited her to read it during assembly.

My mother is a self-made woman, who works two jobs to give me a better life. Every time I want to skip my homework or take a break, I think of her and keep going.

"Me neither." Grace took a long slug of her beer. Her bottom lip drooped, as if the bottle had dragged it out of shape. "How do you think she could buy those houses? I only went to law school because I thought she was investing the last of her savings in my future. Turns out the money was coming from my dad. I must be stupid."

"Who cares if she didn't do it entirely on her own?" He'd read every article about the housing crisis to collect clues on when the recession might end. "She flipped those houses. She worked hard and made real money."

Grace wiped her chin. She'd narrowly missed her mouth finishing the last of the bottle.

"And she lost it too. All because she couldn't be happy with what she had." Grace swept her arm back toward the house. "She couldn't be like your mom, work a normal job to pay off a normal house. Send her kid to a normal school. No, she had to prove she was better than everyone else. And I had to prove it too."

Justin bristled at the mention of his mother, the dismissive summation of her life. "I think your mom rubbed off on mine. We'd have been fine staying in that old townhome we rented after we moved out in fifth grade, and she wouldn't have to work half as hard to afford it."

"What I'm saying is the life your mom has is the one my mom could have afforded on her own, if she'd only stopped wanting so much."

All Justin wanted was a better life for his mother than the one she could afford by herself. At a Blüm meeting in twelfth grade, he'd heard how much consultants made, and he'd spent four years trying to become one. He'd gotten A's in his business classes only to be rejected from the business frats. His internship at a second-rate consulting firm had ended without a return offer. At what point did you listen to the signs? Unlike his friends, he didn't have the luxury to wait and see if the economy rebounded.

"Don't you think it's more complicated?" Justin said. "You don't know what her relationship with your dad is like. I know he'd only call on your birthday, but maybe he wanted to support you somehow. Why does everything have to be black-and-white?"

"Because it's easier." Grace gave him an unsteady smile. "Thanks for listening. Otherwise, it stays stuck in my head."

Justin leaned back on his elbows. "Have you tried working out? I know how that sounds, but I've felt much better since I started."

She attempted to raise an eyebrow and succeeded in raising both. "You sure it's not that new trainer you're always texting?"

"Don't be an asshole."

Justin lay down and slid his arms out by his sides. Against the blanket, the dry grass crackled under his weight. Staring at the bright blue October sky, Justin rubbed his chin, where Raul's stubble had chafed him.

He could hardly hear himself. He might have only mouthed the words. "Is it obvious?"

"It was the one interview subject that wasn't like pulling teeth."

He laughed, the sound faint. He'd gotten bolder, sneaking Raul into every conversation. His friends had never noticed a difference. They'd also never shared a secret shoebox with him, or spent afternoons drawing the fanart they'd found online: their favorite characters in passionate embraces, men with men, with women, in women's clothes, in cat ears and tails. Online at ten years old, the dial-up chawing at their ears, curiosity had felt no different from desire. Those images would have shamed him if he'd been on his own. Instead, he and Grace had stepped off the sheltered edge together.

Grace had told him about her father for a reason. They could step off another ledge now. The wide-open sky made him feel like he was floating. The mirror at his gym gave the same illusion. He lost himself in its reflected distance. This was how Justin had found himself one day watching a black-haired man who was also watching him.

Too much time had gone by after their eyes had met in the mirror. Remembering where he was, Justin had dropped his weights. He'd abandoned his station and gone to settle himself below the bench lift bar.

"It looks like you could use a spotter." The black-haired man had followed him over. He didn't look much older than Justin, but would later admit he was forty. A curl of an accent made his words run together. Justin could have said no. Instead, this was how he'd met Raul Rivera.

"You want more?" Raul had asked, another ten-pound weight in his hand, and Justin, lying on the bench, sweat dripping into his eyes, had said, "I can handle more."

Remembering how far they had come, how natural these once-new rhythms now felt, made Justin's entire body light up.

Grace had not interrupted his story once. He didn't know if he was making sense. He opened his eyes and turned to ask her.

Later, he would wonder what the footage had looked like when he'd grabbed the camera out of her hand. The glossy lens had been pointed right at him. He'd moved too fast to register what his body had done. The camera would have caught everything. The world would have tumbled, the perspective flipped when the camera moved into his grip, then over his head and out of his hand. The viewfinder juddering between the sky and the ground. The camera bouncing across the blanket. They'd both fallen after it, Grace hitting the ground first. She rolled onto her stomach, her elbows and knees digging into the blanket. The slippery fabric gave her no purchase. Justin slammed his body over hers to keep her from getting to the camera. They used to wrestle like this, back when Grace had been three inches taller, and Justin was surprised by the satisfaction that came from being stronger. His panic gave way to anger. How dare she film him. How dare she make him feel this exposed. He should get off her, but he couldn't believe how helpless she'd become. He'd pinned her without trying. The only way she'd get out was if he let her go. He palmed her camera and lifted it up. How easily he could smash it into the ground.

A flash of white-hot pain burst behind his eyes. Justin rolled off, his hand pressed to the side of his head. For a few throbbing moments, he couldn't see. The world came back over-bright and blurry. By the time he sat up, Grace had run to the edge of the yard, the camera clutched to her chest. The beer bottle she'd hit him with lay spinning on the blanket.

"Why would you do that?" He could hardly breathe.

"I wanted to show you, asshole. How you looked when you talked about him."

Too shaky to stand, he said, "We're not doing this movie. Me or my friends."

Grace pushed the hair out of her face. She'd caught her breath, and her expression was calmly defiant. "Go ahead, but unless you're willing to tell them the truth, I wouldn't try it."

She'd pinned Justin in place without lifting a finger. His head was too clouded to think. He grabbed the bottle next to him and slammed it into the grass. Unbroken, it rolled out of reach.

* * *

Secrets bred jealousy. In Diana's basement, the group asked why he hadn't told them about doing a solo interview with Grace, why they'd had to find out from her.

"I wanted to check it out first." The more honest he was, the more believable he sounded.

"What did she ask you?" Vivian put her fist out like a microphone.

"Nothing." Justin pushed her hand away. "She let me talk about whatever."

"Oh my god, please tell me you didn't talk about how much you can squat." Diana was already rolling her eyes.

Justin let the teasing wash over him. His friends riffed on the

BAD ASIANS • 45

imagined interview he'd given—his gains, his macros, his creatine shakes—which wasn't too far off from what he'd said. They knew him so well they barely saw him anymore. A few minutes later, their interest switched to a Facebook photo of Vivian's sorority sisters mooning the camera.

As long as Grace needed the group for her movie, Justin's secret would be safe with her. Afterward he couldn't be sure. He had to tell his friends before she did, but they'd never handled a secret this big. They were too enmeshed, the four of them and their families. What if one of them told their parents? What if one of their parents told his mom? Loneliness closed over him, like a tunnel caving in. He knew his friends too well to trust them.

Justin watched his friends click from one classmate's profile to another's. Someone from college had posted a picture of an apple turned into a bong. Another person had switched their relationship status from *Single* to *It's Complicated*. The surface of everyone's lives was more accessible than ever, scattered with hints to the mystery underneath. He couldn't be alone in his secrecy. If his friends decided to trust Grace, there was no telling what she could pull out of them. He thought of how much easier it was to keep someone's secret safe when they held one of yours hostage.

"Actually," he said, "Grace helped me realize I don't want to be a consultant anymore."

His friends snapped their heads up and Errol muted the Facebook video playing. A high school classmate danced soundlessly beside a moving car with no one in the driver's seat.

"That's huge," Diana said.

"Did she tell you what you should do?" Vivian asked.

"Maybe personal training." The words were out of Justin's mouth before he knew if they were true. "Anyways, if you guys have anything you're trying to figure out, she could probably help."

"What is she, a therapist?" Errol sank his elbows into the couch.

"Just someone who listens." Justin thought back to what Grace had said. "Otherwise, it stays stuck in your head."

* * *

Friday night was creeping into Saturday morning, but the lights were still on in his house. His mother sat at the kitchen table, surrounded by takeout containers from their favorite restaurant. She was too wired to sleep after shifts.

Although she permed and dyed her hair, she looked older than the other mothers. Being on her feet all day kept her too skinny. She was dressed in a baggy shirt and elastic pants, which was what she wore when she wasn't in her salon uniform.

"There you are," she said, a bright smile despite the hour. "Have you eaten?"

She patted his hand, her skin perfumed by her salon's shampoo. He didn't know what she smelled like without it.

"I'm good." He took his hand back to comb through his hair, damp from Raul's rainfall shower. "I grabbed some food at the gym." His hair fell back in his face.

"Let me give you a haircut." She stood up, her knees cracking from the pressure.

"Tonight?"

"When else? Your hair is getting in your eyes."

The problem with never telling his mother no was that to start now would be suspicious. The two of them went down to the basement. His mother threw a cape around his neck. With his hair already wet, she started right away with the scissors.

"Have you found any job openings yet?" Her hand was gentle against the side of his temple. To explain the swelling, he'd told everyone he'd accidentally dropped a weight on his head.

"I'm still looking."

"Take it easy," she said. "There are many ways to make money in America."

She had started cutting hair in this basement after they'd moved back here from Iowa, before being hired at the salon of a woman she'd met through Blüm. In the corner was a small stack of products from the meeting two weeks ago, already half gone. Unlike his friends' parents, his mother wouldn't mind if he lived with her forever.

"Are you dating anyone right now?" She brushed the base of his neck.

"No." He pretended her cold fingers were the reason he'd jumped. She'd never asked him this question before.

"You've been out with Grace an awful lot. It must be nice to have her back home." She stepped around to work on his bangs. When she leaned back to study his face, he was afraid of what she might see. Beyond the spark of fear, he was surprised by how irritated this made him. She was not supposed to care about his personal life. She was not supposed to care about anything.

"Did you know Grace dropped out of law school?" he said.

"More or less." Her voice grew vague. There was the mother he knew, the one who hated the hassle of other people's business.

"Do you know how Mrs. Li feels about it?" He supposed he could call Mrs. Li his mother's only friend, although this didn't mean they talked with any regularity.

"It's not my business to ask," she said. "I'm glad to see Grace. I always thought you two were good for each other."

"Grace says she's gone to ask Mr. Li for money," Justin said. If she kept pushing, he could keep pushing too. "Is that why they never got divorced? You would never do that. You don't even talk to, well, *him*. I forget you're married."

"He will always be your father." His mother put her scissors away and turned on the razor. "Just like he will always be my husband." The coldness Justin had called for traveled over his mother. She was in the room, sharpening the line of his hair, but if he spoke, she would not hear him.

Justin watched his hair bounce off the cape and disappear against the cement. His friends thought he was lucky to have a mother with no expectations. Even their parents thought she was simple to ask so little from life. Meanwhile, his friends were afraid of disappointing their parents because their parents were easily disappointed. What could be simpler than that?

He'd been eight when his father had left their family in Iowa City. His absence had cratered Justin's mother. She would spend hours crying in the bathroom while he kept her company outside. Weeks went by like this before she'd finally moved them to Maryland, where she'd lived before Justin had been born. Her friend, Mrs. Li, took them in. A person who is never disappointed is a person who cannot bear to be disappointed again. He wished he got to be afraid of his mother's disappointment, instead of afraid for her every day.

She was stooped now, sweeping the trimmings with a brush. Justin shook off the cape. He crouched down and took the dustpan from her hand. The back of his neck was cold, newly naked to the world. When he stood up, his mother was waiting. She held an oval mirror between her hands, neither of them looking at his reflection.

"Don't you look good?" she said, as she always did. "Doesn't my son look nice?"

CHAPTER THREE

The first time Grace interviewed Errol, he cleaned his room and then, right before she arrived, threw everything back on the floor. He didn't care if she thought he was a pig. She wasn't someone he wanted to impress. He made things worse, flinging out the pizza boxes stacked in his closet and whipping off the blanket hiding his dirty laundry. The moment he showed Grace through his bedroom door, however, all she said was:

"I love the natural light. Do you mind if we shoot by your desk?"

Errol kept his distance while Grace set up her equipment, and to his surprise, she sat right on his carpet when she was done. She didn't seem to register the crumbs sticking to her legs. Errol's mother had boycotted vacuuming his room when he'd moved back home.

The red recording light blinked steadily. Time played tricks whenever Errol snuck a glance at Grace. Despite the sunlight pouring into the room, she kept on her sweater and hid her knees inside it. As if the over-large cardigan were proof that the clock was rewinding, the twenty-two-year-old in front of him kept dissolving. She looked so close to the way she had at nine, at fourteen, that he felt himself turning back into prey. A lion was useless in water, a shark terrifying until beached. Not Grace. She rearranged the physics of the rooms she entered. Looking down at her in his desk chair, he felt somehow more vulnerable, his skinny throat exposed to her teeth.

"I've been looking forward to talking to you the most." Grace beamed up at him, and what a shock to see that smile when she'd once treated him like he'd tracked shit into the room.

Tucking his chin toward his chest, Errol said, "Are you fucking with me?"

Grace rocked back and forth. She kept her eyes steady on his face. "I know I bullied you when we were kids, and I'm sorry for that."

Errol couldn't believe what Grace had admitted. Growing up, she'd been careful to hide her behavior from the others, and he'd been too proud to tattle. He'd tried to tell Vivian after they'd agreed to the documentary. How Grace would "accidentally" lock him out of her house after school, how she'd tricked him into eating dog food, how she would cough "retard" under her breath.

"Are you sure?" Vivian had said. "I don't remember that. Besides, it was a long time ago."

"This doesn't excuse my behavior at all." Grace peeked out through her curtain of hair. "But I was jealous of you."

"Of *me*?" Once the initial shock faded, Errol saw the logic. Warren had taught him early on that people only spent that much energy, negative or not, on somebody who meant something.

"You got to be messy, and loud, and annoying. You could lose your homework and your shoes and people still praised you. I felt like I had to be perfect. It drove me crazy."

"It's not like I'm this way on purpose." Errol rolled his chair around while he talked, his eyes everywhere except the camera. "An idea comes into my head, and I do it. That's why I'm a fuck-up. I don't think and so I ruin everything."

Those words cycled almost constantly in his head, like white noise made of dark matter, but this was the first time he'd said them to someone else.

"That's not true." Grace's voice struck at this darkness and threw up sparks. He looked at her, really looked at her. The sharpness of her face became a weapon in his favor. "When I heard you quit Microsoft, it was like a light went off. I wouldn't have dropped out if you hadn't shown me the way. Since we were kids, you've done that for me."

Errol's incredible transformation from problem child to prodigy had been the basis for Grace's own success story. For years, everyone had believed there was something wrong with the Chen boy, until suddenly, they had always seen his genius. Einstein hadn't talked until he was five. The signs had been obvious. Grace had learned the unfortunate lesson that tremendous success could save you from yourself and save the dignity of the person who'd raised you. He'd given her the blueprints for a cage, but by quitting Microsoft, he'd also delivered the key.

Grace had taken off her cardigan, as if thinking about Errol had warmed her up. "Who knows if anyone in LA will want this documentary? I might have to work at Best Buy for the rest of my life. It doesn't matter. At least we're doing what we want, and not what someone tells us is impressive."

Goose bumps rose over Errol's arms. He'd barely said anything, and yet Grace had seen him more clearly than either Vivian or his friends, despite him telling them much more. He felt that she knew how at Microsoft he was one of thousands of developers working on one of thousands of components. That the only glory was when someone asked where he worked, and how his parents lit up when they answered. That couldn't be enough, not at twenty years old. From the age of seven, he'd believed he was meant for something greater.

Errol pushed off his desk, the wheels of his chair grinding against the carpet.

"Vivian keeps saying I should go for one of the places head-hunting me." He gave another push, this time off his bedframe, and nearly skimmed Grace on his way back across the room.

"You can't go from Microsoft to some random company," Grace said calmly. Unlike Vivian, who would have placed a motherly hand on Errol's chair, Grace acted like bouncing off the walls was what he *should* be doing.

"Exactly!" Errol spun back to face her. "The only option is to work somewhere better. You should hear the advice people are giving. *You could go backpacking in Europe and freelance to pay the bills.* And they used to call me retarded? I don't want to go to Europe. I don't want to live out of a fucking backpack! I want to be successful, more successful than anyone could imagine." He was breathing hard, braced for Grace's ridicule.

She was smiling with recognition.

"Me too," she said. "There's no turning back now. We have to show them all, don't we?"

For the rest of their interview, Grace walked Errol through the timeline of his life with a perceptiveness that made him feel like she'd been there beside him.

"She got what they couldn't give you," she'd said about Errol's little sister, who was nine years younger. All he had said was that his parents had stopped fighting after Lucy was born. When he'd talked about his former coworkers pulling rank during code reviews, she'd said Harvard had been the same. "When everyone is exceptional, then everyone is average. You end up trying to stand on top of each other."

This must have been what Justin meant when he'd encouraged them to let Grace listen. When she stood up to shut off her camera, Errol looked down at his phone and saw that three hours had passed. He didn't want her to go. For the first time since he'd moved back home, he wanted someone to tell him what to do.

* * *

They scheduled an interview for every afternoon. The conversation, though broken up into days, felt like one uninterrupted stream of consciousness.

"I'm not saying that everyone at Microsoft is a genius, but it's delusional how Diana keeps thinking I could've gotten her a job there. I was an engineer. She's never taken a coding class. What the fuck does an econ degree qualify you to do? The only thing she's good at is bossing people around."

The unspoken rule of the group was that they did not talk shit behind each other's backs, no matter how much they might deserve it. Errol found pockets of resentment within himself that opened at the lightest touch of a question. The way the group treated him like he was their special little mascot. The one so smart he was stupid. Errol hadn't realized how much he had to say until an outside ear gave him permission.

"I'm an outsider?" Grace tucked back her hair.

Like an idiot, Errol had skipped from thinking to saying.

"No, I mean, yes, but it's a good thing." Errol looked up at the ceiling, which he'd dusted for the first time in his life. He'd also vacuumed and done a load of laundry. "It's not normal to be around the same people forever. I mean, I'm dating someone who knew me as a baby!"

Grace perked up, her back straightening. He'd grown attuned to these little movements. This was their third, no, fourth interview now. He could follow her like a boat does a rudder.

"You think it's weird, right? That I'm with Vivian?" Errol's pulse ticked faster against the side of his neck. He was aware of the way his body dared him toward an impulse, although never aware enough to resist it.

"You tell me." Grace leaned back on her hands, her shirt falling against her chest, outlining a form as mysterious to him as Vivian's was familiar.

"Short story short, she asked me out, and here we are." Errol clasped his hands behind his head and swiveled his chair from side to side. "Short story long, she was the hottest girl in our grade. Everyone wanted to date her, and she decided she wanted me. I'd never even kissed someone before. A part of me thought I'd die a virgin. Nobody cared about me winning the Math Olympiad, but suddenly every guy was telling me how jealous he was because I'd landed Vivian."

"I get it," Grace said. "That's why I dated my first boyfriend too."

"Mr. Toyota-san?" Errol had heard the gossip, although he was surprised that he'd retained it.

"Shut up!" Grace slapped him across the knee.

He dreaded seeing Vivian after Grace left with her camera each day. He shouldn't blame her for boring him or nitpick her objectively lovely face. She couldn't help seeming shallow against Grace's depth. If Vivian sensed that he was holding back about his interviews, she was her usual accepting self. Only once did she hint that she'd noticed a change.

"You seem happier," she said, her face pressed to his chest. They were lying on the hill behind his house.

"Nah." He exhaled to see his breath fog the cool air. October was almost over. "I'm just as miserable as always."

* * *

How pathetic was it—he asked Grace, sitting unseen on the floor—that he'd enjoyed taking those tests in school? Skipping two grades and being inches shorter and miles smarter than everyone.

"Remember *The Ugly Duckling*?" Grace said. "The whole point of the story isn't about inner beauty. It's about having been a swan all along and everybody else too stupid to know it."

In the inverse of that fable, his parents no longer recognized him. They'd gone from gloating over his Microsoft offer with strangers to insisting they had no son to people he'd known his whole life.

His first few days back, when they had passed each other in the house, his father would look resolutely away. His mother would mutter under her breath, like a mantra, "Are you stupid? Are you brainless? Are we going to have to take care of you the rest of our lives?" The few times Lucy had asked if he wanted to play a game or watch TV, their parents had hurried her off, treating him like a bum on the street. Errol had stopped leaving his room except to go to Diana's house. He'd learned to time his exits to his family's absences. That summer, if not for his mother chauffeuring Lucy to fencing, debate, art, and something called "early SAT prep," Errol would have been trapped in his room 24/7. Once school restarted, however, and his mother found a new job, avoiding his family grew easier. He went two months without having to face them.

A little over two weeks into his interviews with Grace, however, Errol ran into his family in the kitchen. He'd been in a dreamy state and had lost track of the days. He'd come downstairs to throw away a pizza box when he'd thought everyone would be out of the house. He'd forgotten it was Saturday.

"You're showing your face?" His mother put down her bowl and chopsticks. "Ready to eat something besides junk?" She got up to serve him from the rice cooker.

"I'm full." Errol bent the pizza box in half and shoved it down the trash can.

"Eat what your mother made you," his father said from the table. He'd opened a newspaper when Errol had come in to block the sight of him.

His mother came up behind him, and Errol moved quickly into his seat before she could slap the back of his neck. She dropped the bowl of rice in front of him on the place mat. Feeling his sister's eyes on him, he shoved the plain rice into his mouth. He'd heard laughter coming up from the kitchen when he wasn't around. Lucy was probably thinking how much easier life would be if he weren't part of this family. Well, so what. He agreed. The faster he finished, the faster he could leave.

Behind him, his mother let out a shout. Something wet fell to the ground.

"Look what you've done!"

Turning around, he saw that his pizza box had torn the garbage bag his mother had wrestled from the trash can. The contents had spilled onto the tiles. His mother held the bag by its cinched opening, like a chicken whose neck she'd wrung. She looked triumphant. She'd been waiting for this moment. His father, too good for a mess, tucked the newspaper under his arm and left the room.

"Clean this up." His mother threw the bag onto the ground. Errol didn't recognize any of the trash. Food scraps from a week's worth of meals he'd missed. She grabbed the wet sponge by the side of the sink and shoved it in his face. She crossed her arms, ready to watch him scrub the floor.

Errol picked up the sponge. He felt that pulse ticking like a spur against his side. He swung his arm back and the sponge arced through the air, landing with a slap across his mother's cheek.

He understood what he'd done a moment before his mother went off. All he could do was brace himself. She shoved him hard in the arm, pushed him until he was falling, the chair clattering to the ground. Every time he tried to get up, she knocked him down, shouting, "I should've gotten rid of you! It should've been you!" until eventually he lay still, gripped by the same swirling panic he'd known as a kid that crying would make her madder. He hated her, he hated his father, but most of all he hated himself for feeling anything at all. When his mother burst out of the kitchen, swearing at the top of her lungs, he grabbed the sponge, which had fallen near his head. Without thinking, he shoved it into his mouth. It was not a new sponge. The crusted material tore off with a crunch and he spat the hunk out, depleted.

"Why did you do that?" his eleven-year-old sister asked. They could hear their mother slamming doors all throughout the house.

"What else was I supposed to do?" He'd become a person even children avoided looking in the eye.

* * *

"I'm sorry that happened to you," Grace said later that afternoon. She'd come into the house while he was cleaning the mess, and he'd found himself explaining everything.

For once, she'd set him up on the bed, and she sat across from him, the camera pointing over her shoulder.

"I was being crazy," he said. He was worried about the sympathy in her eyes. That wasn't how you looked at someone you were interested in; it was how you looked at an ASPCA commercial full of abandoned puppies. "Honestly, I like fucking with them. Reminding them that they don't control me."

"It's okay to be upset." She reached out and held his hand.

"I don't need another mom." He squeezed to let her know he was joking. "I already have Diana and Vivian."

He suddenly felt tired of retreading the same topics. He sounded like the parents, repeating gossip and stories until they were no different than a herd of cows mooing in a field. He didn't want to talk about the past anymore. He wanted to start anew. To know how Grace felt about him, about a future.

"If I don't love Vivian anymore, I can't keep lying to everyone." He waited for Grace to move her hand, to give him some kind of sign, either squeezing tighter or slipping away. When she didn't react, he said, "Right?"

The sharp planes of her face went smooth, all emotion locked away. He was afraid of her blankness, could tell that he'd displeased her with his question.

"It doesn't matter what I think," she finally said. "Do what's best for you."

* * *

Confused by his interview, Errol gave into habit. He asked Diana to go on a walk around the lake. From their cul-de-sac, they trekked to the nearby park. Errol looked for the right words to say.

Stopping on the stairs down to the park, Diana turned and said, "Is this about Vivian?"

Errol was too disoriented by her prescience to speak.

"I know it's been stressful with how her parents are treating you." Diana continued down the steps. "I was only teasing about that Microsoft stuff."

The path around the lake was strewn with geese and their turds, soft and grub-like on the pavement. As they picked their way carefully around, Diana said, "I mean, I think it's bullshit that you didn't stick it out. You would've gotten an interesting project eventually."

Just like that, Diana was back on her usual track. Each second took them further away from his destination. Errol planted himself in the middle of the path.

"What if," he said, as if they were in a different conversation. "What if Vivian and I broke up."

Diana was so startled that only half her body turned around. "Are you fucking serious?" She looked like one of Lucy's old Barbie dolls, her torso wrenched back while her feet pointed forward. Her face started to flush and she sat down on one of the benches along the path. "No, really, are you serious?"

"I don't know. Maybe." He walked up to the bench and stood with his eyes cast over her head.

"You guys are supposed to get married," Diana said. "This doesn't make any sense."

The geese they'd been trying to avoid waddled closer, their yodels growing loud. "It makes sense to me."

"Have you even thought about this?" She moved her hands up and down her knees. "This is Microsoft all over again. You know, it's normal to be bored in a long-term relationship."

Errol scratched furiously behind his ear, which relieved some of his tension. Of course she would lecture him. She never believed he could do anything on purpose. "I'm not asking you to—I'm telling you because Grace interviewed me today."

"So?"

"So, I told her . . . what I told you."

A look crossed Diana's face, far from any expression she could voluntarily make, and Errol found himself back at the bottom of the stairs, having bolted the distance instinctively.

"Are you kidding me?" Diana stood up, throwing out her arms as if launching stones at his head. "You told *her* before you told Vivian?"

"I didn't mean to," Errol called back.

Sitting down again on the bench, Diana looked out at the man-made lake carved into the manmade valley. Soon she would say, "For a boy genius, you're a fucking idiot," and he would chafe at the nickname.

Instead, Diana continued to stare out at the lake, her eyes reaching far beyond the other side, as if the milky-green water stretched for miles. Only when she closed her eyes did Errol understand that she hadn't been looking at the water. She had been trying not to look at him.

* * *

Like planets trapped in the sun's gravitational pull, they found themselves back at the mall.

"Alright, ground rules," Diana said when they were parked and fidgeting. She twisted around in the driver's seat. "You're gonna want to shout and dance and kiss a stranger. Do not, I repeat, do not call attention to yourselves. I'm too old to go to mall jail. Grace—you good?"

Grace, who had been staring out the window, nodded and said, "Just wondering if anyone has gum."

"Good call." Diana opened the car's console and unearthed a blister pack of Dentyne Ice.

"This is a bad idea," Justin said in the passenger seat, loudly crunching into his square of gum.

"If you didn't have personal training this weekend, we'd be at a rave," Vivian said. One of her crossed elbows jabbed Errol in the side. Earlier, she'd posted the status: *What's more suburban than doing molly at the mall?*

Vivian leaned over Errol to throw Grace the gum. "Happy birthday, bitch!"

Vivian had insisted on getting molly for Grace's twenty-third birthday. Any excuse for a party. The only one who'd never done this, Errol had no idea what to expect. The internet had told him that radical openness was part of the deal. That, and a lot of dancing. He didn't like the idea of Grace, Diana, and Vivian hopped up on truth potion, and him stranded in the middle.

The parking lot was nearly empty at five thirty on a Wednesday. The gray skies had a flattening effect that made the potholes look 2D. The brown Macy's building reminded Errol of the trips his mother would take to return clothes. She would then buy the same clothes again, for the new promotional price. This was before Lucy was born, when his mother, always between jobs, had plenty of time to bargain and wheedle and fight.

On his other side, Grace caught his eye and said, "Wonder what the sales are like."

A hiccup of hope went through his chest. This was the first time she'd spoken to him since their interview Saturday afternoon. When he'd texted to ask, she'd blamed a busy work schedule. He didn't know if he should take the hint, or if this was a test to pass.

"Come on." Diana shoved the door open with her foot. "Let's get this party started."

When Errol's door handle clicked, the sound was surprisingly crisp. The sensation of the handle was like warm butter on his palm. He felt himself fall out of the car, although he was perfectly steady on his feet. The parking lot was what was tumbling. Images swam fast through the cool air, which had its own taste. The wonder grew, multiplied, and the world crested over his head. When he resurfaced, everyone was grinning. Vivian threw her arms around his waist.

"Errol came up," she said. "What a lightweight."

If the air felt this good when he was motionless, then logic followed that it would feel even better if he moved. He jumped and while his body was left humming in the air, the pavement slapped the soles of his sneakers.

"Somebody control him." Diana was giving him her version of the silent treatment, where she spoke about him instead of to him. Then she was bounding in circles around them, her legs pointed like a compass.

"Whoa." Her teeth clenched with pleasure. "This is good stuff, Viv. Thank your sorority sister for us."

A mother herding what seemed like an alarming number of children came out of the Macy's and toward where they were all now jumping. The car next to theirs beeped, headlights flashing like a warning.

"We should get going." Vivian held her hand out for Errol's.

When she turned toward him, affection rippled across her face. Sober or not, her feelings for him remained unambiguous. He'd never looked into her eyes and been left wanting. In his interviews with Grace, he'd been unfair. Without Vivian, he would believe what his parents said, that he made it impossible to love him. He would always have love for Vivian. He had love for the entire world. When they passed the woman with her brood, Errol stared deep into the mother's eyes.

"You have a beautiful family," he told her.

"Thank you," the mother said, more unnerved than flattered. The children looked not much larger than the shopping bags bursting from her hands.

Errol was too amazed to laugh. He had the entire parking lot to take in, the vibrant humps of the spaced-out cars, the sparkle in their paint. The early November sun was breaking through the cover of clouds, and—how had he not noticed—the mall's windows were still decorated for Halloween! Tinsel spiders and vinyl witch stickers made him think of elementary school classrooms. Behind him, Justin was cracking up, his earlier caution gone.

"*You have a beautiful family,*" he repeated. "I fucking love you, man. You're a freak."

Errol turned fully around, letting go of Vivian's hand. Laughing felt better than it ever had because his laughter was also Justin's. Diana was laughing and Vivian was laughing, and best of all, Grace, no camera in sight, she was laughing too.

* * *

The inside of Macy's was blindingly bright. Diana dragged them out of the department store and through the skylight glitter of the mall. They dove into the warm glow of a beckoning Crate & Barrel. The dimmed bulbs lowered the volume on the constant noise inside Errol's head. His body grew still and sturdy, like the furniture around him.

"Smell these." Diana shoved cinnamon-scented pine cones under their noses. "Feel that." She swept her hand up and down the gold-threaded comforter on a showcase bed.

The calmer he grew, the more hyper the others became. Diana and Vivian climbed onto one of the beds, something that normally he would have done while the others would be watching.

The initial rush had subsided. Errol could feel his face again. He turned to Grace and asked how she was doing.

"Good," she drawled, and they smiled at each other in total understanding.

"You would've had a hard time filming us."

Grace made a box with her hands and framed Errol in the shot.

"Thank you for being so honest in your interviews," she said.

Diana and Vivian were knocking pillows off the showcase bed while Justin cleaned up after them.

"I liked being interviewed," Errol said. "I don't remember you being such a good listener."

Grace laughed, sounding a little deranged in a good and cheerful way. "What are you talking about? I was always listening."

"Yeah, you were sneaky," Errol said. "Diana's up-front, but you'd work people when they weren't expecting it."

"I've been found out." Grace let loose another peal of cartoonish laughter. They were holding each other up, their sides pressed together. Since their interview three days ago, he'd been clogged with worry, barely able to sleep at night. Laughing with Grace, feeling her arm tight around him, made everything feel new and fresh.

"Diana!" Errol called.

"What?" Diana was busy tucking Justin and Vivian in, running around the bed like some demented mother.

"You're the best," he said.

Diana turned around, a look of grudging affection on her face, until she took in his and Grace's sideways embrace. Diana jumped back into the showcase bed and wrapped herself around Vivian.

"If everybody's cuddling now," she said, raising her head from Vivian's shoulder.

Errol and Grace let go at once. Errol could feel something shadowy start to spread, a chest-cold loneliness more intense than his joy had been. He refused to let Diana shame him. Their talk by the lake had made things clear. She wanted him and Vivian to stay together to keep their group from changing. She'd never cared about what was best for him, only what would make her own life easier.

"Let's go somewhere quieter," he whispered into Grace's ear. For once, he knew exactly what he was doing.

* * *

Errol scouted the home furnishing store, which was large enough to pretend that they'd entered a universe of furniture. He pulled Grace into a nearby aisle of Halloween markdowns and through the Thanksgiving display. They went past the kitchen section, where he knocked along a row of dangling pots, and emerged into a sea of dining room tables. They sat down at a small circular table close to the edge of the display.

"Sorry the chairs don't have wheels." She searched the section for another option.

"I'm good." Errol leaned forward on his elbows. "I should take this stuff more often. Look how chill I am."

"If your parents had let you take your ADHD medication . . ." She'd been vocal during the interviews about where she felt his parents had failed him. Nothing he hadn't heard from Vivian and his friends before. For some reason he didn't feel suffocated when the words came from Grace.

"It's mental anyways." He tapped his head. "Mind over matter. Remember Warren Cho got an extra hour to take his tests? He didn't even go to college."

"I think there was more that was wrong with Warren," Grace said.

"He learned English eventually." Errol looked down at his hands. "He was in my AP classes. I heard he got 1s."

His parents had tracked Warren's life like a longitudinal study. He had been proof that giving in to a disordered mind made the subject more unfit for society, whereas Errol, before he'd quit Microsoft, had proven that the best cure was willpower and a fortune reading from Master Yi. No one he knew had gone to therapy; they barely trusted cold medicine, preferring Dr. Song's potions of old tree bark and bitter spice. For their parents, this focus on feelings and unseen pain was as alien as hamburgers had once been. No wonder he'd fallen hard for Grace. She'd shone a spotlight over the hidden hurts that marked his body and had made them beautiful because they were what made him *him*.

"I love you," he said. He really did, and what was more, he loved himself, the version of him that she saw.

"I love you too." Grace looked at him the way Errol had hoped, until she sighed and said, "God, I love molly."

"No," he said. For once, her eyes were the ones bouncing around. He raised his voice to focus her. "It's not because I'm on this stuff. I do love you."

The glow in her face dimmed.

"Oh, Errol." She took his hands, which he hadn't realized were cold until he felt the warmth of hers. "It's a scary time. Everything is going to work out for you. Be single. Be unemployed. Make more friends. The best thing you can do is figure out what you want."

Errol shook his head. "I want to be with you."

"I care about you, I do." Her words smashed around in his skull. What was she saying? "It means so much how close we've gotten, especially after how things used to be. I'm grateful to call you my friend." A flash of fear struck his spine. His hands went clammy in hers.

Her words made no sense. Had they ever? If she made no sense, had he? He heard himself too late, and just like that he heard the things he'd said to Grace in those interviews. Ridiculous, stupid, embarrassing things, and she had nodded along, her camera recording.

"So you never wanted to be more than friends?" He pushed himself back from the table. The chair squealed across the floor. "I don't know what you were trying to do. You get to leave, but I have to live with these people."

"You don't! Not if you don't want to. That's what I hoped you would see. You'll make the right decisions if you make them for yourself, and not for anyone else, least of all me." Grace chewed on her bottom lip. "I'm sorry if I misled you."

She was too smart not to be laughing behind his back. He'd believed that she'd changed when no one truly did, when he was the same idiot he'd always been. *Space Face, retard, Error Chen.*

He knew he'd said all of this out loud when the other customers lowered their heads and hurried out of the section. Grace
looked as if she no longer recognized him. A store employee headed
toward them. Errol's chair toppled backward when he stood up.
He reached blindly behind him, knocking over something else. He
couldn't stand to be in the store any longer, where everything he did
was a mistake. The displays whizzed past him. He thought he heard
Grace shout his name, but then he was back under the bright lights
of the mall, surrounded by noise and distractions.

* * *

Errol's feet were stuck to the floor. He'd escaped to the opposite
end of the mall, where a small, unkempt theater showed the same
three movies all month. He'd bought a ticket for the nine thirty
screening of *Rachel Getting Married*, a movie no one would come
to early. Having tucked himself into the center of the back row,
Errol surveyed the cascade of empty seats in front of him. The
house lights hurt his eyes, but when he closed them, shocks of
rainbow-colored spirals spun like a carnival ride.

In the linty theater seat, Errol found the calm of his mind broken. *I'm a fuckup. I don't think. I ruin everything. I'm a fuck-up. I
don't think* . . . He pictured everyone he knew coming into a theater like this to watch him on the big screen. Of course, the whole
point of Grace's movie was to humiliate him. He couldn't count
the number of times he'd called himself a genius on camera. Had
he really brought up those test scores from first grade? He'd been
making fun of Diana when he'd said it. And what about Vivian?
He'd said that he'd known her for so long that it was like kissing
his sister.

He'd been venting. Grace was the one who'd turned his frustration into something more. All he had was the group, the last ones
left who believed he was worth something.

Errol had sweat through the back of his shirt. Although he didn't know how long ago he'd left the store, enough time had passed for everyone to notice. His pocket buzzed nonstop. One person would call, and five texts would follow, interrupted by another call as two texts flew in. They seemed unshakable, Diana, Justin, and Vivian. He'd only thought of how tired he was of being babied by them. Not what would happen if they tired of babying.

Until Grace had pointed it out, he hadn't found it strange that he only had two friends, three if you counted Vivian. Given how involved his friends were in his life, he didn't think he could handle another one. After graduation, a part of him had been eager to put distance between him and the group, to meet people who didn't feel like they could claim him.

Then, his first day at his job, his manager had introduced him to his team as their new superstar. Only nineteen, and already at Microsoft. In school, everyone had wanted him in their study group when they'd learned of his reputation. His coworkers, however, had been chilly. They had little patience for his questions or requests for help, and much less when he'd pointed out their errors. His second week, his manager had pulled him aside to explain how to succeed in his position.

"I know you're no stranger to being graded on a curve. Here, we have something similar."

Twice a year, he would undergo a performance review, where, relative to the rest of his team, he would be labeled exceeding, achieving, or underperforming. Ranked from first to last, the winners received bonuses and promotions, while those at the bottom were one step closer to being let go. No matter if everyone met their goals or nobody did, someone would be crowned the best, and someone else the worst.

"We want the cream of the crop, which means survival of the fittest." His manager had also been a recent hire. He was in his thirties, and one of the few Asian managers. Their team, on the other hand, was mostly older and white. He spoke to Errol in a conspiratorial tone. "At a company of this size, there's always underperformers."

His team's behavior now made sense. They were in direct competition and his manager had labeled him their curve wrecker, here to help him clean house.

His manager continued, "Don't do what your parents did by keeping your head down. Be loud. Make sure your work is visible. I'm your best friend here, and you'll want to make friends with the other managers too."

His advice was hardly a secret. Rather than collaborating, the other developers ran everything by the supervisors first. Decisions that could have been made in minutes took a week's worth of meetings. Once the work could finally start, Errol found that he had to build on top of convoluted systems written decades ago. Important context was withheld until his code review sessions. Forced to redo his work after each skewering from his peers, Errol grew too frustrated to focus. Deadlines slipped by with no one to remind him.

For the first time in his life, Errol had felt homesick. Running late to work, he would remember Diana banging on his door every day before school, and Justin kicking him awake in class. For years, Vivian's color-coded planner had included his assignments in gold and hers in bright magenta. By his second month at Microsoft, his manager stopped calling him Superstar. By the third, he was introduced to a "Performance Improvement Plan." His coworkers started smiling at him more. Their invitations to lunch were crueler than when they'd frozen him out. They could breathe easier with him at the bottom. He hadn't been honest with Grace because he hadn't been honest with himself. He'd had to leave, knowing what would happen if he stuck around.

How easily he'd forgotten what those three months had taught him. No sooner had he come home before he'd felt suffocated again. In front of the camera, he had taken the group's attention as his due. Worse, he had complained. *They wish they'd been gifted and talented too, but they'll settle for being geniuses by association.*

"Errol Chen!"

A staticky voice boomed his name overhead. Errol ducked as if the sound were a foul ball.

"I repeat, if you have seen a little boy named Errol Chen, please bring him to the security office on the second floor, outside the JCPenney's. Thank you."

Through the poorly insulated walls of the screening room next door, Errol could hear the dance sequence of *Slumdog Millionaire* interrupted. He was being ferreted out via mall intercom. He fumbled for his phone and surrendered his position.

When Vivian poked her head around the theater partition, Errol waved, as if she might not see him. She was alone; she'd asked the others to hang back for a few minutes. His happiness was streaked with guilt. Now he was certain that Vivian was the one who knew him best. He'd had no reason to doubt her. In the seat next to his, both facing ahead, Vivian found his hand across the cup holder.

"What's wrong?" she said. She did not mention the panic he must have caused the rest of the group.

He considered not answering. Unlike Diana, however, who would answer for him, or Justin, who would let the subject drop, Vivian had the bulldogged patience to keep asking.

"I got lost," he said. "Zoned out."

"Classic Error." Vivian gave his hand a squeeze. For once, he felt no irritation at the nickname. He took comfort in its familiarity.

Errol let his head fall against hers, their temples notched almost painfully together. Like nerves regrowing, his skin reacted as if such closeness were new, and when they kissed, he was warmed by the sheer contentment on her face. Vivian may have had her own feelings about Microsoft. She must have wished he'd consulted her before he'd quit, and yet all she'd said was that he knew best. No matter how her parents had pushed, she'd refused to leave his side. She was stronger than he'd realized.

"I'm grateful," he said into her cheek. Today had been a lesson in how frighteningly fast his life could change.

She pulled back. "For me?"

"Of course." His sneakers made a sucking sound when he lifted his feet off the sticky floor and onto the edge of the seat. "I should probably tell everyone I'm sorry for disappearing."

In the spirit of the bewitching day, Justin and Diana appeared around the partition, their voices hushed though the movie was hours from starting. His luck held when Grace was nowhere to be seen.

"You're such an asshole!" Diana yelled when she realized no one else was in the theater. Justin was cracking up beside her, laughing harder than he had in the parking lot. Errol felt like a character in a video game, destroyed by a bad move, only to return unharmed to where he'd started.

Diana and Justin grabbed the seats one row down and sat on their knees to face him.

"Did you like our announcement?" Diana bounced on her seat.

"We had to figure out which one of us could act sober," Vivian said. "And also which one of us could act at all."

"Would you believe Justin won?" Diana lost her balance and caught herself on the back of her seat.

"I wouldn't call it 'winning.'" Justin was deadpan. "I was shitting my pants talking to mall security. You know they carry Tasers?"

"All because you wouldn't answer your phone." Diana turned to Vivian with a grin. "You seriously have to deal with his *bullshit* every day?"

Sensing danger, Errol said, "Should we go watch *Slumdog Millionaire*? This movie won't start for another hour."

"We didn't buy tickets," Justin said.

Vivian yanked Errol up by the hand. "We are not wasting this on a movie. Come on!"

Outside the theater, Errol clocked the manager looking at him, suspicious. Holding on to Vivian's hand, he felt every bit like the lost child his friends had said he was.

"Where are we going?" He was struck by the night sky, the streetlamps. They'd exited into the parking lot. "Are we leaving Grace?"

"I wish," Justin said.

Before Errol could ask what Justin meant, Diana shoved him in the shoulder to look out ahead. The emptying lot wavered with distant moving lights. Diana's car sat alone in the middle of its row. Like magic, the engine turned on.

"She's taking us to the mansion." The cabin light revealed Grace behind the wheel. Diana could not contain the grin on her face. "She's good to drive. She said she didn't take the entire tab so she's basically sober."

* * *

Diana was clearly proud of her insider knowledge. She played tour guide, pointing out, through the scrim of trees and hedges, the massive estates along the unmarked road. No sidewalk connected the houses, which were set far back, the driveways small roads themselves. This was clearly not a neighborhood that trick-or-treated, and everyone laughed when Errol made that observation.

Grace parked and opened the garage door by hand. Right inside was a flashlight, which she passed to the group. She moved as if she could see in the dark, until they were in the kitchen. She fiddled with a large machine on the floor and the room filled with light.

The entire floor was empty, like Diana had described, but Grace had left some signs of life. A plastic bin stacked with tapes sat on the kitchen island, which must have contained hours of footage. A Harvard hoodie was draped over the edge of a pantry door. The inside of the house was cool enough that no one took off their coats.

"Can we turn up the heat?" Errol felt he'd pulled off an innocent tone.

"Here's something to warm you up." Grace slid in her socks down the long hallway connecting the kitchen to the foyer. At the front door, she flipped on more lights. They came down from the vaulted second-story ceiling and splashed the vacant walls with a warm if distant glow.

"You wanted a rave, right?" she shouted to Vivian.

Grace plugged a cord snaking out the wall into an iPod lying on the floor. The walls began to shake with sound, and the group's shadows stretched across the ghostly hollows of the house.

Vivian and Diana grabbed Errol's hands and the three of them slingshot each other across the floor. Their socked feet slid easily against the wood. Justin ran after them and they spun from room to room, until they found their way back to the foyer. The four of them formed a circle by the staircase. Errol's face dripped with sweat. He didn't know how many songs had passed. He left Justin doing dance lunges, challenging the girls to get on his back. In the kitchen, Errol plunged his head under the faucet, drank from the same stream, and used his shirt to towel off. The water still running, he looked at the box of tapes. He could douse the whole thing, destroy weeks of Grace's work. Everything he wanted felt within reach.

He left his shirt on the floor and galloped back. A song the girls must have liked came on because they screamed and threw their hands in the air. Right before he crossed the kitchen threshold, before he felt the press of their skin against his, he saw Grace sitting cross-legged by the front door. A camera had appeared in her hands. Grace peered out behind half-closed lids. She looked as if she knew something the four of them did not.

Then he was back in the huddle. Grace was on the outside looking in. She could keep pointing that camera at them. She could show the group every awful thing Errol had said. He didn't need to wreck her tapes because they had no power over him. She was an outsider, not a friend. The group crowded around him, their hands pushing his bare chest. He was so weird, and they loved him. The circle closed tight, boxing Grace out. She had no idea what it meant to be them.

CHAPTER FOUR

After spending a fitful night on Grace's living room carpet, Vivian climbed eagerly into her own bed. The next thing she knew, her room was dark. Her alarm clock's hands glowed neon.

Downstairs in the kitchen, her mother was on her new phone, engrossed in a game that yelped whenever her finger hit the screen.

"Are you hungry?" Her mother paused her game and walked to the kitchen island. She reached into a green bowl brimming with fruit and grabbed a paring knife to peel a kiwi.

Vivian passed her a mango next. Since she'd moved back home, her parents had been happy to take care of her again, especially since they no longer found Errol up to the job. They had the highest standards for the man she would marry, and for years, Errol had fit them. After he'd quit Microsoft, however, they'd acted as if he'd broken a promise to them all. Vivian was forced to choose between her parents and her future husband, which made her feel surprisingly mature.

"I was on the phone with your big brother," her mother said. "Now he wants two weddings. One here, and one in Korea."

A mango lost its core, the tender ends sliced off and saved for her. Vivian couldn't imagine Errol being this attentive. With him, she was allowed to be the one who did the spoiling.

"Michael can't afford that," Vivian said. Her brother, who was six years older, worked at a Mercedes dealership in Virginia and funneled his money into his various business ventures.

"His fiancée's paying." Her mother huffed. "I told him that's a terrible start to a marriage."

"I love Habin." Patient, grounded, and good with money, her brother's fiancée was the opposite of him, and most of the women he'd dated. Her worst trait was that she made more than Michael did. Their parents found this emasculating.

"She doesn't respect herself." Her mother palmed a red-frilled dragonfruit. "She thinks if she supports a man, he'll stick around." She nudged Vivian's shoulder. "Don't you go thinking the same."

Her mother halved and quartered the fruit. The bright chameleon skin revealed snowy insides covered in tiny black seeds.

"Errol's waiting for the right job." Vivian took the plate her mother handed her, the fruit sliding precariously around. "I'm going to marry him, Mommy. Didn't you support Daddy when he started his own business?"

"I'm the one who pushed him to do it." Her mother picked up her phone from the table and the bleeps of her game restarted. "I let him think it was his idea. They're little boys trying to be big men. Once you know this, you have them."

Vivian thought of what Diana had told her last night at the mall while they'd been trying on plastic jewelry at Claire's, before they'd realized Errol had gone missing. At the time, she'd accepted the news with the poise that extra serotonin afforded. Now she felt a dark hole expanding in her stomach.

"Is that why you work for Daddy?" Vivian asked.

"I work *with* him because your daddy is a flirt," her mother said, one of the more polite allusions that Vivian had heard over the years.

"Is that enough to keep him from flirting?" Vivian thought of the women her mother had told her about. Clients, loan officers, his employees' wives. Not even her mother seemed sure if these were real affairs or her own suspicions. The one they knew for certain was an old coworker of his, before he'd started his contracting business.

"*It takes two to tango,*" her mother said in English, as if delivering a grave diagnosis. She punctuated her words with decisive swipes to her game. "Learn from Mommy's mistakes. Love isn't a competition, and that boy is no prize."

She clucked when she saw Vivian's face.

"Didn't I warn you about this movie?" Her mother stood up and tucked her phone away. She smoothed Vivian's hair off her forehead. "You put a girl like Grace beneath you long enough, you'll see what she does to get back on top."

* * *

In her bedroom after, mouth sour with fruit, Vivian lay down on the rug beside her bed. She looked beyond the tulle canopy at the crystals hanging from her mini chandelier. A painting of a woman at her loom was pinned to her quilted pink bulletin board, along with her homecoming sash and every corsage Errol had given her. She loved her hopelessly girly room, which she'd decorated with her mother when she was eleven. Her friends teased her, calling her mother her best friend. They only knew half the story.

From the moment the doctor pulled her out, Vivian was her mother's spitting image. Everyone said they were like twins born years apart. It was Master Yi who'd taken one look and foretold, "This girl will have her mother's fate."

"From that moment on," her mother would say, "I knew I had to save you from my past mistakes."

Since Vivian could remember, her mother could see her future, which was, after all, her mother's past.

"That girl wants to steal your best friend," her mother would point out, and a few weeks later, Vivian would come home crying. Her mother claimed to feel the injury twice. To see Vivian mistreated was painful enough. To see history repeating itself was a different kind of powerlessness.

Unlike the rest of the group, Vivian had no secrets from her mother, who had heard about Grace's documentary the same night Diana had volunteered them.

"Grace is tricky," her mother had said. "She'll do anything to win. Remember when you were little and she convinced you to trade your nice Disney pencils for her cheap yellow ones?"

Her mother thought her advice leaked through Vivian's ears, but she'd been careful around Grace from the start. She'd watched *The Bachelor*. She knew how editing worked. Grace's intentions might be good, but her success depended on telling a good story. Their first interview, no matter what Grace had asked, Vivian had responded cheerfully. When Grace had thanked her after half an hour, however, Vivian had been offended, even embarrassed. She had heard enough from the others to expect her entire afternoon wasted. She'd bought them both Starbucks for extra energy.

"Is that it?" Vivian asked. Propped in her bed, she felt like she'd failed to measure up.

"Unless you have something to add," Grace said. Her voice floated up from the rug, where she'd sat to dismantle her camera stand. She sounded hurt. Had she guessed Vivian's mother's warning? *A girl like Grace will ask for help, and hate you for giving it.*

"I want to help," Vivian said. "There's just some things I don't want to say on camera."

"Like what?"

Vivian could feel Grace lean against the side of the bed, her interest palpable in that pressure.

Diana's theory was that Vivian's parents had convinced her she was inherently lovable. That was why she was addicted to making everyone love her. Justin thought she was more extroverted than the rest. Errol contributed no hypothesis. How Vivian had explained this to Grace was that his attention had more important places to go, like his coding projects and chess games, than to wonder about his girlfriend.

"Is that so?" Grace had asked. This was a different occasion, the camera also off.

"You can't expect a *genius* to act like a normal boyfriend," Vivian had said, and although she made fun of herself for using that word, she couldn't deny that she sat up a little straighter. "Don't you think?"

Grace shrugged, the bedsheet hitching up by Vivian's leg.

"If I wanted a normal guy, I could have one. Life would be so limited. With Errol—I mean, you're like him, you're supposed to do something special."

Again, the bedsheet shifted. Vivian wasn't delusional. She would never be the center of Errol's world because his world was wider than she could imagine.

"All my life, my parents told me I needed to be taken care of." Vivian thought of her sixty-five-year-old father on a ladder outside her bedroom the other day. He'd been repositioning a floodlight that shone past her window at night. As if she weren't perfectly capable of closing her blinds. "Errol's the first person who needs *my* help. He makes me feel like the genius for scheduling his classes."

"How's the sex?" What should have seemed blunt felt inevitable. Where else was that train of thought leading?

"We've either lived with our parents, or with our friends. I've had so much shower sex, getting wet means something totally different."

When they laughed, they shook the bed together.

Looking up at her ceiling, Vivian wondered if Grace had used what she'd shared to turn Errol against her. Diana had dismissed this last night. If all Vivian had said was that Errol was somewhat useless, that wouldn't be news to him. At most, Grace had deduced that there was enough room between the two for her to squeeze in, which she could have observed from Errol.

What Diana didn't understand was—"No offense, Viv. Why would Grace be interested in Errol?"

Vivian had stared at Diana and the rainbow cat ears she'd put on.

"I mean, I know we joke that he's a genius because he skipped two grades. Honestly, I think he might just be difficult." Diana gave Vivian a pair of shutter sunglasses to try. "Look at it this way. You could've gotten stuck with a lemon."

Over the years, Diana's bluntness had grown harder to handle, but that night at the mall, Vivian had been able to see through her own hurt feelings. All that noise could be boiled down to this: Diana loved her, and no matter how dismissive or overbearing Diana acted, none of this meant that Diana loved her any less.

The same was true for Vivian. Despite how hurt she was by Errol's distance, she loved him still. She might love him more. He'd been so energized these past few weeks, like the dreamy boy she'd fallen for, whose mind could be in multiple places at once. Knowing that his interest in Grace had been the reason didn't lessen how Vivian felt. True love didn't require being loved in return.

"It's too late for me," Vivian had said. Diana had put an arm around her and squeezed.

"These months have been a trip," Diana had said. "We're all looking for an escape. Grace is leaving in January." She'd held her other arm out and pronounced: "This too shall pass."

January was only two months away, but barely two months had passed since Grace's return, and already Vivian was in danger of losing everything. The sad thing was that Vivian had believed she and Grace were becoming good friends. Lying on the rug those afternoons, Grace had made her own confessions. Who else knew about Grace's mother's calls, the nightly deceptions? Maybe she'd only shared those secrets to get Vivian to share hers. If that was the case, she'd underestimated Vivian's own resolve.

Vivian had no other option. She had seen Grace wander off with Errol at the Crate & Barrel, despite Grace saying she didn't know when Errol had left the store or where he had gone. Vivian wasn't special like them. She couldn't compete on a level field. After Vivian's mother vanquished another one of Vivian's father's shadow admirers, she would say, "All is fair in love and war."

Vivian climbed back into bed and looked down at the spot on the floor.

* * *

The next day, Vivian walked over to the Zhangs, where she knew Diana would be alone in the basement. Errol was still sleeping off the molly. Justin was at the gym. Grace had a shift at McDonald's.

Diana had her laptop out, which she closed when Vivian came through the door.

"What porn are you watching?" Vivian yanked off her boots.

With some reluctance, Diana admitted she'd been looking at practice LSATs.

"Thinking of leaving us?" Vivian pretended to sob.

"My parents got in my head," Diana said. "I thought this unemployment thing would last a few months. What if it takes years to find a job? What if I never have a real career?"

"You could marry rich." Vivian lay down on the other side of the couch, her head on the armrest. "Although that's easier said than done."

The basement's popcorn ceiling looked sharp and foreboding. As a kid playing after one of the Zhangs' potluck parties, she used to worry about jumping too high and impaling her skull on a point. Grace had figured this out, and every time Vivian had leapt off the couch, Grace would scream, "Your head was *this* close to getting spiked."

"Can we talk about what happened at the mall?" Vivian said.

Diana slid the laptop onto the ground. "Does Grace know that I told you about Errol?"

"What?" Vivian raised her head from the armrest. "Why would you think that? I haven't talked to her since we took the molly."

"You guys got pretty tight." Diana hid very little, including her jealousy. "You might have wanted confirmation."

"Not that tight." Vivian had to laugh, and Diana fell back, her hands over her eyes.

"Sorry," she said. "I wasn't thinking."

"You know," Vivian said, "a few weeks ago, she tried to make it seem like *you* were the one who was secretly in love with him."

"Gross!" Diana flung her arms over her face. "That bitch. He's like one of my brothers."

While Vivian was quick to reassure Diana that Grace had been totally off base, this was also what she wanted to talk about. If Errol chose Grace, what would happen to their group? What would happen to Vivian? This was the only life she'd wanted, the only life she'd known.

"I'd take your side," Diana said. "If that's what you're worried about. Justin probably would too."

"You said Errol's family." Dust or cobwebs clung grayly to the ceiling spikes.

"So are you." Diana's head hit the other armrest. Her feet scooted out and dug into Vivian's ribs. The cushions bounced with restless energy. "This isn't normal." But she'd conceded the point. "Why'd you two have to get together anyways?"

This had once been Vivian's favorite question. For years Errol had been a friend—a loud, annoying, sometimes smelly one at that—until one day, he wasn't. She'd been racing to class, fighting her way up a crowded stairwell, when someone had knocked the pencil case out of her hand. The case had broken on impact. Her gel pens and scented erasers had ricocheted in every direction. Before Vivian could panic, Errol had appeared, leaping down the stairs. He crawled on the floor, tripping people who got in his way, until he'd collected each of the jewel-colored paperclips in her set of twenty. Mission accomplished, he'd dashed off, leaving her clutching her case, her heart pounding while she called out her thanks. She'd felt both treasured and inconsequential, as if rescued by a superhero who still had the world to save. If she hadn't dropped her case, if he hadn't been taking that stairwell to class, if their parents hadn't been friends, if he hadn't skipped two grades . . . The real collision that day had been with fate.

"It was meant to be," Vivian said.

Diana cracked her knuckles, one at a time. "This isn't a fairy tale, princess."

Vivian lifted her head. Diana's face did not match the easy way she was speaking. She clutched a pillow to her chest, an old home ec project from the sixth grade. Diana couldn't bear to throw away anything that she'd once loved, and the basement was filled with the items of their past. The inspirational dog posters that she'd gotten at the Scholastic Book Fair were practically peeling off the walls.

When Vivian and Errol had made their relationship official, Diana had stared, open-mouthed. Her first words, eventually: "Why didn't I know that?" Years later, the group still shouted this together, and Diana would laugh and say, "Well, why didn't I?" This was what Vivian had told Grace weeks ago. No, Diana was not in love with Errol. She was in love with the group.

"I know a way to get rid of Grace," Vivian said, certain Diana would be on her side. "But I don't know if it's right."

* * *

An hour later, alone in her bedroom, Vivian read through the script she'd written. It would be nine in the morning in Beijing. She dialed the number her mother had given her.

"Good morning, Auntie," she said when Mrs. Li answered the

phone. "This is Vivian, Wang Dong's girl." On her script, she'd written and crossed out, *Your daughter Grace's friend.*

"Hello, Vivian," Mrs. Li said in English. "Why are you calling?"

She'd forgotten how direct Mrs. Li could be. She scanned her script and switched back to English. "I'm sorry for bothering you. I wanted you to know that Grace is not in law school anymore."

Mrs. Li spoke calmly: "I think you've made a mistake."

Vivian had not expected this. Growing up, Mrs. Li was the one parent who always took her child's side, but this wasn't a fight over a toy.

"Ask her yourself," Vivian said quickly. "She dropped out to make movies. She wants to move to LA."

"She's never told me this." A hint of impatience crept into Mrs. Li's voice. She was treating Vivian like a little girl caught fibbing. "I call her every night. I ask her about school."

"Well, I see her every day." Vivian was no longer looking at the script. "I've been to the house in Potomac. That's where she is when you call."

Mrs. Li had already hung up. Vivian didn't know how much she'd heard, let alone how much she'd believed.

* * *

Dr. Song brought the news to Vivian's house two days later. That Sunday afternoon, the good doctor sat in the living room with Vivian's father, the two of them eating pumpkin seeds. Business was good, she boomed. Her client list had never been longer. She was thinking of remodeling the office she shared with her business partner, Master Yi. Vivian set out the tea while her father flipped through his portfolio.

Perpetually sixty, Dr. Song had a tree stump's solidity. She gripped Vivian's wrist, her fingers like thick roots.

"This house is good for you." Dr. Song peered over transition sunglasses that had yet to lose the shade from outside.

"If you tell her that," her father said with an indulgent smile, "she'll never want to leave."

"You'll consult me before you move?" Dr. Song patted Vivian's hand. To her father, she said, "You know Li Ping didn't. I could have told her. That big house of hers is cruel to its women."

"Is that so?" Her father's face remained neutral. His network was larger than anyone's, but he often pretended he had no interest in these topics.

"People never listen to me. I could save them so much grief."

Her father had told Vivian that Dr. Song had been sued last year by a former patient's wife. The wife claimed the doctor's traditional treatment had done nothing for her husband's cancer. Dr. Song had countersued for slander. Both lawsuits had been thrown out, and the man had died in the summer. For months, people had talked of little else. They also kept seeing Dr. Song as if nothing unfortunate had happened. Sometimes, Vivian thought everyone only gossiped this much to stand to be polite in public.

"Speaking of Li Ping." Dr. Song raised her eyebrows. Vivian's father could not help leaning closer. "Did you hear that she's back from Beijing? Perhaps you can recoup those contracting fees. I heard she skipped out on final payments."

"We've been repaid." Her father picked a fragment of shell from his teeth. "By Li Hong, of all people. I suppose they never did get divorced."

"I heard he's made millions from his father's company." Dr. Song gave a cackle and coughed into a handkerchief. "Your wife doesn't have the richest husband anymore."

Her father let out a dull chuckle. "Vivian, why don't you see if your mother needs help."

Heart thumping from Dr. Song's news, Vivian ran back to the kitchen, where her mother was laying out a tray of French butter cookies. Her eyes scanned Vivian's face.

"What's the matter?" she asked.

"Dr. Song says Mrs. Li is back from China." Vivian's heart was climbing up her chest. Everything had unfolded much faster than she'd expected. Her phone call with Mrs. Li was two days ago. She must have gotten on a plane immediately.

"You did the right thing." Her mother put down the tray and took Vivian's hands. "She needed to know what Grace was doing with her money."

"Diana said Grace wasn't using the tuition for anything else." Vivian flushed darker. After what she'd done by telling the truth, she couldn't bear spreading a lie. "She was going to return it to Mrs. Li."

Her mother sucked her teeth. "A girl who would deceive her mother every night is capable of anything."

Of course, they both knew the real reason Vivian had called Mrs. Li. Despite how her mother might have felt about Errol, her support now was unshakable. This alone steadied Vivian's resolve. She took a deep breath and nodded. Her mother picked up the tray and backed through the kitchen door.

"You're a fighter like me." The expression on her mother's face was affectionate and resigned. "Now stop frowning, or you'll get wrinkles."

* * *

Errol and Vivian's seven-year anniversary came two days later. Vivian hadn't wanted to think about celebrating. Errol was the one who'd insisted on doing something, no matter how small. He invited the group for dinner, pizza at CPK, as if nothing haunted their old traditions. He'd been more cheerful after that day at the mall, more affectionate toward Vivian. He could have been basking in that post-molly glow. She'd studied him carefully when he'd learned about Grace leaving town. Instead of looking upset, he'd seemed distracted.

By now, the rest of the group knew that Mrs. Li had returned. No one had been able to reach Grace. She'd left a voicemail on Vivian's phone, but when Vivian had called back at Diana's urging the line was already disconnected. Vivian had visited Best Buy and McDonald's. The manager at each had told her that Grace had quit abruptly. Maybe Grace had made it to LA after all. Maybe she'd saved enough money.

Remembering that voicemail could make sweat break out over Vivian's body. She didn't need the looks Diana was shooting her across the restaurant table. If Diana had thought Vivian was making a mistake telling Mrs. Li about her daughter, she'd had the chance to say something that night in her basement.

Instead, when Vivian had first floated her idea, Diana, high school debate champion two years in a row, had stammered, unable to start a simple sentence.

"I don't know, Viv," she finally said. "You're going to *tattle* on her?"

"What should I do, then?" Vivian asked.

Diana's unwavering opinion was the reason Vivian had come to her in the first place. For better or worse, her certainty was as good as a compass.

Diana had shaken her head. "I can't tell you that."

Avoiding Diana's gaze across the table, Vivian felt a lonely rage at defending a choice she hadn't wanted to make. Diana could pretend she was against what Vivian had done. She'd been all too eager to keep their group together. Resentment struck like a hunger in Vivian's heart. From their booth, she could see where they'd sat back in September, when Grace had been at the head of the table.

"Should we be worried?" Diana dumped sugar in her iced tea. She nudged Justin's shoulder for another packet. "I mean, I think my parents are tough. They're nothing like Mrs. Li."

"Grace is an adult," Vivian said firmly. "What can her mother do to her?"

They hushed when their waiter dropped off their pizzas.

"There's no way she can finish this movie now, right?" Errol's leg bounced and agitated the seat.

Diana shook chili flakes with pointed precision over her slice of pizza.

"I think that's for the best." Vivian found it hard to look up from the table. "She can't make boring footage interesting."

"We don't know that." Justin chewed on his straw. "I mean, I'm pretty sure we talked about smoking weed."

Diana said she couldn't remember what she'd said to Grace. "We spent hours together every day."

"You probably didn't say anything that you haven't said before." Vivian put a slice of pizza on Errol's plate. "You're not very original."

Diana threw a sugar packet at her head. The group laughed in one large exhale.

"The movie was a distraction," Errol said, the usual overflow of his mind breaking the silence. "Now we can move on with our lives."

Justin folded his pizza in half and shoved it into his mouth. The cheese on Errol's fell off when he picked up his slice. Vivian swapped his plate with hers.

* * *

After they said goodbye to the others in Diana's driveway, Errol walked Vivian to her parents' house. Dry leaves swept sideways across their path like little crabs. The night felt too cold to hold hands and they huddled shoulder-to-shoulder. Errol had forgotten a jacket and Vivian felt a stab of guilt for forgetting to remind him.

Seeing Errol shivering next to her, she realized he was dressed in the designer jeans and button-down she'd sent with him to Seattle. Weighed down by thoughts of Diana and Grace, she'd barely noticed his effort. The realization touched her in a spot sore and tender. She'd fought so hard for this relationship that now it felt like work.

They reached her garage, which her parents had left open for her return. To hide from the wind, they ducked into the darkness. She could sense him shifting his weight. All she wanted was to be alone, but it was their anniversary.

She gave his hand a squeeze. The wind blew around them. "Do you want me to sneak you upstairs?"

Errol buried his face in her neck. His cold nose made her squeak.

While Errol stole his way into her room, Vivian said good night to her father in his office, and her mother in the den. She listened for the creaky third step on the staircase, but some things Errol never forgot.

"We had a fun time," she said when her mother asked about dinner.

She kept delaying the inevitable, hoping her excitement would grow. Fifteen minutes passed before Vivian left her mother. Errol only smiled at her lateness. He stood to run the shower while Vivian unzipped her dress.

"Wait," Errol said.

He reached into his pocket. He was holding a velvet box. The shower was meant to cover their voices from her parents. The noise overwhelmed her. She could not clear her ears, could not get the sound of the water out.

Only later, when they retold the story to the group, did Vivian hear what Errol had said in the bathroom before she'd interrupted. Something about how most people had to go around the world to find their person, while he had found his down the block. Seattle had taught him a lesson: Everything he needed was here, and he was an idiot for thinking anything else. He'd spent all three months of his Microsoft salary on her ring because their marriage was his greatest investment.

In Diana's basement, Vivian showed off the ring on her left hand. Despite the dim light, the diamond dazzled.

"We're keeping this a secret," Vivian said. "Until Errol finds the right job."

"Get the fuck out of here!" Justin had shaken off his shock and pulled them into a hug.

Over Justin's shoulder, Vivian saw Diana's face, the pain on it easy to understand. She was certain they were making a mistake.

The mistake was hers. Diana thought she was the only one who knew their secrets. But the instant Vivian had seen that black velvet box, she had confessed to everything. She couldn't get engaged until Errol knew the real her, until he knew that she loved the real him.

They had run the shower for so long that her mother had scolded her the next morning for using up the hot water. The entire room had filled with steam. When Vivian had made her final confession, Errol had gathered her into his arms.

"You did that for us," he'd said. The awe in his voice had washed her cleaner than the tears on her face. "Oh baby, I know, I know that must have been hard."

Hugging Justin now, Vivian looked at the ring on her finger. For the second time in her life, fate had intervened. She felt grateful for the choices that had once brought her shame because life for her was finally beginning. She'd done more than hurt Grace with that one decision. She'd ranked all the people in her life. From that moment on, there was Errol first, and then there was everyone else.

November 1999

Grace unpeels the foil around her Hot Pocket, which she calls
her Cold Pocket because she microwaved it at six in the morning.
Thinking up jokes reminds Grace that she can always keep herself
company. The second lunch bell rings, five minutes after the first, and
the last stragglers squeak their sneakers past the media lab. The media
teacher Ms. Tran has snuck out for a private cigarette. She trusts
Grace enough to leave her unchaperoned with the computers. After
another minute of wondering what her friends are talking about at
lunch, Grace opens her project folder.

While she waits for the file to transfer onto a disk, she drags
the cursor through the long block of footage. Her friends jump and
jerk around, animated as if by lightning. Deep in her lab, she's Dr.
Frankenstein. Fun though it was to shoot the footage, editing is what
holds her captive. For months she has split and spliced until chaos has
merged into order. Entire lunch hours have passed with her fixated on
a tiny ten-second section. Other hours have been forked over to lonely
Ms. Tran, who has taken a special interest in Grace.

Grace first met Ms. Tran last year, in seventh grade media class.
Ms. Tran was a newer teacher, and younger than the others, which
should have made her popular with her media students. Instead, she was

roundly ignored. Her voice is too reedy, her gestures too nervous, and her outfits resemble the smocks they wear in art class. The other young teachers wear tight jeans and curse. They keep the students in place with sharp comebacks and well-styled hair. Ms. Tran, on the other hand, is not someone the students want to be, nor someone they can enjoy being afraid of. During her lessons, the other students play Minesweeper on the computers in her lab. Grace always tries to pay attention.

When Ms. Tran inevitably singles her out the spring of seventh grade, Grace accepts her teacher's offer of extra credit. She stays after school, which means she no longer has to sit alone on the bus while her friends choose seats together. Her class is in its stop-motion unit, and for weeks she edits their choppy felt dolls until there's something close to a story. Ms. Tran buys her vending machine snacks and insists that she take breaks, during which she asks Grace about her friends and family. Grace knows her loneliness is there to distract Ms. Tran from her own. This doesn't stop her from answering.

To talk about either, she has to reveal the secret she's kept since sixth grade, when her mother took a week off from work and brought her to four of the best boarding schools: Lawrenceville, Dalton, Choate Rosemary, and, most prestigious of all, Phillips Andover.

Andover is the top boarding school in America. Fewer than 10 percent of applications are accepted. The statistics mirror Harvard's. Grace and her mother think that to get into one must be a guarantee for the other. Instead of competing with all the other kids in the world, she'll only be up against the three hundred in her grade.

"At least fifty percent of the students won't be able to handle the pressure," her mother has said.

Her mother knows something about pressure. She was the sole girl in her province to win a place at a Beijing college—second tier, but the statistics would astound you. Meanwhile, the kids who grew up in the capitol had a one in ten shot at Tsinghua University, the best college in China. In her mother's eyes, one in ten is a privilege.

"I know what your mom wants. What do you want?" Ms. Tran asks, biting the corners off her strawberry Pop-Tart. A tear bubbles into Grace's eye, as if Ms. Tran has tripped a switch. Lately all of Grace's feelings are twisted, dark and bright. She is grateful to answer even as she hates her teacher for asking.

While her mother liked Andover's brick buildings and championship banners, Grace paid attention to how the students walked in groups. She imagines the freedom they must feel to have no parents there, to live with their friends around them. She is not allowed to tell her friends, who would tell their parents, and then all the Chinese families would be applying.

"These schools care about their numbers," her mother would remind her. "How many Chinese kids do you think they're allowed to take? How many from DC?"

Grace is used to keeping a part of herself walled off from her friends, but one secret leads to another. She cannot tell them about the extra piano competitions, or the practice SSATs. When they invite her to sleepovers and birthday parties, she has to say that her mom wants her to spend her weekends studying. This is also the reason her mother gives to their parents, and Grace is held up once again as the perfect daughter.

When the stop-motion unit ends, Ms. Tran offers to teach Grace how to use a camera. Grace knows her teacher feels sorry for her, which means that she also disapproves of Grace's mother. After her father went back to China, the other parents would take her out for pizza. Grace had loved the attention. Until one day, she'd looked over to see them surrounding her mother. *You are selfish for staying. You're ruining your daughter's life. Your duty is to your husband.* Grace learned that these treats were hiding a punishment for her mother. What did it mean for Grace to accept them?

Soon she knows how to use a camera. She gets permission to check equipment out of the lab and take it home over the weekend. Ms. Tran teaches her how to edit clips together and make the sequence run as seamlessly as if Grace had filmed it that way. They play with scores and voiceovers, and laugh at the cartoonish sound effects that come downloaded into Final Cut Pro. During her mother's end-of-the-year Best Buy trip to pick up gifts for Grace's teachers, Grace notes how much the equipment would cost if she did not have Ms. Tran's favor.

She owes Ms. Tran so much, and yet she can't stop pushing. She makes everything as twisted as she feels. When she notices the cigarettes in Ms. Tran's purse, she asks if she can try one.

"Who taught you how to smoke?" she asks, when Ms. Tran refuses, and Ms. Tran admits she had an older sister. No, *has* an older sister. They no longer speak. They haven't for years. These are her sister's favorites. Were. Ms. Tran doesn't even like them.

"I already smoke at home," Grace says. "If I went outside with my own cigarettes, you wouldn't stop me, would you?"

The next time Mrs. Zhang has one of her Blüm meetings, Grace accompanies her mother. While the women make their deals, she goes into the pantry and nabs one of Mr. Zhang's imported packs from China. The cigarettes palmed, she has an hour to kill. Her entire body prickles at the idea of going down to the basement uninvited, which is why she has to do it. Since sixth grade, this is where her friends have hung out instead of her and Justin's house. She continues to think of her house as shared well after Justin and his mother moved into one of the smaller townhomes in the neighborhood. They rent from Grace's mother, who has bought an entire row of homes. Grace isn't sure what her mother is doing besides buying real estate and earning exciting amounts of money.

"Whoa!" Justin is the first to see her. His excitement is also a warning for the others.

"Shouldn't you be studying?" Vivian is the only one who hugs Grace hello.

Diana hands Grace a can of soda like a good host. "We thought you were bored of us."

"How could she be bored of this?" Errol flips onto his hands and walks upside down toward Grace. She is impressed by his balance, until he seizes her face with his feet and brings her tumbling down with him.

The others burst out laughing. "We should have warned you," Diana said. "He's been finding new victims all week."

Grace's face is warm. Errol's dirty socks are the color of tea. She runs to the bathroom and scrubs her face with hot water. She doesn't mind the dirt, but she achieves the right effect. When she comes out, her friends are careful and quiet.

"Say you're sorry." Vivian pushes Errol by the side of his head. "You little perv. You can't treat girls like that."

"Sorry," Errol says. His eyes have that closed-off look, and Grace doesn't like that he can escape so easily.

"Actions speak louder than words," she says.

"Come on . . ." Justin starts, but can't sustain.

Diana yanks off Errol's socks like a mom getting through one more chore. "Will this make you happy, your highness?" She wipes the socks over Errol's cheeks.

Grace shakes her head, and somehow Diana understands. Justin and Vivian do too. Errol clamps his mouth like an animal sensing danger. Around her friends, everything becomes a chain reaction. Diana half-heartedly dabs the sock against Errol's pursed lips before Vivian grabs the other and grinds it into his mouth. Justin jumps in and yanks Errol back from the girls. The sock sticks out of Errol's mouth like a tongue. Grace is laughing so hard that the others can't help but join her. What choice do they have? With her bad engine, she drives them forward.

Later, in her backyard, her mother at work, Grace smokes her first cigarette. She knows she's supposed to cough, and so she is careful.

She smokes down to the filter without once losing control. Her head lifts with each puff, and she is too light. She has to darken the feeling. She thinks about the basement, and Errol putting his socks back on, a ring of spit around the ankle. She has missed her friends. Her loneliness is not their fault, but the first thing she does is try and hurt them.

When she announces to Ms. Tran that she wants to make a film about her friends, she is excited to have a reason to be with them.

"That's perfect!" Ms. Tran nearly drops her cigarette in her excitement. The two of them are out by the middle school track, behind a low brick wall where they can smoke without anyone seeing. "A short film is exactly what your Andover application is missing."

Grace takes a long, slow drag. Her heart always beats faster when she smokes, but the stupid muscle won't stop thudding.

"It can be a send-off to middle school. Oh my god, and the new millennium! It's fate. I can't wait to help you."

Ms. Tran is right, the horrible bitch. Just like that, she has ruined Grace's one good thing.

"I wish I could let you keep a camera over the summer," Ms. Tran continues. "If you spend September filming, we should have enough time to edit everything after school before your application deadlines."

Grace drops her cigarette and steps on the ember. She's smoked hers too fast. Ms. Tran's is hardly halfway done. The humidity of June clings to Grace's body, and she wishes she could push the air away.

"I can't stay after school next year," Grace says. "My mom wants me to study."

Ms. Tran chews on her lip. Again, that look of pity. If only people knew how ugly their faces became. "How about lunch period? I can pitch in if you need."

"Okay." Ms. Tran is so desperate to be part of Grace's life that Grace makes a vow. No matter how much her teacher begs, Grace will never show Ms. Tran the film.

"Do you know what you want the movie to be about? Besides your friends, I mean." Ms. Tran plays with the ends of her hair. They both know something has shifted.

Grace checks her supply. Since she started bumming cigarettes from Ms. Tran, she has almost a full box left. She tucks the box into the tall grass by the edge of the wall when Ms. Tran isn't looking. She is sorry for everything, for turning someone who wanted to help into someone she despises. She smiles at her teacher, but keeps her eyes on the track.

"I just know I want it to be funny."

CHAPTER FIVE

July 2009

The heat followed them in from the deck. Overwhelmed by the crowd of her future classmates, Diana could barely think. With everyone squeezed inside her father's office to watch Grace's video, the beige carpet was barely visible underneath their feet.

Her father's PC jostled awake and within moments, *Bad Asians* was up on the screen. Diana had moved too slowly for Jennifer, who'd elbowed her aside. No longer in control of the mouse, Diana tried to slip to the back of the room. The people piling in squeezed her further toward the front. Jennifer hit play. Was the video really ten minutes? Diana couldn't deny the truth for that long.

Before she could address the room, the sound of a school bell rang out, along with a loud *shhh* that came from the front row. The black screen rippled like the surface of a lake, broken by white text that floated into sight.

Bad Asian (noun): A term for any Asian American who does not fit their stereotype. Often used by other Asian Americans.

The text sank back down, replaced by a new row.

Antonyms: Overachiever, Model Minority, Filial Piety

Each word bubbled up and sank in turn.

In 1999, we interviewed four good Asian students at Cabin John Middle School, one of the top public schools in the nation.

Nine years later, we spoke to them again to see how the Great Recession has affected their post-graduate success.

Already people were giggling in anticipation. Diana hid her face with her hand. Soon, the undeniable image would stretch out across the computer screen.

Instead: a familiar building. Roosevelt High, where Ann Hua Chinese school had been held on Saturday mornings. The big white bubble of their swim and tennis center. The playground right behind her house. The Kumon Center in Germantown, its quizzical mascot side-eying the camera. Over the montage, someone off-camera spoke, a voice Diana barely recognized. Did she really sound like that?

The camera continued to skim past shopping centers and neighborhoods. Her voice opined: "I got a full ride to Maryland. I was a Gemstone scholar. I graduated magna cum laude. Yet it's been six months and I still can't find a job. At first, I thought I was lucky that my best friends were in the same boat . . ."

There was the Sichuan restaurant staffed by one waiter and one busboy. Next door, the Chinese grocery, where her parents did their weekend shopping.

"You know those crabs in the barrel at the Chinese store?"

Flashes of faded gray linoleum, and aisles stacked with foil-wrapped, vacuum-sealed packages. The seafood counter, and the big crab barrel, as tall as a five-year-old and twice as round. Diana could smell the fish behind the counter, and the damp cardboard soaking up the ice-melt.

"They could escape, couldn't they? The barrels were open. No one was watching them. But you know what happened if a crab got close to getting out?"

The camera zoomed in on the barrel. A claw cleared the rim. The crab's beady eyes peeped up, rotating on their stalks. The camera panned over the opening and revealed a pile of other crabs on which the top crab stood. Their claws lifted, as if in celebration. Then, they grabbed the top crab and yanked it tumbling back down.

"That's what I am now," her voiceover said. "Stuck with a bunch of crabs, keeping me at the bottom of the barrel."

Out of the darkness, there *she* was, in the bedroom where Grace had propped her, sitting on the same bed where she'd minutes ago sprawled out in disbelief.

"You know I had big plans," her video-self said, and before Diana could react, deny, or admit, the image was gone. Against the black screen, the same school bell from the beginning. The sound was uncanny, and in the depths of her body, Diana felt the flutter of memory: collecting, zipping, trudging on to the next class, encased by her friends, by the group. There they were! A clip from the past followed the school bell, one from the time capsule video that Grace had shown them in Diana's basement months ago.

They were in eighth grade homeroom. Mr. Davidson was in the background of the shot, reading his *Washington Post*. The four of them were playing Hearts at a round table. Errol sat on his knees, his elbows knocking against the pile of cards at the center. Next to him, Vivian played with a compact mirror, heavy with bedazzled gems. No one accused her of trying to look at their cards because hers were blatantly bleeding.

"My mom says I should be a lawyer." Diana's younger self dumped another heart card into the pile. Grace must have asked a question, cut out in editing. "I think I could be president. Or a motivational speaker slash doctor, like Ben Carson."

Vivian snapped her compact shut and flipped it open again. "I want to be like Princess Di. Like, royalty, but also helping poor people."

"Drawing comic books would be cool," Justin said without much excitement. He was audibly more stirred up when he lost the hand a few seconds later.

Errol didn't answer, too focused on something off-screen, until a voice nearly inaudible came from behind the camera.

"What about you, Errol?" Grace asked.

Errol looked as if he'd been yanked out of a decades-long sleep. The people in her dad's office laughed louder. Diana wanted to protect this boy on the screen.

"What?" the boy Errol said, and when Vivian repeated the question they'd been given—*What do you want to be when you grow up*—he bent his head back down to the game and said, "Successful."

In the mix of laughter, the scene changed and there was eleven-year-old Errol, now alone, sitting at a desk that had been pulled out into the hallway. A row of lockers stood behind him.

"I guess people call me a genius," the boy Errol said, eyes alternately darting and unfocused, like they were cameras themselves, tracking a subject that never stopped. "It's better than what they used to call me."

Diana heard her voice come in over the scene, which had Errol trying to break the combination to the locker behind him.

"People used to think Errol was, you know, *special ed*, until he got the highest math score in the gifted and talented test in first grade. Not just in our county, but the entire state. They gave him the test for third graders next, and he scored the same. He skipped two grades in one year. Newspapers wrote about him. He was a mini-celebrity. Now he's the good kind of special."

On-screen, Errol grinned triumphantly and yanked down hard on the lock. He was jerked back against the locker. The combination remained unbroken.

All around Diana, people were laughing. Jennifer was wiping tears from her eyes. The video's sound would have been inaudible if Diana had not been right up by the speakers. Were people drunk? What was funny? None of this was supposed to be funny.

On-screen, there was Errol in Diana's basement, almost a decade older, watching his projected self struggle to break the lock. Diana had forgotten that Grace had filmed them squished together on the couch, and she spotted herself at the far end. Her image was blurry, but she could see how hard she'd once laughed, and this wounded her, her own laughter. On the couch, Errol was smiling in his dreamy way.

"Everything comes easy to me. Sometimes I forget to try." Errol on the couch had become Errol on his own, in his bedroom. His walls were covered by whiteboards, which were in turn covered in formulae. "I was at Microsoft for a month before I was bored to death. I figured at least at home I wouldn't have to deal with all those egos. Just Diana's. Has she told you yet about how I was supposed to get her a job? Or how everyone else thought I was retarded? She's acting like she's my mom and I've brought her *great dishonor*. Maybe I'm a bad Asian, but I think there's more to life than giving your parents something to brag about."

Jennifer bumped into her, vibrating like a Chihuahua. Diana fell against the wall by the modem, not hard, but a physical force seemed to tear through her. She understood where this film was going and she heard that horrible voicemail Grace had left Vivian, four seconds long. *I hate you. I hate all of you.*

With a decisiveness that came like divine intervention, Diana wedged her foot behind the modem and kicked out the plug. The video screen plunged into ominous darkness. A white wheel appeared, spinning, spinning. The entire room groaned with disappointment.

* * *

Diana paced in front of Justin, Errol, and Vivian like a general about to present a plan of war. Everyone else was too busy talking to notice, their mouths full of the leftover watermelon she'd brought downstairs. After Diana had cleared out the last of the partygoers, she'd called the group and told them to come to her basement ASAP. It was nearly midnight before Justin was free. Now for the first time in weeks, the four of them were in the same room together.

Right when November had turned into December, Diana had gotten a paralegal position at her mother's friend's law firm. Then in January, Justin had received his personal training license. That same month, Vivian's sorority sister secured her a position at their university donor's office. Even Errol had deigned to take on some freelance work.

By February, through Vivian's sorority network, they'd found an old ranch house in Tysons Corner. The current lessees would let them sublet for a year, which would keep the rent affordable, if split among four sub-employed people. With no better options, the group decided they could share three bedrooms and one bathroom if it rescued them from another year with their parents. Each month since, the money they'd saved had pushed them one step closer to their move-in date in late August. The house became their favorite topic of conversation. Vivian tore pictures from old *Architectural Digest*s that Justin brought back from his mother's salon. Errol found the house's blueprints online and he and Diana had debated the perfect place to install a projector. They'd made it through the winter by dreaming of summer, and by closing the door on Grace. Like characters at the end of a horror movie, they'd relaxed into their new normal when Diana, done waiting for them to finish catching up, shouted that the monster was back.

"Almost two million views," she said. "And counting."

"I've searched her," Justin said after the initial uproar faded. "Online, I mean. I'll type her name in just to see."

"There's nothing." Diana admitted she had done the same. "No Facebook, no MySpace, not even an old Xanga from high school. Until now. She's going by MeMe Productions. The bio says she's in LA. I guess she made it there after all."

Errol took out his laptop. Diana braced for the sound of the school bell, but by the time she'd rushed over to his end of the couch, he was already distracted by the comments section.

Errol's so full of himself, it's laughable.

This is why gifted and talented programs should be removed from schools. They give kids like this Errol guy a massive ego and they crash and burn when they go out into the real world. Sad.

WHAT A RETARD

Justin leaned forward and cleared his throat. "Is there any-thing . . ." He bounced on the balls of his feet. "Anything weird about me?"

"You've got nothing to worry about," Diana said. "You're the fan favorite."

In the video, Justin had come across like a gym bro obsessed with his personal trainer. No one was complaining.

Justin is soooo cute

I hate everyone but that hottie w/ da body

Would subscribe to those squat videos in a heartbeat

"This is so mean," Vivian said, her voice soft. She'd found the video with her new BlackBerry, using the little stencil to flick through the comments. Diana knew what she was reading.

god I know tons of Asian girl basics like Vivian

I'm definitely Asian girl basic. Can I get my boba with 60% sugar

Gretchen, stop trying to make Asian Girl Basic happen! Lolol

When Vivian looked at the recommended videos, she would find a nastier surprise. Already people had made a half dozen remix videos out of Vivian's first appearance. She'd been holding a venti green tea Frappuccino in one hand and her cellphone in the other, trying to find the straw with her mouth while composing a text. The tableau culminated in Diana's voice drawling, "Asian girl basic." All because Grace had prompted Diana, months ago: *What was that thing you called Vivian? You know, the thing you said on our ride after that first dinner? It was so funny! I'd never heard it phrased like that before.*

If Vivian searched herself outside of the website, she'd find the memes too. Diana's voice replaced by blocky white text—ASIAN GIRL BASIC—while Vivian was photoshopped into grocery lines and nail salons with captions like, "I Can Has Diet Pokky?" and "French manicures are for good Asians." Diana was barely on-screen, and yet her voice had dissected her friends neater than a scalpel.

They had all said careless things. What group of friends didn't complain about each other? They had been cooped up, at the lowest point of their lives, with no outlet until Grace came with her questions. What Diana had done was normal. The cameras were the unnatural part.

Vivian and Errol both had the video up. Diana didn't have much time. Soon, someone's curiosity would get the better of them, and Grace's campaign to divide their group would be harder to stop.

"Look, I know it's not pretty," Diana said. For once, she had thought carefully about what she would say. In spite, or because of this, her words came out shaky. "You guys remember what we were like in October. I know there's a lot I said that I wish I could take back. I'm sure I'm not alone."

Diana had to present the greater threat and unite them to defeat it. Over Errol's shoulder, she pointed out the debate raging in the comments section.

Best mockumentary since Spinal Tap

No way, @pbnj91 this is like the marks in Borat, or the Colbert Report. These idiots clearly aren't acting.

The discussion was part of the video's popularity: mockumentary or prank? Diana went back a few pages and tapped the screen, directing her friends toward the comment that multiple others were referencing.

I went to high school with them! They're like this in real life too.

Diana said, "If people think we said those things for real, we're screwed. Every time we apply for a job, or go on a date, that video is going to be our first impression. Either we pretend we're in on the joke, or we are the joke."

Vivian threw her arms out and her BlackBerry smacked Errol in the lip. "That fucking bitch!" she shouted before she registered why Errol was cupping his face.

Relief hit Diana in the knees, and she sprawled over the back of the couch. They'd found their way back to the real enemy.

"Don't worry, it's not all bad," Diana said. She directed them to the comment that she'd nearly missed from user IHeartCarrieYang:

We have to do a collab! Msg me!

Vivian shrieked and Errol clapped his hands over his ears.

"Who's Carrie Yang?" Justin asked.

Vivian was already hissing, "You know who Carrie Yang is. 'What Asians are Actually Thinking'? 'Asian Teen Movie Makeover'? 'March Madness: Dim Sum Edition'?" She took over the laptop and clicked on the profile to show him.

Carrie Yang was as close to famous as a normal person could get. She'd created the videos that had introduced Diana to You-Tube in the first place, a mix of makeup tutorials, confessionals, and parody sketches. Vivian had emailed Diana a link to Carrie's anime-eyes tutorial the other day. There had been over six million views on that video alone.

"We have to do it." Vivian's eyes glittered. "Carrie is my *hero*."

"What're you talking about?" Errol snapped. "Why would we make ourselves bigger targets?"

"People are going to talk no matter what," Diana said. "This way we have a chance to control the story. Would you rather have these comments be about you, or some character you're playing?"

Justin nodded in a way that could either mean agreement or surrender. Errol jerked his head like there was water in his ears.

"I said I didn't want to be in Grace's video." He thumped the heel of his hand against his temple. "Why'd you let her film us?" He shoved the laptop off his knees and Justin grabbed it before it hit the ground. Errol jabbed his finger in Diana's face. "If you'd left her alone, none of this would've happened."

Once upon a time, Diana could chase a person down, yank them by the collar, and sit on their back until they did what she wanted. She was decades removed from those recess games, but she felt a terrible twist at the root, as if she were still chasing, no longer able to catch up with her friends.

"See," she said helplessly. "Grace wants us to fight."

Vivian slipped down onto the ground and rested her arms over Errol's knees. She looked up at him. "Diana's right. Let's get through this. If we do a video with Carrie, everyone will think we were acting in *Bad Asians* too."

They won't think you're marrying a total asshole, Diana almost said. She caught her tongue between her teeth. She wasn't used to fighting with subtext.

"Do it for your fiancée," she said. "If you won't do it for yourself."

Vivian sucked in her lips before she popped them back out. "Please, please, please," she pouted, knuckles under her chin. The sight of her, eyelashes batting, flung a reluctant laugh out of Errol's mouth.

"You trying to be a star?" Diana tried to ignore her own unease. For this to work, her friends had to believe in her excitement. Like shooting the moon, you couldn't flinch, or you'd lose everything.

Vivian threw her head back and shouted, "We're all going to be stars!"

Justin rubbed his head with his hands. "That's one way to look at it."

In unison, Diana and Vivian raised their faces to the popcorn ceiling and howled. Errol took his laptop from Justin and played the first episode of Carrie Yang's *Barbie Chan*. The video had a million more views than theirs. Seconds later, they were laughing while Carrie talked Asian tourist groups into trying a beer bong for the first time. Diana told the group that she would reach out to Carrie, and they used the webcam on Errol's laptop to take a photo. Proof that they were who they said. For the moment, they were distracted into getting along, or at least occupying the same side. They would most likely watch the video once they went home and find new reasons to be hurt and angry, but the delicate truce would hold them together through this larger crisis. Diana had finally learned how to take things one step at a time.

* * *

After her friends had gone home, Diana went upstairs to find her mother washing the last of the dishes.

"Did you tell them?" Her mother turned off the faucet and put the plate in the dishwasher to dry.

Diana was briefly bewildered before she saw the Harvard baseball cap someone had left behind from the party. How lucky that her friends always came through the basement door.

"Not yet." She turned the cap over on the kitchen table.

"How will they find another person to live in that awful house?" Her mother shut the dishwasher, which jangled with the plates and silverware they stored inside it. "You think this is only about you and your friends. What will I tell their parents if they can't move out?"

Diana folded the hat between her hands. Her mother had nagged and moaned at her for months, and now that Diana had given her what she wanted, she'd found another reason to complain. "Tell them I got into Harvard."

"You're twenty-three and you still don't understand anything." Her mother took the hat from her and rounded it back into shape. "You need to think about other people."

Thinking about other people was how she'd gotten in this situation in the first place. She'd said yes to this video as a favor to Grace. She'd applied to law school to make her parents happy. She'd come up with this entire plan to help her friends, and nobody had thought to be grateful. Anyone else with her résumé would be Mother Teresa. Why couldn't people see her as anything but selfish? Because she was assertive? Because she spoke her mind? She looked forward to the day she could be as blunt as the lawyers she assisted, and people would thank her for it.

"They should be happy for you," Diana shot over her shoulder on her way out of the kitchen. "If they're your friends." She made her footsteps heavy on the stairs, but not heavy enough that her mother could call it stomping.

"You think your friends will be happy for you?" her mother called up the stairs, sticking her head past the kitchen threshold.

Diana slammed her bedroom door, catching it right before it hit the frame.

*   *   *

The last big argument she'd had with her mother had been before Diana's first one-on-one with Grace. They'd had a version of the same fight since Diana was a kid. That October, however, Diana's mind, usually locked in place, kept swinging on its hinges. She'd seen old classmates posting about their exciting new careers, often the same people her mother had wanted her to befriend. If she'd made more ambitious, more impressive friends, maybe she'd be with them now instead of sending her hundredth job application.

Her mother had moved next to her, putting on the same gentle tone she used to talk her sellers out of canceling their contracts. Despite this, Diana had leaned into her. She'd smelled like the jasmine in Blüm's latest perfume, and also of dish soap and musky mom-skin.

Pressing her lips to the top of Diana's head, her mother had said, "I don't want you to make the same mistake I did. Do you think I want to sell lotion? Listen to me—the right friends help you grow, and the wrong ones drag you down to their level."

Now her mother's words had been immortalized and anyone who watched *Bad Asians* would think Diana was the one who'd said them.

In the video, her voice had recited, "If you surround yourself with people doing worse than you, you can feel good for a while. You can think, *They're not getting work either.* Meanwhile, other people are getting promotions and buying their first houses. Those people look at you, and they don't think, *She's doing much better than her friends.* They think, *What a bunch of losers.*"

"What does she know?" Grace had said from the floor of Diana's bedroom. "I was surrounded by 'impressive' people at school, and I'd give all that up to have a close group of friends."

Looking now at the spot on the carpet where Grace had sat, Diana tried to remember the satisfaction she'd felt at Grace's admission. To have envy requited was more pleasurable than a confession of love. Or so Diana imagined. She'd never had a serious boyfriend. Sometimes her life felt too full for another person's needs, and sometimes she didn't know how she could trust anyone more than those three. They were the established facts of her life. How else could she have endured them these last few months?

You think they'll be happy for you? Inside Diana, new irritation clustered around old. Since the engagement, Diana had had to watch Errol pretend Vivian was the love of his life, and Vivian pretend she believed him. Even after Diana had filled Justin in on what Errol had done to Vivian, what Vivian had done to Grace, Justin refused to intervene. He would let arguments boil over, no longer in the room despite sitting beside them. Diana had argued with Vivian and Errol so often that there was hardly any water left in the pot. The worst part was that they never argued about anything real. They snapped at each other about what movie to watch, or whose turn it was to go buy beer. Each time Diana decided to face their problems head-on, she chickened out at the last second. She kept thinking there would be another time when they were getting along better, when this rough patch had ended.

Even at their worst, however, look at what they had accomplished together. In February, getting the Tysons Corner house had been a promise. They were going to change their lives. Errol had brought one of his whiteboards to Diana's basement to write out the calculations. How much they needed to cover the deposit, first and last month's rent, and the hourly rates that would help them reach this ultimate number. The jobs they'd once complained about—too menial, too embarrassing, too low-pay—became a means to a brighter end.

"We couldn't have done this without each other," Diana had said the night they'd signed the sublease. Despite the season, they were out by the playground behind her house, their breaths striping the cold wet air. A bottle of red wine was planted into the woodchips.

"Apart, it might have taken months, *years*." Diana shivered and spilled wine across her shoes. "Look at us! We can do anything together."

"Anything together!" Justin had thrust his cup against hers, spilling more wine. They'd already finished three bottles in her basement, which was why they were out in twenty-degree weather. That and the joint in Errol's hand.

Freezing in February, coughing on brittle weed, Diana had been as unable to picture her life in that Tyson's Corner house as to imagine the heat of summer. Whenever she tried, all she saw were her giant dog posters and her family's old wraparound couch. She hadn't known if this meant that she would miss the basement, or that she feared she could never leave.

Now her heartbeat raced through her body like a circuit. Diana felt those worries flushed away. A message had appeared in her inbox from Carrie Yang.

I loved you guys in that video. I'm so pumped you want to collab. You have to come up to New York next weekend. I'll show you around to my favorite places, and we'll film a little. If you guys have fun, we could talk about future projects.

What if their house together had been a necessary fantasy, a lie they'd told to force themselves into motion? If all of them ended up back on the right path, no one would need to live in that run-down house. Justin could start his own personal training business, Errol's freelancing would pick up, and Vivian might be halfway on the road to her own online celebrity. None of this notoriety would help Diana. She'd known this from the start. The plan had been built around the others. Like it or not, and even at their worst, she would always feel responsible for the group.

CHAPTER SIX

According to the Garmin suctioned to the dash, they would be at Carrie Yang's apartment in three hours and thirty-four minutes. Although the GPS belonged to Vivian, they were driving Justin's mother's car to Brooklyn, for reasons out of his control.

Vivian's parents had bought a third Mercedes last year (ridiculous, the other parents had teased, when their garage only had room for two), but her aunt was in town and her parents anticipated a list of situations where two cars would not be enough. Errol's parents were ferrying his little sister Lucy through their own list (squash lesson, pottery class), and needed both cars to give each chauffeur a break. Diana's mother had taken her family's extra car to the Blüm conference in DC and her brothers were learning how to drive that weekend. Yet with one car to spare, Justin's mother had relinquished her Honda without argument.

"Drive safe," she'd told them that morning, waving from the front door and hiding a yawn with her other hand. In a few hours, she would leave to catch the bus to her salon. Saturdays were her busiest. They were also his. He'd had to beg Raul to cover the sessions he couldn't reschedule.

Justin turned the music down and insisted that they be back by tonight.

"Yes, we already promised." Diana cranked the music back up. Her contribution to the trip had been jumping into the shotgun seat with a plastic bag full of their high school mix CDs. They were listening to one labeled HAPPY SHIT. Green Day's "Time of Your Life" blared from the speakers. "I wonder how many views we've got now."

"Over two million when I checked this morning," Vivian said.

A week had passed since they'd learned about the video. How quickly the others had switched from horror to excitement. Justin had tried his best to put the video out of his mind, less to avoid thinking of its contents than to avoid the surge of anger that rose each time.

When Diana had broken the news of *Bad Asians*, Justin's heart had made sloppy thuds against his chest. He'd seen Errol typing into his laptop, and suddenly the video was there. Justin's eyesight had sharpened with pinhole focus. Spotting Errol's name down in the comments, he'd pointed to draw Errol's attention, and he'd been saved from having to watch the video in front of his friends.

Later, in his bedroom, he drank until he could stand to face what Grace had created. Watching on low volume, he had to lean toward the screen. His body tightened each time he heard himself say Raul's name.

"You see how there's this extra curve up here, by my stomach? That's thanks to Raul.

"Raul showed me this move where you take a hand weight between your feet . . .

"This is a protein shake. Raul recommended it, and it tastes like chocolate cake."

Grace wasn't evil. Although Justin's stomach had ached through the ten-minute video, he knew Diana would have said something if Grace had included the moment in his backyard. She wasn't an angel either. The first day of fourth grade, during class introductions, Grace had said, "I live right across the street from school in the big white-and-brick house, and Justin lives in my basement."

She was matter-of-fact enough that no one questioned her. They called Justin "Basement Boy" and never wondered why Grace's mother needed to rent out the basement in the first place. Grace knew the best place to hide a secret was in plain sight. She'd cut his hour-long interview down to a collage of a meathead in love with his trainer. A joke so obvious people took for granted that Justin was in on it too. She'd made a caricature of his confession, and he couldn't confront her without exposing himself.

Her video brought forth another kind of exposure too. Two million people had seen his face, his body, under bright lights, reflected in spotless gym mirrors. The pink birthmark on his chest, the vaccine scar on his arm, the jade necklace his father had given him. In his mind's eye, he'd been a blur. His friends were sharp and vivid. He could draw them from memory if he wanted. Raul's image was so clear that Justin could see him easier than the road ahead. For Justin, looking at his body in the mirror was like judging a suit held in front of himself. When he woke up in the morning, he was as small as a boy until he opened his eyes and sat up.

Now unseen strangers could pick him out of a crowd. That week, the group had gone out to dinner and been approached for photos. The comments section had ballooned with claims of a *Bad Asians* sighting. People triangulated their locations to find where they might live. Someone posted a link to Errol's freelance portfolio. Their parents remained in the dark, but a feeling of unarticulated dread had followed Justin all week, until the comment he'd been waiting for appeared: *Justin goes to my gym!* Replies followed, begging for the name, the address, to which the original poster coyly offered, *PM me if you want to know more.*

Who was *MrUniverse00*? He could be one of Justin's clients, or one of Raul's. Or maybe he was one of the men who would wink when the two of them left the steam room. Justin had gotten careless, certain that nobody from his real life would see. At that gym, Raul had promised people were discreet.

While the rest of the group argued over the current view count,

Justin felt his phone buzzing in his back pocket. Each vibration made his chest pinch tighter. Finally, heads began to dip. No one had slept the night before, and the tires hummed a potent lullaby.

"I hate when people fall asleep on road trips." Diana shot a disdainful look at Vivian and Errol, their hands interlaced while their bodies slumped in opposite directions.

"I don't mind." Justin put his hand over her drooping eyes.

She laughed and batted him away. When that laugh became a face-splitting yawn, she said, "Alright, fine."

She shot her seat back, accidentally clipping Errol's knees, and ejected the CD. "All yours," she said, and turned her face toward the passenger window.

Justin shifted in his seat to slide his phone out and onto his left knee.

Have a safe drive.

I miss you.

I wish I were your car seat.

Please come back already.

Justin loved the formal grammar of Raul's messages, his generational tendency to text in full sentences, with punctuation. Justin, in return, wrote in brief burps of interest:

hey

u awake

nice

"There weren't mixed signals," Raul had said once. "There weren't *any* signals at all!" Raul's head had been on Justin's chest; Justin could feel his mouth moving. "You were completely silent for weeks. Until, out of the blue, you remember what you said to me?" Raul looked up, the devil in his eyes. "*I'm so hard.* I nearly came right then."

The memory cinched a rope around Justin's neck. After a year, his time with Raul was ending. Far later than he would have believed when they'd first started up last July, and with feelings far more conflicted. He would have to put in his two weeks' notice after this trip. He lacked the willpower to end things otherwise, and when he moved in with his friends, he could no longer be out with Raul all night. Unlike his mother, they would demand to know where he'd been, and they would know if he was lying.

They'd believed him, though, when he'd said he was quitting to start his own business. Their enthusiasm had been sweet. In a moment of weakness, he'd admitted he was scared to tell Raul. None of them understood why this caused Justin any grief.

They couldn't know that Raul was barely a month into his trial separation. His wife, Ingrid, wanted to divorce him. At first, all Justin had known about Ingrid was that she had followed Raul from Seville to the States, although she was originally from Berlin. These facts had kept Justin up at night in the beginning, picturing a lonely woman trapped in a country far from home. He'd been shocked to find little pretense between husband and wife. Ingrid was having her own affairs when she traveled weekly for work. The pictures in Raul's house revealed a tall, solid woman with a thick braid of blond hair, beautiful the way a tree was. After he'd seen the pictures, whenever Justin lay in Raul's California King, he would try to find Ingrid's indent in the mattress.

With Raul and Ingrid's coupling clearly transactional, Justin had expected a clean separation. Instead, Raul had gone into hysterics the day Ingrid had announced her decision.

"You'll leave me too, won't you?" he'd shouted at Justin over the phone. It was the first time he'd called for anything besides sex or work. "How can she do this? I gave her everything she wanted."

That night, after Justin had gotten off the phone, he had gone downstairs to find his mother. He had tried to gather the courage to ask her something, only to abandon the idea at the sight of her alone, fixed to the TV that she never turned off. She was laughing at a rerun of *Two and a Half Men*. Something tickled the back of Justin's throat.

His father had also lived a double life, but after he'd made his choice, he'd never looked back. They'd had no contact, unlike

Grace's dad who called her on birthdays. All Justin had was the jade tiger his father had given him before he'd left. Its weight, once a comfort, grew heavy. Standing at his own crossroads, Justin wondered if this was how his father had felt. If, in fact, the man had not been heartless. His sympathy sickened him. He and his father were not the same. His mother would not be left behind again.

When the group asked, *What's the big deal? Your boss should understand*, the longing to tell them stretched a hollow in his chest, on top of which his jade tiger no longer rested. To answer them, he would have to tell not only his story, but also Raul's and Ingrid's, his mother's and his father's. He'd saved up too much. He would have to talk for hours.

* * *

The entrance to the Holland Tunnel at ten on a Saturday was already packed with cars. The lurching and honking woke everyone up. The sound of static also welcomed them to New York. Justin, without realizing, had stayed on the same DC station.

"Jesus, you're a psycho." Diana turned the radio dial. She yanked her seat upright and peered at the tunnel walls. "I can't believe we're going to meet Carrie Yang. Everyone know your roles?"

"Dumb jock," Justin said.

"Delusional asshole," Errol said.

"Asian girl basic." Vivian smiled at Diana in the rearview mirror, her eyes sharp as if staring into the sun.

Diana and Carrie had had another phone call last night, the contents of which Justin already knew, but he sensed an argument brewing between Diana and Vivian. "You're sure she didn't tell you what the plan is for today?"

"Sorry, I didn't ask her for an itinerary," Diana said.

"How can we trust her?" Errol said. "She's going to do whatever it takes to get the most views."

"Exactly. The more ridiculous we are, the more obvious it is that we're 'acting.'"

Unable to stop this argument too, Justin inched the car through the tunnel. The GPS kept repeating, *Lost signal, lost signal, lost signal.*

Carrie lived in a part of Brooklyn that made the group think of their fifth-grade trip to Colonial Williamsburg. The place did feel old-fashioned compared to Manhattan, with low buildings that brought the sky close. The bricks showed their age. Black-hatted men huddled together on the sidewalks, long curls hanging over their eyes.

As the GPS counted down the steps to Carrie's apartment, the energy grew inside the car. The anticipation built and built— would they knock? Would they have to buzz in? How did people do that outside of movies?

But when they turned the last corner, there, on the quiet residential street, was a couple sitting on the front steps of an apartment block. The woman was immediately recognizable, and the brief disconnect between the group's expectations and the sudden reality broke the tension in the car. Without meaning to, everyone relaxed. The worst and best part was over, and sure enough, Carrie Yang had spotted them through the windshield of their car. She sprang up and danced into the street.

"Oh my god, I knew it, she's totally Barbie Chan." Vivian pointed over Justin's shoulder.

Pretty and petite, Carrie looked less like a Barbie than a Japanese schoolgirl with her blazer and short plaid skirt. She wore loafers that were too big for her feet, and a purple Band-Aid above her knee, so small it had to be ornamental. Captivated by her, they forgot about the man who'd stayed seated on the stoop. He had a camcorder out and was following her every move.

"Looks like she's got her own Grace," Diana said. The joke chilled Justin like a premonition.

He found a tight spot between two cars, rolling down his window to see better. Carrie jogged over. He started to say hello when she grabbed his face and planted a big kiss on his mouth.

"God, how are you hotter in person?" she said, her voice a strange valley girl drawl. She tasted like bubblegum, and her gloss stayed sticky against his lips. He felt, with the stoop man's camera on him, that he could not wipe his mouth.

"Nice to meet you," he said dumbly.

Leaning into the car, she said in a stage whisper, "I figured since we only have the day, we should get into character now."

Justin felt the skin along his arms go stiff and bumpy despite the July sun beating hard overhead. He wanted to hold down the horn until this stranger got her perfumed head out of his car. The rest of the group had spilled out onto the street, already acting.

Once in Carrie's fifth-floor walk-up, they gathered inside her kitchen. The rest of her studio was crowded with video and lighting equipment. An unmade mattress lay crooked on the floor. Only one corner of her apartment was neat and decorated.

Vivian pointed to it and whispered, "That's where she films her makeup tutorials."

The kitchen was a stretch of tile with a small fridge and a two-burner stove. A high-top table had been fashioned out of plywood and pipes. Along the table were five shot glasses filled with swamp-green liquid; a large apothecary bottle headed up the line. Carrie picked up a glass, pinky out.

"Gan bei," she said.

"Oh my god, I love Midori," Vivian said.

She was mimicking Carrie's drawl, which made Justin glance at Diana and Errol. He caught the stoop man's camera instead. Vivian had the shot raised to her mouth when Justin sniffed his own. He moved too late to stop her.

She came up spluttering. The green liquid sprayed out of her mouth. Carrie looked into the camera and winked.

"That's not Midori, honey," she said. "This is Green Dragon."

She downed hers with a flourish and did a shivery dance that made her chest bounce.

"What the hell did you give her?" Errol pounded Vivian's back.

"It's weed-infused vodka," Justin said.

"I knew you'd know what it was," Carrie said. She'd already refilled both her and Vivian's glasses. "Bottoms up, babe."

Justin put his shot back down on the table. "Sorry, can't," he said. "I'm driving."

"It's barely eleven." Carrie sidled up to him. "Besides." She squeezed his upper arm with both hands, spanning her fingers to show how they barely met around his biceps. "You're a big guy. One shot must be nothing."

Justin remembered Grace, the camera hidden in her lap, asking him to tell her everything.

He pulled his arm out of Carrie's grasp.

"I'm good," he said, and surprise briefly rearranged her face.

The next moment, she bounded back to the center of the group. She cajoled everyone to lift their glasses and get the day drinking started. For a moment, the camera lingered on Justin before it too followed Carrie's lead, leaving him briefly, wonderfully unseen.

* * *

After the round of shots, the man with the camera introduced himself. He was Carrie's "partner," full stop. His name was Z, full stop again, and yes, this was the name on his birth certificate. His parents had decided the letter was enough, and he was inclined to agree. All of this was communicated in fewer than five words, each one pulled out like a clog from a shower drain. Despite the heat, Z wore black jeans and a black button-down, and when he shook their hands, his fingers felt like ice. His hair fell in his face, which was sharp and triangular. He looked like the fanart Justin used to draw.

"Sorry for springing this on you," Carrie said. Her voice, without the affect, was deep and resonant, smothering the other conversations around her. "Have you tried pretending to meet for the first time? It's fucking impossible! You guys were pro, right, Z?"

Z fiddled with his camera.

"You said you have to drive back tonight?" Carrie asked, and Diana, looking first at Justin, said, "Yeah, sorry."

"I was hoping I'd get you for the full weekend." Carrie cracked her knuckles. "Well, we've filmed under tighter deadlines. Here's what I was thinking."

The group would be their characters in *Bad Asians* and she would be Barbie Chan. She was thinking of calling it *Bad Asians 2: Lost in New York.*

"It's okay if I use your title, right?" she said, and without waiting for an answer, continued, "Awesome, so we have you guys run into Barbie, who you know from some nerdy summer camp."

"Like CTY?" Vivian named the camp that had enchanted their parents by title alone: the Center for Talented Youth.

Carrie was equally enchanted. "I like the sound of that!"

She would lead them on a tour of the city, starting in Brooklyn and moving up onto the island proper. The activities would be liquored up and increasingly salacious.

"I'm hoping we end up at this hilarious Western bar in Midtown," she said. "They have, I shit you not, a mechanical bull. In *Manhattan*! The place is big enough to be an arena."

She cracked open a Diet Coke, which was all her small fridge held, besides a row of glass vials. When Errol asked what the vials were for, she said, "They keep Z alive."

"And I need him alive," she said, her eyes fixed on Z, who looked down at his camera. "He's an editing genius. Don't worry about being funny or whatever. That's Z's job. I've *never* scripted any of my videos. Be yourselves, you know?"

Again, a chill dropped over Justin. He looked around at his

friends, hoping to see some reflection that they had also been spooked, but they all nodded eagerly.

Carrie grabbed her purse off the ground and reapplied her lip gloss. "Alright, first stop, bottomless mimosas, bitches!"

Z shouldered his bag, and with an intensity difficult to dispute, gestured at them with his camera to cheer.

After the brunch restaurant Carrie had picked out, a Polish place that served breakfast pierogies along with coils of kielbasa, Justin made sure everyone finished a cup of water. He had intimate knowledge of the group's tolerance, and at the arcade Carrie took them to next, he pointed Diana toward the bathroom.

The others found the Dance Dance Revolution station and pumped the machine full of quarters. While Carrie and Errol pounded their way through "Captain Jack," Justin wandered off to check his phone by the prize counter. Leaning against the glass case, he saw that he had a message from his mother.

Hope you having fun

He wished she were with him, and in the next instant, he pictured Raul there too, the two of them leading Justin's mother through Chinatown. The image startled and bewitched him, like a colorful bird landing on his shoulder. He was writing to Raul when Z appeared.

"You should get back to the group."

"I'm checking in with someone." Justin looked down at his phone. The barely written message blinked back. He'd lost what he'd wanted to say, not the words exactly, but the buoyant feeling that had made the words possible.

He put his phone away. "Are you dating Carrie or something?"

"Carrie and I are true partners." Z spoke barely above a whisper to prevent the camera from picking up his voice.

"Seems like she's the one in charge." Justin crossed his arms and spoke louder.

"You should know that people are different off-camera." Z gestured for Justin to walk ahead. Justin jutted out his chin and flexed his chest and shoulders, the way a dumb jock would. Behind him, Z's laugh was warm and raspy.

Diana and Vivian were going head-to-head on DDR now that Diana had finished throwing up in the bathroom. Across the room, Errol and Carrie were shooting hoops. Carrie tossed her basketball at Justin and said, "You take over," before skipping off toward the bar.

Justin stood next to Errol and took his shot, the ball too light in his hands. Errol was shooting underhand as always.

"This is kind of weird, right?" Justin purposefully hit the rim to hide his words under the racket.

"What do you mean?" Errol concentrated hard on the basket, the tip of his tongue caught between his teeth.

"It's barely noon," Justin said. "And you guys are getting shit-faced."

"How else am I supposed to get through this?" Sweat cobble-stoned Errol's upper lip. "You should've backed me when I said no. Too late to worry now."

"Just be careful." Justin jerked his head toward Z, who had his camera trained on Carrie. She'd come back from the bar with five tallboys of PBR pressed to her chest.

"Who cares?" Errol said. The game buzzer sounded. "We're supposed to be acting, remember?"

* * *

After Vivian, following Carrie's lead, threatened to shotgun his untouched tallboy, Justin reluctantly drank half. This arm-twisting made him feel well within his right to demand a break for every-one.

"How about boba?" he asked.

Carrie and Z exchanged a look.

"Alright, Mr. Tour Guide," Carrie said, no edge to her voice.

She reminded him of a river, calm and clear on the surface, with a violent current only he could sense. "Let's do Chinatown. I know a place that also serves booze. They set their drinks on fire."

Consulting Z, she decided that the train schedule was "totally fucked" on the weekends. She asked if they could drive up to Manhattan and skip the humid wait in the subway.

Vivian agreed before Justin could say anything, and he couldn't pretend that he'd had too much to drink. Carrie took the front seat and Z squeezed in the back with the others. No one put on their seat belts. Justin looked for cop cars at every intersection while Carrie shouted over the Garmin, bossing him down narrow streets crowded with outdoor wet markets.

A light rain was falling. The sun remained vibrant and shining overhead. Carrie sprang out of the car, her face raised.

"You know what this means," she said. "The devil's getting married."

"Or beating his wife," Z said, so quietly that only Justin seemed to hear him.

Justin understood why Carrie had picked the Hong Kong–style café when every table turned to stare. On their way to the table, whispers trailed behind them.

"I love you, Barbie Chan," their waitress said nervously, as if she'd practiced the line in her head.

"I love you too." Carrie blew her a kiss and, dropping her Barbie voice, asked, "Since we're filming, could you be a doll and comp our drinks?

"Girl, let me see that ring," Carrie said once the waitress had taken their orders. Holding Vivian's hand, she leaned across the table and tapped Errol. "I guess you got over that second-guessing."

"Vivian, you should probably take off the ring for the video." Diana eyed the other tables, where people craned their necks to see into the booth.

"No, keep it on." Carrie bugged out her eyes and held Vivian's hand tighter. "That's *so* romantic! When's the wedding?"

"We're planning on a long engagement." Errol slouched back in the booth. "I had to throw her a bone."

"We're waiting for Errol to find the right company," Vivian said. "Amazon or Facebook."

Diana cut in: "He's awfully picky for someone living with his parents."

"Actually, we're all moving out." Vivian shied away from the act. Her voice grew perkier. "The four of us are renting a house together."

"Oh my god, this is too perfect," Carrie said. "You have to invite me over." A shrewd, almost greedy look replaced the vacuous mask she'd been wearing. She looked like a child counting her Halloween candy.

Justin waited for Diana to shout, "Party house!" as she'd been doing all summer, but she looked intently at their waitress returning with their drinks.

Vivian pulled out her BlackBerry and showed Carrie pictures of the three-bedroom ranch. The entire kitchen was paneled in pale yellow wood, the one bathroom tiled salmon pink. An A/C unit stuck out of the living room wall, the grate furred with dust. The bedrooms were clustered at one end of the hallway. If they tried to walk out of their rooms at the same time, they would be jammed together like pickles in a jar.

"It's adorable," Carrie said. Z loomed over her shoulder, his camera fixed on the images on Vivian's phone. "So retro."

"I can already picture it: *That 70's Bad Asians Show*." Vivian leaned toward Carrie until she rose out of her seat. "What do you think?"

Justin wanted to yank her back down by her belt loops. Vivian had always been this way, the one who would cajole the group to attend a party only to ditch them for a flashier set of friends.

As Vivian leaned forward, though, Carrie was leaning away. Z lowered his camera in time for Carrie to say, "You make one video and you think you're a star."

How quickly Justin turned from impatience with Vivian to sharing the wound of her embarrassment. He opened his mouth. Diana beat him to the punch.

"Aren't you dating your own camera crew?" she said.

Carrie's upper lip bulged when she swiped her tongue across her front teeth, shifting like a boxer ready to strike.

"Mama bear." Carrie took a delicate sip of her drink. "Taking care of your cubs. What're they going to do when you leave them next month? Or, oops, was that supposed to be a secret?"

Diana put her glass down, the *thunk* traveling up Justin's fingertips. He was too surprised to get his words in order, and Vivian, never one to assume she'd been left out of the loop, was fervently denying on Diana's behalf.

Errol was left to ask the necessary question. "What is she talking about?"

Diana stared down at the table, tracing the ring of condensation her glass had left. Justin had seen countless teachers on the opposite end of Diana's glare, their anger wilting over her refusal to look away, and when she couldn't meet any of their eyes, he was suddenly afraid.

"I . . . I got into Harvard Law," Diana said.

Justin's brain went down the wrong circuit, *No, Grace got into Harvard Law*, and he felt himself start to say those words, the press of his tongue against the roof of his mouth.

"Yes!" he shouted. He threw his arm around Diana's shoulder and jostled her until her head bounced out of its lowered position. "That's amazing! Why didn't you tell us sooner?"

"You said you only applied to schools near DC." A shimmer of hurt warped Vivian's words.

"I was embarrassed," Diana said. "I thought I wouldn't get in. I almost didn't. I must've been the last person they let off the waitlist."

"Seriously," Errol said. "At this point, they're trying to find someone to pay the tuition."

"Well, it's not like you *just* got off the waitlist," Carrie said. "Didn't you tell me on the phone yesterday that you threw a welcome party?"

Faced with a direct question, Diana could not back down.

"I found out in June," she said. She squared her shoulders and shifted her gaze, no longer looking at Carrie. Justin glanced over, and there was Z, or rather his camera lens, dilated and shiny. "I thought it might bum you guys out to hear that I was leaving for Harvard."

Vivian scoffed. Justin wasn't sure if she'd caught on or was genuinely reacting. "You thought we'd be jealous?"

"You couldn't pay me to go to law school," Errol said.

A sharp buzz traveled up Justin's leg, sustained and insistent. He could excuse himself and let them fight, but the other tables were watching.

"A round of sake bombs." He lassoed his finger over his head. "To Diana, no longer a bad Asian!"

This was where he left them, table reverberating from their pounding hands. He made his excuses with his phone already pressed to his ear.

Plugging his other ear to block out the subway train rattling across the Manhattan Bridge, he said, "What's up?" He circled the car, inspecting it for new dings.

"I couldn't read your intake notes at first. I think I deciphered your chicken scratch. Sorry to interrupt. You having fun?" The question came out slightly muffled. Justin could picture Raul with his cheek squashed into the gym office's couch, an oblong pancake of sadness.

"My friends are driving me crazy."

"Come back home," Raul said.

"I *am* by the car." Justin jangled the keys in his pocket.

"What've you been doing?"

"Filming. Drinking. Not me. I'm DD." Justin checked behind him, back at the café's entrance. "They're wasted and it's barely three."

Justin understood then that he was upset, that the shock over Diana's news had flaked off. She had lied to them for weeks. They had made promises! Sacrifices! She wasn't allowed to leave when he'd chosen to stay behind. The claustrophobia of that ugly little house wrapped around him. He had done what other people wanted. For his trouble, Grace had stolen his privacy, his friends, his last gasp of freedom. They had even taken his mother's car!

"Are you there?" Raul asked.

"Yup," Justin said. That feeling from the arcade came over him again. He didn't want to lose it. "I wish you were here."

Raul laughed, surprised. "You must really like me."

"I like you the most," Justin said, the closest he'd come to telling the truth.

The rain had gone, if it had been there at all, leaving the smell of washed asphalt, nearly dry from the sun.

* * *

After the Chinatown café, Carrie took them uptown to a steakhouse called Carmichael's and ordered a round of martinis. Justin urged his friends to get the porterhouse, or the cowboy steak—something to soak up the gin, the sake bombs, the cheap beer, the champagne, that terrible green vodka—but he no longer felt the same sheepdog-ish drive to herd them away from disaster. While he didn't like steak, and certainly couldn't afford the cut he ordered, the act of cutting and gnawing granted him a reprieve. This was why men ate steak. For as long as he chewed, no one would ask him to talk.

His friends couldn't stop talking. They ignored their food, their words spilling over each other. Justin was no longer listening. He kept turning over the offer that Raul had made.

"Move in with me," Raul had said over the phone. "You want to live in that tiny house with a couple, and a stranger?" A new option had presented itself, a way to keep both his lives intact and apart. "You've seen my house. I don't want to live there alone. We could work out a rent if you require it."

Somebody, Diana, pelted a dinner roll at his head. The bread left a kiss of grease on his wrist where he blocked it.

"What're you doing?" He looked around to make sure their waiter hadn't seen.

"I assed you a quess-chon," Diana said, and burst out laughing at the mess of a sentence she'd made. She'd been drinking faster since Carrie had revealed her Harvard news, and also pushing Vivian and Errol to keep up.

Justin shoved another chunk of steak into his mouth.

"I asked," Diana tried again, "if you were gonna be a professional body builder." A flick of panic lit up Justin's backside. She was setting him up to announce his new business, one he was no longer sure he needed.

With her sharky grin, Carrie said, "I mean, what's the goal here? You're obviously an overachiever, even at the gym. What're you lifting those weights for?"

Justin cut savagely through the two-inch rib eye, the meat wriggling on the plate. "Just killing time, I guess."

"Like in prison?" Carrie lifted an eyebrow too cleanly, as if she controlled even herself through puppet strings.

"No, like a hobby," he said, in that guileless way that made other people laugh. Being the butt of a joke usually brought it to an end.

Carrie laughed without taking her eyes off him. She wasn't done. Justin had been counting and Carrie had had two drinks more than anyone. Yet while his friends were blowing bubbles in their water, Carrie was draped across her seat, languid as a cat.

He had made himself a target, resisting Carrie all day. In squashing whatever fight might have flared up at the Chinatown café, he had crossed her again. Justin looked at the bleeding meat on his plate. She could do her worst. After this dinner, they were done.

He would corral the group back into his mother's car and grab a few takeout bags in case there was nausea on the highway. Soon the day would be over, rinsed away like the days before. Time, once so stagnant he had to fight to move ahead, now ran so fast that all Justin had to do was hold on.

"You can turn Diana's empty room into a personal gym," Carrie said.

Justin caught the camera by accident and looked away. "I don't work out at home."

"Why not?"

He picked a shred of steak out of his back teeth. "Don't like to sweat where I sleep."

Everyone was laughing too hard. Errol hugged his stomach like it hurt while Vivian sprawled over his back. Diana upset the over-filled water glasses. People stared at their table.

Sated, or bored, Carrie turned her heavy lashes away. Displeasure flashed across her face.

"Jesus, you guys are lightweights," she snapped, her Barbie voice gone. "You need to sober the fuck up. We can't use any of this."

Like children scolded, his friends shrank in their seats. The quiet that dropped over the table startled them. They had not heard the noise they were making until its absence echoed back.

"We're done here," Carrie said to their hovering waiter, who swooped in to drop off the bill. He also tossed a stack of napkins with a gesture both indifferent and appalled.

Justin raised his hand toward the waiter before he could fly away, and with the same hand pointed to his plate of half-eaten steak.

"Can I get a box for this, please?" he said, too quietly for the waiter to hear. The waiter's face collapsed in impatience. Justin panicked and barked, "A box!"

"You don't have to yell." Carrie turned to the others, sweet Barbie again.

His friends cackled and yelled his name, as if he'd been in control of his own rudeness, as if he weren't sweaty from the narrowed glance the waiter threw his way. With the clarity of the sober observing the drunk, Justin understood that he had felt on display well before Carrie had planted that sticky kiss on his mouth. This entire year, the more space he'd tried to carve out, the harder his friends had teased. It felt like all they did anymore was laugh at him.

Justin's face flashed cold and hot. He thought he saw Z shift the camera away. The grip on Justin's throat eased and he received the takeout box from the waiter with a forceful and polite "Thank you very much."

* * *

Carrie grandly paid the entire check, which must have cost well over four hundred dollars. Shocked by this generosity, Justin allowed her to suggest one last stop on their way out of Carmichael's. To be in a small car with his friends yammering on for the next four hours was not worth the possibility that one more drink, one more bar, might knock them out. Throughout college, Justin had found himself in the position of taking care of the group whenever they got too drunk. In his memory, he'd had a lot more fun.

"I know the perfect place." Carrie pointed down the block.

At the corner, a neon sign glowed. He could not read what the sign said from that angle until he saw the horns jutting out.

"I don't know if this is a good idea." Justin peered into the bar, where sure enough a mechanical bull stood at the center of a padded ring.

"Come on, it's one drink," Carrie said. "I'm not making anyone ride a bull. Z needs a different backdrop. Plus, it's well-lit and quiet."

Justin checked the time. Five past eight on a Saturday. They probably didn't turn on the bull until there was a crowd.

Carrie shouldered open the swinging saloon-style doors. Justin beelined for the bar. The faster they got their drinks, the faster they could finish them. He didn't want to see what might happen when New Yorkers who liked country music finished their dinners and came calling.

When he returned with the cans, only Z was at the table. The others had gone to the bathroom.

Left alone with the camera, Justin asked, "How did you and Carrie meet?" He wanted to make the footage unusable. He didn't expect Z to respond.

"College." Z lowered his camera and put it on the table beside them. "We were in an acting class at NYU."

"You act?" Justin was surprised by the ease with which Z spoke, so different from that morning.

"Oh no." Z smiled with his lips pursed together. A private joke? Or self-conscious about his teeth, which overlapped like playing cards. A dimple appeared in his right cheek.

"Why did you take the class?"

"To find actors to work with." Z cleared his throat, as if unused to talking this much. He snuck a glance at Justin to gauge his interest. "That was back when I was trying to make a short film every week."

"That's impressive."

"Well, they weren't any good." Again, that dimpled smile. "Except the ones Carrie was in. She's an amazing actor and she has the best ideas. That's why more people have seen her least popular video than all my films combined."

"Must be nice to ride her coattails," Justin said. He'd meant it as a joke, but he heard too late how crass it sounded.

Tightness came back to Z's shoulders, and with it the damned camera. He shrank behind the device, muttering the same thing he'd said at the arcade. *True partners*. The rest of his words were drowned out by the sudden cacophony of the group returning. Diana and Vivian were skipping arm in arm. Behind them, Errol was talking intensely to Carrie, his muscles tight along the sides of his neck.

At the table, everyone sniffled with secretive glee. They talked over each other, their words no longer slurred. Z trained his camera on them, and Justin also stared. He didn't understand where they had gotten this new burst of energy.

"Your friends needed some waking up," Carrie said. She flashed a small packet of white powder tucked into the waist of her skirt. "You want a sniff?"

Justin backed away until he was out of Z's frame. His friends were on coke for the first time in their lives while shooting a video that millions of people would see. He could understand Errol's impulsiveness, and Vivian's need to please, but the Diana he knew would never have allowed this. His friends wanted to lose control and there was nothing he could do to stop them. The jolt of fear was replaced by cold logic. He'd tried his best. He could only keep them from dragging him down too.

"It'll be good for you two to get your own place anyways," Diana was saying. Her voice was raised and confident. "You need to figure out whatever *this* is before you get married. Marriage is serious. It's legally binding."

"Is that what they teach you at law school?" Errol said.

Oblivious to the shift in temperature, Diana teased, "Don't act stupid."

"According to you, I'm not acting."

With Errol's eyes traveling from Vivian to Carrie and heading toward him, Justin saw the moment where he should step in. He looked off at the other end of the room.

Another small group had come in a few minutes after them. They had taken one of the empty tables closest to the bullpen. One of them was dealing out a deck of Magic cards. What a funny thing to do on a Saturday night. Leaning his back against the table, his body breaking out of his circle, Justin wished he could go over and join them. He'd forgotten that he'd loved Magic once. His friends had made such ceaseless fun of the game that he'd quickly given it up.

He'd thought that their teasing had started this year. Now he remembered a different story. His entire life, he'd tried to fit in with the group, to change or hide anything they didn't like. His clothes, his art, his friendship with Grace.

If he told them about Raul, they would find a reason to make fun of him too. The way he styled his hair. The fact that he was married. His age. His goddamn name. Raul was not the problem. Nor the gym, nor anything else his friends had teased him about. Justin being different from them—that was the problem. Justin dating a man. Justin having less money. Justin having no father. They couldn't tease him for the real reasons he stood apart. They couldn't let him forget either.

Vivian and Diana were shouting. When had this happened? The party across the room looked over from their card game.

"You're the reason people are writing those awful things about us." Vivian stabbed her finger at Diana. "You ruin everything and then you leave?"

"Why do you think I'm here right now?" Diana's tallboy foamed at the mouth each time she banged it on the table. "At least I try to fix my mistakes."

"We could sue you for slander. It's a good thing you're going to law school. You'll learn there are consequences."

"Consequences!" Diana threw up her hands, as if the word were a rock flung at her face. "God, you are such a hypocritical, shallow, spoiled—

"Asian girl basic," Carrie said into Diana's ear.

"Asian girl basic!" Diana parroted.

"Don't call her that." Errol's entire body twitched, like an animal rustled out of its den. "If anyone's basic it's you. You don't give a shit about law school. You'd pay to pick up turds if you got a Harvard degree for doing it."

Z was next to Justin now. "Can you step in?" he said under his breath. He held his camera steady.

"I thought this was what you and Carrie wanted." Justin stared at the TV mounted above the bar, eventually registering that he was watching a baseball game.

"Says the guy who got engaged to someone he wanted to dump." Diana's voice grew pinched and superior. She wheeled back to Vivian. "I said what I said in that video, but you know you're the reason she made it. You threw her under the bus, you threw *us* under the bus. And all for this fucking retard?"

Justin stepped back into the circle despite himself. He'd never heard that word from Diana. Before he could tell her to cut it out, he caught Errol's expression. The shame on his face was too familiar. Justin had to look away. Diana needed to turn around; she would stop if she saw what she'd done.

Diana kept her eyes on Vivian. She had a sneer on her face. "Your one job was to marry well, and it looks like you can't even do that."

Vivian set her beer down with great restraint, and then shoved Diana so hard that she crashed to the ground.

Carrie dropped her voice an octave and hollered, "Asian girl catfight!"

If Z hadn't hissed, "Carrie, stop," Justin would have believed one of the bartenders had given the shout.

Carrie threw her voice again. "I saw them doing coke in the bathroom!" Her face was like a clown's, rigid with delight.

Justin couldn't move, couldn't turn his head, let alone follow Errol when he ran to separate the two. He heard the struggle to keep Diana from throwing herself at Vivian, Carrie shouting at Z, "Don't drop the camera, dickhead! Keep it steady!"

Something hit Justin from the side. He sprawled across the table. Errol had collided into him, and his hands furiously dug through Justin's pockets. Justin squirmed out of reach, too surprised to grab him. Errol raised the car keys triumphantly over his head. He shouted at Vivian to hurry up and made a mad dash toward the street. Justin raced after him, shouting—*For fuck's sake,*

Errol, stop! Don't you fucking dare! Errol! Errol! He was already out of the bar.

Justin burst through the saloon doors in time to see his mother's car on one side of the street, and then, a glitch in the system, somehow all the way on the other. One front wheel was popped up on the curb, the other dangled over the street. The bumper had crumpled around a fire hydrant. Justin heard himself yelling. Errol stumbled out of the car.

"Oh shit." Errol stared at the damage. "I'm sorry. I'll get it fixed. Don't freak out."

Justin slowed down. His breathing was steady despite sprinting down the block. He could almost believe he was calm. He walked around the car to get a better look at the front. The bumper hung off at an angle. Errol was babbling. All Justin could hear was the underground sound of his blood rushing through his ears. Errol shut right up when Justin moved toward him. His hands sprang up to protect his face. Justin grabbed the keys dangling off Errol's thumb and got in the car. He turned the ignition and heard the engine start.

Lurching off the curb, the car separated its bumper from the fire hydrant with a screech. Justin deduced that the car could run. In fact, it was running fine. A smoky odor came through the air-conditioning, but by the time Justin hit his first stoplight, the smell was gone. In the rearview mirror, the street had cleared of people. The clock read nine. In his pocket, his phone seized with vibrations.

His mother needed the car. That was what he would say. He was not driving away, he was driving to her, driving to Raul. More calls came until he switched off his phone. He found a radio station that was bearable. Miles later, he remembered the Garmin. His finger hesitated over the screen and then he made his selection. Turning back was not impossible, but far beyond the work it would take to keep going home.

PART TWO

FOUR YEARS POST-GRAD

2012

CHAPTER SEVEN

July 2012

That summer in Detroit, trapped on the couch with a broken leg, Errol found himself thinking about friction. The concept had irritated him since the first grade, back when his father would keep him at the table after dinner and turn everyday objects into homework. One day, he'd slid a glass across the table and asked, "Why did it stop moving?"

Errol knew the answer, but he spun the question around in his head. *What if the glass didn't stop? If the world was round, wouldn't the glass end up back where it started?* He imagined himself in a world without friction, a world he could skate on as if every surface were ice. A running start and then he'd glide past the Great Wall, the Pyramids, skim across the ocean.

"Without friction, we could slide around the entire world," Errol said, forgetting to answer. He'd found a loophole to the predictability of his father's lessons.

"Without friction." His father knocked his knuckle against Errol's head. "The only direction you would slide is down."

Now Errol understood all the pleasures of a frictionless world. He'd spent three years sliding through one. After New York, he and Vivian had fallen in with her former sorority sisters who'd stayed in DC post-grad. They were part of the growing EDM scene, and Errol had been surprised that these straight-A students popped ecstasy like Tic Tacs on the weekend. Back in college, he'd dismissed them—too uptight for real friendship. He also hadn't been interested in making friends. Without Diana and Justin around, however, he enjoyed the lightness of these new bonds, the way the conversation rarely dipped past the surface.

Although the Saturdays that year tended to blur together, one night stood out starkly from the others. It was early October. The venue had been packed. Unlike his new friends, Errol had no idea what DJ was up on the stage. He drank from a water bottle laced with molly. When he offered Vivian a sip, she shook her head and looked nervously at club security. Most of the people crammed around them were also Asian. They stared, trying to place the two of them. With the blinding strobe, however, no one was sure enough to approach.

Bad Asians had been out since June, and four months later, they were still getting stopped. People loved to tell him that Errol was their least favorite character. He'd seen the photo Diana had posted of her and her new classmates. *Good Asian goes to Harvard!* He hadn't heard from her after she'd served Carrie Yang a cease and desist. Clearly, she was feeling secure that the sequel would never be made. If she didn't care about being recognized, neither did he. Everyone here was a bad Asian, spending their Friday night dancing instead of working overtime. Like him, they must have grown up under too much pressure. They needed a little help feeling connected, feeling *good*. His life was an example of a new way to be. They needed him to guide them.

"You're different when you're on this stuff," Vivian said later that night when they were lying in bed.

"You don't like me like this?" Errol had wrapped himself around her like a koala bear. He couldn't get enough of the smell of her hair.

"No, I love it." Her voice shrank in its confession. "I wish you were like this all the time."

"Me too." Whenever Errol closed his eyes, he saw flashes of light.

He sprang up and grabbed his laptop off the nightstand.

"What're you doing?" Vivian sat up.

"I'm applying for a marriage license." The idea had come to him with startling clarity. "It'll be ready in a week." He talked quickly to keep Vivian from interrupting. "It's almost our eight-year anniversary, which means we've been engaged for a *year*. Who cares what our parents think? They don't control us. It can be our secret. When they accept that you and I are forever, we'll have another wedding."

Vivian crossed her arms. "Let's see if you feel the same in the morning."

Errol kissed the top of her head, and she buried her face in his chest.

"We're getting married," he sang.

Vivian laughed and shook her head. His joy was too contagious. He grabbed her hands and pulled her to her feet. They jumped around the room, singing every wedding song they knew. Of course, he'd feel the same the next morning. He'd feel this way for the rest of his life.

* * *

Their witnesses were Tracy, Vivian's Theta big sister, and Tracy's boyfriend, whose name Errol could never remember.

"You can't tell anyone," Vivian said to their witnesses, over their celebratory dim sum. She thumbed through the photos Tracy had taken on her new iPhone, which was as good as a digital camera. "If my parents find out, they'll flip. These are too cute. I wish I could post them."

"Bad Asians elope," Tracy said. "The internet would go crazy."

Errol picked a fight later that night. "You made me look stupid in front of Tracy."

Vivian stopped editing the photo on her laptop. "What're you talking about?"

He held his ring finger up like a lewd gesture. "You don't want the internet to know you're married to that loser from the video, that's fine. Why the fuck would you tell Tracy and her boyfriend that your parents hate me? I already have to hide my shit in this apartment in case your mom drops by. You won't wear your rings out in public. Can I have one part of my life where people don't think I'm a fuck-up?"

"Don't yell." Vivian twisted her wedding band. She was already near tears.

"I'm not yelling." Errol touched his throat. "I might have raised my voice."

"I know your parents like to yell," she said. "Mine don't. If this is going to be a problem in our marriage, we should find a therapist."

Errol didn't need a therapist to tell him that he and Vivian were different. She called her father "Daddy." Her parents let her live in their new investment property rent-free. In Vivian's family, people fought and got over their hurts by morning. In Errol's family, an argument didn't end until the worst thing had been said. Did Vivian know that? If she was such an expert on his family, did she know that having him meant his mother couldn't complete her PhD? That his delayed speech had cost them thousands to treat, and three years later, when his mother fell pregnant again, that they couldn't afford to have the baby? He could no longer count the number of times he'd heard his mother shout that she'd made the wrong choice.

"She'll say she should've gotten rid of me. That's when I know we're done fighting."

"I had no idea." Tears dropped onto the collar of Vivian's white dress. "I thought they were strict, but not like this."

Errol had to hide his face with a throw pillow. He was embarrassed that Vivian was crying for him. He'd exposed his family not for sympathy, but to stop her from threatening therapy. All therapists wanted were your secrets. He couldn't imagine telling a stranger he was the biggest mistake his parents had made. He could barely believe he'd told his own wife.

The next day, Vivian wouldn't leave him alone. At breakfast, she kissed him whenever their eyes met. Errol felt brittle, as if he'd been robbed in broad daylight.

"Could you chew more softly?" he snapped.

Vivian put down her cereal and held his hand. "Oh babe, of course."

He could sense something familiar hidden in her tenderness. Before, he'd been too smart to be held responsible. Now, he was too messed up.

* * *

Tracy's boyfriend said weed would help Errol sleep, and he'd have some the next time Errol bought molly. After Vivian had her first panic attack and nearly crashed the car, Errol prescribed her a joint to calm her nerves. They made a ritual out of smoking. For a few months, they rewatched old childhood shows. They got lost walking around Bethesda. They ate Oreos with chocolate icing, ramen with ham—the kind of food they'd dreamed of when they were kids.

They burned through their supply. Their tolerance grew. Vivian kept falling asleep during *Reading Rainbow*. Errol would nudge her awake, and she would insist she hadn't been sleeping. Eventually, he left her alone. His thoughts raced no matter how much he smoked. He hated that time had become something to kill. What else was there left to do? They could get a dog. They could have a baby. Errol switched from children's shows to horror movies.

* * *

Their circle started traveling to festivals to get their EDM fix. Vivian stayed home. Although she hated her job, she never took time off. She was worried they'd find out she was replaceable.

"Don't fall in love with a hula hoop girl," she said when he kissed her goodbye.

The next afternoon, sitting on the edge of Detroit's downtown plaza, Errol gave a bearded white bicyclist twenty dollars for a molly-laced Poland Spring. He felt rundown from the eight-hour drive, which they'd made in the middle of the night. Everyone else had researched the DJs playing that Memorial Day weekend, as if they might get quizzed when they arrived. All this group did anymore was talk about concerts they'd gone to and concerts they'd missed. Maybe they'd always been this way and Errol had gotten sick of the sameness. He had tried cutting out weed, quitting alcohol, adding cocaine. He couldn't get back to that lightness he'd once attained. He was even getting sick of molly, not the immense rush of joy, but how cheap it felt once his serotonin resettled. He thought about throwing the water bottle away; then he plugged his nose and drained it.

The festival had four main stages, and the idea was to dance around and sample the beats. Once Errol finished his drink, his ass stayed planted. This was nothing like the stuff he normally took. He forgot he was at a place called Movement. He barely saw the dancers and their dirty sneakers. For hours, he talked his head off. Pure light poured out of his mouth. He befriended the bicyclist who'd circled back to find Errol exactly where he'd left him. The bicyclist brought him to the hotel room where he and his friends were staying. None of them had heard of *Bad Asians*, which had been out for almost a year. When Errol went to pull the video up on his phone, he saw that Grace had accrued a following of over 200k subscribers. She'd posted pages of videos, many more popular than the one Errol was in. He took this as a sign. He told the room the video no longer existed.

The bicyclist found an afterparty and they took a van with a bumper sticker that read, "My dog is an honor student." They left the van by an open loading dock, which everyone climbed onto without hesitation. They rode up three floors in a freight elevator.

When the doors buzzed open, Errol felt he'd been transported to a college house party. He danced to the same music he'd ignored earlier that day, with the same people who'd avoided him on the ground. Almost everyone was white and in their early twenties, except for a group of middle-aged Black ladies selling chicken nuggets to whoever had cash.

"I'm thinking of moving out here," he said to the people he met. He was half lying until he wasn't.

"You have to!" They were adamant. Most of them had moved here in the past few months. They'd heard Detroit was rebuilding.

He followed a group to somebody's loft. The sun peeked over the horizon. He slipped his wedding ring off while he sat on the roof and listened to everyone's summer plans. Everything they said was something he'd never heard before. Stories of a Disney World knock-off in Hamtramck, a Prince museum in a DJ's house. He could feel the springs coiling beneath his skin, the power building in the stillness before the jump. The effortlessness of motion.

* * *

Eight months after he'd moved to Detroit, Errol wound up at a Coney with a guy who said he'd drive him home if they stopped first for a snack. The guy ordered a Salisbury steak that came out looking microwave gray. He kept asking Errol if he wanted a bite. The carriage was turning back into a pumpkin in front of his eyes. Errol felt the expanse of the strange, carved-out city. That voice was loud in his head, telling him he was worthless. He'd recently turned twenty-two in a warehouse with strangers. He had no real job, no real friends, a family that hated him. He was separated from his wife, and he'd been married for less than a year. After Errol had gone back to Maryland to break up with Vivian, there was no one to ask him to come home. He was flooded by an impossible longing. He missed their long walks, her easy tears, how her hand found its way into his hair. He'd give anything to listen to her endless gossip.

Someone had offered him a line of coke on his way out of the party, and he was talking nonstop. Light was no longer pouring out of him. He felt like a toy monkey wound too tight, forced to bang his cymbals until his cogs gave out.

"Sounds like you've got some stuff to resolve." The guy waved his Salisbury steak around on his fork. "I've got acid if you want it."

Back at home, Errol sucked on the square of paper that Salisbury had sold him. He felt nothing for a long time, and he fell asleep waiting for something to happen.

He woke up around noon and was out the door to grab breakfast when his body went floppy like a rag doll. Moving was a revelation. He threw his body around, amazed that he never lost his balance. His face was inches from the floor each time he caught himself. Somehow when he'd fallen asleep, he'd halted the oncoming trip until the door to his consciousness reopened. He struggled to read his phone until he saw that the screen was locked. He tried his apartment door and found the same conundrum.

He was wearing his house flip-flops and what he'd gone to sleep in, his shirt from last night and a pair of mesh shorts. He'd only meant to go to the 7-Eleven downstairs. He jammed a credit card in the door, the way he'd seen it done on TV, and succeeded only in tearing the plastic.

Errol went out on his floor's public balcony and barely felt the cold. The clouds above him swirled with good humor. Each apartment window had a metal grille nailed to the bottom. His apartment was the second window to the right of the balcony. He liked to keep his window cracked open. If he stood on one of the balcony tables, he could easily clear the partition. This was no different from the monkey bars at the playground.

He tested his weight on the top bar of the first metal grille, his feet hooked to the table's edge. The cold bit at his hand, but the metal held. Nothing moved or squeaked in protest. He swung his feet onto the grille's bottom bar. He kept his knees tucked, his hands and feet close together. The wind blew the clouds away from the sun, which warmed his back. The window glittered, and he saw himself, big-eyed and grinning.

He inched along the grille until he reached the end. He blinked, testing his perception. The space between the windows was wider than they'd seemed from where he'd stood on the balcony. He stretched and reached; his hand barely grazed his window's grille. The only way forward was to jump. He sank back into his heels and aimed. For a split second, he was in flight. Nothing tethered him to the building. He landed strong, both hands snatching the top bar like a gymnast, but when he swung his feet up onto the bottom bar, one of his flip-flops slipped off. For the first time that morning, Errol looked down at the street ten stories below. He started to laugh, amazed at what he saw, and then, he let go of the railing.

He landed smoothly onto the private balcony of the apartment under his. He'd forgotten that certain apartments had their own. He picked up his fallen flip-flop. Looking through the balcony doors at the apartment inside, he saw no furniture, no signs of life. He tugged on the handle of the balcony door. Like a blessing, the door slid open smoothly. Inside the empty apartment, thoughts of what could have gone wrong rose like ghouls grabbing at his feet. Errol refused to let them catch him. He'd defied gravity. He'd found a new way inside. He ran back to the floor above to try his luck a second time.

* * *

A few months after he'd discovered the balcony trick, Errol's sister Lucy called to say that their family was touring the University of Michigan during her spring break. Errol was less surprised that Lucy was looking at colleges in ninth grade than that his parents were considering a state school besides Maryland.

"It was their idea," Lucy said over the phone. "They want to know if you're free for lunch or dinner. We'll be driving by Detroit on our way to Ann Arbor and back."

His parents were coming to spy. Almost two years had passed since he'd left Maryland or seen his family. He hired a housecleaner and ended up paying her for a full day of work. He had a friend come over and tell him what else to change. She pointed out that a bare mattress on the floor was a red flag.

"How do you get any girls?" She picked up a half-full trash bag slumped on the kitchen floor.

"We're usually too fucked up to care." He didn't like how that sounded. "Also that window thing. They seem to like that."

After discovering the unlocked balcony below, he'd throw himself out of his window at parties to shock his friends and impress girls. Lying on the balcony, he'd hear the screams from above. He'd laugh so hard that no matter how chaotic he'd left things, someone would hear him and look down.

Errol told Lucy they could park in his apartment lot. He would take them out for dinner. At seven on the dot, his doorbell sounded.

"You look awful," his mother declared when he opened the door. She gave his shoulder a hard pat.

His father agreed and quizzed him on his sleep schedule, his diet, the quality of his BMs, while going to his fridge to check its contents.

"Why, this is empty!" his father cried.

"I eat out a lot," Errol said. The housecleaner had thrown away leftovers so old that Errol couldn't remember where he'd gotten them.

His parents hadn't changed—they looked the same in their khakis and polos—but Lucy had shot up to nearly his height. She'd gotten her braces off and swapped her glasses for contacts. Rolling a cooler into the room, she shyly unlaced her sneakers, which were drawn over with Sharpie.

"We knew you weren't eating right." His mother revealed that she'd packed the cooler with food from their favorite Chinese restaurant.

Errol didn't want it. He could buy his own food. He was almost twenty-four and his parents still didn't trust him. When Lucy asked to use the bathroom, his mother said to wait until they were at the restaurant. She wrinkled her nose at Errol and said, "I'm sure your pee is everywhere."

"I cleaned," Errol said too loudly. "Go use the bathroom."

His parents continued their list. His apartment was on the wrong side of the building, north-facing and therefore empty of natural light. Besides, he should've bought the condo rather than rent, although if he was buying, he should know better than to invest in a one-bedroom. They moved from his apartment to him. Why was he freelancing? He was no better than those men waiting outside the Home Depot for work. Vivian had put up with it because Vivian was a saint. He needed to go to the gym. His back was too weak. His posture was worse than ever.

Getting ready to leave, his mother noticed his trick window, open wide. "A pigeon could fly in." She went to close it. "Or you might fall out. You're stupid enough to make that mistake."

"I'm not going to fall out," Errol said. He slipped out the window. "See?" He bounced back and forth on the grille.

His mother's face went white. She slapped Errol's father on the back, unable to make a sound.

"Get back inside!" his father barked. He went over, ready to haul Errol in, until Errol put his hands up and balanced on the balls of his feet. His father stopped in his tracks.

Errol looked down, tempted to show his parents how little they knew. He'd installed a dashcam to catch people's reactions and he could picture the video already. A scream made him lose his balance and he grabbed the sides of the window. Lucy had come out of the bathroom to find their parents begging him not to jump.

Chastened, he crawled back inside. His mother rushed over and slapped him hard on the head.

"Next time, you better jump." She flung herself out of the apartment, shouting, "See if anyone cares!"

His father held Lucy's shoulders, which trembled slightly. He said softly, in her ear, "We're leaving, treasure, don't worry."

"What about dinner?" Errol had meant to sound hard and sarcastic. His question came out confused. He didn't know why he'd gone out the window anymore.

After his father slammed the door behind him, Errol leaned his head out the window. He couldn't see which tiny figures were theirs. He'd never asked Lucy how she liked Michigan or how school was going. He'd barely talked to her at all.

* * *

After his family's non-visit, he lost interest in his window trick, and besides, everyone already knew it. Spring passed, and at that year's Movement, he collected new friends. For the Fourth of July, he invited them to watch the fireworks from his building. They grilled on the public balcony, charcoal smoke mixing with weed. Hours later, people grew restless. Despite two years in the city, Errol only learned then that Detroit's fireworks went off in June. A compromise with the Canadian border. Back at his apartment, people had their phones out, looking for another party. Errol didn't want them to go. Almost everyone he knew in Detroit was there in the room; it was a city that people kept leaving. He was smoking, straddling the windowsill, when he pointed at the sky.

"Hey," he said. "It's starting!"

With everyone looking, he toppled over the sill. He didn't think to sight the balcony. The fall was that simple. He wasn't diving through the window. He couldn't miss the balcony below.

On the way down, however, he crashed through an antique glass table that his new downstairs neighbors had set out. The glass shattered into pieces so long and thin that he didn't feel how many points went through him. He woke up in the ER, two medical interns tweezing the glass out. He didn't know who'd called 911. During the psych eval, he said he'd lost his balance during a party. He said he hadn't experienced any suicidal ideation. He offered the dashcam video for evidence, which no one checked. They let him go home in a taxi.

* * *

Through the black fuzz, the sound of a phone ringing. His phone ringing. His phone never rang, not since he'd broken his leg.

Errol struggled to sit up on his couch. "Diana?" Almost three years had passed since the last time they'd talked.

"It's been forever, right?" she said. "Did I wake you?" She sounded like she was smoking, which she used to only do when she was back home. Her voice was like a porthole he could peer through. He pictured her striding down the hill of their old neighborhood.

"Are you at your parents'?" He took a stab.

"I'm guessing you've heard." The flick of a lighter and a deep inhale. Another cigarette? "Also your parents have been trying to reach you. I was afraid you'd changed your number."

"Oh shit." After his parents' visit five months ago, he'd figured out how to block their calls and texts. His parents must have seen his insane hospital bill. Except Errol hadn't used their insurance. Hence the bill. Before he could relax, Diana yanked him back to attention.

"Have you been listening?"

"Sort of." Errol probed the swollen folds of his eyelid to displace the tug in his chest. Many people asked him that question. Only Diana was genuine. "I haven't heard anything. I mean, I don't know what you're talking about. What leak? Whose cellphone? And what the fuck is mouse mix?"

"Mousemix, as in Mousemix91." If Diana was repeating herself, which she almost certainly was, she displayed no impatience.

Again, that tug, stronger, sweeter. Errol closed his eyes to listen better.

Mousemix91 was a twenty-one-year-old known for his vlogs about his family's farm. A month ago, he'd posted a video where he accused Carrie of slipping roofies in his drink to film him passed out at her party. He had woken up with a terrible headache and no memory of the night before, and Carrie had told him that he'd had too much to drink. They continued shooting their collab. A week later *City Girl/Country Mousemix* came out and he was horrified to watch his unconscious image moved and manipulated by people he'd thought were his friends.

Some of the other partygoers, YouTube creators with their own followings to protect, had quickly come out with videos. They apologized for their actions while insisting that Carrie had misled them. They made a petition to get Carrie banned from the website, or at least have her videos demonetized.

"I thought for sure that was the end for her." A deep drag on the other line, followed by a ragged cough.

Instead, Carrie Yang had fought back. She'd released videos that revealed messages between her and Mousemix where he wrote that he "would do anything for views." She dropped in stories about the other creators who'd come out in support of Mousemix.

"I mean Jigglyruff hires minors to be her 'unpaid interns,'" she'd said in a video titled *About Last Night Part 6*. "So maybe y'all should be looking into that."

Those creators took down their initial videos and replaced them with public apologies to Carrie. A handful reported seeing Mousemix open his eyes at the party and wink to show that he was pretending. This story gained enough steam that Mousemix posted a picture of his blood test to prove that Rohypnol was found in his system. Although he'd inked out his private information, someone had deciphered his home address and released it anonymously on Reddit. Carrie Yang had come out with a somber video soon after. Mousemix was receiving death threats. His entire family had had to move off their farm. While she loved her fans, this was a step too far.

"I'm still healing." In the video, she'd used a Q-tip to dab tears from the corners of her eyes. "But we've all been twenty-one once. We have to be more forgiving."

Diana had followed the story obsessively, which was how she knew that Carrie Yang had been winning. Not that the tide of public opinion had shifted in her favor. Rather a different tide had been ebbing. A month was a long time to care about a story with no neat answers. Last week, Carrie had posted a makeup video with no mention of current events and her viewers had let her.

Someone must have wanted people to pay attention again. To see Carrie Yang punished.

"I thought I made them delete the only recording of that night in New York. I didn't know there was cellphone footage." Diana mentioned the website where Errol posted his balcony jumps, a forum well-known for underground hip hop and bar fight videos. The terms and conditions were laxer than for YouTube, which was why Carrie could not get the video taken down.

He opened his laptop and typed in *Bad Asians*. The muffled country music in the video's background jarred him. He hadn't remembered there being any music. He paused the video. Three years was enough time to forgive Diana for that night. He didn't need to relive what he'd clearly forgotten.

"That's why my parents are trying to reach me?"

Diana was back in Maryland for that reason. She'd wanted to tell her parents in person, which she'd done that morning. Her mother had forced her to go to the other parents' houses and apologize. She'd had to sit and watch both the cellphone footage and *Bad Asians* with them. She'd recently finished with Errol's parents. The chain-smoking made more sense.

"Do you know who did this?" Errol checked the user account, which had been created a week ago. The account name had no hits on other websites. He inspected the IP address, which told him the person lived in the greater New York area and nothing else. "If you send them the same cease-and-desist that you sent Carrie, that could get them to take it down."

Another deep drag. Diana's voice grew calmer. "It's from Carrie's cellphone. She has no idea who leaked it. Turns out she'd play it for people at parties and pass her phone around. Anyone could have sent themselves the video or hacked into her cloud."

"You've talked to her?"

"That's why I'm calling," Diana said. "Her PR team has a plan. The five of us get on camera saying it was a scripted scene from a collaboration we decided not to post. Make some shit up about not wanting to promote underage drinking. Thank God you were twenty when it happened. We'll apologize for the content. Make it clear that we were the ones who decided not to put it out there, and that there are real consequences to people sharing this video without our consent. Justin's got his start-up and Vivian's a wedding planner. There's my law career to think about. I'm sure you have a life you don't want to ruin because of some stupid shit we did three years ago."

Errol glanced at his crutches by the couch. He imagined hobbling to the elevator and folding himself into his car. He'd ease out of the lot, using his left leg to work the pedals. Once he got to the highway, he could cruise control the ten hours to New York.

"Are Justin and Vivian going to be there?" He hadn't said those names in years, and he wanted to say them again. "Are Justin and Vivian in Maryland?"

"I was going to call them right after you. I figured you'd be the hardest to track down."

Errol clamped the phone between his shoulder and cheek, grabbed his crutches, and heaved himself up. He jolted forward too roughly. Pain stabbed up his leg, and his balance gave out. He sank back down, having reached the end of his couch.

"Are you alright?" Diana asked.

"I don't think I can get to New York." He was panting from the effort, sweat beading his forehead. "I . . ." Three years sat between them like a big, black stain. He used to be able to tell Diana anything. "I just can't get out there. I'm sorry."

"That's fine," Diana said, after a pause. "You can film your video separately. We'll release them together."

Errol had not looked in the mirror since he'd left the hospital, outside of what was reflected on a dark laptop screen. From these brief glimpses, he'd frightened himself. He imagined millions of people seeing his black eye, the gashes and scabs on his face, his unwashed hair. He imagined his parents.

"I can't."

"It won't work without you." Diana's voice trembled. "My law firm called. They're threatening to rescind their offer."

Errol's body burned hotter than his phone. This was the closest Diana had come to asking for help, and the most she'd ever needed it.

"It's on camera that I'm coked out of my mind, using that word. People are saying I should be disbarred. That anywhere I go they'll get me fired."

His helplessness made him sick. He could smell himself and the odor was dizzying. After his accident, he couldn't shower without someone to help, and the last volunteer had stolen his pain meds. The level of trust he'd put in other people felt astonishing. He'd gone to abandoned parking lots with hundreds in cash. He'd followed strangers into houses without plumbing. He thought he'd had no choice in leaving Vivian, leaving home. Hearing Diana hold back her tears, he understood what having no choice really felt like.

"You have to believe me," he said. "If I could, I would."

He turned his phone off before she could call him back. Head throbbing, he found the dashcam video he'd been avoiding. What had other people done when he'd needed their help that badly? On the couch, Errol fast forwarded to the moment he did his window trick. At regular speed, he played the tape and watched the initial panic. People ran to the window and looked down. They must have spotted him on the balcony below because their movements slowed. Some other people came to the window to see for themselves.

Errol nearly missed the first person who slipped out of his apartment. In the video, heads turned at the closing door. No one took out their phone. Maybe they were afraid of being questioned by the police. Maybe they didn't want their night interrupted for some guy they'd met at a festival. Another person left, then another, and then everyone at once. Within five minutes of his accident, his apartment was empty. The video ran on, the flickering image the only movement.

Errol threw his computer to the ground. It clattered across his floor. The screen flashed like a lightbulb burning out. Another impulse he'd given in to, masquerading as a choice he'd had to make. He closed his eyes and pictured the highway again. He was on the interstate, heading for home. He wasn't falling to the lowest point. He was Space Face, Boy Genius, Error Chen. If he kept going, he'd end up right where he'd begun.

CHAPTER EIGHT

Vivian's phone rang in the middle of the photoshoot. Diana again. The call went to voicemail. Soon after, a text appeared.

You're for sure going to the screening?

Before Vivian could stuff her phone away, Diana followed up with, *WE NEED GRACE!!!*

Vivian could not imagine communicating with anyone like this. Diana had called her six times yesterday to confirm that Vivian would carry out the plan.

"Remember, it's the DC Watch Out Festival," Diana had said the last time she'd called. "If I could do it myself, I would. All we need is a statement that we were acting in her video. Beg if you have to." She'd had to raise her voice over the noise from the street. She'd gone back to New York early, ostensibly to see Carrie, but Vivian had heard from her mother that Diana was meeting with her law firm.

When the scandal had come out, Vivian's mother had been furious on her behalf. At the next Blüm meeting, she'd confronted Diana's mother in front of the other women.

"She admitted that her daughter might lose her job over her disgusting behavior." Her mother had been breathless at the discovery. "That woman has always pretended to be too good for us, and now look, she's already losing sellers. The two of them deserve it."

Vivian should have sided with her mother, the way her mother had done for her, but she could practically feel Diana's panic in her own teeth. Yet each time Diana had called, she'd failed to mention how her career hung by a thread.

Vivian could have pretended she didn't know how badly Diana needed this video to work. They weren't friends anymore, and if Diana wanted Vivian's help, she could ask for it. In the end, Vivian had agreed to the video without forcing Diana to admit the truth. She'd even thanked Diana for being the organizer. She'd felt protective of Diana as she hadn't in years. Her pride was all she had left.

Vivian wasn't any different. She had waffled the entire day on what she would say to Grace at the festival. She should tell Grace that she and Errol had broken up, that the group no longer spoke. Grace would find this karmically fulfilling, and time and fame should have made her more forgiving. She had millions of subscribers. She'd been a guest at the Oscars. Then Vivian would remember the voicemail Grace had left her, like a shock collar going off. In the end, the idea that Grace might do Vivian a favor out of pity was no more bearable than Grace refusing to forgive her.

Vivian silenced her phone. She was at work. She should be focused.

After the cellphone footage had come out, Vivian had asked the other planners at her agency to take her weddings for the month, but she'd felt obliged to keep her former Theta big sister Tracy's on her calendar.

She was currently surrounded by people she'd known in college, whose approval she'd desperately craved. The bridesmaids had been juniors and seniors when Vivian had rushed, and years later she still watched their faces. The groomsmen were fraternity brothers too, part of Alpha Kappa Psi, the Asian business frat that had rejected Justin twice. Vivian remembered them calling Justin a loser behind his back while Vivian, to her shame, had laughed. Driving into DC, Tracy had promised that no one would bring up the bar video, but Vivian could sense the whispers, and why not, she deserved them.

At least while they posed on the steps of the Jefferson Memorial, Tracy's wedding party was too wilted to gossip. When Tracy had first told her about wanting this photoshoot—*With the Washington Monument in the background!*—Vivian hadn't had the heart to share that every prom group at her high school had the same artistic vision. Tracy's wedding party had flown in a day early to avoid the weekend crowds, and they'd been out in the swampy heat for two hours in tuxedos and floor-length gowns. Despite their insistence that they were fine to try another angle, they must have harbored some objections. Vivian didn't miss this quiet group resentment, the fine print of friendship, to ignore anything that could not be changed.

Vivian had gotten every tourist out of the shot when the photographer called for a break. He capped his camera and pulled out a pack of Camels. A spray of clouds had blocked the sun, and they could not possibly continue. The photographer, Jake, had a weary way of talking that made Vivian nervous to contradict him. That and the fact that he was in his mid-thirties, lived in New York, and had shot for *Vogue*. He worked for the fashion magazine where Tracy was an editor. The group dropped their poses and tried to enjoy the paltry shade of a muggy July afternoon.

The bridesmaids aired out their strapless blue chiffon gowns. Some peeled the jackets off the groomsmen's sweaty backs. Everyone except Vivian clumped in a circle, including the photographer who ducked down in the center to sneak his cigarette. He was unexpectedly comfortable as the sole white person in the group. Being tall and ten years older probably helped. The single bridesmaids were especially welcoming.

While Vivian stood off to the side, she thought she overheard the words *Bad Asians*. Someone was already filling Jake in on the gossip. Vivian walked down the memorial steps. She could sense the questions hovering like mosquitos before they bit.

"Is she still with Errol?" The wind had picked up and Vivian could hear everything the wedding party was saying.

"I don't know." That was Tracy, to her credit.

Her fiancé, who'd been the other witness at their courthouse wedding, said, "That little dude was always on something. I mean, you saw that bar fight."

As if he hadn't sold Errol everything he'd taken that year. Vivian looked up, squinting at the clouds outlined by the sun. The wind blew again, and the smell of cigarette smoke overwhelmed her.

"Sun's back!" She strode up the stairs and glanced down at the photographer hunched in the middle of the wedding party. "Would you put that away? We're going to get kicked out by security."

Jake put up his hands and stubbed the cigarette out on the side of his boot. He called everyone back to their places.

A half hour later, while the bridesmaids stripped down in the back seat of her car, Vivian helped Jake collapse his lightbox. She'd seen him wrestling with his equipment, and she'd gone back up the memorial steps to help, an apology for snapping at him earlier.

"I hear you're the best wedding planner in town." Jake slipped the lightbox into its bag, a cigarette clenched between his teeth. He spoke and puffed out of the same side of his mouth, an anthill of ash growing by the second.

"Tracy says that because I gave her a discount."

Jake checked his camera bag one more time and zipped it up. "Sounds like I got the job for the same reason."

He looked approvingly at Vivian. A part of her blossomed at his favor. Playing with the chain of her necklace, her engagement and wedding rings hidden beneath her clothes, she requested one of his cigarettes.

"Are you working the actual wedding?" Vivian leaned toward his lighter. His arms were tattooed down to his fingers.

"No way," Jake said. "This was a favor."

"I don't think you can call it a favor if you're getting paid." She had smoked in front of enough bathroom mirrors to know that the way the smoke streamed through her lips was a subtle but undeniable suggestion. Jake watched the smoke rise like a screen over her face.

"Fair enough," he said.

"Too bad." She tilted her head down and let her hair fall over her eyes. A second later, she peeked up through her bangs. Jake looked back, a little dazed. Vivian was already tired of smoking. Like this conversation, what she craved was the initial strike and flare, that first deep breath to draw in the flame. Once the flame caught, every breath was a foregone conclusion. She could never predict when she would miss Errol acutely.

Her attention flew to the bottom of the stairs, where the bridesmaids emerged from her car. They could gossip all they wanted about her to Jake. Here he was, no less interested. She watched them watch her say, "I was hoping you'd be at the wedding."

"Why's that?" he asked. Already he was grinning; already he knew what he'd won.

"No reason." She let her voice trail off, and like a door slowly closing, she waited for him to reach out and push his way in.

Typing Jake's number into her phone, she saw that Justin had finally responded to her question.

Maybe

Depends on work

Vivian nearly put in the wrong number for Jake, who caught the mistake and teased her for making his name "Jake Wedding."

"I know a lot of Jakes," she said, setting him up.

He leaned in to hug her goodbye. "Sure you do."

She made things so easy for these men, for everyone—Diana, her clients—and so difficult for her own desires.

"Actually." She tugged Jake by the elbow. "Why don't you come to a screening with me? A friend of mine made a documentary."

"How do you know I don't have plans?" Jake asked.

"You don't seem like the type." Vivian swished her way down the white granite stairs. She didn't bother looking back.

* * *

In the car, Vivian went through Justin's response in her head. His commitment to being noncommittal infuriated her. Over the years, he had artfully dodged her attempts to keep in touch. As if being part of the same friend group was all that had held them together.

The first time she had reached out was after she'd been recognized at a wedding. She'd called Justin from the coat closet. This was over a year after the video had come out, but the experience had still felt rare since the donor office where she'd worked had a median age of fifty. Then, in the mania of her and Errol's breakup, she'd become an event planner's assistant without realizing that most of those events would be weddings.

Giddy and tousled, as if a strong breeze had blown up her skirt, Vivian heard Justin pick up. Without saying hello, she went straight into the story.

"You'll never believe what happened!" A bridesmaid had asked for a photo. Her ex-boyfriend had a crush on Vivian from that video, and he would die if he saw that she'd been at this wedding. Someone had found a straw and stuck it in a flute of champagne. Vivian had had to re-create a pose so iconic that other people coached her into striking it right.

"It'll probably be online before the wedding's over," she said, and Justin, laughing in a newly deep grumble, said, "It's definitely already been posted."

Vivian had felt some small release, like a hidden corset popping open.

"I miss you." She'd stared at the row of wool coats.

"I miss you too," Justin had said.

They'd promised to grab dinner and catch up, but each time Vivian had tried, Justin had gamely avoided her.

She would write: *Are you free this week?*

A week later, he would reply, *Sorry, work was crazy*

Vivian had heard that Justin was at a biomedical start-up, which gave his excuse some plausibility.

That sucks, how about this week?

To which he answered, *Not great*

What could she do with that? She'd put herself out there enough times that when the cellphone footage had first leaked, she'd waited for Justin to reach out. The whole point of knowing someone for their entire life was to get the help you needed without asking. Then Diana had told her that Justin hadn't agreed to the video statement yet because he hadn't been in the cellphone footage. Without Errol, they needed Justin more than ever. It was better not to push him. That morning, however, Vivian had given in and texted him. She couldn't face Grace by herself.

Looking over at Jake, Vivian regretted her hasty invitation. She hadn't wanted to show up to the screening alone. Bringing a guy she didn't know was hardly less pathetic.

At a parking garage down the block from the Georgetown theater, she forked over forty dollars and grabbed Tracy's wedding gown.

"Should I be worried about my camera equipment?" Jake asked when he saw her with the garment bag.

"Losing the bride's dress the day before the wedding is a chance I refuse to take."

Approaching the theater, Vivian gripped the garment bag so tightly that Jake faltered when he tried to take it from her hands. She apologized and thanked him in the same breath. Without the bag, she felt defenseless. The line into the theater was nearly down the block. She'd thought she could sneak in and hide in the back. With this crowd, she was sure to be recognized.

"Quite a turnout for a documentary," Jake said while they waited to cross the street. "Not the usual suspects."

Most of the people in line were younger women, wearing clothes appropriate for the late July weather. Among them was a small contingent of serious-looking men dressed in black.

"She also makes YouTube videos," Vivian said. Clocking the look of recognition that crossed Jake's face, she added, "I didn't know what I was getting into when I agreed to be in those. It's embarrassing. I know I said she was my friend, but I haven't talked to her in years. That's why I didn't want to come alone."

"Got it," Jake said. He handed her his sunglasses and draped the garment bag over his shoulder to block her partially from view. The traffic lights changed. They stayed across the street and watched the line march into the theater. "The people making real documentaries must hate her."

Vivian was embarrassed by the spike in her mood. "Because she's a sellout?"

"You can't sell out if you were always for sale."

Vivian bumped her hip against his. "No wonder she's popular."

The line disappeared into the theater. Jake put an arm around her shoulders and gave her a squeeze. "I bet you a drink this movie is terrible."

* * *

The death of the pig was disturbing enough. The squealing had been horribly human. If she hadn't been sitting next to Jake, she would have put her hands over her ears, like some people in the rows ahead. The informational pamphlet had cheerfully intoned that Grace Li's first experimental documentary short combined the gonzo journalism of the great Iris Chang with vivid imagery-as-critique. None of this had prepared Vivian.

A man hacked away at the pig's body, breaking it down into pork, and the sounds of metal against bone faded under the female voiceover.

"They tied Old Tse up, forcing him to kneel on the ground. One of them took out a bayonet and hacked at his head."

"Jesus," she heard Jake mutter, and the urge to whisper in his ear rose and fell in one breath. The subject of the documentary rendered it impossible to make fun. Who knew? Jake seemed like the kind of person who spent his free time watching difficult documentaries. Like the group of men who'd sat themselves up front, their boots propped on the stage below the screen.

When the pig was dismantled, the man gathered the other animals he'd dismembered earlier and brought them into the dilapidated farmhouse kitchen. The window looked out onto the dusty patch of blood left over from the butchering.

"Apparently some quirk of human nature allows even the most unspeakable acts of evil to become banal within minutes, provided only that they occur far enough away to pose no personal threat."

The man diced green onions and garlic by the fistfuls. A limp red cockscomb stuck out of an earthenware pot. If this was the kind of movie Grace was making, the last few years had not softened her at all. Vivian felt punished by the images on the screen, as if it were her fault for watching.

When the credits rolled, Jake whispered, "What the fuck was that?"

"I think that was art." The pleasure of teaming up made Vivian catch the giggles. The rest of the theater managed a tepid applause. The lone row up front gave standing ovations.

Jake was on his feet too. He offered Vivian his arm. "I believe you owe me a drink."

She stayed seated. "I have to talk to her after."

"She'll ask what you enjoyed," Jake said. "You don't seem like you'd be good at lying."

The lights came up, and the applause grew louder. Grace had come out on the stage for her Q&A. From the back of the theater, Vivian only saw the bold strokes of her transformation, but she could tell that Grace cut the perfect image of an indie filmmaker. The half-shaved head, the dramatic eye makeup. Her jumpsuit was tailored to fit her tall, column-like body. Her platform boots made her even more imposing. Vivian was wearing a floral romper with gladiator sandals, an outfit that had seemed cute moments earlier.

Vivian tried to drag Jake back into their seats, afraid of being seen. He stayed standing, no longer willing to humor her.

"Come on," she said, her smile nervous.

"I'm going for a drink." He handed her the garment bag that he'd kindly held the entire movie. "When you're done here, you can join me."

Vivian sank down, the weight of the wedding dress laying over her like a lead vest. At the front of the theater, a festival organizer handed Grace a microphone. When she greeted the crowd, the audience cheered, having forgiven her for the treatment to which they'd been subjected.

"Thank you so much," Grace said. "This documentary has been in the making since I was in middle school, when I first read Iris Chang's *Rape of Nanking*. I wanted to explore the spectacle of other peoples' misfortune, how we can rationalize away any violence, how the story of the past can't help influencing how we perceive the present. In many ways, it's my most personal project yet."

She went on to thank everyone who was in the film. The festival organizer announced that Grace would take a few questions.

An audience member with bright red glasses walked up to the microphone stand.

"My name is Rachel Liao, here reporting for *BuzzFeed*. I'm also a huge fan, Ms. Li, and have been since *Bad Asians*."

Vivian sank down further in her seat. She hadn't realized there would be journalists in this audience, and she recognized the name. A Rachel Liao had emailed her twice last week.

The organizer interrupted: "We're only taking questions about the movie . . ."

"It's no problem," Grace said. "I'm happy to talk about *Bad Asians*. This is off the record, by the way."

The smooth way she handled this made Vivian prickle with envy. She'd felt the same itchiness when she'd seen photos of Grace at the

Oscars that winter. They hadn't been widely distributed because she'd been the guest of a nominee—Harris Yu, who'd gotten his start on MeMe. Vivian's mother had found them anyway. Grace had worn a black Versace gown with a sleek, sensuous train that flicked after her like a dragon's tail. She'd fit right in with the celebrities on the red carpet.

"I wanted to know," the journalist continued, "I mean, *Bad Asians* was a landmark. It was the first time I saw me and my friends in something like a show or a movie." She hesitated, but when she spoke, her voice was steely. "Given the recent cellphone footage of the *Bad Asian* actors, why haven't you made any comments on their behavior and what it represents for our community? Don't you have a responsibility to your Asian American fans?"

Splinters of ice traveled down Vivian's fingers. Not from the question alone. Grace's eyes had found hers at the back of the theater. She'd known Vivian was there all along. Her gaze locked with Vivian's. Gradually, a different message became clear. Hardly able to believe that they were communicating, Vivian slowly nodded. Grace lifted the microphone up to her mouth. With everyone's attention up front, Vivian slipped out of the last row and through the exit without notice.

* * *

Hiding in the restroom, Vivian wanted to put this strange experience behind her and return to her date with Jake. The journalist's question had reminded her that he wasn't fazed by her notoriety. He hadn't left the theater because she'd been an idiot on the internet; he'd left because he'd run out of patience. What a surprise to realize that online rage didn't have to bleed into her reality. She wanted to make him look at her the way he had on the memorial steps, to have someone's interest in her be simple attraction.

The restroom door swung open, and people surged in, enough

that a line soon formed for the toilets. They were too busy discussing Grace's Q&A to wonder why one stall stayed locked.

"What'd you think of that movie?" asked one girl.

"Sickening," someone else said.

"Just like her responses," another person added. "If she's not against that behavior, she's for it."

"I'm boycotting her videos," the first girl declared.

"I mean, if she makes more of her usual stuff, I might still watch," someone new chimed in from the stall next to Vivian's. "I keep waiting for a sequel to *Starter Pack*."

"Oh my god, is that the one where the guy custom builds a girlfriend?"

Vivian had seen that one. She'd watched a few of Grace's most popular videos when they came up in her recommendations and had been dismayed by how much she'd liked them. They had been light, romantic, surprisingly sentimental at times. The opposite of how she thought of Grace. The movie today was a closer match, as angry as *Bad Asians*, but without the humor to hide it.

The crowd slowly dispersed, until Vivian was alone. A few minutes passed before the restroom door reopened. A pair of platform boots stopped outside her stall.

"We need to talk," Grace said through the crack in the partition. "There's a bar in the hotel where I'm staying. It's the one down the street."

Before Vivian could agree, the boots spun around, and the door shut behind them.

* * *

The hotel was a tony establishment with uniformed bellhops. They kept trying to take Vivian's garment bag. By the time she got away, Grace was already seated at the bar, talking to the bartender. Off-stage, she still had an aura of importance about her, as if she were somebody who deserved your attention.

"I'll have a Beefeater martini, up, with a twist," Grace said, and the bartender shot back, "I'm jealous, that sounds delicious."

"Treat yourself to one." Grace put her card down on the bar. "And whatever my friend is having."

"Make it three." Vivian tried to copy Grace's breeziness.

"What a surprise to see you in the audience," Grace said. The temperature of her voice was at the border between cool and chilly.

"I'm sorry you had to deal with those questions." Vivian draped the garment bag over the stools next to hers. "You're here to celebrate your new movie. Which was amazing! Intense, in a good way. And instead of people asking you about your work, you have to answer for . . ." The bartender set their drinks down. "Anyways, thanks for defending us."

Vivian popped a Pepcid to shut herself up. Grace played with the lemon peel floating in her drink.

"I didn't defend you." A vein Vivian had never noticed was popping out of Grace's forehead. "What I said was that it's easy to think that we know someone because we hear one story about them. Or we see one moment in their lives. The same reason people are outraged is also what made them look up to you in the first place. Judging you helps them decide what they think is right or wrong. It's a terrible thing we do to other people when we turn them into the side characters of our own stories." Grace swiveled in her seat to face Vivian.

Here was her opening to beg Grace for help, but Vivian was suddenly tongue-tied. How could Grace lecture her when she'd forced Vivian to play a character for years? The moment she'd shared with Justin over the phone had been the first pebble in a rockslide. It seemed every wedding had someone who recognized her. She would try to put off the interrogator, who was always tipsy and loud, but her politeness spurred them to ask their most impolite questions.

The excitement would pull in more guests, more identical questions, which she would have to answer again or someone else would be delighted to answer for her.

"She said she hasn't talked to Errol in *years*," they might extrude in a whispered shout, their liquored breath hot against her necklace.

Now there was more footage. More proof of her wasted devotion. She dreaded returning to work and facing the new questions that would be repeated until they too turned old.

"I'm sorry," Vivian said, the strength of her drink searing the back of her throat. "What do you think *Bad Asians* was doing? Did you think about what happened to the rest of us? What's happening right now?"

"Exactly what about that cellphone footage is supposed to be my fault?" Grace put her elbows on the bar. She sounded so genuine that it was hard to believe she was.

"I'm not sure," Vivian said. The distress in her voice surprised her. "But you can't pretend that these things aren't connected. If I hadn't done what I did to you, you wouldn't have made your video, and we wouldn't have let Carrie push us into that awful fight. If any of us had leaked the video, maybe I'd understand why, but whoever did it has nothing to do with us. They're ruining our lives for no reason. Diana is about to lose her job!"

Vivian took a big gulp of her martini. "We would help you, is what I'm trying to say, if things were reversed. We would feel like we owed you that much."

"Carrie Yang is a bad person," Grace said softly, looking away. "I've been in the same circles as her for years. I know people who worked with her, who've been abused by her. Whoever is trying to take her down has a reason."

The bartender dropped off Grace's card and the receipt. Vivian hadn't seen her ask for the bill.

"I have to run. I've got dinner with the festival organizers." Grace tipped back the rest of her drink.

The harsh tang of alcohol had numbed Vivian's tongue, that useless lump. Diana was depending on her to act in her place. What would Diana say if she were here? Despite years of absence, Vivian heard the words perfectly in her ear.

"If you don't come out with a statement saying we're actors, that our collaboration with Carrie Yang was scripted top to bottom, then I wonder if that *BuzzFeed* journalist would be interested to know how unscripted *Bad Asians* really was."

Grace put her glass down hard enough for a clean note to ring out against the counter.

"Seriously?" Grace sounded wry. That forehead vein was pulsing. "History repeats itself."

"I know you." Vivian was surprised to find this was true. "I knew when you found me in the theater that you wanted me to sneak out. I knew to hide in the bathroom until you could get away from the crowd. And I know you've been waiting this entire time for me to play that card. That's the only reason we're talking."

Grace tried to interrupt. Vivian raised her voice.

"*History repeats itself.* It does when you don't give a person any other option. You of all people should know that."

Grace leaned close enough that the freckles on her half-shaved scalp were visible.

"I'm never going to talk about *Bad Asians*." She grabbed her card and shoved it into her bag. When she slid off her stool, she seemed the smallest bit unsteady. "If you or any of those vultures talks about me, you'll be hearing from my lawyers."

Her platform boots pounded out of the bar. Vivian was left with her mostly full drink. Again came the voice that she'd thought was Diana's, but was in fact her own righteous anger. The reason Grace could afford those lawyers was because of the fame the group had given her, because she'd capitalized on every opportunity. Vivian had seen the video tie-ins with brands. Grace could pretend that she didn't court media attention, but the product placements in her videos, the digital collaboration with MTV—those didn't come without her chasing. Grace posted a new short film on You-Tube every week. She'd featured the most popular creators in them. She'd acted more ravenously than their whole group combined, and here she was, accusing them of being hungry.

"Everything alright over here?" The bartender took Grace's glass and wiped the counter.

"Totally." Vivian put on a cheerful face. "She had an important dinner to get to."

"Is she famous or something?" He lowered his voice.

"No." Vivian downed the rest of her martini. "She just makes YouTube videos."

* * *

The wedding dress back in her car, Vivian waited for Jake. She was feeling reckless after her hurried drink. When she'd texted him to meet her at the hotel bar, he'd told her he was headed toward the parking garage. Vivian had decided to take this for a challenge. If Grace wanted to treat their confrontation like a brief interruption to her night, then Vivian's evening was also just getting started.

"Do you have the hostage?" Jake emerged from the elevator bank. The sight of him sent a nervous flutter down Vivian's stomach.

"No sudden movements." She thumped the back of her car. "If you want to see your equipment safe and sound."

Jake leaned his shoulder against the hatchback, which put them eye to eye. She'd forgotten how intoxicating this was, the moment an uninterested man gave her his full attention. Jake dipped his head down and Vivian lifted her face to meet him. The delicate choreography of their first kiss over, he moved his hands up and down her back, gripping her by the waist, her hips, her ass, her legs. Each shiver of sensation yanked her back into her body.

He pushed her against the back of her car. The rear windshield wiper bit into her shoulder. He kissed the side of her neck, grazing her necklace in a way that felt dangerous. From over Jake's shoulder, the parking garage was empty. She watched the lighted number above the elevator to see if it would descend. He ran his hand over her romper, looking for an opening. His ink-heavy hand went up the leg and slid her underwear to the side. He rested a finger inside her, not moving it up and down, but pinning her in place, like a page he didn't want to lose. She was doing the moving, grinding against the palm of his hand. The elevator was silent. The garage was dark. Little urgent noises escaped from her mouth.

A sudden roar of sound plastered them against each other. Light blasted from a car across the row. Vivian twisted away from Jake. She hid in the space between her car and its neighbor. The phantom driver squealed his truck down to the lower exit.

"What the fuck." Vivian came out of her crouch.

"He didn't see anything," Jake said.

"How do you know?" Vivian yanked at her clothes. The air around her turned solid. She was panting. "That fucking pervert. Fuck! What if he was recording?"

"It'd be too dark to pick up anything." Jake craned his neck. The truck's taillights disappeared.

Tight, everything was too tight. She knew this feeling now. Since her first one on the highway with Errol, these attacks would ambush her, like having a sack thrown over her head. A part of her was always waiting, dreading, praying. Her heart kicked against her ribs. Her airways shrank. All the blood had gone up in her ears. She was sliding down, legs numb. Bracing, bracing.

"You're okay." The trunk slammed. "I have you." A car door clicked open.

She was lifted into the air and set in the passenger seat. Jake wiped the sweat from her face with the hem of his shirt. "Tell me three things you see."

Her breath was just out of reach. She squinted at the dim parking garage. "A car, another car." Her eyes focused on the tattoo creeping over the neck of his shirt. "Lisa Simpson."

"Good, now how about three sounds."

"Your laugh." She must be calming down if she had the space to feel embarrassed. "I mean, you laughed when I said that thing about your tattoo." Her chest ached once her heart had slowed down. "My big blabbermouth. And sirens, outside."

He grinned down at her. "Now move three body parts."

She handed him her car keys and touched her own hot cheek. Weak, but urgent, she pulled him down for a kiss, clinging to the neck of his shirt. Grateful because he'd saved her, and because he kissed her back. That he still wanted her after that.

In Vivian's condo above U Street, Jake filled a glass with water and brought it to her on the couch.

"Could you stay?" she asked.

She was determined to rescue the night. Her panic attack had only lasted a few minutes. She hoped her face was making the right expression, flirty instead of bleary. Her head was heavy, as if filled with mud.

"I could." Jake sat next to her, his hand on her knee.

Vivian straddled him. When she closed her eyes, the room spun. She copied everything he did, biting what he bit, and when he leaned back, she thought he'd caught her.

"Listen," he said. "I want you to know that I'm not looking for anything serious."

Something about the smugness of that statement made Vivian tug on her necklace and pull out her rings.

"Me neither," she said. "I'm married."

"Whoa." Jake shrunk away and put his hands up. "Seriously?"

"I haven't talked to him in two years," Vivian said. "I told you so you wouldn't worry."

She was lifted into the air and set back down on the couch. Jake stood up, shaking out his legs. He looked for his phone, checking that he had his wallet and keys. She needed him to say something, to stop ignoring her.

"He was in the videos with me." She fell back on the couch and swiped her hand across her eyes, her palms streaked with makeup. "I don't know why I told you. I don't know what I'm doing." She looked up at him, her body laid out. Open, vulnerable, inviting. She watched his eyes move over her.

"Jesus," Jake said softly. "Those videos did a number on you."

He leaned down to tuck a strand of hair behind her ear. This was what she'd thought she'd wanted. Vivian turned away to bury her head into the couch. For once, when it made all the sense in the world, she couldn't cry.

"You'll sleep this off," he said, sounding gentle. Who knew what expression was on his face.

"Please don't tell Tracy," she said.

"What's there to tell?" he said. "We hung out. Nothing happened."

When her front door shut with a rattle, the tears finally squeezed through. All of it was more than she could handle—not only Jake, but the photoshoot, the screening, the journalist, Grace, that man in the truck, and the constant reminder around her own neck that the love of her life had left her. She used to be the one who put things back together, who cleaned up the messes other people made. She felt as weak as her parents had always warned her she was.

Her phone buzzed against the coffee table. Vivian twisted around and her stomach twisted with her. Diana was calling. Diana, who'd needed this plan to work.

Vivian had failed her twice, once by losing Grace and again by forgetting who would suffer the worst consequences. Vivian grabbed the phone. She would have to answer. She wouldn't run away like Errol, like Jake, like Justin. She twisted her necklace around her throat until she could barely breathe.

She would answer, by the next ring.

Or the next one.

CHAPTER NINE

Diana had made it onto the last Amtrak back to DC. She thought about trying Vivian again, if only for the distraction. The gash on her knee had stopped bleeding. Her nose continued to trickle. She leaned back further in her seat.

The train hurtled through the dark and Diana stared at the ceiling. The day's decisions spread out in front of her, trailed by the choices that had led her there. The first time she'd met Weston. The name tag she'd worn at orientation. The morning she'd walked into Carrie's apartment. For the first time she could remember, Diana had nothing to do except think about what she'd done.

* * *

That morning, Diana had told her boyfriend, Weston, not to make her breakfast.

"I know you're nervous." He'd looked up from his emails. "But you need to eat."

His face was red from his razor, and the curly hair she'd asked him to grow out was tamped down by gel. While Diana had long ago given up on making herself more presentable, she admired Weston's daily efforts. By the time he returned in the evening, he'd be back to his stubbled, frizzy-haired self. And Diana would know if she had a job or not.

"I'll throw up if I do." She pushed away the bowl of oatmeal he'd set in front of her. "You have no idea how I feel right now."

"I never said I did." He kept his tone light, but his shoulders tensed.

She used to love the alertness of his body when he caught wind of an argument, and how her own body would react, like they were two dogs chasing down the same scent. After the cellphone footage had come out, however, they'd become one dog chasing its tail, going through the same points until they became pointless.

"I wish I could get this over with already," she said.

The hiring partner, Vic, had initially wanted to set up a call. She'd strong-armed him into a meeting that afternoon. Her mother always said it was harder to reject someone in person.

"I'm stuck with clients all day." Weston put the spoon against her lips. "But I'll try to get out early and catch you after."

"Or I could come early." Diana let him feed her although her stomach cramped. "If you sat with me before it started . . . I know I'd feel much better. I'm sure Lisa would stash us in an empty conference room if I brought her a latte. I could bring you coffee too."

"The office has coffee."

"And it's terrible." Diana tried to smile. She put up her hands. "Okay, I'll stop asking."

"I'm sorry." Weston placed their bowls in the sink.

"Don't be." Diana wrapped her arms around him.

The back of his button-down was damp with sweat, despite how calm he acted. He'd been this way toward her bar exam too, certain that she'd pass and then unable to sleep the night before. A part of her was moved. Another part wondered if this meant she should keep pushing. "You've done so much for me already."

"I love you." He gave her a tight squeeze. "And they loved you as a summer associate. Vic said you were his favorite from the entire cohort. If you tell him what you told me, I know they won't hold some thirty-second clip against you."

Diana tried to ignore the sting of shame that came whenever she remembered how she'd behaved that night, especially what she'd called Errol. She'd been close to apologizing to him over the phone, but at the last moment, the words had escaped her. She focused now on the looping argument that Weston had restarted. His car was arriving in a few minutes. She didn't have time to counter that the scripted angle was stronger, or to hear how foolish it was to team up with Carrie Yang, who'd put her in this situation in the first place.

What she wanted was for Weston to pull Vic aside, the way he had when she'd been up for summer associate, but the fact that he'd vouched for her once was why he couldn't do so again. He had his own reputation to protect. What remained unspoken between them was that if he loved her enough, he'd put his own career ambitions on the line. The rebuttal was there too—if she loved him enough, she wouldn't think to ask.

"I don't know what to do with myself." She handed him his messenger bag.

"You could unpack."

Diana looked at the boxes they'd driven up from her parents' house. Weston had had to stay in the basement even though they were moving in together.

"I could do that."

Weston shrugged on his suit jacket and kissed her goodbye. "Put up those awful dog posters you like."

* * *

Emerging from the subway, Diana rechecked the street signs to make sure she was in Williamsburg. She'd spent last summer in

New York without once leaving Manhattan. She'd barely ventured beyond Midtown, where her law firm was located. In three years' time, the black-hatted men had been replaced by boys with black beanies. The bushy beards remained the same. The old brick buildings now sported enormous murals. The subway station was wedged between a fancy bagel shop and a casual sushi bar.

Turning off the main drag, Diana was transported back to that moment in Justin's car when fantasy had met reality. This was the street where Carrie had danced in her Barbie gear; the stoop where her creep boyfriend had filmed it.

She punched in Carrie's apartment number and a second later, the door buzzed open. The feeling of déjà vu continued to press in the higher she climbed. At the fifth-floor landing, she reached for the doorknob, an uncanny instinct, before she stopped herself and knocked.

The door flung open, and Diana was dragged in by the wrist before it slammed shut again, nearly catching her heel.

"Were you followed?" With her back toward Diana, Carrie Yang was all shoulder bones and rumpled fabric. She'd pressed her face against the peephole.

"No, I don't think so."

When they'd talked on the phone that morning, Carrie had sounded serene. Yes, the gossip papers were reporting that she'd lost her sponsors, and that YouTube was threatening to deactivate her account. And yes, there were rumors that an ambitious state prosecutor was considering a case against her. Those were stories, and Carrie was certain that they'd get ahead with a better one.

In person, however, Diana could feel the electricity coming off Carrie, the way lightbulbs buzzed when the voltage was too high. Empty energy drinks and coffee cups littered the studio apartment. The mattress on the floor had too much laundry and video equipment piled on top for Carrie to have slept on it recently.

Satisfied that no one else was coming up the stairs, Carrie

whipped around. Despite her franticness, she looked no different from her videos. Her makeup was expertly applied. "Where are your friends?"

"I didn't say they were coming today." Diana narrowed her eyes. "You told me you wanted me to meet your PR team and talk out their strategy in person."

"Jesus, still the fucking ringleader." Carrie was going around the room and shaking every opened can. "You think it'd be obvious that if we were meeting with an entire *team* that we needed everyone present. I guess they're sending you to do their dirty work again."

"We could do a conference call." Diana flushed.

She was glad that that Z guy wasn't around, in part because of how small the studio already felt. No matter where she moved, she found herself in Carrie's way. The place seemed laid out to make you feel like an intruder.

"Please tell me you brought a disguise." Carrie had found an energy drink that she hadn't finished.

Diana looked down at her purse, which held a suit set and a pair of heels. "Just my clothes to meet with my law firm later."

Carrie pulled a trunk out from the closet and threw it open. Wigs spilled out, along with a rainbow of colored latex and sequined fabric. "You're lucky you weren't recognized."

"It's a big city." Diana took the light brown wig Carrie thrust in her face.

"Bitch, you know it takes one person with a phone."

Carrie pulled on a wig cap, and for an instant, her head became a skull, the sharp points of her face too pronounced. She ducked behind the trunk, pinning and adjusting, and when she flipped her new hair over her face, she looked like a siren emerging from the ocean.

Diana looked like one of the monsters from that goth family on TV, her wig swallowing her face. The little round sunglasses Carrie added to her outfit didn't help the resemblance.

"We stand out more than ever." Diana stared into the giant mirror propped against the back wall.

"Not with these." Carrie handed her a clipboard and put an empty conference lanyard around her neck. "Nobody will see us if they think we're asking for money."

At the mouth of the subway station, heading to Park Avenue where the PR firm's offices were located, Diana marveled at the way people's eyes slid over them while she waited for Carrie to finish her phone calls. From her side of the conversation, she seemed to be tracking someone down. Diana pictured a hunter checking her traps, growing hungrier by the second.

"Any news?" Carrie asked, and then, "Did Z reach out?"

Diana felt a lurch. The image she'd been avoiding flashed in front of her eyes. Z and Carrie asleep on that dirty mattress.

Diana waited until they'd transferred at Fourteenth Street in Manhattan before asking, "Is Z joining us?"

"We're not together anymore." Carrie pulled at her wig, which had gone askew. Her shoulders dropped. "He broke up with me after that Mousemix video."

"I'm sorry," Diana said. She'd never seen Carrie without her defiance.

"The thing is, he *knows* I didn't do anything wrong. That little twink roofied himself." Carrie glanced up and caught Diana's expression. "Surprising, right? Acts like he's Dorothy fresh off the farm. He's been coming to New York to do poppers since he got internet famous."

"Why'd Z break up with you, then?" Diana wasn't sure how much she trusted Carrie's account.

"He got spooked." Their subway pulled into the Thirty-Third Street station and Carrie moved toward the doors of the car. "He found out who leaked the video, but he's afraid to tell me. Says he doesn't want any more blood on his hands. As if he's ever had the guts."

They were moving with the flow of the crowd when Carrie

stopped in the middle of the subway stairs. Diana was forced to stop behind her.

"I need you to understand that I did nothing wrong," Carrie said. Her eyes were wet, dappled by the shifting tunnel light. The thought occurred to Diana that Carrie should re-create this exact look when they sat down for their statement video.

Somebody clipped Diana's back with the wheel of a stroller and shot her a dirty look. She tried to move up the stairs, or at least out of the flow of traffic. Carrie grabbed her by the shoulders.

"I would never drug somebody. You guys consented to everything we did. We had one wild night, and that's what the footage showed. It's crazy how people have bent it to fit their own story."

"Right," Diana said. She kept being bumped as the crowd split behind her, while Carrie remained untouched. For a moment, she hoped Carrie *had* drugged their drinks. "Although that's not what we're saying. We're saying it was scripted. That's our story, right?"

"Of course." Carrie turned back around. She strode up the rest of the stairs. "We've got to fight fire with fire."

* * *

The buildings on Park Ave were taller versions of the stately pre-war constructions they had all around DC. The offices of Carrie's PR firm were in one of these beige-and-brick facades. When Diana tried to follow Carrie through the large mahogany doors, however, Carrie told her to wait outside. She didn't want her team to charge her extra when Diana hadn't brought anyone else.

When Diana had called Carrie that morning after Weston had left, she'd been looking to do anything but wait around. Clearly, all Carrie had wanted was company for this trip. She couldn't exist without someone watching or recording.

Sitting on one of the metal benches that lined the avenue, Diana looked east, where a few blocks away in Midtown her fate was being decided. Where Weston was too, probably eating a protein bar for lunch. Anything to rack up more billable hours. She imagined what he would say when she told him about this wasted trip later. She hoped they'd both be in the mood to laugh.

They'd met a year and a half ago, during a networking event that Diana had organized. The newly elected Social Chair, she'd gotten an impressive number of alums to make the drive up from New York. The room had been packed and she'd been taking a victory loop around the reception area. At the bar, she'd accidentally made eye contact with her study partner AC. He was with an alum and Diana was forced to join them when AC called out her name.

"Weston mentioned being interested in digital copyright. I thought you'd want to talk to him."

When AC was nervous, he blinked too fast. He was intent on proving that nothing was awkward between them. The previous week, Diana had politely turned him down when he'd tried to kiss her in the library. Originally from Bangladesh, AC was sweet but looked sixteen, baby-faced and gangly.

"Are you also interested in the subject?" Weston asked.

Diana couldn't remember from her list if this was a first or last name. His name tag told her he'd graduated two years earlier. Unlike AC, who looked uncombed and wrinkled in his suit, Weston was overly buttoned-up, down to the shoes he'd tied too tightly.

AC shook the hair out of his eyes. "Diana was in a viral video called *Bad Asians*."

She wished she hadn't rejected AC so nicely. It was one thing for her classmates to know and another for an alum who could be a networking contact.

"Haven't seen it." Weston crossed his arms, his stiff sleeves riding up to reveal wrists covered in curly hair. "Maybe you can show me sometime."

His tone was unimpressed, as if Diana had been the one bragging.

"It has over five million views," Diana said.

"Let me guess. The person who made the video became ubersuccessful and you feel like you deserve a cut?" Wisps of hair also poked out of his starched collar. Although Weston's head was neatly buzzed, he must have been matted like a wolfman underneath his clothes.

Diana felt her face go red and she hadn't had a sip to drink. "I never said—"

"You're better off making your own content." Weston interrupted. "Even if you tried to get that video taken down, someone else will repost it. Unless it's child porn or a snuff film, our internet overlords aren't doing jack shit to scrub their servers."

"I heard 'child porn and snuff films.'" A second-year law student named Christina poked her head into the group. She was one of Diana's friends from the Diversity Board. Following behind her was Patrick, a 3L.

"Diana wants to get *Bad Asians* taken down," AC said.

"No, I'm trying to understand why Weston here is against digital protections." Diana headed off Christina's excitement. While she barely saw Christina outside of Diversity Board meetings, she somehow knew that Christina and Patrick were hooking up despite Patrick's fiancée back in North Carolina. She'd thought Chinese people ran their mouths. At Harvard, people went through gossip like they were trying to launder it.

"Just a thought experiment. Let's say I finish filming *Bad Asians* and decide I no longer want to be in the video. It hasn't been edited, let alone posted. Don't I have the right to my own image? I feel like these kinds of cases are going to get more popular. It's cheap and easy to make a video and post it online. Little kids are doing it. It's not some professional production with a union for everyone. Isn't there some legal way to protect these amateurs?"

"If they were worried, they shouldn't have gotten in front of the camera," Christina said. "You have to be smart about what you put out there."

"I have Facebook, and I treat it like it's my résumé." Patrick flashed a brilliant, empty smile. He reminded Diana of a handsome horse.

Diana rolled her shoulders. Back in high school debate, the more she tightened up, the worse her arguments got.

"Right," she said. "I'm sure those firms are going to love your engagement photos." She turned back to Christina. "But you can delete those images. They belong to you. Or what if, another thought experiment, you and Patrick hook up, and he says, *Wouldn't it be hot if we filmed it?* You're caught in the moment; it seems like a fun thing to do. The next morning, you sober up and ask him to delete it. What happens if he refuses? What happens if he says he's going to send that video to everyone you know?"

"Why the fuck would I do that?" Patrick clenched his formidable jaw.

Weston elbowed his way back into the conversation. "You're moving the target. This isn't a pornographic video you're talking about. It's probably some silly sketch. Who owns the footage? Whoever owns the camera. Anyone can buy a nice point-and-shoot, take a picture of some girl in a cool outfit, post it on their blog, and make money from ad clicks. If they're not selling the photograph itself, they don't owe Ms. Cool Outfit anything. That's called being a good businessman."

More people gathered around them, an eager jury. Except this wasn't a court case. This was like the arguments her parents and their friends would get into when they'd had too much to drink. The way to win was to be the most entertaining.

"We're getting lost in abstraction," Diana said. "Let's take on a real case. Everyone here knows Carrie Yang?" She looked meaningfully around the group. Before Weston could dismiss her, she said, "For those too old, Carrie Yang is one of the most popular creators on YouTube. And, according to my sources, her subjects are often coerced into taking illegal substances and then filmed in compromised situations. That's how she gets her viral moments—alcohol, weed, cocaine, and sometimes with minors." She smiled at Weston. "You're saying, with your expertise in the field, that because Carrie owned the camera, it's not illegal, it's good business?"

Weston's brow dropped, aware of how his words might be misinterpreted.

"I don't know if this thought experiment is useful if you keep adding on to it." He excused himself to refill his drink.

Applause and laughter filled the space where Weston had been.

"You showed him." AC bumped his fist against Diana's, and then asked if she had plans for the rest of the night.

The rush of victory ebbed away with the crowd. Diana hurried after Weston and caught up to him in the hallway. She couldn't believe she'd embarrassed an alum whose presence alone was a favor.

"Look, I'm sorry about that," she said. "AC's an idiot. He brought up a sore subject. I shouldn't have taken it out on you."

Losing the fight had rumpled Weston, but he didn't seem angry.

"Is he your boyfriend?" He put a hand in his pocket and looked down at the carpet.

"He wishes," Diana said without thinking.

Weston had a goofy untrained smile, as if he'd never seen a picture of himself. "That's good. I'd hate to think that's how you talk to your boyfriends."

No one had flirted with Diana before, including AC, who had leapt for her mouth without warning. In high school and college, she'd been told she was too intimidating for guys her age. She'd asked out her own prom date. If not for all the tales of hookups she'd heard in the last year and a half, she might not have known what Weston was doing. Had been doing, she also realized, before the crowd had gathered. She liked that he softened the sharper she got. She would find out on their first date that he'd also been raised by ambitious immigrant parents, who had changed his name from Vladimir to seem more American. His aggressive manner hid how he looked after the people he loved. He was supporting his younger sister through college and saving up to buy his parents a house. Through him, Diana could accept the paradox in herself. They could care about others deeply despite caring about themselves the most, which was why their first meeting would come back to haunt them. Weston had remembered, after the cellphone footage came out, exactly what Diana had said.

"You knew this would happen. You let me put my reputation on the line." His head had been in his hands, his laptop pushed to the edge of his bed. The only way to convince him that she hadn't knowingly put him at risk was to confess what she'd done to the real recording.

The double doors of the PR offices suddenly burst open, and Carrie was in front of her again, her face enraged, as if she had seen the memory in Diana's head. Then she thrust her phone in Diana's hand.

"Take my picture." Carrie ripped off her wig and shook out her hair.

Bewildered, Diana switched the phone into camera mode. Carrie crossed one leg over the other, bent slightly at the waist, and brought both hands up, her middle fingers framing her face.

After Diana snapped a few, Carrie grabbed the phone back. Looking over her shoulder, Diana saw her on Instagram posting the photo. The caption she was typing read:

Never apologize for being yourself. You have to be your own woman and stand up for what you believe in. History will reveal everything.

"Wait," Diana said, and Carrie jerked her head up.

"Shit, you should be in the picture too." She looked around for someone to take their photo. Diana yanked her by the arm. Beneath the expensive cotton, it was like holding on to a bone.

"Absolutely not," she said. "What the hell happened in the meeting?"

"I fired my PR team." Carrie snatched her arm back. "They're pitching fucking apologies."

"What're we going to do?" Passersby glanced over. Diana's clipboard was no longer enough of a shield.

Carrie looked at Diana like she was slow. "We're going ahead with the video. This doesn't change anything."

Diana almost mentioned Grace, her possible involvement, but it was too tenuous to give Carrie hope. To check in, Diana called Vivian, and when she didn't answer, texted her a reminder, the message far more certain than Diana felt.

When she looked up, Carrie had dug a prescription bottle out of her purse. She shook out two pills and dry swallowed them.

"What're you taking?" Diana asked.

"My ADHD meds," Carrie said. She inhaled deeply and leaned her head back, hands outstretched and fingers curled like a yogi.

Unease grew in the pit of Diana's stomach. Carrie was fraying at the edges. Diana checked her phone. Her meeting was an hour away, and after that Instagram post, she couldn't risk having Carrie near the firm.

"I should head out," Diana said.

Carrie snapped out of her trance. "I thought we were meeting with those lawyers."

Diana's confusion was slowly replaced by dread. Carrie seemed to be living in a different reality. "No, they're not representing me. They're . . . deciding whether to hire me."

"You're a lawyer!" Carrie hit her forehead with the heel of her hand. "That means if we find the person who leaked the footage, you could make them take it down."

Diana was struck again by the vertigo of the present and past colliding. Errol had said the same thing on the phone.

"I could at least pressure them," Diana said carefully. "You'd have to get Z to tell you first."

"You could force him, right? Say he's harboring a fugitive if he doesn't?"

Diana started to correct her and then thought again. People didn't understand what the law could and couldn't do. Diana's law school education had not only given her fluency in a complex language few others could speak, but it had also taught her that every accepted idea could be overturned. Their professors had debated the imprisonment of pedophiles, employed the Socratic method to unravel what made a rape a rape. What was a lie if it got Z to tell the truth?

"Let me think about it. See if you can find Z first."

She'd learned a thing or two from Justin. If her meeting went the way she hoped, she would remind Carrie of this moment when she hadn't said yes or no.

* * *

In the lobby of the firm, Lisa the receptionist hugged her hello and offered her a drink while she waited. Diana's strategy was to pretend she was an honored guest, and not a kid in trouble. She asked for anything iced, which meant she was stuck with a glass dripping condensation on her skirt.

She thought about what Carrie had asked. She could still remember what she'd written in that cease-and-desist three years ago, cobbled together from what she'd seen as a paralegal. She had stayed up all night in a disgusting Times Square motel and all morning outside a copy shop. To hide her lack of knowledge, she'd picked the most expensive paper the shop sold. She could have wiped her mouth with the letter, it was that cottony.

Only to find, outside the door marked 14, that the paper was too thick to slip through the crack. She had been about to knock when some instinct had her try the doorknob first. She might have remembered the day before, seeing Carrie push the door open without using a key, or she might have been lucky. The doorknob turned, and Diana stepped over the threshold, forgetting that the apartment was one open room. Right in front of her, Carrie and Z were sleeping. She remembered that Carrie's face was buried in her pillow, her naked shoulders thin and pale against the sheets. Z, however, slept on his back, and his eyes were half-open. She'd thought he was looking right at her.

Diana didn't know how long she stood there, but something must have broken her paralysis—Carrie smacking her lips, or the A/C unit switching on. Once it was clear that Z wasn't going to jump up, Diana had turned to go. That's when she saw the familiar black strap. The camcorder was right there on the little key stand by the door. Looking back at Z, she had lifted it up. He was so still he hardly seemed to be breathing. Her other hand held the letter, flimsy in comparison. She walked very slowly down the stairs. No one came after her. She hooked the strap over her shoulder. At the first garbage can, she looked around before throwing the camera into the yawning mouth. She'd texted her former friends that Carrie had deleted the recordings thanks to Diana's quick thinking, and that the cease-and-desist had worked because Errol was underage. No one had replied to her message. She could've gone to jail for trespassing, for theft, for destruction of private property. Her entire life could have ended right there.

"Diana!" A booming voice from behind startled her. She spilled iced coffee on her skirt.

She quickly covered the stain with her purse and turned around. Vic, the hiring partner, clapped her on the shoulder. A big-bellied man with a cherubic face, Vic was boisterous under any conditions. His gladness indicated nothing.

"I need to get used to your hellos again," Diana said.

Vic laughed and swept her into his office. His desk was covered in strange souvenirs. Next to his computer sat a baby shark preserved in a bottle and a rose dipped in gold. He grabbed his ever-present bag of sunflower seeds.

They chatted about his kids, and the next vacation he was planning. Minutes passed, and the small talk took on a nervous edge. Vic, used to being the nicest partner at the firm, kept cracking jokes while Diana grew quieter. She felt like a mouse cornered by a cat too squeamish to finish the job.

"Look." Vic swallowed another mouthful of seeds, which he ate with the shell and everything. "You put us in a tough spot with that video coming out."

Diana felt her spine go liquid.

"I know, and I'm sorry for putting the firm's reputation at risk," she said. "The public response has completely twisted the truth."

"Who cares about this firm? We're fuddy-duddies." Vic brushed off his hands. "You're smart, hard-working. You'll succeed wherever you go."

A deep ache spread across Diana's chest. "If I can explain—"

"Diana, my dear"—Vic fiddled with his suspenders—"if there were any way we could keep you on, please know I would've done it."

"The video was scripted. We decided to scrap the project three years ago because we felt it was problematic."

"The problem is not the video." Vic's tone sharpened, a reminder that he hadn't gotten this far without his own killer instinct. "It's not why did you make it, or why did you say what you said, but why do we know about it at all."

"The reason it was leaked is because . . ." Diana felt like she was sliding down a cliff, scrabbling for somewhere to grip.

"Carrie Yang, yes, and regardless of whether the allegations against her are true or false, you have been pulled into association with her."

The finality of this statement hit her with a thud.

"You still have a bright future." Vic stood up. "You'll get the most glowing reference letter from me."

Diana gathered her purse. The entire time, she'd managed to cover up the coffee stain, as if that had made any difference.

"I appreciate you meeting me in person," she said. "I know you could have easily done this over the phone."

"Come see me any time," Vic said. "I mean it."

He walked her past reception, out to the elevators in the hall.

"It's like I told Weston," he said while they watched the numbers climb. "If there'd been cameras on phones when I was your age, I'd be in a Thai prison rotting away."

Diana snapped out of her daze. Weston had tried after all. He'd waited until the last possible minute, but he'd fought for her. She'd underestimated him, and now, queasy and heart-thundering, she wanted nothing more than to climb into his arms.

"I'm glad he talked to you," she said.

The elevator doors opened, and Vic put out his hand, chivalrous to the end.

"It's truly a shame," he said. "We really thought there was a chance this could blow over."

* * *

Diana had planned to call Weston, but when the elevator doors opened, Carrie was in the lobby arguing with the security guards.

Diana hurried over. She wasn't trying to lose her reference letter too. "Is there a problem here?"

"See, I told you I knew somebody." Carrie was wearing a different wig, a short bob with red highlights. Diana hadn't seen her bring an extra one in her purse.

Diana dragged Carrie out of the building. "What are you doing here?"

"Z is going to help us!" She looked so genuinely pleased that Diana softened.

"That's great," she said. "But we need to figure out what to do about this footage. I don't know if saying it's scripted will work, not when there's this other controversy around you."

"Z will know what to do." Carrie hailed a passing taxi. "He's done it before."

Diana was pushed into the back seat. Carrie flashed the address to the driver. Diana caught a glimpse. They were going to the Lower East Side, where Z was staying with a friend.

After fighting blocks of rush hour traffic, their taxi pulled up to a street full of head shops and tiny underground bars. While Carrie waited for her change, Diana stood on the curb. For some reason this neighborhood was eerily familiar. Had she come here to eat during her summer program? These didn't seem like the kind of restaurants the firm liked to choose.

Passing a tiny three-stool restaurant advertising soup dumplings, the answer popped into her head. One of Grace's YouTube videos had been in a store like this, the one where a daughter went back in time to meet her mother as a little girl. Over there was the sex shop from *Starter Pack*, when the guy needed the right measurements to program into his new girlfriend.

"Which friend Z is staying with?" Diana asked. What were the chances Grace and Z knew each other?

"One of his cunty film girls," Carrie said. "He's never let me meet them." She pressed a buzzer.

Diana forgot that she might be in Grace's neighborhood when Z opened the door. He'd lost weight and his already-thin frame looked emaciated. Purple shadows hung under his eyes, which darted around, as if marking the possible exits. Carrie flung herself into his arms, somehow already sobbing. Holding her back, Z looked at Diana over Carrie's shoulder. He had an expression she couldn't read, somewhere between resigned and frightened.

"Thank you for helping us." Carrie checked her makeup in the mirror that hung over the shoe rack.

"Carrie," Z said. His voice faltered. "I never said that."

"Why else did you call?" Carrie asked, her voice babyish, lips pouting.

Z looked at Diana again. "I'm sorry."

"Why are you apologizing to her?" Carrie looked around at an invisible crowd. "I'm the one you put through hell."

"You know you deserved it," Z said with a sudden flash of anger.

Carrie shrank back, tears in her eyes. She was like a shapeshifter confounded, unable to find the best disguise to get what she wanted. She and Z stared right at each other. Something passed between them, and Carrie's mask fell.

"What the fuck did you do?" Carrie pulled off her wig and threw it at Z's feet.

Diana could suddenly see beyond the makeup—the hollow cheeks, the feverish eyes. What was painted on and what was the real Carrie.

"I don't care what happens to me." Z kicked the wig away. "Everyone needs to know who you are."

Faster than Diana could react, Carrie pulled the mirror off the wall and smashed it across Z's face. His head whipped back, and he crashed to the floor. Carrie swung the mirror again and Diana grabbed it out of her hands before she could bring it down on his back. The mirror slipped from Diana's grasp and the glass shattered against the floor.

Carrie had jumped on Z while Diana was busy kicking the shards away. Carrie was hissing something into his ear. She clutched his shirt in her hand and pulled his face closer. When Z pushed her away, she hit her phone against the side of his head.

Diana grabbed Carrie around the waist and Carrie jerked her head back. The room disappeared in a burst of white light and Diana's nose ran hot with pain. Vision blurry, Diana felt herself pulled up by her armpits. Carrie was dragging her out of the apartment with unnatural strength.

"Stop, somebody help!" Glass scraped across the floor. Whatever was running down Diana's nose was also streaming from her knee.

"Get-the-fuck-out—" Carrie heaved her farther with every grunt.

When Diana fell into the hall, she wrapped her legs around Carrie's and pulled her down with her. The door slammed behind them. A dead bolt slid into place.

Thank God Thank God Thank God went the sound of Diana's heart. Blood gushed from her nose with every beat. A neighbor had come out, was threatening to call 911, and Carrie leapt up, was already down the stairs, was gone, gone, gone.

* * *

Back in the apartment, Diana and Z found the first aid kit and cleaning supplies.

"Grace told me what's been happening." Z swept up the glass. His face was already swelling where the mirror had hit him. "She ran into your friend Vivian in DC and . . ."

"Wait, is this her apartment? I didn't know you two were friends. She has a lot of plants." Diana was giddy and lightheaded from the adrenaline rushing through her veins. Weston had the same bookshelves and couch, which meant Grace shopped at Ikea like everyone else their age. Instead of books, Grace had stacked tiny, meticulously labeled tapes, like the ones she used to feed her old camera. "Are you sure you're not concussed? God, remember when Russell Crowe supposedly threw a phone at that hotel receptionist? We thought it was funny. Isn't that fucked up? Wasn't that a real phone too? Like a landline?"

Her voice was nasal from the rag stuffed up her nose to stanch the bleeding, and this made her want to talk more, hearing how silly she sounded. Nothing else seemed to matter. Her knee might need stitches, but her nose wasn't broken. She was okay. Z was okay.

They'd convinced the neighbor not to call the police or the EMTs. Z was sure that Carrie would stay away, unless she wanted him to file a restraining order, a public record the internet could dig up easily.

196 • LILLIAN LI

"I'll take the video down," Z said. "I wasn't thinking straight. You don't understand what she—" He broke off and focused on picking up the smaller shards that the broom had missed.

Gravity reasserted itself, and with it a sinking feeling. "Has she done this to you before?"

"Not like this," Z said.

Diana bent down beside him, wincing from her knee. "I had no idea." He had been the silent guy with the camera. She'd never considered that he might have been silenced by somebody.

"It's not an excuse." Z helped Diana stand up. He dumped the glass from the dustpan into a paper grocery bag. "I did the things she told me to. And didn't do the things I should have."

He half closed his eyes and Diana recognized the dark stillness inside them.

"You saw me that morning," she said. "I knew you had, but, when you didn't move . . ."

Z had an unexpectedly gentle smile. "When you took my camcorder, I wanted to cheer."

Diana laughed until the next logical step fell in place. "She must have blamed you when she woke up."

Z played with his hair. The neck of his T-shirt gaped where Carrie had pulled it. "I could have left. Martin—that's Mousemix—he was the wake-up call. Not that she dosed his drink, God, can you believe that? I didn't do anything. I helped her film those follow-up videos, helped convince her fans to back her. Then she released his private information."

Diana had been sure that a stranger on the internet had found and posted Mousemix's address. She hadn't considered how much easier it would be for someone you knew to leak that information anonymously.

After they'd restored Grace's living room back to order, Z insisted on paying for a cab to drop her back at Weston's.

"I'm sorry," Diana said. Z looked up from washing his hands. "I made all these assumptions about you."

"I did ruin your life," Z said.

"A bunch of lawyers ruined my life," Diana joked.

Z walked her outside and hailed a cab at the corner. She told him to thank Grace, and for a moment they stood, uncertain, before they both opened their arms to hug goodbye.

With the driver staring at her face in the rearview mirror, Diana remembered to check her messages. She expected a few from Vivian, from her parents, and, of course, from Weston.

But they were all from him. None of them made sense.

I'm so sorry. I'd do anything to take it back.

Where are you? Are you okay?

All the way back to that afternoon, when Weston had written:

I didn't think they'd fire you. I wanted to get ahead of the story. Please call me. I can explain.

With a stab of clarity, Vic's words came back to her: "We really thought there was a chance this could blow over." Only now, she knew what he'd meant by "we."

Weston had ratted her out to save himself. If not for him, the firm may have never found out. For all the hateful threats online, no one had listed her information. The cellphone footage hadn't made national news. She'd believed that a mob of strangers had more to gain from her pain than the person she thought had loved her.

"Can I change the drop-off point?" Diana asked. She gripped the handle of the door. "Or let me out. I made a mistake. I'm sorry. Please, can you let me out?"

She was in the middle of the city. Her nose was bleeding again. A few blocks away, she saw the glass drum of Penn Station. She would not cry. She would not give Weston one more piece of her tonight. Fighting the crowd, she limped into the hub where so many railways crossed, including the one that would take her home.

Hours earlier, she'd been amazed that Weston had put her above himself. The truth was, she could not imagine making the same choice. Now the opposite was true. The selfless thing to do would be to go back to Weston and let him explain, to forgive him for a mistake that she also would have made. The smart thing would be to cut him out of her life.

Looking up at the ceiling of her train, she traced the exact track that had sent her hurtling toward this moment. Every selfish decision where she'd come out better than someone else. No wonder Vivian had stopped answering her calls and Justin had never picked up. Why Errol's explanation was simply that he couldn't. The ones who had put her first, she'd put second too many times. The people left in her life were just like her. Crabs in a barrel. Her first day at Harvard was the last moment where she could have switched her track, tried to find people who were kinder than they were ambitious. If she had a time machine, would she have chosen differently? Forgone the popularity her choice had brought her, the influence and access? To lose her status or to never have it? You couldn't escape yourself any easier than you could escape your fate.

That first day at Harvard, at her section's orientation mixer, she'd hung back while everyone else grabbed a name tag and marker. She hadn't caught anyone's eye yet. Jennifer was the only person from her party who was in her section, and she'd promised not to say anything. There was a chance nobody else would recognize her.

Name tag in hand, she studied the blank space. Her section leader had asked that everyone jot down an interesting fact about themselves. She could already see what other people had written. Someone had served in the Marines. Another had won Miss Texas. One person's name tag read: *Climbed Mt. Everest to raise money for LGBT rights.* As if summitting the tallest mountain in the world wasn't enough.

Students were forming tight, exclusive circles. Diana felt like the last person to turn in her exam. She wasn't artistic like Justin or pretty like Vivian. She wasn't even that smart, not compared to Errol. She had stood out in school because she had focused on standing out, like every other person here at Harvard.

She'd taken an enormous risk to ensure that no video would

threaten her place here. Now she faced a different danger. She'd forgotten that once you secured your place, you looked around to find your standing. She was surrounded by future senators, attorneys general, Supreme Court justices. They had no reason to pay attention to her.

"I couldn't sell Blüm by relying on people who wanted to look like me," her mother had once said. "No lotion can do magic. But I was a diplomat's daughter. Your father's father once operated on Deng Xiaoping's son. I'm selling the opportunity to talk to me, to be associated with somebody important."

Diana remembered the party she'd thrown, and how people had clustered around her. Those who hadn't seen the video had found her interesting because other people thought so. Diana uncapped her marker. She knew how far she was willing to go to be a success. She'd learned that morning in New York.

I'm a Bad Asian.

She didn't bother to write her name. The people who didn't know it soon would.

Before the name tag was fully stuck to her shirt, someone's hand was on her arm.

CHAPTER TEN

YouTuber Carrie Yang Has Reportedly
Checked into Rehab

Rachel Liao
BuzzFeed News Reporter

Posted on August 10, 2012 at 3:36 p.m.

Popular YouTuber Carrie Yang issued a statement on her Instagram on Friday morning announcing that she will be checking into a live-in rehabilitation facility located in the Rocky Mountains of Utah.

"I have been abusing prescription drugs and alcohol for almost six years," Yang, 28, wrote in a caption accompanying a picture of a sunset over the Brooklyn Bridge. "It began with Adderall to keep up with the pressure of generating new video content and spiraled quickly from there."

Yang, known for her Barbie Chan character and makeup tutorials, apologized to her four million subscribers. "I'm ashamed I let my demons take control. Creating videos for you was my reason for being. It also became the justification for my addiction."

The apology has touched a chord, receiving over ten thousand likes in less than twenty-four hours. One-time collaborator Paulette Cho (known by her handle Paulywaugs) commented, "Proud of you for prioritizing your heath!" Oscar-nominated actor and producer Harris Yu wrote, "@ilovecarrieyang, you have nothing to be ashamed about. Your videos have brought millions of people joy, and now u need to take care of U (sp)."

Two weeks earlier, Yang had uploaded an enigmatic Instagram post that had fans speculating about her mental well-being. This followed recent allegations made by fellow YouTuber Martin Simon (known by his handle Mousemix91), and leaked cellphone footage from a never-published YouTube video with the actors of the 2009 viral hit *Bad Asians*, Diana Zhang, Errol Chen, and Vivian Wang.

"It's a shame that a deleted scene from a short film we never made has been released without our permission and turned into a topic of public speculation," Zhang, Chen, and Wang wrote in a joint statement they released to BuzzFeed News. "We hope to move on from this unfortunate incident and ask that people allow us to return to our lives as private citizens."

Simon's representatives did not comment when reached by BuzzFeed News.

More from BuzzFeed

YouTuber MeMe Production's First Short Film Hits Festival Circuits

Justin clicked out of the website, relieved that his name remained unpublished. A month since the video had come out, he still hadn't been connected to that night. Only his shoulder had been visible in the footage. The moment his face would have swung into frame was when the clip abruptly ended. For years he'd wondered if he should have stepped in to stop that fight. The public scrutiny his former friends faced had dissolved his uncertainty.

While he'd been studying the article, waiting for a customer to find her order number, his email queue had ballooned up to double digits. He clicked through the support tickets, assigning each the right color flag, and re-sorted by importance. On their end, the customer was finally ready. Unmuting his headset, Justin swallowed the almonds he'd been chewing. Vijay preferred their office manager stock the crunchiest snacks.

"I see you now." Justin dragged the order page over to his second monitor and opened one of the easier email tickets on his laptop. "Looks like it should arrive in two days." He made a note on his iPad to follow up on this order and email a coupon if the shipping ended up delayed.

"I'm glad you love our OG Green," he said. "I was with our CEO the day he came up with the blend." His phone set showed no incoming calls, and when a customer stayed on the line to chat, they were usually a little lonely. He amended the note on his iPad to call with the coupon offer and copied over the phone number on his screen.

Across the room, Vijay performed a large yelping sneeze. "I think someone's talking about me."

Justin double-checked that he had muted his headset before shouting back, "I'm telling them that you used to bench sixty."

Through the glass doors of their underground office, their Marketing lead Thomas emerged. He was carrying stacks of pizza, the first indicator that it was evening. Their basement office operated like a casino, time unobtrusive amid the steady hum of activity.

Justin got off the call, recommending a flavor called Mucho Macho Mango—"We call it 'Mmmmm' down at HQ." When Thomas came by with a money jar, Justin dropped in a few bills. He refused the slice Thomas offered.

"Seriously?" Thomas's pink cheeks showed beneath his blond beard, which made him look like a boy in disguise. "Don't tell me you're fasting."

"I've got dinner waiting," Justin said. Thomas gave a jealous, good-natured groan. "It's only Sunday dinner with my mom."

"Exactly," Thomas said. "I wish my mom was here to cook for me. Invite me over sometime. Moms love me."

Thomas moved off to the next desk. Out of their company of thirty, almost everyone was here, although Vijay was adamant that no one had to work weekends. Justin hated leaving early, although what "early" meant was hard to say when there were no set work hours at BOD. Other people clocked out when their job was done. Justin's job was endless. He ran Customer Support by himself, with part-time help from Vijay's cousin Adi. Vijay had awarded Justin "All-time Grinder" at their last company retreat, a trophy that tickled Raul and Ingrid endlessly.

The alarm rang on Justin's phone, and he took off his headset. He closed and unplugged his laptop, experiencing the usual tug of concern that he was leaving someone in a pinch. He slipped the laptop into the sleeve of his company backpack. He could tackle more emails later tonight.

Walking by Vijay's desk, which was right by the office entrance, Justin held his hand out for a quick goodbye. Vijay pulled out an empty chair.

"I've got something I want to run by you." Vijay leaned forward and lowered his voice. Up close, his gelled hair looked like a woodblock carving. "I'm getting some serious VC interest from SF."

"That's great." Justin made the face of someone who was very excited.

"They're telling me it's time to move out to Cali." Vijay opened his bloodshot eyes wide, displaying how hard he'd worked for this. "This is it, man. This is what we dreamed of."

"California dreamin'." Justin's stomach churned from caffeine and too many mixed nuts. "Are you sure? I mean what about the team?"

"Thomas is in, and PJ, and Brad. If we leave some people behind, that's fine. All I care about is my core four."

Justin stood up and pulled Vijay into a shoulder bump. "Congratulations, man."

"Congratulations to you, brother," he said. "Once we get that green, you'll be running your own team. No more headset, no more tickets. Hell, I think you'd make a great VP, if you want it."

"All-time Grinder." Justin tapped his chest on his way out the door, not sure what he was saying anymore.

"ATG!" Vijay was elated as if the news were fresh. When had Thomas heard? On his way out to grab pizza? The order could be as random as that. Or Vijay was letting Justin know where he stood?

When the office elevator opened on the ground floor, Justin emerged into a darkened world. On his way to the parking garage, he passed Everyday Fitness, where the whir of treadmills and the smell of chlorine made his head hazy. He'd first met Vijay there, and Raul. The branching path of his life could be traced back to this gym, as central as his mother's house. He couldn't move to the other side of the country. Not with his mother alone in her home. Not with Raul and Ingrid together in theirs.

Since college, he'd eaten Sunday dinner at home. The route from work to their usual restaurant to the house was so engrained that in a blink he'd gone from one garage to another. He hugged his mother, who unhooked the takeout bags from his fingers. She turned the TV down, the table already set with empty bowls. They split their disposable chopsticks in unison.

"Tell me what you did today." His mother rubbed her hands, stiff from her scissors. Justin thought about the California news.

"I had sixteen customer calls and closed twenty tickets," Justin said. "I answered more than that, but there's always a back and forth with emails."

"So many!" She would be impressed if he'd handled only one.

He picked out the cashews and peanuts that wound up in his bowl, the nuts being his mother's favorite. When he offered them to her, however, she shook her head.

"It's nothing serious," she said when he pressed her. She prodded the side of her jaw, which was slightly swollen. "I got a tooth pulled last month, and the area keeps getting infected."

"You got a tooth pulled?" He'd seen her every Sunday. "You didn't tell me."

"Yes," she said. "On my day off."

"I could've driven you," he said, instead of the questions he wanted to ask.

"My friend Gerald was free." A salon customer. His mother had no friends. She turned her attention back to the TV. A rerun of *Everybody Loves Raymond* was playing. His mother drifted away on waves of studio laughter.

Bending over his bowl, Justin ate while his mother pushed her food aside, no longer hiding her toothache. He told everyone that he enjoyed these Sunday dinners, as if that meant they couldn't also be a chore. He could have been making a gourmet meal with Raul in their newly renovated kitchen while Ingrid played them some obscure band and made them listen, really listen, to the rhythm section. He and Raul would tease Ingrid for being too cool, then he and Ingrid would laugh over Raul's kitchen gadgets, which would lead the two of them to poke fun at Justin for oversalting his food. Before them, he'd never known how quiet his mother's house was, besides the blaring TV, the captions eternally scrolling. Justin wanted to take the remote out of the napkin holder and turn the damn thing off. He saw his mother every week, and yet she didn't know that he'd learned how to cook a perfect steak. Or that drums were the backbone of a song. He relied on her not to ask about the big things in his life, but she could have asked about the little ones. He'd had to hear from Diana that his mother was aware of *Bad Asians*. The Sunday after Diana's apology tour, his mother simply said, "Tell me what you did today."

He in turn had kept his questions to himself. He didn't ask about her day off because there was a chance that she'd simply slept, the way she had when he was younger. The last time he'd asked why she was so tired, she'd told him she missed his father. Everything was only a few degrees away from that man. Since his decision years ago to take off his jade necklace, Justin's memory of his father began the day he'd left, and his mother had locked herself in the bathroom. Perhaps his mother knew that the love that defined her was one that he did not understand or respect. No matter what he did for her, or how hard he worked to make her happy, that bathroom door would stand between them.

When he couldn't bear these thoughts any longer, he said, "You need to go back to the dentist. I'll call them tomorrow."

"I'll call," she said. "You'll be busy at work."

"Let me know when your appointment will be." She wouldn't ask the right things. She wouldn't take her discomfort seriously. "I want to come with you."

"Okay." She placed the leftover cartons back in the plastic bag. "Then why don't we skip dinner next Sunday? You can go home and have dinner with your roommates." She turned the volume down on the TV and looked straight at him. "You can't spend all your time with me."

"I don't," he said. He'd thought she knew that these Sunday dinners were for her. Any other mother would be grateful. He took the bag of leftovers, his face growing hot. "My company might move to California."

His mother shifted in her chair, like a bird disturbed by a strong wind.

"How exciting," she said. She turned back to Raymond on TV, stuck between choosing his wife's side or his mother's.

They hugged goodbye at the lip of the garage. He turned his car on in the driveway, keeping it in park. He waited to see if his mother noticed. She had already pressed the button for the garage door to come down, its metal pleats folding her up like a fortress.

* * *

On his way out of the neighborhood, he drove by Diana and Errol's cul-de-sac, and Vivian's street soon after. He didn't know how they were doing beyond the voicemail Diana had left after Z had taken the footage down. If his mother had heard news from the other parents, she'd kept it to herself. Even so, this weekly drive meant he was never far from thinking of the group. No matter how much he'd moved on with his life, he couldn't stop circling back to where he'd started.

After the trip to New York, Justin had allowed himself to fall in love for the first time. He was rewarded a month later by Raul dumping him to reconcile with his wife. Without a place to live, Justin could not afford to quit Raul's personal training team, or so he told himself. Raul was careful not to overlap their appointments. Justin had come to the gym anyway on his days off, hiding in the cardio room and walking on the treadmill for hours. His chest ached without reason. His hands shook when they gripped the weight bar. He had never known such weakness.

During this low point, Justin had started training Vijay Patel, who was more interested in Justin's diet than in lifting anything himself. Unathletic, but energetic, Vijay was easily distracted during their sessions. He complimented Justin's physique, his manner, his way of instruction. Justin had played at the idea of hooking up with a client. In his fantasies at night, he'd quickly go through the motions with Vijay and languish in Raul's reaction, finishing off with their feverish reunion.

After two months of attention, Vijay had put his hand on Justin's shoulder at the end of their session.

"Hear me out," Vijay said, and Justin prepared himself to accept whatever came next.

"Bio Organic Design—B. O. D." Vijay had spelled out the rest while he did butterfly stretches on the mat, so inflexible his knees touched his shoulders. "All these supplements and protein powders. Don't you wonder what chemicals are inside them? What if I told you I have a proven recipe to build muscle fast, and increase your metabolism, with an ingredient list a third grader could read?" Vijay's pitching abilities were strong. What he was missing was a body for evidence. He had a binder and a business plan he could present, but Justin had already agreed.

Justin's first days at BOD were spent in Vijay's parents' basement working out on a Bowflex and taking packets of powdered supplements. Justin's urine samples, his literal blood and sweat, had gone into fine-tuning their OG Green powder. A part of Justin believed that he'd misled the findings. He'd grown stronger in the basement not because of B12 or zinc, but because the day he went to quit, Raul had begged him not to leave.

Justin's fantasies had been less imaginative than the reality. In the gym's office, Raul had fallen to his knees. When they'd gotten up off the floor, he had a bigger favor to ask.

"Ingrid wants to meet you," Raul had said, his arm thrown around Justin on the office couch, as if to pin him from leaving.

Justin had remembered his old curiosity, lying in Raul's bed, trying to find Ingrid's shape in the mattress. Her heavy braid, her broad hips, how real and solid she'd looked in those faded pictures.

"And then I can be with you?" Justin had asked.

He'd buried his nose deeper into the side of Raul's head, his heart torn between sinking and soaring. The reality of Raul's need had been apparent when he'd let Justin ruin his perfectly sculpted hair.

* * *

Justin arranged to meet Ingrid at a used bookstore in Adams Morgan. He came into the store expecting to find her at the front. When minutes passed with no Ingrid, he asked the desk clerk if he'd seen a blond German woman. The clerk slowly pressed his finger to the sentence he'd been reading and gestured toward the entire store, as if to say that Ingrid was all around them. Justin walked quickly past the sections, barely glancing down the aisle of each one. If he missed Ingrid, this "meeting" would still have to count.

It only took a glimpse. The passing sight of her in the dim light yanked him backward like a hook. Her hair was out of its pictured braid and formed a menacing cloud of curls, chaotic where Raul's waves were lawful. She wore what looked like an oversized fisherman's jacket and her shoulders filled the width of the narrow aisle. A stack of books was by her feet. She dropped the one in her hand on the pile and looked up to catch Justin staring. She did not return his smile. Yards away, her hostility was clear. Thinking of Raul, Justin entered the stacks to greet her.

"I'm sure there's black mold in this dust." She went back to the wall of books and then caught herself. "Pleased to meet you." She extended her hand, her face to the shelves.

Her hand was soft, and she was slow to withdraw it. She raised her chin and glanced over.

"Do you read?"

"I draw." He didn't understand why he'd offered her this. He hadn't drawn in years.

She dug through the pockets of her big coat.

"Show me." She shoved a pen and an old receipt into his hands.

Justin thought of drawing her, but he was afraid of her derision. He wanted to surprise her, and in doing so, he surprised himself. He drew the clerk at the front, nose-deep in his book, and added qualities to enhance the clerk's true nature. He made the nose long and thin like a branch and added leaves. The glasses became more owlish, and feathers grew around the eyes. A ruffled collar appeared, a cloak of wings. When he looked up, he caught Ingrid watching, and she gave him a tiny smile, her front teeth peeking out.

"I think we're done here," she announced, quickly reshelving her stack of books. Before Justin could be relieved or disappointed, she pushed him ahead. "There's a coffeeshop next door. I don't like coffee, but it's a nice place to sit."

Ingrid spoke for the group. She had a cosmopolitan accent, neither entirely German nor anything else, and her questions sounded like commands. At the coffeeshop, she said, "It's late. You want some mint tea." He was happy to oblige. He waited for her to do the talking.

Instead, Ingrid took him in, the way Raul had that first day at the gym. She sat back, luxuriating in the plushness of the armchair. Justin had assumed that Raul was the main mover behind this meeting. Ingrid seemed unlikely to be moved by anyone.

"You wanted to meet me?" he said.

"I did," she said. "I don't like upsetting Raul, and without you, he was very upset. I want to see how we might have everything."

Justin kept his face blank. He enjoyed hearing that his heartbreak was shared. The sharpness of his pleasure revealed that he remained angry with Raul, despite his gratitude over their reunion.

In Justin's nighttime imaginations, he'd had Ingrid dying or cast off a hundred times. Sitting in front of her now, he wanted to know her better. He'd closed one door when he'd fallen in love with Raul. He wondered if he'd closed it completely. She ordered a pot of tea for them to share, and poured him a cup, attentive to each action as if performing a secret ritual. The steam from her tea turned her face pink. She had a snout-like nose and big, white teeth. She wore her body like an expensive fur, slinky and fluid, and when he asked her questions, she spoke in full paragraphs.

"I don't understand hobbies," she said. "Why do something to pass the time? I'd rather do nothing. In fact, I like sitting by a window and being bored. It's not that I don't want to be entertained— please invite me to dinners and parties—but sometimes, if I haven't been bored in a while, I'll stay home. I don't know how many people have tried being home alone while the people you adore are having fun without you. Raul says he'll lift weights out of his range because he enjoys the way he aches after. I think it must be the same. I'll never know because I think exercise is another name for a hobby."

Raul preferred a dialogue. He had worked hard to draw Justin out and when he was with Raul, Justin heard how his rusty words grew oiled, his mouth a machine that could not be neglected. Yet from that first meeting with Ingrid, Justin came to learn that his body, down to the tiny twitches of his face, could communicate better than words.

On their way out, Ingrid had opened the coffeeshop door with a sweep of her arms. She'd held the door in place for Justin to walk through it. When he'd passed her, his head ducked, he could not help glancing up. She'd understood and they'd blocked the entrance like two teenagers. Justin had never kissed Raul in public like this and he lost himself to the freedom. A moment later, recognizing the guilt paling his face, Ingrid had said, "Don't worry. Raul knows this was a possibility."

The next day, Raul had alluded to what Ingrid had made direct: "Ingrid enjoyed your date."

For a year, Justin saw Raul when Ingrid traveled for work, and took Ingrid out when she came back on the weekends. While Raul gave him home-cooked meals and the pleasure of somewhere to return to, Ingrid expanded his world with museums and art house movies.

His attraction to Raul was like hunger. Simple, predictable, impossible to deny. What he felt with Ingrid was closer to fascination. Despite the new things he'd had to learn to sleep with Raul, it was sex with Ingrid that made him most aware of his body. He'd discovered the nerves at the tips of his fingers, the pressure exerted by the end of his nose. Thinking of Raul alone turned him on; with Ingrid, it was the two of them together.

That year, he'd felt more divided than ever, three different Justins hiding under one skin. The one with Raul, the one with Ingrid, the one with everyone else. He couldn't keep sectioning off his life. No one knew him completely, least of all himself. He had to choose, but he couldn't trust that his choice would satisfy him. Not when he knew how easy it was to be with a woman. Or that to deny his desire for men felt like starving.

He was surprised when Raul and Ingrid invited him to dinner for his twenty-fifth birthday that March. In the red-walled tapas restaurant, scenes of bullfighting on all sides, Justin readied himself for a couple whose marriage had nearly ended.

When they arrived, however, they were laughing. Raul took Ingrid's coat and said to her, "Doesn't he look handsome?"

Ingrid stuffed her gloves in her handbag and put a cold hand to Justin's cheek. "Happy birthday." She looked back at Raul. "Do you remember when we were twenty-five?"

That night, Justin learned that Ingrid and Raul had attended the same international boarding school in the Swiss Alps. They'd fallen in love when they were freshmen. Ingrid pulled up her sleeve to show Justin the stick-and-poke tattoo he'd mistaken for a freckle, and the matching one on Raul's shoulder.

"We're bound for life," Ingrid said. "That's what we've had to learn."

Far from jealous, Justin was intrigued watching how comfortable Raul and Ingrid were with each other. A new option presented itself, too outlandish to say out loud. Justin could be the stabilizing note that created the harmony between Raul's and Ingrid's extremes. Without him there, Justin could picture Ingrid ordering for the table and Raul stewing that he hadn't had time to look. Raul charming the waiter and Ingrid muttering that small talk was for small minds.

Now Ingrid rattled off classic tapas dishes that Justin *had* to try, and Raul added a few novelties that had caught his eye. They chatted about work, Ingrid and Raul each giving advice on how BOD could market itself better, with Ingrid analyzing the business model and Raul offering his entire gym network. To the other diners, their table must have looked only a little strange. A glamorous couple celebrating their younger, scruffier friend. For the first time in years, Justin felt like one person living one life without anyone blinking an eye.

"I hate to drop you off in that opium den," Ingrid said at the end of the meal. "Why not come home with us. You already spend all your time there."

When Ingrid went on work trips, Raul would insist that Justin stay over, and Justin was sure the three strangers he lived with used his room when he was gone.

Raul clarified Ingrid's suggestion. "You said your lease is almost up. We have extra room. I know it's unorthodox—"

"Oh, please, let's not bring in the orthodoxy!" Ingrid clapped her hands. Justin reached under the table to touch her leg. He bumped Raul's hand already doing the comforting. Before Justin could yank his hand back, Ingrid clamped his fingers and Raul's between her knees. The tapas place had very small tables, even relative to the size of their plates.

"Oh my god, we could be on a poster," Raul said.

Justin had laughed so hard that he'd upset his glass of sangria.

An hour later, he had come back to the dank room of his shared house. Highway traffic whined outside his window. Out on his desk was the Kleenex box he'd hidden in his closet, empty and tipped over on its side. When Justin went to throw away the box, he found the missing tissues wadded up in his garbage can. He sat on the very edge of his bed, afraid of what the blanket might be hiding. If he'd gone to sleep that night in an unsoiled bed, if he hadn't had that sangria, if he'd said no to the dinner invitation . . . if he hadn't left his friends in New York, if he'd kept his mother's car at home—he could keep tracing the chance decisions of his life until he was too paralyzed to make any choice at all. He called the only landline he knew besides his mother's. He packed what would fit into his gym bag and prepared to leave everything else behind.

When Raul and Ingrid arrived twenty minutes later, they rolled a fleet of Ingrid's stylish suitcases up the driveway of the house. Justin had waited by the door, trying to collect himself. He hadn't asked for these suitcases. These two dazzling people had known exactly what he needed. When Raul had taken the gym bag from Justin's shoulder, he'd been too grateful to speak.

* * *

Justin unlocked the front door, his dinner leftovers in one hand. The house was quiet, but when he walked into the kitchen, Ingrid and Raul were sitting side by side at the table. Their backs were rigid and the air between them was tight.

"Is anyone hungry?" he asked. Only Ingrid turned around.

"You're home early." She rose stiffly and gave him a kiss. Before Justin could return either the kiss or her question, she'd left the room. Her footsteps pounded up the stairs.

Raul deflated in his seat. His head fell below his shoulders.

"I'm sorry," Justin said. The plume of hair bobbed back up.

"What are you sorry for?" Raul turned. The skin around his eyes was thin and worn, and for once, he looked like a man in his forties.

"I should have stayed longer at my mom's." Justin had lived with them for a year without realizing that they might have reasons for wanting him out of the house.

"Don't be ridiculous—this is your home too," Raul said.

Justin hated when Raul spoke to him like everything was simple. As if the home was not in Raul's and Ingrid's names, as if he hadn't been kicked out before. Justin did not even own the suitcases in which half his belongings were still packed.

"How was work?" Raul asked. "How was your mom?" He pulled Justin into his lap.

Justin had chosen Ingrid's side without realizing. Contrite, he kissed Raul's forehead, his cheeks, the divot below his nose.

Raul sighed into Justin's mouth. "That's exactly what I needed." He pressed his hips up against Justin's leg.

"My mom got her tooth pulled without telling me." Justin was uncomfortable talking about his mother, but more uncomfortable with the alternative. They couldn't go to Justin's guestroom if Ingrid was upset upstairs. She would think they didn't care about her feelings.

"Today? Is that why you came home early? I'm sure she could barely chew." For someone who loved sex, Raul was happily distracted by good conversation.

"Last month." Justin rolled off his lap and sat in Ingrid's chair. "As far as I know, all her teeth could be fake."

"She'd tell you if something was wrong." Raul rubbed Justin's knee. "My grandmother was the same way."

"The one who died of breast cancer?" Ingrid had come downstairs with a lot less noise than she'd gone up. She emerged from the hallway and leaned against the threshold of the kitchen. "The one who told everyone when the lump was the size of an egg?"

"She didn't know any earlier," Raul said. "I don't think eighty-year-old Catholic women are touching their breasts every night in the shower."

"This woman was famous for giving birth without making a single sound. She had her rosary and a piece of wood. They showed me the wood, with the teethmarks and everything. She nearly bit through the damn thing and they passed it around like it was a piece of costume jewelry."

"I've found that making a big commotion isn't the only way to get through a hard time." Raul massaged a knot he'd found in Justin's thigh. Justin stayed quiet while Raul dug his knuckle in harder.

"You're hurting him." Ingrid leaned her elbows on the counter.

The knot popped loose, and Justin breathed out a hum of pleasure, which he hadn't meant to do. Raul patted his leg like it was a dog.

"Let's go to bed," Raul said to Ingrid. "I'm tired."

Ingrid undid the plastic bag and pulled out the leftovers. She waved her hand in the air, pouring the cashew chicken onto a plate. Raul gave her wide berth on his way upstairs, as if she might reach out and swipe him.

Ingrid went into the living room, where she curled into her favorite spot on the couch. Justin watched Raul's back disappear around the corner before he followed her.

"I can't believe you and your mother eat this every week." Ingrid shoveled the cold chicken into her mouth. "Your country has some of the best food in the world, and you choose this cornstarch junk?"

"Maybe you can take me somewhere better."

She sank further into the deep corner of the couch. When she leaned her head back, her hair sprang around her face like ivy.

"What if we got a place together," Ingrid said. "No Raul allowed."

216 • LILLIAN LI

Justin played with the tassel on the pillow he'd pushed into his stomach.

"You two work in the same building. I'm always traveling. When do we get alone time anymore?"

The floor creaked overhead, followed by the sound of rushing water.

Some nights, lying in the guest bed, Justin counted how many months he'd loved Ingrid, how many he'd loved Raul, the numbers thin and shaky. When he counted the years Raul and Ingrid had loved each other, however, the wobbly stool turned stable and trustworthy.

"I should take you out more when you're home," Justin said. "I dropped the ball. I can talk to Raul if you want. I don't know if we need another house."

"We adore you," Ingrid said. "You know that, don't you?"

What he wanted her to say was that they adored each other. He depended on the marriage they'd built; it had become his compass home. He had the horrible premonition of moving to California with BOD, of Ingrid meeting him during layovers to fuck in airport motels. How easily they would devolve into something careless and selfish. The three of them had recently planned a vacation to New Orleans. They considered one another at every point. Ingrid liked live jazz. Raul was nervous around water. Justin had never eaten an oyster.

"I love you guys," he said. The tassel broke off in his hand.

Ingrid scraped her bowl clean.

* * *

"I know you're in Nola that week." Vijay pointed to the next month on their shared team calendar. "Can you move your vacation? There's an angel investor that wants to meet the executive team. He's got a sweet retreat in Joshua Tree."

Vijay looked like he wanted an answer now. He'd caught Justin on his way to the bathroom, which was already an urgent situation.

"I'll have to check with my roommates." Justin shifted in the spare seat.

"Have you thought more about the big move?" Vijay swiveled his chair until they were knee to knee. Nearly a week had passed since he'd first brought up the subject.

Justin crossed his legs, trying to think.

"I'm worried about my mom," he said. "She recently had dental surgery, and there's complications. She doesn't have anyone besides me."

"Bring her with you." Vijay turned to check his email. "I'm sure we can afford to pay for her relocation costs."

"You're kidding, right, Vij?" Justin said. "Would you bring your mom to California?"

He squinted at Justin's question. "She doesn't need me to."

The screen shone in Vijay's glasses. He pulled up the program they used for their office chat and typed in Thomas's username.

"Look, why don't you talk to your people," he said. A small *ding* rang out a few desks away. "I think I've told you what you need to make a decision."

Friday was the one day of the week when Raul's break at Everyday Fitness lined up with Vijay's cousin's part-time schedule. Justin made sure Adi was logged into the phone system before he went up to the first floor to meet Raul.

The gym had installed a new smoothie bar with a few high tables where people could stand and eat. Justin ordered a shake with BOD's Berry Belly. His stomach had been upset recently.

After the fight on Sunday night, the next few days had been full of jokes and research for their trip to New Orleans. Raul had made his famous tortilla Española, flipping the layers of egg and potato to great applause. Ingrid had gotten a haircut that made her curls as light as bubbles in a bath. On Wednesday afternoon, Raul and

Justin had dropped Ingrid off at the airport, where she had blown kisses through the sliding doors. Raul had fallen asleep in the passenger seat while Justin drove them home. He'd stumbled to bed, complaining of a headache, and slept through the night, sixteen hours when he normally needed five. When Justin had asked, Raul admitted he'd been staying up too late. He wouldn't say why. Had Raul and Ingrid kept up a facade during the day while fighting in bed? Justin had the guestroom where one of them could have retreated. Justin was at home when they could have aired their grievances.

Now Raul was well-rested, leaning across the smoothie bar's high table. Chewing on a fruit leather, he caught Justin up on the new clients he'd signed, the fitness program he'd been fine-tuning.

"I'm going to get even busier." He arched and cracked his back. "I'll have to hire another trainer. You know I'd rather have you."

"You might," Justin said. "Vijay wants to move the company to California. There goes my job."

"You wouldn't move with them?" Raul had his neck canted to the left. He stretched thoughtfully for a few seconds. "Are you sure you've thought this through?"

"I can't leave you and Ingrid," Justin said.

"You know." Raul kneaded his thumbs against the bridge of his nose. "Ingrid doesn't think we're being good to you."

"You've been so good to me." Justin stabbed the straw in and out of his smoothie.

"She's been regretting how we brought you into our life just because we thought . . . we should have everything."

Justin pressed his knuckles hard into his stomach. "We do have everything."

"I agree." Raul grabbed his other hand. "Oh honey."

"I have to go check on Adi," Justin said. "Sorry."

He threw his smoothie in the trash, the lid popping off and making a mess for somebody else to clean.

* * *

Saturday morning, before his mother's salon opened, Justin picked her up for her dentist appointment. She gave him directions and took out a baggie of grapes, which she offered him at every stoplight.

"I'm surprised the dentist works this early on a Saturday," he said.

His mother fussed with her hair in the passenger mirror.

"I'm going to see Dr. Song," she admitted, naming the Chinese medicine woman who didn't believe in chemo.

"You can't be serious." They were already on the highway. "She's not a real doctor."

"The dentist is the one who gave me this problem." His mother worried the skin off a grape with her fingernail.

"Your mouth is full of bacteria." Justin thought about driving his mother straight to the ER. He had no better idea for how to help her. "This infection could spread. It could go to your brain."

"I only have an hour until my first client," she said. "Take the next exit and turn right." Unable to argue with that, he followed her directions to Dr. Song's practice.

Dr. Song and her partner Master Yi shared an office space in a business park in Quince Orchard. A bagua mirror hung by the front door. Above the door, a bell rang out when they entered a waiting room where acupuncture posters hung above jade carvings. The receptionist who greeted them was overly familiar with Justin's mother.

"Is this your boy?" the receptionist asked. "You didn't tell me he was so handsome."

While the receptionist walked his mother into one of the inner offices, Justin took a seat in the waiting room. He checked his phone for his mother's symptoms and read through websites with dire messages about gangrene and sepsis.

"Justin, what a surprise!" Master Yi's long, thin head poked through the receptionist window. He came out into the waiting room with a smile on his face. He wore a loose tunic and drawstring pants, as if he'd come from doing tai chi in the park.

"How are you, Master Yi?"

Master Yi claimed to have "the sight." Justin had no idea how much the man could see. He took the seat across from Justin and crossed his legs with a swish of fabric. People said he had studied Peking opera in his youth, and when Dr. Song wasn't by his side his movements had an extra flair of drama.

"Any accidents this year?" Master Yi studied Justin with a solemn expression.

Diana used to do a spot-on impression of Master Yi and his method of mystic interrogation. *When's the last time you moved your bowels?* she would ask with her hands together and sleeves touching, and after one of them gave a laughing answer, she would nod gravely. *Somebody close will betray you.*

Justin told Master Yi nothing had happened. He was having a noneventful year.

"Your zodiac sign hasn't had any good years in a while," Master Yi said, his vision confirmed. "No bad years either. This year, however, you must be cautious. You have two lucky stars, but also—how do I explain it to you—something like a disaster."

"I guess I'll be careful," Justin said. "Thanks for letting me know."

Master Yi smiled at him with great sympathy. "Careful won't help you in this case." He leaned in and lowered his voice. "This year, you're going to have an accident, and from what I see, you will shed anywhere from a little to a lot of blood. This year, you will also have good fortune, and everything you do will succeed. The accident is the only thing blocking your luck."

Justin had been to enough Blüm meetings to recognize when someone was trying to close the deal. He was meant to ask what he could do to prevent the accident, and then he would be in Master

Yi's grip. He checked his watch. His mother's appointment should be ending.

"Usually when I do these readings, these unfortunate events are incredibly difficult to counteract." Master Yi kept trying. "In this case, I'm pleased to say the solution is very easy."

"Okay." Justin adopted the blank stare that Errol had excelled at giving when he was fed up with a conversation.

Master Yi had a melodic laugh, the kind that reminded people he'd been an opera singer. "I know you'll listen carefully."

Right when Master Yi finished explaining, the front door opened, and the bell rang out. A woman in her fifties came with a large gift basket.

"Now what's this?" Master Yi swanned over to his client and the two left the waiting room in a flurry of gratitude and excitement.

An extra sensitivity coated Justin's body, as if he'd finished watching a horror movie. He was suddenly aware of the pan flutes playing on the speakers overhead, and the soft gush of water from the miniature fountain beside him. A door creaked open past where Justin could see.

His mother appeared, a paper bag in her hand. She looked happy, as if she'd learned that all her worries were unfounded.

* * *

For the first Sunday in years, Justin took a slice of pizza from Thomas and said his mother had canceled dinner to recover from dental surgery. In truth, whatever Dr. Song had given his mother had cured the infection overnight. He turned the alarm off on his phone and kept answering email tickets. Did the carryout girl at their usual restaurant wonder at his absence? Did his mother enjoy her sitcoms without him breathing down her neck? People slowly trickled out of the office. The ticket queue continued to refill.

It was nearly midnight when he pulled into Raul and Ingrid's driveway. A familiar car was parked in front of the house. Justin crept quietly in through the front door, afraid to interrupt, but intent on catching whatever was happening.

In the kitchen, Raul sat with Tye and Pru, whom Justin had met at a few dinner parties. Tye was thirty, and Pru in her late fifties. Justin knew they were the couple that had helped Raul and Ingrid open their relationship. Tye had been in the lifestyle for nearly a decade while Pru was a more recent convert. Tye was usually the languorous, sarcastic one, and Pru so excitable that her homemade earrings caught on her fingers. Tonight they were twinned in consolation—patting Raul's hand, shaking their heads. An open bottle of whiskey and three empty glasses were on the table.

"Is everything okay?" Justin asked.

Their heads shot up.

"Oh my god, look at the time." Raul stood and collected the glasses. "I've kept you two far too late."

"Everything's fine." Pru took Tye's hand and gathered her purse.

"Are you okay to drive?" Raul fumbled the glasses and they clanked dangerously into the sink. "Whoops, must've had a little too much whiskey."

"We're good," Tye said. "Just think about what we said."

"Take care of yourself." Pru gave Justin a hug. He resisted her soft arms, the way they knew something he didn't, but what he resented was Tye pretending he wasn't there.

They were out the door before Raul had finished washing the glasses.

Justin leaned a leg against the kitchen stool. "What were you guys whispering about?"

"Very adult stuff." Raul copied Justin's joking tone. "I wanted a little company. You've been at work all weekend."

"Vijay's got us working harder now," Justin said.

"You must be exhausted." Raul wiped his hands on the dishcloth. "Let's go to bed." He came around the counter.

"Did Tye give you good advice?" Justin asked.

"A gentleman never kisses and tells." Raul slid his hands into Justin's pockets. With a hiss, he yanked his right hand back out. "Shit, what was that?"

A pinprick of blood welled up along his cuticle. Justin pulled out the sewing needle he'd forgotten was there.

"Jesus, you're like the urban legend." Raul laughed at Justin's blank face. "Too young for that reference, huh?"

Justin thought of the way Tye and Pru had hurried out, the conversation they must be having on the car ride home.

"Tye's not that much older than me," Justin said. "He acts like I'm a kid who doesn't understand anything."

Raul let out a deep breath. "In some matters, Tye does know more."

"Did he tell you I'm the problem?"

Raul pulled on Justin's belt loops. "I'm sorry. What's going on between me and Ingrid is much bigger than that."

"I'm not part of this?" Justin pressed his thumbnail into the pads of his fingers. He was calloused everywhere he touched.

"You are—" Raul cut himself off. "Look, I don't want to talk about this without Ingrid here." He put Justin's hand on the inseam of his pants. "Do you know what I feel like doing?"

Justin followed Raul up the stairs. He kissed Raul urgently against the door of the bedroom, but when Raul headed toward the bathroom to prepare, Justin asked if he could go first.

Door locked, he held the needle up to the light. He ran the hot water to sterilize it.

"You need to take control," Master Yi had said in his office lobby. He'd held his thumb and pointer finger close together. "Pay a little blood now and you'll save yourself from something much worse. You could floss and be done with it or prick your finger with a needle. You see how easily you could fix this?"

Chinese superstition was so concerned with the inevitability of suffering. The only way to avoid pain was to inflict it on yourself.

Last night, Justin had flossed roughly and spat clear into the sink. On his way to work today, he'd seen Raul's sewing kit out after he'd repaired the tassel Justin had snapped off the pillow. He'd taken a needle and forgotten it.

No matter how hard Justin pressed the needle into his fingertips, the point left indents that quickly sprang back. His hands shook. He was losing his nerve. He had thought that it was easy to bleed. Raul's finger had done so without trying. Justin had nicked himself countless times shaving, scraped his knuckles on weights. Accidents happened all the time.

He grimaced at his reflection in the mirror, avoiding his eyes. He brought the needle up to his gums. The skin there was thin enough to see through. If he did nothing, the pain would still come. It had come for Carrie, for his former friends, for his mother. He couldn't wait to be blindsided. He was twenty-six and had never been in control of his life. Like water finding a crack, he went wherever he was needed.

Raul was waiting in the bedroom. Ingrid was in her hotel. His mother was watching TV. Throughout the day, Justin would catalogue where everyone must be based on their schedules and routines. Sometimes he would imagine the exact room they were in, who they were with, what they were doing. He would turn the vastness of other people's worlds into model globes in his hands. Yet if he'd asked himself where he'd be tonight, he could not have guessed the needle in his hand. He was as unpredictable as anyone he'd loved, as capable of leaving them gasping. How willing was he to change his life? He was still holding the needle up to his mouth. His arm ached all the way into his chest. The easiest part was coming. Pain came and went. What you suffered were the consequences.

PART 3

EIGHT YEARS POST-GRAD

2016

𝕿𝖍𝖊 𝕹𝖊𝖜 𝖄𝖔𝖗𝖐 𝕿𝖎𝖒𝖊𝖘

Grace Li Is Not a Good Asian

By Rachel Liao

JANUARY 17, 2016

On Wednesday January 13, popular YouTuber Grace Li sent shock-waves through the internet when she posted a video titled My Finale. In the four-minute video, she announced she would no longer be posting on the platform that made her a household name for viewers below a certain age. Ms. Li's channel MeMe Productions has garnered more than 2.6 million subscribers since she shot to fame with the viral video Bad Asians in 2009. Over the past seven years, she has uploaded to the platform nearly every week and in her frank video statement she pointed to this grueling production schedule as one of the reasons she has decided to step away.

"I'm tired," she told her fans, who call themselves Me3's. "It's not fun anymore, or meaningful, or fulfilling. Maybe it never was, but I felt like I wasn't allowed to stop."

This statement is particularly poignant given the themes of her short films: the promise of success if you do everything right; the way others' perceptions shape your own desires. In New Shoes, a woman receives praise, romantic propositions, and a promotion once she puts on a pair of designer heels. After the whirlwind day, she limps home, her feet bleeding in the shoes she can no longer bear to take off. In Starter Pack, a name-brand-obsessed man custom builds his perfect girlfriend, only to find out she's identical to what his friends have also made.

Ironically, these videos skewering the trappings, and trap, of success have made Ms. Li incredibly successful, garnering her not only a loyal international fanbase, but also a brand partnership with Apple (she does her editing on iMovie and has recently started shooting on an iPhone 6) and California Pizza Kitchen, a frequent setting for her films. Most impressive of all, she has been tapped to direct the movie adaption of former MeMe regular Harris Yu's best-selling memoir Coney Dog, based on the Oscar-nominated actor and producer's childhood in Coney Island. The news, announced in November of last year, was a watershed moment for YouTube creators, who often struggle to be taken seriously by traditional media.

This directorial opportunity, combined with My Finale, *has led Ms. Li's fans to speculate that she is purposefully distancing herself from her YouTube past. In a think piece published on* Jezebel—*now retweeted 22k times—the author Jennifer Lo writes:*

"I can't help feeling like I've been ditched. In some ways, I have. Maybe what Grace Li is rebelling against is not herself, but the popularity we've bestowed upon her. She has outgrown not only the art she's making, but also her audience. Like our best friend who has found a cooler group of kids to play with, MeMe is breaking up with us all."

The proliferation of these opinions is why Ms. Li agrees to meet with me and set the record straight.

"The thing is, I'm not MeMe," Ms. Li says while we walk past lines of people waiting for dim sum in Chinatown. "MeMe is a brand, not a person. It's almost funny how lost everyone is. They think that subscribing to my channel means that they can claim me as their friend. They have no idea who I am. The majority wouldn't recognize me if I were sitting across from them."

Next to me, Ms. Li cuts a striking figure in knee-high boots and a suede trench. Underneath, she wears a structural dress that looks like it could stand up without her. Her skin is airbrushed smooth, her hair blown-out and glassy. She seems to have walked off a magazine cover, a stark difference from the scrubbed down, almost plain look she adopted during her My Finale *video, the first time she's shown her face on camera.*

Alter egos are not new territory when it comes to celebrities. Beyoncé has Sasha Fierce, Eminem has Slim Shady. They are a way to protect one's real identity from the warping pressures of fame. In Ms. Li's case, however, her alter ego is all there is, which may be why there's so much slippage between herself and MeMe. She is notoriously private given that she operates in the oversharing milieu of social media. In the Personal section of her Wikipedia page, it states that she lives in New York City. Only now is the real Grace Li standing up and speaking freely.

Over daytime whiskey sours at a banquet hall turned bar, she tells me about her childhood growing up in Montgomery County, which was memorialized by Alexandra Robbins's best-selling book The Overachievers.

"Everything was a contest. From the grades you got and your test scores, to how well you behaved, how good your Chinese was, how pretty you were if you were a girl, and how tall if you were a boy. Every aspect of

you was scrutinized and compared, and that's all I knew for my most formative years."

Did this overtly competitive culture prepare her to compete for attention online, a commodity that eludes most creators and corporations?

"I don't know if my childhood 'prepared me.'" From the window of the bar, we can see a small park, where children frolic among senior citizens. *"Except by making me more desperate than other people."*

Her hometown of North Potomac is also notable for having one of the highest percentages of Asian Americans in the country—one out of every four people, when the national average is 4.8%, or one in every 20.83. Her unselfconsciously all-Asian casts are a touchstone for her fans, including yours truly, who often cite her videos as the first time they saw themselves in popular media. While she may have been negatively shaped by how she grew up, don't the best parts of her also come from this place? Ms. Li bristles at the question, although not in the way I expect.

"Seeing yourself in those videos is supposed to be a wake-up call, not a comfort. I wanted my Asian American viewers to think critically about how they grew up, and what influences their choices. Are they chasing success for the sake of it? Are they doing whatever their parents tell them? Asian Americans are the most educated demographic with the highest median income, and yet we're also the least politically active. It's sickening how complacent and materialistic we can be. We have an incredibly important presidential election coming up this year and civil rights protests all over the country. Meanwhile the people I grew up with are posting about their new condo or designer bag."

Ms. Li is quick to say that she doesn't include all Asian Americans in her statement. At the same time, she questions whether the familiar immigrant narratives of sacrifice and struggle—such as the movie adaptation of Coney Dog she's directing—truly apply to the upper-middle class Chinese families she grew up around.

"It's a total myth that our parents came to America to give us a better life. They came because they wanted money for themselves. They wanted to be rich and powerful, but you couldn't be a millionaire in China in the '80s and '90s. Their friends who stayed back in China became the one-percenters there, often by exploiting their workers. That's why our parents raised us to seek success and money. We're not the model minority, we're one degree away from being the white supremacy."

From our window, we watch a little girl play with her grandmother and I point out that cultural and generational differences should also be considered. Isn't it a universal truth that parents everywhere are trying their best?

"How did your parents raise you?" *Ms. Li has an eerie level of focus, almost merging with the person to whom she's listening. You're not talking to a therapist but to a magic mirror.*

A half hour later, I'm crying, not because of anything terrible my parents have done. The very opposite. I am overwhelmed with gratitude, and yes, also guilt, for the life they've made for me in America. If it's a life they chose, that doesn't erase how hard they had to work for it. Yes, their sacrifice could have been a calculation. Maybe they understood that they alone would not be able to achieve success in a new country, that they must pour their ambitions into me. Regardless, everything I do, I do for them. At least, those are the things I'm willing to publish.

Ms. Li is sympathetic, but she's in a different place.

"The guilt has kept me quiet for my entire life," *she says.*

We've moved to another bar in the neighborhood where hand-written posters advertise karaoke rooms in the back, although our vantage point is blocked by boxes of fortune cookies.

"I grew up believing I was raised by a single mother who'd scraped together enough money on her own for my education. Until I found out my father was paying for everything back in China. I thought that was the end of my debt to her. I could pursue my dreams and not hers."

The family bombshell led to Ms. Li dropping out of Harvard Law and making the video that would become Bad Asians. *Her near-immediate success seemed like a sign that she had made the right choice. Now she sees that she was repeating with film what she'd done with school.*

"I had never stopped trying to make her proud." *Ms. Li has switched to baijiu, a rice grain alcohol popular in China, which she shoots back every time she reveals something personal.* "I would call her every week and give a little report on my numbers, my sponsors, how much money I was making, how much money everyone else was too."

The moment of reckoning came when Ms. Li had her weekly call with her mother. Ms. Li had just come back from a doctor's appointment with prescriptions to treat a stomach ulcer and insomnia. Over the phone, her mother announced that she was moving back to Beijing to care for her father, who'd recently suffered a heart attack. Despite living on separate continents for the last twenty years of their marriage, her mother felt she had a duty as his wife.

"Never mind that he's been living with another woman that entire time." Ms. Li finishes another baijiu and gestures for the check. "I saw clearly what it looks like when you live your life for someone else. That was my wake-up call."

Ms. Li realized she'd been making these videos to warn her generation of overachievers without hearing the warning herself. Now she hopes that her act of rebellion will pave the way for others to follow.

Our conversation is interrupted by the owner of the bar. He cajoles us to try out one of his karaoke rooms. We take up his offer of a free song. I let Ms. Li choose, and she hardly flips through the catalog before picking what feels like an appropriate anthem. Together we belt out Linkin Park's "In the End," screaming the chorus—"I tried so hard and got so far / But in the end, it doesn't even matter"—knowing that for one of us, at least, you have to fall to lose it all to understand what does and doesn't matter.

Related Coverage:

January 25, 2016 *Popular YouTuber Slammed for Calling Asian Americans "Complacent and Materialistic"*

January 27, 2016 *Backlash Against Popular YouTuber Leads to Fans Burning Merchandise*

January 28, 2016 *Asian American Groups Call for Boycott Against Popular YouTuber*

February 1, 2016 *Actor Harris Yu Announces New Director Amidst Controversy*

CHAPTER ELEVEN

May 2016

To get out of his car, Errol had to grab on to the door, his right leg buckling beneath him. Twenty-three hours on the pedal had worked the muscle into jelly. He'd surprised himself with how quickly he'd made the drive from Texas. He'd budgeted three days. Long drives did something strange to his brain. The internet said this was road hypnosis. He'd have to run that theory by his psychiatrist. All he knew was that the highway had gone dead quiet in the pre-dawn hours. He barely had to think to keep going.

The front door opened and his mother appeared. She hid her surprise at the sight of him. He'd forgotten to let his family know that he'd be arriving that day. Or arriving at all, for that matter. They sized each other up like two cats meeting in a backyard. His mother was wearing pajamas with rabbits dotting the fabric. She had more gray in her hair. She let his appearance go without comment. Four years had passed since her visit to Detroit. Since then, they had done their talking through Lucy. His little sister had found him on Facebook a few years ago and they had kept up a spotty correspondence.

For a horrible moment, Errol convinced himself that Lucy's high school graduation was two days ago instead of two days from now. That was why his mother wasn't saying anything. When she let him through the front door, he looked for deflated balloons and other party debris until he bumped into the graduation gown hanging in its packaging. Nine times out of ten, he kept his schedule straight, but there was always the possibility that he'd forgotten something.

His mother caught him looking at the cap and gown. "Lucy will be happy to see you."

Inside the house, which had accrued more instruments and sporting equipment, Errol followed his mother into the kitchen. She put a bowl of leftovers into the microwave without asking if he was hungry. He sat in his usual spot, where a stack of textbooks was propped.

Handing him the hot bowl, his mother said, "Of all the places to sit."

She moved the stack of books to the kitchen counter and cleared the microwave timer. The clock read three. Earlier than Errol had expected.

"Are you sick?" he asked.

"Do I look sick?"

"You're not at your office." He couldn't remember Lucy mentioning if their mother had quit her job.

His mother grabbed the rag by the sink and wiped around vigorously. "Is there something wrong with the food?"

He dug in with the chopsticks she'd given him. "Did you retire?"

"Your sister's in school. You think I could retire?"

Errol could feel the pressure building in his mother, the way some people's bones hurt before bad weather.

"Did you get fired again?" He never liked to wait for his mother to blow up on her own. "You lasted longer than usual."

His mother suddenly looked distracted. She gestured toward a stack of black binders. "I'm studying to get my real estate license."

When he reminded her that she'd once called salespeople prostitutes, his mother said, "Mrs. Wang got her license a few years ago, and she's making more than her husband." She riffled through the tabs of the binder on top. "If *she* can sell houses, imagine what someone with my brains could achieve."

"So, Mrs. Wang is helping you?"

"I'm helping her. I'm showing a house for her client in—" His mother checked the microwave clock and the sleepy daze fell from her face. "Half an hour! I still need to pick up the keys. You're always distracting me."

Errol hadn't been around his mother in years, but he remained the scapegoat for her problems. "Go get them then." Errol stood to grab his suitcase from the car.

"I have to get dressed!" His mother hurried him toward the door. "Make yourself useful. You remember which house is theirs."

Errol stared at his mother in her rumpled pajamas. She was sending him to knock on Vivian's mother's door as if she had no memory of how things had ended. As if she herself hadn't told him that breaking up with Vivian was proof that he was too stupid to be helped.

"I'd be happy to go see my mother-in-law." Errol punched the side of his leg to stop the impulse, but the sentence was out.

"Hurry, hurry!" His mother hadn't heard. She was already running up the stairs.

* * *

In the five minutes Errol took to walk over, his mother must have called Mrs. Wang. She was waiting on her front porch, stouter than he'd remembered, as if her new profession had made her more solid. She threw her arms out wide to give him a hug where only her hands and his shoulders touched.

"Your mother says you surprised her by coming back home for Lucy's graduation." Errol hadn't heard such rapid-fire Chinese in years. "We're so proud of her. Princeton! Your mother said the happiest day of her life was when Lucy got the news." Mrs. Wang stepped back to take another look at him. "Still too skinny. I heard you're in Texas, not Houston, but . . . Aspen?"

"Austin," he said.

Not a city where he'd intended to stay, but the years passed easily there. He'd taken a shine to the simplicity of their good times, happiness no more complicated than cracking a beer and listening to live music.

Errol told her that he worked for a well-known company. They matched people with the right jobs. Mrs. Wang was unfamiliar with the name.

"Why would anyone want to live in Texas?" Mrs. Wang pulled a face. "It's too hot. I suppose the taxes are lower."

He explained that Austin had become a tech mecca in recent years. Some people called it the new Silicon Valley. He usually made this statement ironically.

"Your mother said that the house you bought last year is worth forty thousand more than you paid for it."

Errol had posted a picture online, but he hadn't told Lucy his new address. His parents must have searched some real estate website until they'd found a match. He'd have to be more careful. A few years ago, you could post anything and believe it was private. The only way information spread was if you told another person.

"It's a starter home. I'm thinking of buying more properties to rent." The idea had not occurred to him until then. He'd been happy with his ranch home, had filled it with instruments he'd eventually learn to play, and was growing a vegetable garden. Although, he may have forgotten to ask a neighbor to water it.

Mrs. Wang thought more properties was a very smart idea. Many of her clients were young Chinese kids like him who were investing in real estate. Errol mentioned he'd also received plenty of equity when he'd been hired, making bank on the acquisition that occurred a few months later. He left out that he'd said yes to their first offer, needing the health insurance to cover complications from his broken leg. He let Mrs. Wang congratulate him on negotiating such a good deal. How quickly he'd fallen back into impressing other people.

"How's Vivian?" he asked, unable to help himself.

Mrs. Wang grew in stature, like a bird fluffing out its feathers. "She's gone and left us for New York, although I suppose I shouldn't complain. It's not Texas! And if she wants to keep expanding, she has to go to the best city. She has a . . . I can never remember what it is. It's like a radio show."

"A podcast?" After the cellphone incident, Errol had an alert attached to everyone's name. He already knew what Mrs. Wang was trying to find on her phone.

"Yes!" Mrs. Wang took out a pair of reading glasses to peer at her screen. "I think she should do a talk show next. She was made to be on TV. Everyone thought that girl Grace was the star. My Vivian is quickly outshining her, especially after she made such a fool of herself in that article."

Errol had also read Grace's profile in the *Times*, and the follow-up covering the backlash. At first, he'd been perplexed by how carelessly Grace had acted. After years of controlling her image, she'd managed to antagonize not only her fans, but also people who'd never heard of her. She'd gotten drunk with the journalist too—Errol could read between the lines—and that had to be why she'd brought up her mother. Despite the articles and comments focusing on what she'd said about Asian Americans, he'd been more shocked by what she'd revealed about her family. This alone had tipped him off. The more he thought about Grace, the more he recognized himself, and the illusion of control when you were the cause of your own fall.

Mrs. Wang found Vivian's podcast—*You Say I Do*. She tapped her finger on the ranking, sixth in Dating and Marriage, which translated into hundreds of thousands of listeners. Errol was not one of them; it felt too much like peeping through the windows of Vivian's house.

"Her boyfriend Brian helps her with the show." Mrs. Wang's smile looked briefly strained. "It's been six years, hasn't it? I hope that doesn't upset you."

Like waking up to a hangover, whatever pain Errol felt was justly deserved, and yet still a nasty surprise.

"They're planning a trip to Paris, and you know what that means!" Mrs. Wang held up her ring finger. "I'm sure Vivian was worried. They've been together almost four years."

Errol grew more disoriented. Their stalemate over their marriage had seemed like a sign that neither of them had found anything serious. That was his reason, at least. He didn't understand what she'd been waiting for if she'd had Brian all along.

"He works on Wall Street and owns his own condo in Chelsea. She's not living with him, of course. She's got a nice apartment of her own near Chinatown. Oh!" Mrs. Wang poked her head out further and waved down the street. "I think that's your mother's car coming."

"She needs the keys to the house," he said, not ready to have their conversation end.

Mrs. Wang dropped them in his hand. "Be nice to her this weekend. It's difficult when your child graduates and leaves home. This time of year was already tough."

"I came back home after graduation," he said. "Nobody was happy about that."

"She's always worried too much," Mrs. Wang said. "I think switching to real estate will be a good change of pace. Get her out of the house. Out of her head. It's good of you to help."

His mother's car squealed into the cul-de-sac. Errol walked backward toward it. "She seems to help herself fine."

"Remember." Mrs. Wang lingered at the door. "As hard as she was on you, she's five times harder on herself."

At the end of the driveway, Errol handed his mother the keys through her window. She grabbed his wrist and told him to get in the car.

"You've made me later." She waved at Mrs. Wang and peeled off, cursing the speed traps that forced her to slow back down.

"Why am I going?" They passed Lincoln Elementary, and Errol craned his neck out of habit to look for Justin's old house.

"You can pick up Lucy from her debate competition," his mother said. "It's in Falls Church. She's up first, and afterward she can do her homework in the car instead of around those stupid people."

Stupid people was what his mother called her former coworkers, former managers, his father's colleagues, Errol's own friends. It was what she called anyone who didn't meet her ever-changing standards. Errol didn't see how his mother could be harder on herself than she already was with perfect strangers.

"She's about to graduate," Errol said. "What homework does she have?"

"She's taking classes at the community college," his mother said. "So she can have a head start at Princeton."

"Those credits won't transfer. You should let her hang out with her friends. What if this is the last time they get to see each other?"

"If she has any sense, it will be." His mother sucked her teeth and shoved Errol to the side. Something crumpled beneath him. A bunch of flyers he hadn't seen, wrinkled by his weight.

Errol braced himself, but his mother threw the flyers into the back seat. With every delay, he grew tenser. It was painful to be sitting in a car so soon after his marathon drive. His legs danced, unable to stretch out. He fiddled with his window, buzzing it up and down, waiting for something to set her off.

His mother looked over, although not at him. She was looking out his window, her face almost soft.

"When you were three," she said, "you threw your clothes out of the car window on the way to daycare."

"How did I do that?"

His mother laughed. "The A/C on our minivan was broken. Some piece of shit car your father bought off another graduate student. I had the windows down. It was this time of year and already unbearable." She looked over at Errol and frowned. "We were late because you'd thrown a huge tantrum." She brightened again. "I was driving on the highway, like this, when another car started honking and chasing me down. I thought we were going to die. Then it was this old lady who stopped when she'd caught up. She must have seen you naked and realized who was throwing clothes out of the car. You even managed to take off your shoes."

Errol laughed too. He rarely heard stories of himself in this kind of light. The best memories belonged to Lucy. His mother gave a small sigh, like someone setting down a heavy load.

"That was a horrible day," she said, face half-blurred in remembering. "I had to bring you to the abortion clinic. I wasn't the only one there with a child. That surprised me. You think it's stupid teenagers who get into trouble."

Errol twitched in his seat. He'd thought this was a happy memory. He'd thought his mother might say a normal mom thing. She still knew how to throw him off balance. He scratched hard at his neck. The itch was too deep to reach. Everything was too much, the inside of the car suffocating. They were going seventy, but he buzzed down the window. The rush of wind engulfed him. He stuck his head out and let grit fly into his eyes. When he pulled himself back in, his mother replaced her foot on the accelerator, having let the car slow while the flow of traffic sped past them.

* * *

At the Virginia house, his mother shut her door and left the keys in the ignition. The more miles Errol put between them, the calmer he grew. The streets turned unexpectedly familiar. He must have been to Eisenhower before, the high school where Lucy's tournament was staged. Most likely Diana had had matches there when she had been the star of the debate team. Errol used to tag along as an excuse to avoid his family.

Walking into the auditorium, he remembered Diana behind

the podium, running circles around the other side's argument. Where Diana had been, his baby sister stood spotlit at the front of the stage. She looked too young to be wearing a blazer.

"If this was a question of morality, we wouldn't be having this conversation," Lucy half-said and half-read. In trying to sound like a serious adult, she enunciated her words too crisply. He could tell that she'd memorized the speech, but she couldn't stop looking down at her pages. Had Diana been this young? The realization reached through time, and when he remembered the last year of their friendship, he also remembered that she'd been twenty-three.

And he'd been twenty, with the awe of someone who'd looked up to his friend since he'd been a baby. Her disappointment over Microsoft had hurt worse than his parents'; he hadn't been able to stand it. Not when she was the one who'd said he was destined for greatness, that his mind was one of a kind. Every time she brought up him quitting, he singled out how shallow she was, how obsessed with status and money. The more he undermined her, the less her opinions should have mattered. Instead, he'd gotten angrier. He'd felt betrayed to find out that the person he'd worshipped was no better or wiser than him. Which, of course she wasn't. They were two and a half years apart. Easy to forget when she'd protected him as if she were much older.

Small whoops alerted Errol that the debate was over. Lucy's side had been declared victorious. When she went to hug her debate partner, she caught sight of Errol waiting in the back. She stared, her face slowly turning into a mask of adolescent horror. Errol regretted every impulse that had led him to this auditorium. If he'd had his own car, he would have driven back to Texas.

The next team took the stage to set up their notes at the podium. With the focus back at the front, Lucy hurried over to Errol. He'd been heading toward the exit.

"Is Mom okay?" she asked with unexpected urgency.

"She's fine," Errol said. "She's showing a house."

Lucy nodded and straightened her shoulders. "That's good," she said, and then remembering her manners, "Thank you for coming home for my graduation."

The moment had passed to greet one another. They stood awkwardly for a few moments, before Lucy went back to grab her things. When she said goodbye to her coach, the man looked at Errol for a long time, as if he might be called upon for a police description. To be fair, Errol had grown his hair out until it touched his shoulders, and he'd been experimenting with how long his facial hair would get.

Out in the parking lot, Lucy climbed into the back of the car. She spread out her textbooks and neatly gathered the scattered flyers, tucking them into the seatback pocket. Minutes out of her competition, she was doing homework without complaint, like a horse calmly taking its bit and saddle.

She had no idea that she'd never again be this unmarked by her choices. That she could throw those textbooks out and defer college, go abroad, blow her savings. She could spend a year doing the opposite of what she was supposed to do, and none of those detours would matter. She would end up roughly where she was supposed to be. She had no sense of what permanence was, and that meant she was safe from its talons. He would give anything to go back to a time without regret, and here she was wasting it.

"Are we going to pick up Mom?" she asked in the middle of highlighting a sentence.

Too busy watching her, he'd forgotten to start the car.

"Don't you want to take a break?" he asked. "You just won your debate."

She gave this some consideration and said, "Okay." She capped and uncapped her highlighter, staring fixedly at the gearshift in front of her.

He backed out of the parking lot before she could reach over and reverse the car herself. He asked her about school and her friends, hoping she would explain why she'd looked frightened to see him. Lucy might be a naturally fearful person, or maybe he should've gotten a haircut in the last year. That didn't explain why she'd asked about their mother.

"Is something wrong at home?" he said.

Lucy plucked at a Post-it stuck to her textbook. She weighed whatever was on her mind, determining how much to trust him. "Mom's depressed."

"I see." Errol fiddled with his phone to map them back to the Virginia house. Sometime later, he thought that Lucy might be serious. He looked at her in the rearview mirror. "Actually?"

"I think so." Lucy took a bite out of the Post-it, so quickhanded that Errol almost missed it. "She's been crying a lot. She says it's allergies. Dad found out she stopped going to work."

"She did that all the time when I was growing up." Errol thought of the little rabbits on his mother's pajamas. He hadn't looked twice. "You're not used to it because she never freaked out with you. It's normal."

Lucy stared at him in the rearview mirror and said, slower, "She's depressed."

"But why?"

"There doesn't have to be a reason."

"No, why do *you* think she's depressed." Somehow, he was sounding like the younger sibling.

"Maybe it's not a big deal." Lucy retreated. "But she did this when I was growing up too. Not when I was little, but since you've been gone. It's the worst in the spring."

Errol had never tracked their mother's behavior, the same way he'd never paid attention to their father's lectures. If it rained every day, what did it matter if it was a storm or a drizzle?

"What does Dad think?" he asked after she'd gone back to her homework.

Lucy scratched her chin with her Post-it and took another secret bite. "He thinks she needs to exercise."

* * *

Earlier, when Errol had left the Virginia house, another car had been waiting in the driveway. Returning, the driveway stood empty. He'd been gone for less than half an hour and his mother had already scared off the buyers. He waited for his mother to come out until Lucy said, "You should probably go get her."

"Right." He slowly unbuckled his seat belt. "You stay here and finish your homework."

His mother had left the door unlocked. At some point, the current owners would return. Their living habits peeked out through the fresh paint on the walls. Their magazine subscriptions, their photos in the hall. The faint smell of dog was in the carpet padding the basement stairs. Errol took his time exploring the house; he'd already guessed where his mother was hiding. One strike against Austin was that there weren't any basements. He'd missed that underground feeling where entire afternoons could be spent lying on the carpet and avoiding his parents.

How unfair that even with a family like his, there were reasons to return, and none for the friends that had once sustained him. He thought again of Vivian, their years of separation. Maybe he'd been waiting for a serious relationship. Or maybe he'd stayed married because he'd wanted something more substantial than the invisible ties that tugged when he passed by Justin's house, or the school stage where Diana had once stood. A good reason to reach out when he was finally ready.

His psychiatrist would say that he didn't need an excuse to contact Vivian, or the group. Today's technology offered many opportunities. The truth was, Errol wanted both the connection and the distance, as if the latter preserved the former instead of eroding it. The people he loved were turning into portraits, the flesh-and-blood entities into strangers. But no matter how much he wished to see them, he was also afraid. The possibility remained that whatever had caused his old group to break apart would always be there, built into the same code that made them work in the first place.

On the second floor, at the far end of the hall, he walked into a guest room full of mismatched furniture. His mother was asleep in the canopy bed someone must have outgrown. She'd kept her shoes on and dangled them off the side while she curled in, facing the wall. Her head was under the pillow. He didn't know what it was like to be this tired and still picky enough to choose the cleanest bed in the house.

He sat down on the ground, at the foot of the bed. He thought of Grace again and his unexpected empathy, so different from his glee years ago when he'd heard that she'd dropped out of Harvard. He'd assumed that Grace was in control that entire time, yet every surrounding circumstance should have told him she was spiraling. Perhaps she hadn't known herself. He had also fallen apart while thinking he was invincible. His psychiatrist had suggested that Errol had been depressed those three years when he was rarely sober.

"I used to throw myself out of a window for attention," Errol had joked. "Would a depressed person do that?"

The difference was that Grace had been breaking down for much longer than three years. She'd gone nearly a decade without help. No wonder this was where she'd ended up. Looking at his mother, in her own damaged state, he couldn't pretend not to understand her anymore. He could no longer be angry without also being sad.

He thought of his sister out in the car, slowly eating the paper that surrounded her. His father at work, reading up on the science of exercise, but not on antidepressants. Sometimes this was what it looked like when people were trying their best.

"You should get up," he said. "You're scaring Lucy." His mother huddled her shoulders closer and refused to listen.

Poor Lucy. No wonder she had sounded like a real adult. Errol stood up and went back out in the hall. At the top of the stairs, he crouched by the fake rubber tree, too big for the pot that held it. He could go back to Austin where happiness simply happened, or he could stay and make life hard again. He looked down the stairs, like a kid at the top of a waterslide. The plant and its pot were so light that they bounced when they fell, and the crash was perfect—a crystal-clear alarm. Maybe the only people you could fault were the ones who didn't try. In the guestroom, his mother opened her eyes.

CHAPTER TWELVE

Vivian's mother called again while she was getting ready for dinner. Vivian put the phone on speaker.

"I've been trying to reach you—you'll never guess who's back home." Her mother's fast-paced chatter filled the bathroom. "Your first love! He came for Lucy's graduation yesterday, and he's planning to stay the summer and work remotely."

Her mother could despise someone for years and romanticize them the second they were out of the picture.

"Is that so." Vivian stared at the mirror. The girl looking back was turning red. If she admitted she already knew, her mother would demand to know how, and why Vivian hadn't told her.

"When are you coming home for a visit? We see your brother every week." Her mother's tone sharpened. "That ex-wife of his is dragging out their divorce." She peppered Vivian with questions about her boyfriend Brian and if she thought he'd bought a ring. "There's a house in our neighborhood that will be on the market next month. If you get engaged soon, we can buy it."

"I have to go. I'll call you later." Vivian spent another five minutes disentangling from the call, hearing again about the renovation her parents were planning, the favors her mother was doing for Mrs. Chen, and how Errol's sister had given a great speech as the valedictorian.

* * *

"I'm sorry I'm late." Vivian slid into the empty seat at the brasserie where a Monday crowd had gathered for mussels and frites. She smiled apologetically at the waiter who slipped her a menu. "Can I get a Beefeater martini with a twist?"

Grace raised her eyebrows. "Hard day?"

Vivian told her about the phone call. "It made me more nervous about going back home to meet Errol on Thursday. Another secret to keep from my parents, and from Brian."

When her drink arrived, Vivian took a long sip. "I already feel more human."

Grace looked at the glass. "I wish I could join you." When Vivian raised her own eyebrows, Grace looked down at her menu with great concentration.

"We should talk about the podcast a little bit." Grace studied the specials. "So we can write this off as a business dinner."

One more thing Vivian had to keep secret from her mother. After the *Times* profile, and the backlash that had followed, Grace had stopped her projects and quit drinking. Besides an hour with a therapist twice a week, she found her days and nights too free. She'd asked Vivian if she could help with the podcast. "Help" had turned out to be an extreme understatement. Initially a way to advertise her wedding planning, Vivian's podcast had grown in popularity once Grace became her producer. Not only had Grace's ideas been popular with listeners, but she'd also used her connections to get Vivian more press. Grace had stayed in touch with the journalist, Rachel Liao, who had been enormously apologetic about the response to her profile. She'd known Grace was getting a little too drunk, but public personas were rarely so unfiltered on the record. She'd been a freelance writer at the time, scrambling for jobs, and the *Times* had been her big break. Shortly after the article came out, she'd been hired on as a staff writer. As a favor, Rachel wrote about Vivian's podcast for the Wedding section. Five months later, Vivian was making enough from ad revenue alone that she'd quit event planning entirely.

Over dinner, Grace proposed that their next episode's theme could be outdoor weddings. She knew someone who had gotten married at a camp in Vermont. She'd see if the couple would agree to an interview. How about a segment on the wedding favors too? Like homemade mosquito spray. Personalized water bottles. That way the guests stayed hydrated and didn't throw up in the woods. Speaking of, you'd have to have access to a bathroom. They could do a fun piece on decorating porta-potties. And as always, Vivian would end with updates on her quest to get engaged to Finance Daddy (Finn for short).

"What're we going to do when you get engaged?" Grace dipped a fry in the butter sauce pooling in her dish.

"Is it too meta to talk about planning my own wedding?" Vivian asked.

"You could talk about already being married." Grace grew wistful. She loved a good story. "Now that it's almost over."

"No way, my parents listen to every episode." Vivian broke open a mussel and plucked out the meat. "And Brian."

"So? They know most of it's made up." Grace spent the rest of dinner trying to persuade her. The only time Grace was pushy was when it came to her work.

"Okay, business dinner's over." Vivian pushed her plate aside. She hadn't been able to enjoy her martini with Grace eying it all night. "Tell me what's wrong."

Grace put her hands over her face. "I looked up Carrie Yang again."

At the height of the backlash, Grace had discovered that Carrie Yang was back online. Over the past few months, Carrie's rebranding had become a fixation. After Carrie had completed rehab in 2013, she'd stayed in Utah and gotten married. She was now one of the top Mormon mommy bloggers on Instagram. Carrie had succeeded in part by rolling her controversy into her origin story: She'd found religion, and she'd been rewarded with a God-fearing husband, two perfect boys, and a baby girl on the way. She posted pictures of Easter brunch and her children's birthday parties, but her long captions also included stories of her debaucherous past, titillating an audience that had never had a beer, let alone lines of K at a kink club.

"It's not that she gets to come back after everything she did." Grace tore at the corner of the paper tablecloth, spotted with butter sauce and ketchup. "It's that she would want to. Every time I think about making something again, I think about everything getting dug up to haunt me."

"Of course you do."

Grace had gotten death threats and anonymous phone calls for months after the profile had come out. Worst of all, a former fan had found Grace's apartment and knocked on the door for an hour. Grace had moved in with Z soon after. Months later, she was still afraid to put her name on a lease. For years, Vivian had avoided Z despite him being one of Grace's closest friends, but the level of care he'd showed these past few months had won her over.

"It feels like I can never get beyond my lowest point." Grace moved on to the other corner of the paper tablecloth. "Like I'll have to answer for that awful choice forever."

"It's only been six months," Vivian said. "Trust me, people forget faster than you think."

"They'll forget me faster if I disappear." Grace looked up from her ripping. "I've decided I'm deleting MeMe. I'm done. Maybe I'll go back to law school."

Six months ago, Vivian would have been wracked with guilt. Ever since she'd contacted Grace's mother in Beijing, she'd felt responsible for everything that happened after. This irrational feeling hadn't gone away just because they'd become friends. Vivian used to worry over every problem Grace brought up, going out of her way to try to fix them. Something as small as missing a meal would lead to Vivian delivering dinner the next day. Recently, however, Vivian had felt a shift between her and Grace, an unexpected equalization. What the profile had shown her was that Grace could make her own mistakes. That she was both more and less than what Vivian had made her.

Vivian had gone to Grace's apartment the day of publication and found her friend pale with regret. That was the first time she'd seen Grace cry. Each day after had at least one moment of open weeping. Her shell had cracked, and the real Grace was oozing out, one who no longer had to be careful. She was still cagey about her relationship with her mother—all Vivian knew was that they were talking again, if no longer once a week—but suddenly Grace was admitting to her secret YouTube account, from which she would write snarky comments on her competitors' videos. She would make large sweeping proclamations about becoming a monk and get mad when Vivian and Z teased her. Her fixation with Carrie Yang was something that past Grace would have never admitted, and now it had become a shorthand for a very bad day. All of which meant that when Grace told her she was going back to law school, Vivian could react like any good friend.

"You can delete MeMe." Vivian slid her card into the bill holder and handed it to their waiter. "But you can't stop making movies. Don't forget what I told you—you're supposed to do something special."

"Maybe I already did." Grace put her elbows on the table and rested her chin in her hands. "I'm out of ideas. I didn't even want to direct Harris's movie, not that it matters anymore. I just didn't feel like I could do nothing."

Vivian took the check back from their waiter and clicked the pen against the table. If Grace could hear how silly she sounded. She'd brainstormed an entire podcast episode minutes ago. For Grace, ideas were not a finite resource. Otherwise, she could not have made a short film every week. Good ones too. Vivian

thought about *New Shoes* every time she considered buying sti-
lettos.

"If you were making a documentary," Vivian said, "and your
subject was a former YouTube creator who wanted to delete her
incredibly popular channel, how would you shoot it?"

Grace shook her head, but her eyes slid up, thinking.

"I guess I'd have them do it on camera," she said. "Although it's
too boring if it's one person and a computer."

She waved her hand, dismissing the idea. Her fingers tapped
against the table. She grabbed the pen from the bill holder and
sketched a rough layout on the cleanest part of the paper tablecloth.

"I'd get some of her old actors or collaborators in the room.
Maybe do a big dinner where they get to talk and tell stories. Like
a reunion. Lighting would be tricky, but we could make do with
fewer angles. No individual shots, which could set that party mood
if everyone is crowded together. That would be the beginning."

She drew circles for the people, the cameras and lights as squares.
With Grace focused on the drawing, her face was wide open. Vivian
was amazed at how easily she could read Grace after years of thinking she was an enigma.

"Just one scene?" she asked.

Caught, Grace attempted coyness. "Even if I wanted to make
something longer, I don't have enough money."

"Consider me an investor." Vivian leaned back and crossed her
arms. "Thanks to you, I have the money."

A half hour later, Grace sat on the lip of Z's tub, a bedsheet
wrapped around her neck. They'd picked up a box of bleach at the
drugstore down the street. Vivian plugged in the razor.

"Another filmmaker taught me this," Grace had said in the
drugstore line. "It takes a year to grow out a buzzcut, and another
year if you factor in what I dyed. If I don't have my documentary
finished by the time I have a work-appropriate haircut, I'm finding
a real job."

In the bathroom, however, Grace's nerve was fading.

"Who's going to want to watch a documentary of me?" Grace looked down at the scissors in her lap. "What do I even have to say? This is so egotistical. I'm going to look crazy for two years for no reason."

"You dropped out of Harvard before you knew what you were making the first time." Vivian tested the razor, which hummed like an insect caught in a screen. "You moved to LA with a bunch of footage and nothing else."

Vivian combed her fingers through Grace's hair. In the last four years, Grace had grown her undercut out. Her hair fell past her chest. She looked too much like the lawyer she was in danger of becoming.

"You're our star." Vivian put her hand on Grace's shoulder. "You do things that don't seem possible. People are going to want to know the real you, and how you got this way." She gave Grace the scissors. "Most importantly, this will look great on camera."

The magic words. Grace bunched her hair in her fist and drew the scissors across in one furious slash. Her hair fell like a sheet of glass, shattering across the tub's bottom. Grace dropped the scissors and closed her eyes.

"Will you help me do the rest?"

Vivian turned on the razor. She felt its thrumming down in her stomach. Grace could pretend she was talking about her hair. Vivian had read between the lines. She'd been waiting for this moment since she'd seen the layout sketch and counted the five circles. Really since she'd read the email Errol had sent her. If *Bad Asians* had never been made, she and Errol would have eventually broken up. Diana would have gone off to Harvard and lost touch, and Justin floated off in his own orbit. Everyone said that friends grew apart, especially the ones you'd known when you were younger.

If those relationships had ended naturally, would that have hurt less? Would Vivian be thinking of them today? What she knew was that people had far less patience for an ordinary friendship's end, while they'd let her nurse the pain of that video forever. Some blast sites were large enough to allow a memorial. What a strange concept—turning destruction into a place worth revisiting. Grace's new project was no different. Seven years later, the same video that had broken them apart had the power to reunite them.

"I'll do you one better." Vivian brought the razor to the nape of Grace's neck. "I'll make sure I get you the others."

*   *   *

The Chinatown bus wove through the other cars like it was being chased down the interstate. Leaving her life in the driver's hands, Vivian listened to Grace's edit of the last episode they'd recorded. The buttery quality of her voice was all thanks to Brian. He'd turned one of their closets into a podcast studio and outfitted her with the best equipment. A trader by day, and well into some nights, he liked to keep himself either busy or unconscious. After Errol's email arrived late Saturday night, Vivian had struggled to find the right excuse for her sudden trip to DC that wouldn't send Brian into a flurry of helpful activity. She'd used her brother Michael and his impending divorce. A brother-sister bonding trip. Since Michael worked weekends, she could go down on a Wednesday without arousing suspicion.

On this podcast episode, Vivian had answered listener questions about planning a DIY wedding. She'd interviewed her old hook-up Jake about how to light your own wedding photos. They'd done a matchmaking segment where Dr. Song and Master Yi had paired two people up based on their birthdays and OkCupid profiles. Her Finn story had been cribbed from her Theta sister Tracy, who'd let her repurpose a quest to sleep with a long-distance boyfriend, one that ended with a tampon plucked out in a parking garage. Vivian's mother would be calling her when that episode dropped. Brian had insisted that her fans would love it.

This closing segment had also been Brian's idea. Half the tweet replies Grace sorted through each week centered around Finn, and predictions of who he might be. Like Grace, Brian had a knack for identifying what people wanted, and a gift for delivering without judgment. Their first month together, he'd handed over his phone and told Vivian to press her thumb against the biometric sensor.

"In case you need to use my phone," he'd said. "You don't have to ask me first."

Their relationship had progressed as if project managed. Their fifth date, he'd brought her to a friend's birthday party. At the three-month mark, they'd driven up to Connecticut to see his parents, a nice white couple who had adopted Brian from China when he was a baby. A week later, he'd treated her parents to dinner at Le Bernardin and rented a car to drive them to buy groceries in Flushing. At nine months, she moved into the condo he'd bought years ago with his signing bonus from Berkshire Hathaway. While his college friends had had their Wall Street offers rescinded, Brian, like his condo, was recession-proof. The two-bedroom had since doubled in value.

In suggesting the Finn segment, he'd essentially proposed, and the trip to Paris they were planning for their Season 2 finale had settled the question. Vivian had never met someone this commit-ted to the task of making her happy. Compared to him, she was always underperforming.

The stories she told about him, about Finn, were the only times she got to pretend Brian was inept or disappointing. She could tease him without worrying that he'd be spurred to self-improve. He'd once repainted the walls because she'd called them "Brian Beige."

Sometimes, after a string of late nights where Brian came home asleep in a private car, Vivian would go to a bar and flirt with some-one hopeless. Baristas who also played in a band. Doe-eyed poets and gauge-eared club promoters. Boys who promised romance in exchange for too many chances. Like the cigarettes she bummed, she'd rediscover that she'd lost the taste for them. She would flick them away and go back to healthy living.

She blamed Errol for this restlessness, Brian's kindness at odds with what she'd been taught to expect in her first and longest relationship. She'd thought this was why she kept delaying the divorce, to see if for once Errol would take responsibility. Except, he had, and yet the resistance remained. Whatever the feeling was, it wasn't love, despite sharing a stubbornness that would not give way to reason.

A few hours later, the bus pulled into a parking lot and heaved its own sigh of relief at arriving in one piece. Vivian's brother's Mercedes idled among the less ostentatious rides. He got out of the car, wearing a Gucci suit tailored to hide his growing belly. Diamond studs glittered in his ears. If Vivian hadn't known Michael, she might have found him impressive.

While she sat in his car, he waded through the crowd of bags to find the Louis Vuitton fake he'd given her at Christmas. Her brother had not been this gallant when they were kids. She couldn't have predicted then that in her time of need now, he'd be the first person she'd call.

"What's up?" he asked when he slid into his seat. "What'd you do, and why can't I tell our parents you're in town?"

"It's a long story," she said.

When they'd lived in the same house, they had been like rival spies in the epic war to be their parents' favorite. Any bit of information could and would be used against the other. Their relationship had shifted once Vivian moved to New York because Michael had their father's mind for business. Over dim sum on Mott Street, Michael had revealed that for the last ten years, he'd visited her new city regularly to buy high-quality designer fakes to resell back home. Shipments could come in at any time; he needed a trustworthy go-between when he was stuck in DC.

By confiding in her, her brother became Vivian's confidante in return. When their parents came to visit, she brought them to see her "apartment" in Chinatown, one of the Airbnbs Michael managed. After Michael heard about Brian's almost-proposal, he'd volunteered to take her to his favorite diamond place on Canal. It was cash only, and a quarter of the price if you knew how to haggle.

"Does it have to do with Brian?" Michael pulled out of the parking lot. "You better not have broken up."

"Definitely not." Vivian leaned her head against the window. Everyone worried that she would let Brian slip through her fingers.

"You guys elope? What about Paris? Don't tell me you let him spend 10k on a ring."

"I'd never let him do that," Vivian said. "Especially when I'm already married."

Michael laughed politely, as if he hadn't quite heard. Vivian pulled out the ring Errol had given her almost eight years ago. She'd hidden it in the one place Brian would never look: a box labeled "Secret."

Her brother had preached ad nauseum about the wonders of German engineering. Vivian's head still jerked back when he braked without warning.

"Holy shit." Michael waved an apology to the car honking behind them. He took the ring and held it up to his eye. "You're fucked. That kid is going to take you for everything you've got."

"He's not!" Vivian dug her finger into his armpit. "Not every divorce is like yours."

Michael thrashed against his seat belt, yanking her hand off him. He clamped his arm tight across his ribs. "I'll crash this car if you don't stop. You want that airbag to break your nose?"

Vivian feinted another jab to scare him. "It was Errol's idea. We'll sign some papers and be done. We don't even need lawyers."

"Jesus, didn't you learn anything from me?" Michael gestured at the high-rise apartments coming up around the bend. "I can't even move out of this dump without making her suspicious. You know she tried to get me audited?"

"You deserve it," Vivian said. "You're worse than Daddy."

Michael could pretend all he wanted that his ex-wife was crazy. More than a few times in New York, some glammed-up woman had greeted Michael on the street and given Vivian the cold shoulder until he'd introduced her as his sister.

"I'm sure you told Brian all about your trip back home. Should I let him know the real reason?"

Michael's car squealed up the spiraling parking structure. He cursed his way into a tight space between two Humvees.

"These things should be fucking illegal." He leaned over to check that she had space to get out of the car. His expression softened and he gave her forehead a poke, right where her brow was furrowed.

"Meimei, you know I'll keep your secrets."

For a moment, she relaxed under his protective gaze. She could not help being soothed under somebody else's wing. Her brother, the shark, sensed an opening.

"Now could you tell Brian to link up with my Fendi contact tomorrow?"

*　*　*

Vivian had wanted to meet Errol at a neutral location, and since Michael refused to let her drive his Mercedes, they decided on a Cosi off the red line in Friendship Heights. Vivian didn't want to be the first one there, heart pinging every time the café door opened. She planned her route accordingly and showed up exactly twenty minutes late. Errol was already there, sitting by the window. Through the glass, she could see the remains of a sandwich beside him.

She barely had time to register that she was in front of her estranged husband. She was too mortified that she'd left Errol waiting long enough for him to finish his lunch. She spent their first minutes together apologizing. He'd stood when he'd seen her come in, and they hovered uncertainly over his table.

"I also assumed I'd be late," Errol said. "That's why I got here an hour early."

The straightforwardness of that statement made Vivian laugh, which melted some of the tension. She slid into the chair across from him, aware that the small café table meant their knees were nearly touching.

"I like your hair this way." Errol studied her face.

"Thank you." Vivian tucked a strand behind her ear. She'd cut her hair into a chin-length bob years ago. She'd forgotten that she'd once worn it long.

"It makes you look older." Errol threw out his hand. "In a good way!"

"You've changed your hair too. All over."

Errol stroked his chin, gathering his wispy goatee between his fingers. "I did No Shave November and realized I hated shaving."

Vivian could have spent the entire afternoon describing what had changed about him. She felt like a kid, captivated by what must seem ordinary to everyone else. Errol barely fidgeted. His hands stayed in their pockets. His eyes remained steady on her face when she went on a long tangent about opening her own wedding planning business and starting the podcast. After they'd traded notes on who they'd kept in touch with from high school and college, they both looked down at their coffees. Vivian could see Errol readying himself to bring up the divorce.

"There's one other person I've stayed in touch with," she said. "You remember Grace?" The understatement gave her the giggles. "Of course you do. Actually, we've gotten pretty close."

Errol blinked as if he'd been asked a trick question. "How the hell did that happen?"

"I don't know if Diana told you . . ."

After their tense encounter in DC, Vivian had been surprised to learn that Grace not only knew who had leaked the cellphone footage but had also persuaded Z to take it down. When Vivian moved to New York the next year for a fresh start, she'd reached

out to Grace and they'd gotten together for drinks. Beefeater martinis with a twist. Maybe the timing had been right. They'd wound
up going back to Grace's apartment. A little drunk, the two of
them had laid down on the floor. It was still Grace's favorite place
to talk and think.

"It felt easy. I don't know. Am I weirding you out?"

Errol dug his hands deeper into his pockets. "How can you
trust her?"

"The same way she can trust me," Vivian said. "It's not like I
forgave her right away, but also . . . you can be around someone,
and feel close to them without completely forgiving them for hurting you."

She hadn't been thinking about the two of them until Errol
went stiff in his seat.

"What's it like to have that kind of person back in your life?"
He chewed on a thumbnail.

"Sometimes complicated. It's also a different relationship. A
better one, if you're lucky."

Again, that resistance. No longer rooted in the idea of divorce,
but at the thought that she might call Errol her friend. Who
wouldn't be resistant? He'd dumped her and left her waiting for
years. She'd have kept waiting if she hadn't grown up, if she hadn't
realized that love was more than what one person could bring. In
that time, he'd grown up too. Somehow this thought came closer
to hurting.

The sun through the window was heating up her knee, and
when she shifted out of its light, she bumped into Errol.

"You hitting on me?" Errol's jokes were never funny, but they
made her laugh. Like a pressure valve releasing.

"So that article," he said. "Have things blown over with her fans?"

She was surprised he knew about the controversy.

"Not yet," she said. There would be no better time. "She's thinking she might make a documentary about it. About herself, for
once."

Vivian was producing the film, which meant seeing if Errol and the rest of the group would sign on for the one scene where Grace deleted everything. Interviews too if any of them were willing.

Errol's stillness was more disconcerting when she had to wait for him to speak. Finally, he said, "Do you feel like you owe her?"

How to explain that what had once felt like a debt looming overhead had become a tab opened in good faith? "I feel like I have a chance to help a friend when she needs it."

"A second chance to help." Errol looked around the café. "What if I wanted to produce? What does a producer do?"

Vivian reached into her purse and took out the ring. She slid the velvet box across the table.

"They help make the project happen. Invest some money. Get the right people."

Errol opened the ring box and bugged out his eyes. "I forgot how much I spent on this thing."

Vivian brought up Michael's diamond contact on Canal. The resale value on a used engagement ring wasn't great, but they might get a couple thousand.

"Being a producer means I'd have a say in how the film is made?" Errol asked. "Or would we need a contract?"

She had missed the speed of Errol's brain, and how much faster it made her own thinking. For all her brother's worrying, he'd provided them with a perfect plan. A younger Vivian would have called it a fairy-tale ending. A diamond ring to summon a crew of helpers. A years-long spell finally breaking. It was all how you told the story.

"What do you say we find a lawyer?" Vivian asked. "I think I know a good one."

* * *

Diana's LinkedIn told them that she worked for the same small firm where she'd once been a paralegal. They specialized in probate law and their offices were in Gaithersburg. Vivian called Diana to say she was in town and asked if she wanted to meet near her firm for coffee. Unfortunately, Diana was running straight from work to something she called "an Own Your Narrative seminar."

"You could come," Diana said. "In fact, you have to. It's life-changing stuff, especially for people like us."

"Errol might join too." In fact, Errol had already gone home to take his mother to the doctor, but Vivian wanted to see how forgiving Diana was.

"The more the merrier." Diana didn't skip a beat. She sounded like her usual brusque self, more cheerful perhaps. The lack of curiosity was disconcerting. "The best part is I can use my referral code to get you guys in for free."

Apologetic about his absence, Errol had let Vivian borrow his car. Vivian wound through the private road that led to the country club address Diana had texted her. The green lawns on either side grew into the hills and valleys of a golf course. The road was hemmed in by low stone walls, reminding her of Grace's old neighborhood.

A large sign for the seminar greeted her in the lobby, and gold-embossed arrows were there to guide her. Vivian, who'd set up events like these, noticed the attention to detail. She walked down the hall, passing a large dining room with floor-to-ceiling windows, where men and women drank cocktails in their golf polos. Cutting through their laughing conversation, Diana's voice was audible even at the end of the hall. Moments later, there she was— standing outside the seminar room's doors, talking on the phone.

She could've been on her way back from mock trial rehearsal or debate club semifinals. She was wearing a dark suit and carrying the same ratty messenger bag from high school. Vivian thought of meeting Carrie Yang for the first time, how the reality of the person was always smaller than what she'd made up in her head. She walked down the hallway with steadier steps.

"The story you tell yourself is the story you end up living," Diana was saying. "What theme are you seeing in your journals?"

When she caught sight of Vivian, Diana opened her mouth wide and pantomimed an excited greeting.

"It's important that you're structuring your daily gratitudes in a three-act." She pulled Vivian into a hug while humming her agreement over the phone. "Once you shape the story, the story can shape your life."

After she hung up, Diana flung out her arms as if ready to hug Vivian again. "Holy shit, isn't this a reunion? Where's Errol?"

"He had a conflict," Vivian said. She felt that old urge to tease. "He probably heard the word 'seminar' and got antsy."

"Well," Diana said mildly. "There will be more opportunities."

She led Vivian into the seminar room, where she plucked the Reserved signs off three seats in the front row. The large space was full of other people in business formal. Many had notebooks out on their laps. A few feet away, a raised platform acted as the stage, a whiteboard the only object on it. *Own Your Career Narrative* was written in neat cursive.

"You're so lucky," Diana said. "Matthew Kean is delivering this seminar."

"Who was that on the phone?" Vivian asked.

"One of the people I'm coaching," Diana said. "She's on the 'Own Your Dream Narrative' track. I've got eleven clients right now and rotating more in every day. I'm still in training, but once I get five hundred hours, I'll be certified, and once I reach a thousand, I'll have a chance to join the executive cohort and work directly with Matthew. You know he runs these seminars internationally? He was in Tokyo last week."

"Wow," Vivian said. "How long is this seminar, by the way?"

"Three hours." Diana stood and the room exploded into applause.

They turned to face the back of the room, where a large man strode down the aisle. He shook the hands of the people who reached out to him. When he passed Diana, he gave her a jaunty salute.

"Good to see some old friends," he boomed. "And new ones too." He looked right at Vivian. "Welcome."

Beyond his height, his looks should have been unremarkable. Wide-set eyes, a softer jawline, light brown hair styled with mousse. His attention, however, made Vivian sit up taller. He held her in his gaze as if he knew she was thinking how corny this was. Somehow, through that moment of sustained eye contact, he told her he was in on the same joke, but that he thought she might be surprised. She couldn't look away after he'd moved on. She watched him scan the room, his eyes briefly catching each person they passed, until he'd snagged the entire audience in his net. What she'd experienced was likely what everyone else had too, and if he looked her way again, she could confirm it.

"I'm Matthew Kean." The applause restarted, and his voice rose over the noise. "Who here would like to tell us a story?"

Diana's hand shot up, clipping Vivian in the shoulder. Matthew helped her gallantly onto the platform.

"I'm Diana Zhang," she said to the audience. "When I first heard about Own Your Narrative, I thought I was at the end of my story. I'd had my high-power job offer revoked, I'd lost my closest friends, my boyfriend, and, worst of all, my sense of control." Vivian ducked her head when Diana spoke about *Bad Asians*, but no one in the crowd murmured in recognition.

Behind Diana, Matthew wrote on the whiteboard. He'd drawn a graph, and along the X-axis, he'd jotted down the events Diana had mentioned.

"Then a coworker told me about Own Your Narrative. I attended my first seminar. Cassandra Jacobs was leading it."

"Cassandra's the bomb," Matthew interjected.

"I learned how to think of my life in acts."

While Diana explained how every life event held the material for what could come after, Matthew drew a line on the graph that sloped upward, like the hills of the golf course outside.

"With the workshop's help, and later Matthew's book, *Thematic*

Materials, I reframed what I'd thought was proof of my failure into key themes to understanding my true story."

The points on the X-axis had sprouted their own lines, connecting them to the themes Diana listed: involvement, education, independence, collaboration.

"Take those themes together, and what it spells out is clear. I've started training to become an O.Y.N. coach, to transform my selfish tendencies into a desire to serve. The events that once gave me all this shame now help others break free from their own restrictive narratives."

Matthew had circled "O.Y.N. Coach" multiple times on the board, and then he wrote, "The End???"

"Let's give Diana a big round of applause," he said. People had already leapt up for a standing ovation.

"It's been a joy these past few years to see Diana shape her story." Matthew put his hand out to help Diana off the stage. "I can't wait to see what twists and turns are in store for her."

He announced their first exercise would be modeling Diana's example and sent them off in pairs to "graph your life." Diana took Vivian back out into the hallway. She was flushed from her time onstage, the strands of hair at her forehead damp with sweat.

"That was amazing," Vivian said. She was talking faster than normal, the energy of the room contagious. "I could never get up and deliver a speech like that."

"It's an awesome community," Diana said. "Did you bring a pen and paper?" She riffled through her messenger bag. "If not, I carry extra."

With Diana watching, Vivian had no choice but to draw her graph. This exercise was a strange but useful way of catching up. Its novelty left little room for awkwardness. Diana looked over Vivian's shoulder to give prompts and other instructions. That same urge came back to tease her old friend.

Vivian wrote down "Married Errol." From behind her, a murmur of surprise, but as on their phone call earlier, Diana held back her questions. What Vivian hadn't been able to see over the phone, however, was how unconsciously Diana leaned forward. Vivian wrote down her friendship with Grace, the profile, the fallout that came after. Diana's hair was brushing across Vivian's cheek. When she finished writing the plan for the documentary, Diana lost her balance.

"Do you have any questions?" Vivian's hands were on Diana's shoulders to keep them both from falling. The normalcy of the touch was startling.

Inside the seminar room, Matthew called people back to their seats. Diana looked nervously past the threshold, calculating her own patience.

"I could tell him there's an emergency." Diana pressed the corner of her phone into her forehead. "This counts, right?"

When Matthew called out again, that anxious look was back on Diana's face, an expression Vivian had rarely seen. Diana used to be the one who strode ahead, who gave Vivian the push she needed.

"It's such an emergency that we didn't have time to tell anyone." Vivian headed down the hall, and after a moment's pause, Diana reluctantly followed.

Right before they stepped out of the front doors, Diana gripped Vivian's arm. "Maybe we should finish the session."

"I don't know what the seminar is teaching you." Vivian threw the doors aside. "But you won't want to miss this story."

CHAPTER THIRTEEN

When Diana got out of her car, Vivian's was nowhere to be found. Minutes passed, and tired of waiting, Diana went up to her office. She found Vivian's number before putting down her phone. Thanks to O.Y.N., she'd gained a handle on her tendency to overstep, to do what she thought was best. She was going through the standard boundaries exercise—Had Vivian said she was lost? Had Vivian asked her to call?—when she heard a knock. Whipping her office door open, she stared into a Starbucks tray. Vivian held it with a nervous smile.

"I figured you might want coffee."

"My hero!" Diana grabbed the tray with both hands and raised it over her head like a trophy. "Holy shit, you got a Frappuccino?"

Vivian lifted her drink. "Don't laugh. The green tea frap is still my go-to."

Diana gestured at her office. "I have no right to laugh at anyone."

Her office was like the site of a prank. Every seat and surface was taken up by stacks of folders and loose papers. In the corner, she'd stacked pallets of energy drinks, bought in bulk at Costco. Last year, she'd started her 500-hour "hero's journey." Every free moment was dedicated to coaching or finding clients. Her apartment looked much worse.

Sinking into the chair Diana had cleared off, Vivian said, "Where would you like me to start?"

Diana held up her left ring finger. She couldn't believe Vivian had to ask.

Vivian told Diana the story as if for the first time, revising the narrative while she spoke. According to Vivian, the marriage had been a desperate attempt to erase their doubts about each other. Or rather, it had come from a mutual effort to pretend everything was normal, and at the same time, out of a need to graduate into the next stage of life. At the end of the day, they were too young to get married.

Vivian had expected to feel transformed when the judge on duty decreed them husband and wife. Instead, a few weeks after the courthouse ceremony, she'd had her first panic attack. One moment she was driving Errol home from one of his raves, and the next she was swerving onto the shoulder. Errol had dumped out the contents of the plastic trash bag in the car and placed the opening over her nose and mouth to stop her hyperventilating. She'd screamed at him to get off her, that she couldn't *breathe you fucking idiot I can't breathe.* They'd sat on the side of the highway, the car shaking whenever a semi roared past.

"And then he said, 'If you couldn't breathe, you wouldn't be able to yell like that.'"

"For fuck's sake, Errol," Diana said. "So you dumped him for good?" At some point, Diana had heard from her mother that Vivian and Errol had broken up. She'd pretended she didn't care to hear the details.

Vivian pulled down her cheeks. "No, I couldn't do it."

Diana must have looked exasperated because Vivian put her hands up in surrender. "I was clueless, okay? I kept wondering, 'Why do I feel unhappy?' And it's obvious now—I felt unhappy because that's what I was."

She had started smoking weed every night to keep Errol company.

He would put on a horror movie, and she would pass out with her makeup on. They limped along for a year, too numb to notice their own unraveling.

Errol broke up with her the Friday after one of his out-of-town raves. Until this point, Vivian's retelling had bordered on vague. Here the details sharpened. Diana understood. Some memories you tried hard to suppress, and others you went over too often.

Friday had been Vivian's favorite night of the week. She could look forward to zoning out for the next two and a half days. She'd already taken off her bra and put on her elastic pants. She'd been scrolling through the menu of a nearby Indian restaurant when Errol had appeared in the doorway of their bedroom.

"Do you want the garlic naan?" she'd asked, and he'd said, "I've been thinking . . ."

She had been so excited by the menu that she had finished his sentence, "Why not get both plain and garlic?"

He had looked at her, confused, and she had laughed. "Sorry, not what you were thinking?"

"No." He hunched closer to the doorframe until he was clutching it with both hands. He drummed his fingers. "What if we took a break?"

"From weed?"

Vivian grimaced, reliving how long she'd taken to catch on.

"Why should you have to finish what he'd started?" Diana said. "Good for you making things harder for him."

Through O.Y.N., Diana was familiar with the memories you punished yourself with, and the release that came, like a pop in your ears, when you cut your younger self a break. Vivian's emotions were usually all over the place, but she grew calmer while she considered what Diana said.

"After that, he moved out." Vivian took a pensive sip of her drink. "We stopped talking. I guess I figured that we would deal with things eventually."

"Deal with things?" Diana said. "It's been six years. Did you think you'd get back together?"

"I don't know." She sounded nostalgic when she told Diana that she had been certain Errol was the one. Overwhelmed with tears that awful Friday night, she hadn't asked if this meant divorce, and Errol had used words like "space" and "time." As if them belonging together was a done deal, and only the journey was up for negotiation.

"What—are you still in love with him?" Diana couldn't keep the challenge out of her voice. She'd often wanted to talk to her O.Y.N. clients this way, to get to the point already.

"No." Vivian's voice wobbled. "I love Brian." A hitch tore through her words, and she covered her mouth with her hand.

"I was so sure about Errol," she said, laughing a little at her tears. "I know it's crazy we waited this long. What was I thinking? I'm sorry, I don't know why I'm crying."

Diana pictured a raging fire slowly burning down, until the smallest wisp remained. Of Vivian watching over that flame for six long years, and then, in one accidental breath, finding it extinguished.

"I know how much you loved him." Diana wished that she'd been kinder. "You've got nothing to be sorry about."

"I really did," Vivian said. "I think that's why a part of me doesn't want to let go. Yeah, I was an idiot, but I'll never love anyone like that again. Not even Brian, who deserves it more."

"That's for the best." Diana unearthed a box of tissues from one of her desk drawers. "You should imagine the love you have for Brian as the kind of fire that warms your home. Not one that'll burn down your house."

"Or start a catfight in a bar." Vivian carefully dabbed her eyes. "Yours sounds more poetic."

Despite all her O.Y.N. training to keep her negative emotions in check, Diana allowed herself to feel jealous. Not of Vivian, but of her younger self. Flawed as she was, she had also once loved at the top of her lungs. Had it been seven years since she'd been that person? They had more ground left to cover. She took out the graph Vivian had drawn and tapped at the end of the X-axis.

"Now tell me how you got from there to here."

*　*　*

Diana picked up her takeout order from the Thai restaurant near her apartment. She was starving, her conversation with Vivian going on until nearly ten. She'd needed to push back her check-in with Cassandra. She would have canceled if she hadn't had to explain why she'd snuck out of Matthew's seminar early.

By the time Diana kicked off her shoes and cleared a corner of her kitchen table, she had thirteen minutes to eat before the Skype session. She could use that time for a quick resetting meditation, or she could look at her phone. The pad see ew was starchy and sweet. As was her Instagram feed. An engagement, a wedding, a new house, a tropical vacation. Her thumb skimmed past each post, hardly registering what she'd seen.

Out of habit, she tapped on Grace's Instagram page, or rather MeMe Productions. It had over a hundred thousand followers. If Vivian was to be believed, one day soon, they would type in the handle and find that nothing remained. The think pieces and Reddit threats would circle a missing center. The *Times* profile would become an archive.

When Diana had read that profile in January, the first thing she'd felt was vindicated. Grace having her unfiltered thoughts exposed to the public—was there a more karmically fitting punishment? Although it was a setback in her training to sink into comparative thinking, for months, Diana had cheered herself up by reading about Grace. As O.Y.N., and Cassandra, had predicted, however, this narrative was designed to make Diana feel small.

"She was a functional alcoholic, until she wasn't," Vivian had said in Diana's office. "Not to mention with her production schedule, she was hardly sleeping or eating. Then she has this huge fight with her mom right before the interview. If any of those elements had been missing, she'd probably be back to making MeMe videos today. Can you believe she says she's grateful?"

Leave it to Grace to show Diana up again. She was like those buffalo that Cassandra loved to cite, how they would run straight into a storm because they'd figured out this was the shortest time spent in the rain. As if that should convince Diana to agree to this documentary. She knew if one of her clients presented this problem to her, she'd encourage them to leap wholeheartedly. These were the challenges that got you into your next act. All very well to advise when she was safe on the other side. Looking over the cliff herself, she understood how unhelpful she'd been. She'd thought that three years at O.Y.N. made her an expert. Humility was her least favorite plot twist.

Diana opened her laptop right as the burbling ringtone played. Cassandra's face filled her screen. A white woman in her forties with cat-eye glasses and henna-ed hair, Cassandra looked like a pop art print.

"How was the seminar?" Cassandra asked.

Diana demurred: "It never gets old seeing Matthew in his element."

She remembered the thrill of Matthew recognizing her when he'd walked up onstage, like being back in school, the teacher's best student.

"I heard you had to leave early." Cassandra touched the sharp wing of her glasses. Her ability to question without asking was a tactic Diana liked to copy in her own coaching sessions.

"You remember me telling you about my childhood friends?" Diana chewed on the tip of her pen. "One of them, Vivian, came to the seminar with me. She had some big news. They're making a documentary about that viral video I was in. She wanted to know if I'd participate. Be a producer."

Cassandra was scribbling down notes. The pale part in her red hair bobbed on the screen. "This is very exciting."

"Is it?" Diana drew spirals in her notebook. She should be mapping out a decision tree. The doodles felt better. "I guess it's happening no matter what. I need to be proactive."

"That's defensive thinking," Cassandra said. "The answer is right in front of you. Visualize it."

Diana closed her eyes. Her dinner, too quickly consumed, bubbled in her gut. She remembered having to move back home again after leaving Weston and New York, except this time she'd been alone. Her law school friends had called once to get the story and never again. She'd lost touch with everyone back home. For months, she'd slept through the day, her eyes only snapping open at night. Her hurried breathing echoed in her ears during those midnight hours. She became afraid to leave the house in case she ran into somebody she knew, or somebody who knew about her.

Her parents, to their credit, had been kind. Her mother especially. She didn't blame Diana for the loss of her seller base. To rebuild, her mother had had to go back to cold call recruiting. She would approach strangers when she stopped to get gas. Watching from the car, Diana had decided that if her mother could start over at sixty, she had no excuse. The prestigious firms had shut her out, which left thousands of no-name places that might say yes. Her life moved forward. She found O.Y.N. through a coworker and signed up for a free trial. At Diana's first workshop, she met other people like her who had lost the futures they'd worked hard for, from jobs, to lovers, to children. Rather than hide their misfortunes, however, they clambered to share them with the group. She'd been especially struck by the workshop leader, Cassandra, whose husband had left her after her cancer diagnosis. She told her story with a level of detachment that rivaled a Buddhist monk's. It was hard to believe she was the same person who had thrown a brick through her ex-husband's windshield. Diana wanted Cassandra's control, her elegance and calm. Most of all, she wanted to turn her cautionary tale into an example that others could follow.

The harder Diana worked and the more literature she read, the closer she came to accepting that her life would be measured by everyone she'd helped through coaching. Some nights, however, when Diana stayed awake thinking of what she'd lost, she felt like those people on the news after a flood or fire. Disoriented in this new reality, unable to piece together the moment before and the moment after. She'd never thought it was right to interview those people on TV.

"I don't know if I can go through it again." Diana opened her eyes.

"This is your opportunity to show how much you've grown," Cassandra said. "You can stay where you are—I know how hard you've worked to get here, it's true—or you can move to the next level."

"Don't you mean the next act?" Diana asked. The only time Cassandra talked about levels was when they discussed the training program.

"That too." Cassandra smiled patiently. Although if she were really patient, Diana shouldn't have been able to see her acting it. "I assume this documentary will want to show how you've progressed since the original video came out, and this would be not only a way to reclaim your story, but also to share how Own Your Narrative was the key factor."

"Matthew would let me talk about O.Y.N.?" Their organization was careful about what information they put out in public. Diana's training contract had stated that any unapproved mention of O.Y.N., including on social media, called for automatic disqualification from the program. In today's world, opportunists were looking to steal Matthew's ideas, or to call the seminars cult-ish. As if when you found something that changed your life you weren't supposed to actually change it.

"He trusts you to represent us." Cassandra looked down at her notes. "You also mentioned that you could be a producer. That sounds like a position of greater control."

Diana was taking notes now too. "I could also write the contracts and get final cut approval. I could make sure the focus is on O.Y.N. and not on me."

"Just like when you tell your story at seminars and with your clients." Cassandra leaned back, satisfied. "You see? This is nothing like your first or second experience with being on camera. Sometimes, if we stay too on the surface, certain thematic materials might look the same. That's why I'm here to help you push deeper."

"You said this would get me to the next level?" Diana gripped the sides of her chair. "I have hundreds of hours left before I reach certification."

"How do I explain." Cassandra drummed her fingers on her laptop, the red polish flashing at the bottom of the screen. "Part of the hours system is to give you the experience you need, but it goes both ways. Your clients benefit too. The more clients you reach, the more people learn about the program, the more lives we can change. Every person who watches this documentary is learning, which means your reach grows too.

"Look at my platforms. I started out like you. One-on-ones, personalized sessions. When my abilities increased, my social media accounts were approved. I found that I could make those same connections in a video, a tweet, a photo. The people I train who become trainers themselves—they are also extending that reach.

"That's the thing we try not to reveal too early to our trainees." Cassandra leaned in, as if they were sitting across from one another. "The hours program isn't linear. It's exponential. Do you think we'd ask anyone to give up a thousand hours for free? No matter how amazing our program is, that's exploitation."

Cassandra showed Diana her notebook. On it was a circle in the center with lines connecting it to smaller circles, each with their own connecting lines. "It's like the rays of the sun. We shine outward together to warm the entire world."

Diana pictured herself not facing a camera, but how a viewer might see her on-screen. Like Cassandra, the story she told would be completely at odds with how poised and polished she seemed. At the bottom of the frame, a ribbon would unfurl to read: *Diana Zhang, Lawyer and Executive Coach*. She'd been aware and afraid of how quickly life could change. She'd never considered how it could change for the better.

"You're on the fast track," Cassandra said. Her face was full of pride. "The moment we met, I told Matthew to look out. That one's a superstar."

* * *

The final piece was Justin.

"We have to go all in," Diana said over the phone. After her talk with Cassandra, she'd pulled an all-nighter to plan. She was more energized than if she'd slept.

Vivian, who was on the early bus back to New York, yawned and said, "I haven't even had my coffee."

"It's simple, if risky." Diana paced in her living room, kicking aside piles of clothes that got in her way. "We put everything in place. Grace, her cameras, have them set up. Then we go to Justin."

"I was thinking we could use my parents' house." Vivian perked up. The plan had roused her too. "They're doing a second-floor renovation in a few weeks and they're going to Italy to avoid the construction."

"That's great," Diana said. "But we need a location that's so close to where he lives that it would be more effort *not* to participate."

"Justin has lunch on Sundays with his mom," Errol said, the first time he'd spoken during the conference call. Diana had assumed he'd fallen back asleep. "Lucy's seen his car when she takes walks around the neighborhood. He still drives that old Honda Civic."

"We've got our date." Diana wrote on the whiteboard she'd Velcro-ed to the wall. "Vivian, tell Grace the plan and let me know what she thinks. I'll get the contracts drawn up."

"If it's a Sunday, Grace will have to come down that morning," Vivian said. "She edits the podcast Saturday nights. I can get there earlier and drop off some of the equipment."

"Why don't we stay the night at my parents' house." Diana double-checked her calendar.

Her mother, who'd won her first promotion in years, would be traveling to Hawaii to receive her honors at Blüm's Leaders Gala. "It'll only be my dad there and he won't notice. Minimize the amount of back and forth. Reduce errors."

Her logistical reasons were less than sound. She didn't want to admit that she was too nervous to spend the night before by herself, and she couldn't host Vivian in her disaster of an apartment. She'd meant for the one-bedroom to be a waystation when she'd broken up with Weston, but she'd renewed the lease year after year. Perhaps to avoid dealing with the boxes of law school mementos that she'd unearthed last night in her flurry of planning. Emboldened by her conversation with Cassandra, she'd opened the first box. She'd pulled out a photo from Halloween, when she'd run into a group of 2Ls dressed as *Bad Asians*. Beneath that her professors' recommendation letters for a fellowship she'd decided not to apply for, in part because she'd wanted to read what they'd written. They'd described her as "talented and driven," "guaranteed to go far," and "full of enormous potential." When she'd reached the Cartier bracelet Weston had bought her after she'd gotten her summer associateship, Diana had shoved the boxes back into her closet. Like the ancient pathogens trapped in glacier ice, they had the potential to be lethal if released.

In the weeks after the conference call with Vivian and Errol, however, Diana relapsed into wondering what her life could have been. She'd heard some of her classmates were clerking for Supreme Court justices, others were making millions, or entering politics. Weston was a dad now; he'd married one of his coworkers. On the phone with her O.Y.N. clients, she listened to their stories of envy. She redirected them to focus on what they wanted, not what they didn't want others to have.

"Don't be a jealousy junkie," she warned them, a fraud in disguise. "Don't feed the beast. The worst story you can tell yourself is, 'What if.' The best, 'What's possible now.'"

She asked Cassandra for more clients, ones in different time zones. Every hour she logged was one more step planted in the only life she had.

The night before the shoot, Diana had a call with an American expat in Korea. By the time she met Vivian outside her parents' house, her dad had gone to bed. He'd left the basement door unlocked.

Creeping upstairs, Diana had a funny urge to confess: "I used to wish I could live in your house." Admitting this petty thought gave her surprising relief.

"No way." Vivian looked pleased. "You never came over."

"You had all this room. And the best stuff." Diana grabbed a sleeping bag from the upstairs junk closet. "I didn't want you to get a big head."

Unfurling the sleeping bag, Diana was hit by a wave of BO. The bag must have belonged to one of her brothers.

"I can sleep on the couch—" A yawn split her face. "Sorry, I've been up since five."

"We could share the bed like we used to," Vivian said. "If that's not too weird."

After brushing their teeth, they got under the covers. Diana switched off the light. Vivian turned her head, her pillow rustling in the dark.

"Should we talk about boys?"

The urge to giggle seized them, despite Diana's unease. She hadn't dated anyone after Weston. The cycle restarted in her head. A dad! It had hardly been four years. Meanwhile she'd re-downloaded one of those apps and swiped left on everyone. Every bad habit she'd thought she'd suppressed was bubbling back up to the surface.

"Tell me about this Brian," she said lightly.

"Everything I tell you, you'll hate," Vivian said. "We met when I first moved to New York. He's a trader on Wall Street and there's truly nothing wrong with him."

During a sudden thunderstorm her first year in New York, Vivian had found herself stuck under an awning in Chelsea. Brian had stopped to offer his umbrella. It turned out he was heading in her direction. They'd walked the six blocks back to her apartment. A week later, she'd found out he lived next door from where they'd met. He'd been on his way to buy a sandwich at his local bodega.

"Ooh, Chelsea," Diana said. "Is that a big deal or something?"

Vivian shoved Diana, and they elbowed each other back and forth. In the dark, under the covers, Diana had no sense of how old she was. The bed felt as large as it had when they'd been kids. A dog barked from someone's backyard and a chorus of neighborhood dogs rose to meet it.

"He doesn't know the real reason I'm here," Vivian said shyly. "Or about Errol."

"If he's so great, why didn't you tell him?"

"Because he'd have taken care of everything." Vivian kicked her foot out from the covers. She sat up and plumped her pillow with sharp chops of her hand. "Like with the divorce. He would've hired the lawyers, filled out the paperwork for me. He'd track Errol down if he had to."

"Jesus, is he a fixer?" Diana rolled over onto her side. "Blink twice if you're engaged to a contract killer."

Vivian draped her hair over her face. "That's how he is. He's the perfect one, and I'm the fuckup."

Diana didn't realize how gusty her sigh was until the hair blew off Vivian's face. "Walk me through that logic?"

"I think I understand how Errol must have felt being the mess everyone had to clean up. I know I don't deserve Brian, but who wants to feel that way all the time?"

Diana fell back onto her pillow. "Anyone that obsessed with fixing other people's problems must be crazy. I should know."

"Everyone loves him. He's perfect!"

"I swear, you jump from A to Z. You think you don't deserve Brian because he's perfect. You think he's perfect because he takes care of your problems. What about his problems?"

"He doesn't have any."

"There you go." Diana slapped the bed. "Everyone has problems. Your man is messed up too. A lot more messed up than you if he's hiding it that well."

"You should meet him first before making these grand statements."

Diana cackled. "I'll bet you a hundred dollars I can break him in an hour."

The tenor of their conversation softened. Diana realized how close they'd come to fighting. She never shied away from arguments—she enjoyed throwing herself against someone and seeing how they both held up—but this teetering sensation, the subtle way frustration rose and rarely broke, was something she'd only felt with three people. The longing that crept over her was different from what she'd felt all month. Gentler, a reminder of what she'd had rather than what she'd lost.

"Even if he's this superman," Diana said, "I'm glad you didn't get Brian involved in our plans."

"Why's that?" The air-conditioning clicked on and ruffled the bedroom curtains.

"We don't need his help." Diana resettled the blanket over them. Vivian tucked her foot back under the covers.

Diana had pictured time travel as a machine, a vehicle that people rode, like the car that had brought her home. Instead, it was time that traveled, like electricity through a circuit, through her and Vivian, the bedroom preserved since the '90s, and Errol sleeping next door. People knocked on the doors of their childhood homes hoping to close this circuit of shared history, to feel running through them a flicker of who they'd once been. Lying on the spot where she'd lain a hundred times, with the friends she'd lain beside, Diana was afraid that if she moved, the spell would be broken. Electricity had also felt like magic once. Now, she couldn't live without it.

* * *

A car door clicked open and slammed shut in the distance. The sound telescoped into Diana's ears, from barely audible to screaming loud in an instant. She was suddenly, irrevocably awake. Looking out the window, she saw Errol locking the front door of his parents' house. She tapped on the glass, and he looked up. She couldn't help smiling at his hippie hair and scruffy goatee. She held up a finger and climbed over Vivian's sleeping form.

"What's with the outfit?" she asked as she strode over her front yard. She was in her pajamas, wearing her father's jacket and her mother's mules. The heels sank into the wet grass.

"I'm a working professional now." Errol walked to meet her at the end of the shared drive. He was dressed in a button-down and khaki trousers. His car was a recent model too. When they hugged, she was pleased that he'd put on a little muscle. That meant he was exercising.

"My mom told me you're a software engineer down in Austin." She was surprised by how glad she was to see him doing well, and yet how disappointed she was too, that he wasn't doing better. "That corporate grind."

She'd thought she was being subtle until Errol groaned a little.

"It's not where I imagined myself, but it's a lot better than where I was." He looked down at the crumbling asphalt. "I'm sorry again about not being able to come to New York."

"I'm sorry too. For asking, for everything." Diana dislodged part of their driveway with her toe. This was the closest she'd come to apologizing for what she'd called him in that bar. "Carrie was nuts. I don't know what I was thinking."

"Let's both plead temporary insanity for our early twenties." Errol twisted the tail of his goatee, and Diana felt the grace of what he'd spared her.

"I can't believe you drove from Texas." Diana nudged her shoulder against his. "Take a plane."

Errol cracked his knuckles. "I like driving."

The rear door opened. Mrs. Chen stuck her head out and waved.

"Good morning, Auntie!" Diana called in surprise. She hadn't realized Mrs. Chen was in the car.

If Diana's presence kept Errol's mother from voicing her impatience, her continued waving made the message clear.

Turning back to Errol, Diana whispered, "Where are you taking your mother?"

"To the hospital," Errol said after a beat of consideration. "She has a consultation with an Alzheimer's specialist."

Diana's hand went to her mouth. "Oh my god."

"Don't worry, she doesn't have it. She just doesn't want to admit she's depressed." Errol's back stiffened. "Shit, what time is it?"

When he heard, he ran to the car and reversed it down the drive. The conversation would have to continue when he got back. Through the window, Mrs. Chen was a fizz of hair and hands. Her shouting matched the rev of the engine as they raced out of the cul-de-sac.

* * *

Back in the house, Diana's father had prepared a bountiful breakfast, with fried dough and cut fruit. He poured Diana and Vivian bowls of hot, sweetened soymilk, brewed in a gadget that spoke Japanese. Diana couldn't remember the last time she'd seen her parents apart, or rather her father without her mother. She hardly recognized this voluble man inhaling food in one breath and grilling her about Mrs. Chen in the next. At potlucks, her father had seemed too engrossed in eating to speak.

"From what I've gathered, Mrs. Chen's been going to doctors all month," Diana's father said between large bites of his scallion pancake. "You said it's Alzheimer's this time? She must think there's something wrong with her brain."

He was skeptical. The other week, Mrs. Chen had cited the exact cost of pork ribs over the last five years while complaining about inflation. Regardless, it was nice to see the relationship improving between her and her son. Perhaps because of the nature of these appointments—Diana's father guessed there might be sedatives involved—Errol had been driving his mother to them. Diana's father would see the two on his way to work.

He gave Vivian a solicitous grin. "I'm sure you're glad not to have her for a mother-in-law. Otherwise, that would be you up before dawn."

Vivian's collarbones began to flush. In a minute, she'd be red in the face.

"You two were a sweet, young couple." Diana's father made satisfied noises draining his bowl of soy milk. "I would go on my morning walks and see you holding hands on the playground. Green hills and clear water couldn't have been a more lovely sight." Her father waxed poetic, dipping into his trove of scholarly sayings. Soon he would ask them if they knew the story behind the proverb.

"A walk sounds good, Dad." Diana indicated with her eyebrows that Vivian should stay behind. Her father had revealed himself to be as big a gossip as her mother. Diana had to keep him away from any reunion between the two sweethearts. "I haven't seen the neighborhood in a while."

"My heart flower is in full bloom." Her father sprang up. "My busy daughter wants to walk with me."

Diana felt guilty watching him hurry to clean up. Her parents would talk about how she hadn't gone on a date or a vacation in four years, but they'd never asked her to come home, nor her brothers. Kevin was in California and Tim in Shanghai, both working hard for their next promotion. Surely her parents missed them. She took her father's hand when they left the house, and he tucked it under her arm. His smile was wide enough to show his missing molars.

They took a right onto the main road that bisected the larger neighborhood and walked toward the community lake. A few minutes in, her father paused as they passed the back of Vivian's parents' house. He visored his hands over his eyes.

"What're you doing?" Diana grabbed him by the arm when he tried to step closer.

"There's a van in their driveway."

Luckily, Grace and Z were nowhere to be seen.

"It's probably the renovators." To distract him, she asked what was new with Mr. and Mrs. Wang.

Her father let himself be led away. "You know that Mrs. Wang got her real estate license?"

With her longtime roots in the community, she had quickly become the go-to agent for their suburb. Not many people knew, however, that Mrs. Wang was the new breadwinner of the family. Over the past few years, Mr. Wang's company had lost most of their contractors. With WeChat's popularity, the contractors could advertise their services on their profiles. The rumors of underpayment hadn't helped. Perhaps ten years ago, Mr. Wang could have picked up the slack, but it made clients nervous to see a man in his mid-seventies hefting cinder blocks over his shoulder.

"This renovation is their biggest yet. The entire second floor! I think they want to hide that his business is failing."

More interesting was that Mrs. Wang's success had turned Mr.

Wang into the doting, nervous one. Where he'd once treated his wife with a distracted indulgence, he now stayed glued to her side while Mrs. Wang held court at parties.

"We call her Big Sister Wang," her father said. "Your mother thinks she acts like a lady gangster."

Mr. Wang was not the only one flustered by Mrs. Wang's transformation. Diana's mother had been nonplussed to hear that one of her Blüm sellers had asked Mrs. Wang to recommend an acupuncturist.

"Your mother's used to being the first person that people consult," her father said. "Would you believe that Mrs. Chen is Mrs. Wang's right-hand woman?"

Diana, who had seen the parents as a unified body, learned that Errol's and Vivian's mothers had never gotten along. Nothing had happened between them, as far as her father knew. It was a mismatch of personalities. Mrs. Wang was a classic Southern flower, sensitive and cunning, and Mrs. Chen a typical Northern brute. Tensions had grown when Errol and Vivian had started dating.

"Chen Yu didn't think Vivian was good enough for her son." Her father had slipped into calling the other parents by their names, dropping the honorific. "Wang Dong used to say Errol was her future son-in-law. Chen Yu never returned the favor."

"She acts like Errol's the worst thing that's happened to her," Diana said.

"She's an exacting woman," Diana's father said. "Until he quit Microsoft, he was her pride and joy. You should've heard how often she would mention him skipping two grades. She found a way to work it into every conversation."

"We'd better hope she doesn't find out Vivian's in town," he said, as if he weren't the only person who could tell her.

They'd finished taking a lap around the lake. The air was heavy with wet heat and patches of sweat had spread across her father's shirt. They sat down on a bench, and Diana remembered the day Errol had told her he wanted to end things with Vivian. He'd needed a friend, and she'd chosen to give him a lecture. This morning she'd fallen right back into her old patterns. It was easy to be a detached coach with her O.Y.N. clients, to meet them where they wanted. The hard part wasn't that Errol had changed, but that she hadn't changed as much as she'd thought.

As if he'd read her mind, her father said, "How long has it been since you kids were in town? Are you having a reunion?"

"Something like that," she said.

A goose flew from one side of the lake to the other, touching down with a honk. The water skittered out in parallel trails and the goose swam over to the little bridge where a family tossed pieces of bread. Justin had loved feeding the geese. He would squirrel away the group's bread rolls during lunch. One day, tired of him begging for hers, Diana had asked the lunch ladies for a donation. That afternoon, they'd hauled a garbage bag full of stale rolls over to the bridge and half-clogged the lake in the process. The way Justin had smiled! His teeth had taken up more and more room until the rest of his face was as squished as the bread.

"How do you stay friends with the same people for so long?" she asked. The parents had first met in 1985, longer than she'd been alive.

"Live next to each other," he said. "People like convenience."

He swung himself up from the bench while she was still laughing and offered her his hand. "Do you want to see where it all began?"

They took a detour through the part of the neighborhood where the old townhomes sat. Diana had rarely gone to see where she'd spent the first five years of her life, outside of visiting Justin when he and his mom had briefly lived there. The townhomes in front of her had hardly changed over the decades. They looked old although not decrepit, the paint sun-faded, and the concrete steps sturdy despite the cracks.

"That reminds me!" Diana's father took out his phone and opened his WeChat. He scrolled through until he found the post

286 • LILLIAN LI

in his feed. "The Professor scanned a bunch of old photos. Look at how young we used to be!"

He thumbed through a series of digitized photos that Dr. Chen had posted. The fathers playing basketball, Mrs. Chen and Diana's mother sitting on a couch, all of them eating hotpot around a table with mismatched chairs. There seemed to be no reason the photos were taken, the people merely an excuse to use the camera. The only posed one was of the five mothers lined up in the parking lot.

"That was the day Yu Zhou and that husband of hers left for Iowa," her father said. Diana could see a UHaul at the edge of the frame. "You should've seen how much the women cried. It was like she was going off to war."

At one end of the row was Errol's mother, Mrs. Chen, the only one not pregnant. She cradled a volleyball as if it were her belly, which was probably why the other women in the photo were laughing. They were younger than Diana was now, and while she felt distant from their lives and responsibilities, the way they laughed together was familiar enough to ache. Mrs. Li, at the other end of the line, had her head tossed back, her body at a slant, ready for the group to catch her.

Diana tapped the screen. "I didn't know you all were close with Mrs. Li."

Her father put away the phone. "We were," he said. "It's regrettable how we acted back then. We had just come from China. We carried Chinese values with us."

Diana couldn't believe how little sense she'd had of this drama that had engulfed her parents. He told her that when "the kids" had been in third grade, Mr. Li had decided he was done with America. The grand experiment had failed, and he and his family would move back to Beijing.

"Who could blame him?" her father said. "Here, he was an accountant, and over there, he was going to be CEO of his father's company. China's economy was prospering. The quality of life had completely changed after we'd left. It made perfect sense on paper."

Mrs. Li had refused to leave. She'd loved the freedom of the U.S., the ability to get her mail with her house slippers on and not be reprimanded by her neighbors. Americans didn't ask her what her parents did or tell her how to raise her daughter.

"*Americans mind their own business,*" her father quoted. "Which isn't true. There's simply more space here. Although that's also a kind of freedom."

The other parents had sided with Mr. Li, and they'd forged their own campaigns to get Mrs. Li to see the light. She couldn't separate her husband from his daughter, and Grace from her father. She had to think of Grace and the life she deserved, which Mrs. Li could never afford on her own. She wouldn't even be able to support herself. Every conversation eventually led back to this topic, until Mrs. Li refused to speak to any of them. This hadn't stopped them, not when they were sure they were right. They switched over to helping Mr. Li in more intrusive ways, recommending lawyers, real estate agents, and finally social workers. Diana had believed Grace and her mother had distanced themselves from the community because they thought they were superior. What a shock to discover the role her own parents had played.

"We got too involved," her father said. "Now we know better. Everything is very . . . intense when you're young. You burn out fast if you don't learn to slow down. With friends, and with work too." He gave her a meaningful look.

They were back in their cul-de-sac. Errol's car was in the driveway, and though Diana was soaking with sweat, she told her father she was going to stay outside a little longer.

Sitting on the steps, she thought about how her father was right to say the parents had trespassed against Mrs. Li. At the same time, it was easy to cross the line when the line was always moving. When was walking into someone's house without knocking an intrusion, and when was it a sign of trust?

Her clients asked her for help, and she offered exactly what O.Y.N.'s framework of exercises said was appropriate. Which wasn't bad, just transactional. This was the first time in a year that she'd scheduled no client calls. The silence of her phone was unsettling. She missed the flurry of activity, but not any one person. As involved as she was in their lives, once their free twelve-week trial was over, the relationship ended too. The ones who paid for additional classes were moved to more experienced coaches. She moved on just as quickly—you couldn't reach five hundred hours if you became too invested. And being too invested, in others, in herself, was why her life had fallen apart.

"What're you doing out here?" The front door opened. Vivian and Errol flanked her on the stoop.

"Just taking a moment," Diana said.

Vivian placed a cold can of Coke against the back of Diana's neck. Errol held out a hand to pull her up. All the times Diana could remember overstepping with her former friends, she could also remember when they'd given each other exactly what they'd wanted.

O.Y.N. had drawn up tidy lines to color between, an instruction manual on how to be better. But what did O.Y.N. have to say about how big her father had smiled that morning, the crow of his voice when she'd called last week? He could tell her that he missed her, that he wished she'd come home more, or she could save him the breath. In the end, she couldn't change who she was without changing what she did best.

* * *

The three of them crossed the street to Mrs. Yu's house. Justin's car was parked along the curb. Grace and Z had remained at the Wangs to finish setting up. They had their phones in case reinforcement was needed. Diana had calculated that their plan had a 50/50 chance of success. The others found this pessimistic.

To Diana's shock, Justin opened the door thirty years older, fat, and bald, with Mrs. Yu right behind him. Not until Mrs. Yu introduced the man as Gerald did Diana accept her mistake. The idea of Mrs. Yu with a boyfriend had seemed less likely than Justin aging at the speed of light.

"Sorry, Mrs. Yu," Errol said. "We don't mean to interrupt lunch. We were in the neighborhood and wanted to talk to Justin."

"There's no interruption," the unfamiliar man said. He undid his shirtsleeves and began to roll them up. "I haven't started cooking."

He grinned at them as if he'd been expecting guests. He spoke Chinese in a twangy accent and the outline of his undershirt was visible beneath his collared button-down. He was like a cowlick that sprang up no matter how much gel you applied.

"You could make a banquet meal in thirty minutes," Mrs. Yu said with teasing admiration. "Justin!" she called down the hall.

Although her soft voice barely traveled from the room, Justin burst into the foyer at the sound. Maybe because of how quickly he was moving, or his spandex-y clothes, he reminded Diana of a bobsledder, nimble and sleek. On second glance, he looked dried out, almost shrunken, with bags under his eyes and drawn, hollowed cheeks.

"Did you need the kitchen, Gerald?" he asked the man, not registering the others' presence. His mouth was pursed tight, an expression that for Justin was practically scowling.

"Hi," Diana said, startling him. Justin shook his head at the three of them, as if to clear his vision.

"Isn't this amazing?" Mrs. Yu clapped her hands to her cheeks, agog at how much they'd grown.

"What're you all doing here?" Justin crossed his arms. He'd stayed at the threshold of the kitchen, keeping his distance. Diana shot Vivian and Errol a look. Her calculations had not been conservative enough.

"Let me show you which vegetables I want you to use for lunch," Mrs. Yu said to Gerald. She led him out to the garden growing on the deck, another new addition.

The four of them sat at the dinner table, Justin fiddling with a remote that for some reason was in the napkin holder. Vivian, who was closest to the project, did the talking. There were years of gossip and intrigue to catch him up on, but Justin paid little attention. He checked his phone, the fitness tracker around his wrist, and the additional pedometer he had clipped to his waistband.

"Wow," he said, dry as a newscaster, when he heard that Errol and Vivian had gotten married. The news of Grace deleting her channel aroused an extra blink. By the time they told him that Z would be assisting the shoot, his eyes had drifted out the window.

On the deck, Gerald and Mrs. Yu filled a plastic bag with green beans.

"What's with that guy?" Diana asked, and then berated herself. This was her priority? But Justin jumped to attention.

"Right?" He looked positively poisonous. "She's cut his hair for years. After my dad died, he started coming over here."

"I'm sorry about that," Diana said, months too late.

She'd thought about reaching out when she'd first heard from her mother. Too much time had passed with her debating if that was appropriate. A condolence card was lost somewhere in her apartment.

"I'm probably overreacting." Justin had taken her to mean the Gerald situation. "He's just a general manager at his family's Peking duck restaurant."

The deck door opened, and Mrs. Yu came through laughing and swatting Gerald, who held up the bag of beans as a shield.

"Don't mind us," Mrs. Yu said. She touched Justin's hair tenderly. "You should go have lunch with your friends. How rare is it that everyone is back in town at the same time?"

"They're not here for lunch and I still have to fit in my run before I stop by the office."

"We're setting up to shoot at my parents' house," Vivian said. "One scene, half an hour, tops. Diana's drawn up contracts to make sure we have final say on how our images are used. It may not be used for anything—Grace hasn't decided."

"When have we heard that before." Justin stretched his biceps behind his head. Everything about him was sharp and unrelenting. While Vivian and Errol had both steadied over the years, Justin had pushed himself toward the extreme end of his younger detachment.

"Grace might quit filmmaking," Vivian pressed. "We're the first thing she's been excited to shoot in months."

"She's been through a lot since that article came out," Errol said. "Before then, if we're being honest."

"We can't shoot this video without you." Diana felt her urgency joining the others.

"I don't know," Justin said, his classic answer. You could work with a no. Fighting with Justin was like punching water.

"If you don't want to miss lunch, what about dinner?" Mrs. Yu fussed with Justin's hair. "Gerald could cater. Wouldn't that look nice on camera?"

Justin hunched his shoulders up to his ears. Vivian asked Gerald his price, and Gerald protested that he should pay them for the free publicity for his side catering business.

"He'll need help in the kitchen," Mrs. Yu added, almost an afterthought. "Justin, if you can't go to the Wangs, I'm happy to."

Gerald was delighted by the idea. His little sous-chef. His sexy assistant. She could be his business partner. Now that she worked at the salon part-time, they could fill their weekends with spectacular events. They could cater abroad! He listed the countries his business would take her. Justin cleared his throat.

"No, you stay here, Ma. I'll go."

"If you're sure . . ." Mrs. Yu wandered out of the room.

Justin looked after his mother like an unhappy child who'd been tricked into trying broccoli. Diana felt laughter bubbling up in her throat. She fought to keep her expression straight and put her hand on Vivian's elbow to stop her from shaking.

Gerald, oblivious, named the dishes he could make before announcing he would go to the store after lunch. From the other room, her voice wafting in like a flute, Mrs. Yu volunteered Justin's assistance.

Diana broke first. Vivian and Errol collapsed like dominos around her. They kept setting each other off until Diana put her face down in her arms.

"Laugh it up," she heard Justin say. "Let's all tease Justin." With her eyes closed, he sounded like the old him, too annoyed to act like he didn't care.

Diana lifted her head. For once, she wasn't thinking about O.Y.N., or about Grace taking down *Bad Asians*. The group was here. She reached out for Justin's hand, ready to convince him their story hadn't ended.

CHAPTER FOURTEEN

In the passenger seat, Justin's mother's boyfriend breathed loudly through his mouth. Gerald had sinus problems—it couldn't be helped. At the stoplight, Justin passed him a tissue, which the man used to hock something from the back of his throat. Now the man's phlegm was in Justin's car.

What should have been a short drive to the store had doubled when Gerald had requested that they stop by his family's restaurant. They'd gotten stuck in Sunday traffic on the way back home. Justin hadn't been able to check his phone in half an hour. Who knew how many messages had accrued.

The car in front inched forward. Justin ran his thumbnail under the seam of the driver-seat window. Half an hour shouldn't feel like a long time. He'd realized how often he looked at his email when Diana had clocked him on her way out the door.

"You have some client breathing down your neck?" she'd joked, waggling her own phone in solidarity.

The only person breathing down his neck was Justin himself, and everyone who'd graduated after '08. He'd already been hamstrung by his years of sub-employment. Spending the bulk of his twenties working his company's help desk had put him further behind. Four years ago, he'd missed his chance to become the head of Customer Support. He'd quit his job in a desperate bid to save his relationship. By the time he'd come back, single and shell-shocked,

BOD had secured $6 million in funding. They had also moved their headquarters not to San Francisco, but thirty minutes away in Bethesda. Vijay's cousin Adi became Justin's boss. Adi, who'd worked the help desk part-time during college. Adi, who was five years younger.

Since then, Justin had carved out a managerial role, which meant his queue of tickets became a revolving door of trainees. No sooner would he get someone comfortable enough to support customers on their own before they'd message him that they'd found a better job. He worked from seven to eight Monday through Friday; he'd stopped counting how many hours he put in over the weekend. When he wasn't working, he was training for his next marathon. He'd had to exchange Sunday dinner with his mother for a quick half-hour lunch, otherwise he'd be buried by Wednesday. For years he'd believed that this extra work would be noticed. And it had, but not in the way he'd wanted.

That Friday, he'd joined his old work friends for their executive board lunch. Vijay had booked the glass conference room, the leaders visible for everyone else to watch. Justin had spent most of the time fighting that out-of-place feeling. While the table chatted about their weekend plans, he tried a gratitude exercise. He should be grateful that his team continued to grow exponentially, even if his workload grew with it. He should be grateful that he was friends with not only the CEO, but also the heads of Product, Marketing, Sales, and R&D. It shouldn't matter that they'd once been on the same level. He was thanking the universe for the chickpea burger he'd bitten into when Vijay had turned to him and asked, "Are you a volcel?"

Despite being the CEO of a multimillion-dollar company, Vijay forgot that when he spoke, everybody listened.

"What's a volcel?" Justin asked, his mouth full to seem more casual.

"Voluntary celibate," Vijay explained, demonstrating what casual truly looked like.

According to Vijay, voluntary celibates were known for incredible creative output. With their sex brain turned off, these men could redirect that energy into their work and personal growth. They retained purity of mind, and regained good posture, cured of the primal hunch that marked the male orgasm.

"Nikola Tesla was a volcel," Vijay continued. "And Gandhi."

Brad (head of Product) looked up from his bag of chips. "Didn't he sleep next to naked women to test himself?"

Vijay raised his hands up to the ceiling. "That might be the most volcel thing I've ever heard!"

Vijay proceeded to lay out the reasons Justin could claim the seat next to Gandhi. They'd known each other for seven years. That was hundreds of weekends recounted between them without mention of a date or a one-night-stand. Vijay had seen Justin in spandex. In a totally homosocial way, he knew what Justin was working with. Did he masturbate? Or did he keep himself totally dammed up? With their eyes on him, Justin had tried a cryptic shrug, which everyone in the room decided was confirmation.

PJ (head of R&D) mentioned that their recent Net Promoter Score was close to 100. He clapped Justin's shoulder. "All thanks to the loads you chose not to blow."

PJ was technically Justin's boss's boss.

Vijay mused over the idea of a chastity pledge, which was met by outsized shouts of "No way" and "Not for a million dollars." The people sitting outside the conference room looked up, envious of what was happening behind the glass doors. Justin would have traded places with any of them.

Soon, Vijay's enthusiasm gave out.

"The flesh is weak," he said, shoulders slumped. "I couldn't do what you do."

Stitched in the soft cotton praise was an errant thread, sharp as wire. The heads of his company did not admire him; they were astonished. His silence over his personal life was not a shield but a vacuum that they'd filled with their own stories. In their eyes, he had opted out of a basic human urge, and in doing so, had become less human. For his hard work to go unrecognized was one thing. For it to be labeled freakish was unacceptable.

"I don't talk about hooking up," Justin said. "Because I don't think you guys could handle the truth."

"Story time," said Thomas (head of Marketing). Over the years, he'd continued to grow out his beard, which carried the same pink tint as the cheeks hidden underneath.

"It started after college. I had no job, tons of free time. I was either working out or picking up people at the gym." Justin talked through another massive bite of his chickpea burger. "Let just say, a lot of threesomes. Sex in public bathrooms. I had an affair with a married woman."

"Our Justin's a homewrecker?" Vijay planted his hands on the conference table and thrust his chair back and forth. "You kinky devil."

"I mean, her husband wasn't fucking her." Justin grabbed a napkin and gave his mouth a hard wipe. His helpless anger four years ago had become a brittle shard he carried, like a splinter of glass wedged under his skin.

"Don't make him feel bad for having a good time." Brad emptied his bag of chips into his mouth. "My girlfriend once gave me a handjob in a movie theater. During *Twilight*."

"Big deal," Vijay said.

"You watched *Twilight*?" PJ snorted.

"Her little sister did. Did I mention she was sitting on the other side?"

More hooting ringed the room. Everyone wanted to compete for the wilder story. Thomas had had sex in a graveyard—"On a tombstone!"—and PJ had gotten a blowjob in a stairwell. He'd rushed to finish before his upstairs neighbor walked past his floor. "I was literally counting the steps."

"Here I thought you were spending every weekend with your mom." Vijay gripped the back of Justin's chair and shook it.

Justin stood up and brushed the crumbs off his lap. "Anyways, duty calls."

Inside the conference room, the leaders had looked at him with the same envy as their employees outside. Justin had made his way back to his desk, clutching his trash in both hands. The red onion from his half-eaten sandwich had stunk up the entire office. He'd left early and run the fifteen miles to his apartment.

The smell of onion permeated his car now too, along with garlic and fermented black beans, thanks to one of the buckets Gerald had brought from the restaurant.

"My mom hates this smell," Justin said. Gerald looked over in understandable surprise given that Justin had not spoken to him since lunch.

"What do you mean?" Gerald asked. "Your mother loves my house sauce."

"She doesn't like onions or garlic," Justin said.

Gerald chuckled. "Your mother eats onions and garlic all the time."

"She doesn't." Justin heard the strident tone in his voice. "You haven't noticed? That's why we never eat anything garlicky during lunch."

"Your mother grew up in Shandong. She eats onions and garlic." Gerald's eyes practically twinkled. "She worries they make her breath smell bad. I told her I *love* the smell. She's too embarrassed to eat them around anyone else."

"That doesn't make sense." When had Justin become "anyone else"?

"She's a complicated woman." Gerald rubbed his chin slowly. "Maybe someone told her she smelled bad."

Justin turned onto Vivian's street at too high a speed. A loud clatter sounded out from his trunk: Gerald's loose equipment, including, for some reason, a portable lazy Susan. The man couldn't be bothered to put his pans and ingredients in a box, and he had the confidence to call Justin's mother a "complicated woman." He thought getting his hair cut by the same person for ten years meant he'd known her for a decade.

After parking along the cul-de-sac, Justin opened the trunk and stacked the materials in the most efficient order. Gerald grabbed a spatula and a taro root. His hands effectively full, he went up to the house.

Vivian opened the door and greeted Gerald politely, calling him Uncle and showing him to the kitchen. Justin followed them and dropped the equipment on the counter.

"How're your parents liking Italy?" He hugged Vivian hello.

"They're sending fifty pictures an hour," she said. "I shouldn't have taught them about selfies." She swiped through her phone and showed her parents' faces blocking whatever view they'd thought they'd captured. "They might as well be at Costco. You think Gerald will take your mother on a vacation?"

"Please don't put that idea in his head," he said.

The doorbell rang, and they moved back out into the hallway. Vivian greeted Diana and Errol, who each held two bottles of wine.

"Anyone want an aperitif?" Diana waggled a bottle.

"God, yes," Vivian said. "Let me grab my Pepcid."

While the three of them rooted around for a wine opener, Justin split off. Part of him wanted to joke around. Another part was heavy with foreboding. This once familiar house was covered in plastic to prepare for the upcoming renovation. He batted his way through the maze-like rooms toward the bathroom.

Pushing through the partitions, he came face-to-face with a man on top of the toilet lid. His pants were around his knees. A needle was poised over his leg.

"Shit, sorry!" Justin moved to close the bathroom door and tangled himself in a loose sheaf of plastic.

"It's okay." The man stood, his face jarringly familiar. "It's insulin. I'm not shooting up or anything."

Very little had changed about Z, including his all-black clothes, although the color was softer, almost faded. Justin kept looking.

He needed a sign that he was in 2016, that Gerald's van hadn't burst into flames on the interstate and sent them into purgatory.

"What's going on?" he asked.

"I'm assisting Grace with the shoot," Z said. They both looked down at the pants around his knees.

"I should've knocked," Justin said.

"I should've locked." Z smiled.

Justin remembered the overlapping bottom teeth, the dimple in Z's right cheek.

Z cleared his throat. "I'm glad you're here." He sat back down on the toilet lid, looking for some place to put down the needle. "I wanted to say I'm sorry. About the stuff with Carrie. And the cellphone footage."

"It's okay." A lingering question resolved itself. "You cut me out of the clip. I appreciate that."

"I wished I'd never posted it." Z's head was bent, his hand in his hair. "I wasn't thinking how it would affect anyone except Carrie. It was like I was obsessed. Looking back . . ." His other hand jerked the needle through the air. "I don't recognize that person."

"I can understand that." Justin avoided looking at the needle, his stomach turning at the memory of another bathroom. He should get out, but he'd grown too dizzy. He closed his eyes and leaned his shoulder against the doorframe.

"Are you afraid of needles too?" Z had a soft, dry laugh. With his eyes closed, Justin thought of the little Zen garden on his office desk, the way the sand rasped through the hand-sized rake.

"You have to do that every day?" Justin opened his eyes a fraction to look at Z.

Z shook his head. "Three times a day. Mostly, I'm on autopilot. But sometimes, if I'm in a new place, it's like I remember what I'm doing." His hand hesitated over his leg. "Do you mind if we keep talking?"

"Well, you're better off without Carrie," Justin said.

Z's laugh grew raspier, as if he knew what Justin was really asking and he was afraid he had no answer. "You know, she's famous again. She got her happy ending."

Justin didn't know what had become of Raul and Ingrid, if they'd stayed together or broken up. He thought of Master Yi's words. *Pay a little blood now.* He hadn't; he'd stayed, and years later his socks were covered in rusty patches, twenty-mile runs blistering his feet to pulp. He bled and he bled and every morning, he woke up feeling no less cursed.

He was jolted by Z grabbing his hand.

"Sorry," Z said. "You looked kind of sad."

"I'm okay." Justin gave Z's hand a squeeze before slipping out of his grasp.

"You know, Carrie used to do my shots."

"I always thought she'd make a good nurse." Justin liked making Z laugh. He hardly had to try.

"Now or never." Z flexed his fingers and jabbed the needle into his thigh. He quickly swabbed the area and put the needle in a bag labeled BIOHAZARD.

"I don't know if Carrie will get what she deserves," Justin said. He was no longer feeling nauseous. "That doesn't mean you won't."

"She wasn't well." Z looked at the bathroom wall. "That's what I have to remind myself."

When they made their way toward the kitchen, Justin could still feel the weight of Z's hand, and the jingle his belt had made when he'd buckled it.

"Uncle Gerald," Vivian was saying sweetly. "We need to shoot soon. I have to get back to New York. Z, tell him we don't need to fill the entire table with food."

"Six dishes is more than enough," Z jumped in. "Especially with the lazy Susan I saw in the hall. Did you bring that? Very smart. I can mount a camera on it."

Justin joined Diana and Errol, who were refilling their wine. He accepted the glass Errol offered.

"We were talking about your dad." Diana swirled the wine in

her glass. "I'm sorry I didn't reach out. I didn't know if you wanted me to."

"That he died?" Justin had absorbed the shock of his father's passing with ease. This absence was no different from the one he'd shouldered for years. At work, people kept expecting him to cry. They'd encouraged it. He'd taken a few days off to seem normal. He'd found an ultramarathon a few states over to pass the time.

"*Fuck you*," Errol pretended to read off his phone. "That was probably the last thing I texted you."

"What he means," Diana cut in, "is that we've been out of touch. I know you weren't close with your dad. I thought you wouldn't want to make a big deal of it."

"Thank you." Justin pressed his thumb into his chin. "Nobody else gets that."

Vivian came over. "Justin, Grace wants to see you in the dining room. To make sure the seating works with the lights and cameras."

Justin passed by the adjoining kitchen on his way to the dining room. The constant cleaver-thunking and wok-banging made Gerald sound as if he were pretending to cook. Before he could peek in, Grace stuck her head out into the hall. Whatever he'd planned to say to her vanished at the sight of her bleached, buzzed scalp.

"You like it?" she said ruefully. "It's my deadline to figure out what I'm doing with my life, before I have to face reality."

Justin followed her into a room crowded by cameras and large white boxes on tripods, which Grace said would supply their light. Cords snaked like vines across the floor, taped to the carpet. Grace pointed to a chair, and he sat down. She went behind the camera that faced him and adjusted its position.

"How have you been?" she asked.

The scream of a blender replaced the banging woks. Justin wasn't sure if he was allowed to move. He flicked his eyes over to the kitchen. "The more time I spend with him, the less I understand my mother."

"I think your mom knows what she's doing." Grace looked conspiratorial. "Apparently Gerald used to bring flowers to the salon, and she told him to spend his money on Blüm hair products."

"Who told you that?" Justin jerked up and banged his shin into a table leg.

"My mom," Grace said. "They're always on WeChat together."

Justin was struck by Diana's famous phrase—*Why didn't I know that?* He crossed his arms. "I'm surprised you and your mom are talking."

In the next breath, he regretted this. When he'd read the profile, he'd tried to imagine speaking about his mother that way. The thought had followed him for months, at turns horrifying and alluring.

Instead of bristling, Grace scratched her head. "Not at first, but I've learned more about her in the past six months than in the thirty years before. It's the first time we've been able to be honest."

This stung him, like antiseptic on an invisible cut.

"Are you okay?" Grace was too observant.

In the kitchen, Gerald erupted into a coughing fit that rivaled the sound of the blender.

"We're good here, right? Because I need to check on that." Justin jabbed his hand at the noise. "Is he trying to blow up the kitchen or something?" He rushed into the hall and threw open the kitchen door.

He was blown over by a gust of heat that burned his throat, his nose, his eyes. Gerald, through hacking coughs, waved at him in alarm.

"There's too much spice! Get out!" In his hands was an industrial blender, shining red with broken chilies. Justin couldn't stop coughing, his eyes overwhelmed by tears.

"What are you doing?" He grabbed the blender from Gerald to throw in the trash, and his face was raked over by the fumes rising from the blender's open top.

Gerald's meaty palms clapped down on his shoulders. The

blender was no longer in Justin's hands. He wiped his eyes and the fire in them grew hotter. Someone put a wet towel over his face, and he was led out of the kitchen. Gerald clucked in his ear about the dangers of Sichuan chili peppers.

"I'm used to them," Gerald said. "And you heard how I was hacking. You'll be fine. Your face will burn for a little longer."

Gerald pushed Justin down, and he felt the sofa receive him. He kicked a little when Gerald tried to position his legs across the cushions, but he submitted to lying down, the cold towel covering his face. His eyes pulsed and leaked hot tears.

"Will you make sure he's okay?" Gerald asked Grace. His heavy footfalls receded out of hearing.

"I'm fine," Justin said. His nose was stuffed up. "Go back to work."

"Z will take care of it."

Justin peeled off the towel to see his way out of the room. His face burned too much without it. "This is going to ruin the dinner shoot."

"It'll be fine," Grace said. "Your eyes might be swollen. If you're self-conscious, we can put some spoons in the freezer and bring the swelling down."

"I was trying to get out of doing this," Justin said. Frozen spoons did sound nice.

Grace's laugh came from below him. He pictured her sitting on the ground beside the couch. "You should talk to your mom about your dad."

Justin said, "Are you serious?"

"She might surprise you." A rustle from Grace shifting on the carpet.

"You get to say that." Justin pressed the towel hard against his face. "You won't be the one who deals with what happens."

The burn had died down to a dull throb. His entire face pulsed.

He thought about that conversation with his mother years ago when she'd cut his hair in the basement. *He will always be your father. Just like he will always be my husband.* The inexplicable principles of her own heartbreak had not only frozen time, but also frozen her within it. After his own break-up with Ingrid and Raul, however, Justin had come to understand.

He too had become consumed after they'd asked him to leave. Raul had sat him down one Saturday morning, a few weeks after their trip to New Orleans. Justin had quit his job to be able to go, which he'd announced to Raul and Ingrid at the airport. The entire trip had been awkward, the three of them talking politely about the food, the jazz, the houses, and when they'd returned Raul had been reluctant to show Justin that month's training schedule. The day Raul had knocked on his bedroom door, Justin had known. They'd never treated his room like a separate space before.

"We weren't ready," Raul said. "We were too new to this. Opening things up. There's too much we need to fix about ourselves. We shouldn't have let you quit BOD. I have other trainers you could work for. I'd be happy to refer you."

As if Raul didn't know that everything Justin had done was meant to make this conversation impossible. He'd staked it all: no job, no friends, nowhere to stay. He was as dependent on them as a child.

"Take however long you need to find a place for yourself." Raul's hair was unstyled that morning, Justin remembered. It had looked like a misshapen helmet. "We're happy to pay the rent for the first month if you need. We're going to make sure you're okay."

"Where's Ingrid?" Justin interrupted. "Why isn't she here?"

Raul looked surprised. "She felt—we felt that, well, it started with you and me."

"I need to talk to her." A low, desperate part of him had thought that emotional Ingrid would be easier to persuade.

Raul had sent Ingrid in. She'd looked small and defenseless, sitting cross-legged on the ground. This tactic had felt familiar although it would be days before Justin would tie it to Grace.

"Don't forgive us." While Raul offered their explanations, Ingrid had taken their blame with so much fury that Justin felt the need to comfort her. "We did a horrible thing." Her nails dug into the palm of her hand. She pounded her fist into her head.

"I'll be okay," he said, afraid she'd hurt herself. "I knew this wasn't permanent."

Being dumped by one person was like someone tearing down a wall in your house. But two walls? Two contingent walls? Everything had fallen around him. The first night in his new studio, he'd been so sick with grief that he'd cut a thin line into his stomach. The blood he'd been too afraid to shed at Master Yi's first warning had welled up on his skin with ease. His head had cleared. He could breathe. The next morning, he threw out anything with a blade. He could no longer trust himself. Out of work, he ran every day to keep himself busy, coming back to the apartment only to sleep. When he met Vijay for coffee to beg back his job, he'd lost enough weight that he'd had to pretend he'd gotten pneumonia.

The first time Raul had broken up with him, Justin had stuck around like a dog locked out of a house. The second time, he knew better. He left himself no room to think about the pain. The same way he rarely thought of his old group of friends, or Grace, or his father. He'd learned to run his head empty. To lose himself in work. He and his mother were the same. When fire burned you, you didn't dive back in; you starved it of any oxygen.

"She stays loyal to him for twenty years, won't hear a bad word, and as soon as he's dead, she's with Gerald?" Saying this aloud gave Justin unexpected satisfaction, like scratching a mosquito bite he'd been gallantly ignoring.

Grace pushed her finger against the side of his head. "You're too protective." This wasn't a compliment.

"I thought my mom was through with relationships," Justin said. "I mean, I stopped trying to date four years ago . . ." His heartbeat bounced into his ears, saying those words out loud. "She's never dated at all. Why'd she wait this long? Did she think she was married to my dad? It makes no sense."

"Our parents rarely do."

"I'm worried," he said. Who else could he tell? Vijay? Thomas? "When my mom told me about Gerald, I was against him before we'd even met. You know how she's been . . . not depressed. Just a sad person. For as long as I can remember. What kind of guy would be attracted to that? Is that awful for me to think?"

In the next room, Gerald was calling that dinner was done.

"Your mom isn't the same person she was when you were nine." The couch sank from where Grace lifted herself up. "Besides, if she were as sad as you say, do you think she'd want you to be like her?"

Justin's embarrassment shimmered over his body like heat. All these years later, Grace still had the keys to his house. If she asked him, really asked him, about Ingrid and Raul, Justin wasn't sure he'd be able to stop talking.

"By the way." When Grace put her hand on his shoulder, he didn't lean away. "Z asked if you were single."

Justin took the towel off his face. Grace had left the room. The cloth was warm in his hand.

* * *

Gerald unveiled the dinner, and Justin noticed that Vivian and Diana held back their praise, a show of loyalty that was touching. Errol complimented every elaborate plate, from the fried whole fish to the duck stuffed with sticky rice. Grace was also kind, telling Gerald the food would look great on camera.

The lazy Susan was almost too big for the table. Everyone looked at the food to avoid looking at each other.

"What does the director want us to do?" Diana asked Grace.

Z gestured that the cameras were rolling. Justin reached for Vivian's plate.

"You don't have to do that," Vivian said.

"Justin's always been the polite one." Diana passed her plate up too. "Extra duck please. And don't skimp on the stuffing."

The table remained quiet, and the sound of the serving spoon scraping was interrupted by a colossal sneeze from Gerald in the kitchen. A small fit of giggles rippled through the group.

Then Grace said, "Remember how we met in fourth grade?"

Like a relay, each person knew when their part was coming. Diana took the first leg, and then passed to Errol, who did his impression of Warren Cho.

"It's not racist if a Chinese person does a Korean accent," he said. Diana looked at Grace.

"We can cut it out in editing." Grace gestured to Vivian, who gamely told the story of the chase. She detailed the rocks flying, and how, when Diana and Errol had first sprinted away, Vivian was sure she'd been left behind for a sacrifice. She'd chased after them out of pure spite.

"I wanted to beat the shit out of you guys," Vivian said.

Vivian's part had everyone laughing the hardest—something Justin hadn't remembered. Perhaps she'd changed the way she told the story. Vivian hadn't been the funny one. She was the peace-keeper like him. She smoothed the way for others to be the star. Now, she was radiant from the attention in the room. She was Vivian and she was also different from the Vivian he knew.

It was Justin's turn. "I didn't see them." Z directed one of the cameras toward him. "I heard them. They were screaming their heads off. I went out to the garage to see what was happening."

His mother would leave the garage open in case her clients wanted to park inside. He'd crept down the garage stairs to spy before he recognized who was screaming, and why.

"The way I saw it, I could do nothing and watch them get stoned from the safety of my house, or I could hide them and be on Warren's shit list forever."

Diana threw her arm around him. "Aren't we lucky you saved our lives?"

"Actually"—Justin looked over at Grace—"I wasn't the one who made that decision."

He hadn't been alone in the garage. He and Grace had been spying together. Watching Diana, Vivian, and Errol come over the hill, Justin had tried to sneak back inside. Grace had grabbed him by the collar.

"Tell them to run in here," she'd said, and shoved him out of the garage.

Justin had stumbled onto the driveway and sprinted back to safety. In his memory, he hadn't said anything. Later, he'd told everyone that he'd shouted, "In here!" No one had questioned him or wondered how he'd gotten the garage door to close when the switch was all the way up the stairs.

"Why didn't we know that?" Diana asked. She looked from Justin to Grace. "You acted like you were too stuck up to hang out with us."

Grace fluffed the hair on her head. "I'd promised my mom that I wouldn't get too close. She thought you'd only want to be my friend to get our secrets for your parents."

That was why she would avoid the group when they came over after school, and hiss at them to be quiet. She'd been afraid that if Justin's mother found out, she would tell Grace's mother, who would force them apart. While the group played in the living room, Grace would sneak down to eavesdrop on their games. Sometimes, she brought a book into the kitchen and pretended to read, until she couldn't help getting involved in their fun.

"I blamed you for being like your parents, but look at me. I believed anything my mother said."

"It's pretty crazy that for two years we went to your house every day after school," Vivian said. "While our parents thought we were at home studying."

"Well, guess what Justin's mom told me yesterday when we were back in the house. *I miss hearing you kids laughing upstairs.*"

Diana nodded at the looks of surprise around the table. "We tried so hard to be quiet. She knew we were there the entire time!"

What else did his mother already know? Justin looked at Z and felt a stab of improbable hope. For the first time in years, he had no desire to check his phone. He noticed Diana wasn't checking hers either. She was too busy shouting, "Guess what I found out about my dad? He's a *huge* gossip! Way bigger than my mom."

They were aware of their real lives waiting after this meal, but they continued to suspend their disbelief. Justin wanted Gerald to bring out sliced oranges, toothpicks, cups of green tea. This was why the parents' parties shared the same endings. Any excuse to stay at the table was necessary when people enjoyed each other's company but could not take it for granted. They had work the next day, children rubbing their eyes, plates unwashed in their own sinks at home. Still, they'd stayed for another round of cut fruit, another bag of melon seeds, submitting to the hospitality. Sitting in their parents' places, they had not prepared for this kind of silence to fall, not for lack of things to discuss, but for want of a reason to stay and keep talking.

"I think it's time," Grace said. She reached underneath the table and pulled out her laptop. Z moved a camera directly behind her, pausing to re-angle the ones on either side of her chair. He changed the camera's shutter speeds to avoid the flickering of the computer screen.

When the setup was finished, Diana went to stand by Z. Slowly, the rest of them followed. Grace navigated to the website and dove through the layers, going deeper behind the scenes of her public image until, in plain type and with little fanfare, the word "Delete" came into view.

"Are you sure?" Justin couldn't help asking, and Diana hushed him without much force. They'd seen those remarkable numbers. Once-in-a-lifetime proof that Grace had done something special, something people strove and starved to achieve, and like some moral in a story they were too young to understand, she was throwing that success away for a future with no guarantees.

"Ready?" Grace asked. The group took a collective breath to answer.

"All good on my end," Z said.

Their breath released in an embarrassed quiver, right when Grace hit the button.

Would she turn around, cry, shake, laugh? They watched her as if they were one body. When she did face them, Grace looked the same, if a little tired. The way a hostess did after a party. She thanked them for the time they'd given. Justin clapped, and the others joined in. At least they'd gotten a second shot at a proper ending.

Gerald cleared the table and the group helped Grace and Z dismantle the equipment. They worked quickly to the sounds of Gerald washing the dishes.

While the others piled equipment into the van, Justin went back to the dining room to reset the chairs. A needless task, but this room had held them together. The tablecloth remained and the story of the night could be read from the stains. Of course, everyone was right outside, making conversation around the van. Yet here he was, apart from the others.

Z appeared in the doorway, holding the chunky Nikon that he'd also used to take photos during the shoot. "That was a great dinner."

"I ate too much." Justin rubbed his stomach like a fool.

"I thought you said you guys weren't friends anymore." Z clicked through the photos, holding the camera display close to his face. When he found what he was looking for, he moved next to Justin. He tilted the camera. "This is my favorite."

It was the video he'd taken when the food had been cleared away. Z had mounted his Nikon on the lazy Susan and spun the wheel while the camera was recording. Their faces came and went like a carnival ride, the equipment suddenly visible in the background. Z sped through the video, which made it more dizzying.

"Here it is." He let the rest of the video play. The lazy Susan slowed down. The group had forgotten its presence because Errol had spilled water all over himself. Each of them had sprung into action, napkins in hand, and begun patting him dry in unison. When they'd realized, they'd sunk onto him, laughing. The camera crept past the huddle until all that remained was the laughter.

Z's dimple flashed. Like a teardrop in the sand. Something clicked on in Justin's brain. The urge to touch Z's skin. His entire body responded as if tugged by little strings. He kissed the dimple. When Z smiled, the dimple sank in deeper. He gripped Z's chin. Their lips pressed together. Z held Justin's head right where his cowlick sprang out. Raul used to smooth down that insistent part when Justin got up in the mornings. Ingrid would always mess it back up. More memories came, too close and too soon. Justin jerked his head back. His chest ached where it had pressed against Z's camera. He wiped the sweat from his forehead, but more poured out. Z's hand was on him. Justin moved away.

"This isn't for me," he said. The pressure in his chest lifted. "I'm sorry."

Z looked down, his hair concealing his face, and he gripped his camera like it might hide him. Justin remembered that night in New York, at the Western bar, when he'd watched Z bloom and wilt in a matter of seconds. Before Justin could apologize, a clatter of metal rang out.

Vivian, Diana, and Errol were crowded in the doorway behind him, picking up the equipment they'd dropped. Caught, Diana pushed the others back into the hall. Z had already shoved past them, his body hunched small. The front door slammed shut a few seconds after.

"We didn't see anything!" Diana shouted.

"We'll be outside," Vivian added.

"Sorry we cockblocked you, dude," Errol said on their way out the door.

This shook a laugh from Justin, like hidden fruit from a tree. None of them had seemed surprised. This would have horrified him eight years ago. Now he wished he could enjoy the relief of all of them knowing. For that kiss to be what his friends thought they'd seen, an intimate moment interrupted.

The pull to touch Z had been shocking after years of feeling nothing at all. A different kind of intrusion. Every nerve in Justin's body sung and stung at once. That moment of stillness, pressed against Z's chest, had taken Justin farther than four years of motion. What terror he'd felt, to be flung into those memories. He couldn't separate the good from the pain. He'd tried to scramble back to safety. Now he knew it was too late. He couldn't forget again if he tried. He remembered the first time he'd kissed Ingrid, the way their bodies could speak. With Raul, how fear had nearly swallowed him whole before desire had saved him. He missed them so much, but most of all, he'd missed all this *feeling*. He wanted to touch Z again. He wanted to cry. He wanted, he wanted, he wanted.

* * *

Justin walked into the kitchen for water. Gerald was wiping down the counters with a rag that must be making them dirtier.

Drinking from the tap, Justin felt a little better. His chest was less tight, and he could breathe in the smells of the hot kitchen. This close, Gerald was a pungent mix of alliums and cooking oil.

"My mom really likes garlic?" Justin asked.

"She loves it." Gerald's face was made for smiling. Like a dog, his mouth fell open when he was happy.

Justin's life was not the only one he'd frozen. He thought of the parties his mother had missed, and the ones she would no longer have to. Without him noticing, her life had gotten easier. She had friends. She'd paid off her house and cut back on her hours. She was in love with Gerald. She would be okay without Justin. Maybe the question had been if Justin would be okay without her.

Out in the dwindling sunlight, Justin looked at the line the others had formed to pass the equipment up to the van. He went to the front and peered through the open side door. Only Grace was inside.

"Where's Z?" he asked.

She swiped her nonexistent hair out of her eyes. "He called a ride to the bus station. Said he forgot he had to be back in New York early. I told him we'd be ready to go in an hour or so. He was pretty insistent."

"So he's gone." Justin leaned against the sliding door of the van.

Grace studied him. "Holy shit," she said. "Did you guys . . . ?"

"Yup," Errol said, and Diana elbowed him in the side.

"It's not a big deal," Justin said. "I just wanted to apologize for something."

Vivian broke out of line. "You've got to catch him!"

Grace crawled out of the van, waving her hands. "Stop, stop, stop."

"There's stuff to pack." Justin picked up a loop of cords.

Diana pushed her way to the front of the car. "If you need to get there fast, you should have Errol drive." She climbed into the shotgun seat before Justin could stop her. "I'll navigate. What's the address?"

"I don't know." Grace slammed the van door shut from inside. "It's a Megabus. There's two different stations."

Vivian had taken the second row next to Grace. Justin was pushed into the back. Over the headrest, he could see Vivian search for something on her phone. "I think the easiest thing is if I give the headquarters a call."

They left with half of Grace's equipment lying on the lawn, the front door to Vivian's house wide open.

"I bet some neighbor sends my parents a picture of their front yard," Vivian said while waiting on hold.

"Gerald will deal with it," Grace said. "I already messaged him on WeChat."

Vivian sweet-talked the operator into finding Z's ticket form, and Diana rerouted them to Gaithersburg when she heard the address. While Vivian was transferred to the bus driver's cell, Errol raced through a yellow that had technically turned red seconds ago. He claimed to know where the speed traps were from driving his mother around.

"Hi, hello!" Vivian turned around and gave Justin a thumbs-up. "You're the driver of Bus 33C leaving Gaithersburg for New York Penn Station?"

"Can't you drive any faster?" Diana said to Errol.

"This van won't go over sixty," he said. He pressed the pedal until the engine growled. "Never mind, sixty-five."

Everyone was in their element while Justin sat useless in the back. No one had asked if this was what he wanted. He should shout at them to stop, to turn the car around. He didn't know what they were expecting. Z was some guy he'd kissed. This wasn't a fucking rom-com. An entire bus full of people would be forced to wait because his friends couldn't stay out of his business.

Nothing he thought could interrupt the momentum thrumming through his veins. The words wouldn't leave his mouth. Looking in the rearview mirror, Justin remembered the image of his friends shrinking into the distance the night he'd raced out of New York. Back then he'd thought that they were chasing after his car, that he was driving it home, but the van they were in was not what was hurtling them down this busy road, and Z was not their destination. The force of his friends was what propelled them. Seven years ago, that same force had pushed him to run. Now, against the odds, across all that space and time, the distance between them was closing.

Errol swerved through cars and Diana hit his blinker for him.

Vivian, her eye on Diana's navigation app, told the driver, "We'll be there in two, no, one minute. Can't you wait an extra minute?"

Diana crowed the last instruction, "Turn left up ahead and we're there!"

An idling coach bus heaved exhaust into the air. The driver was in his seat, phone to his ear. Errol screeched the van into the space right in front of the bus.

"Now, you don't have to park there," the voice on Vivian's phone scolded.

"We'll be quick. We need to give our friend something he forgot." Vivian turned around to face Justin. "What're you waiting for?" She pushed the van door open and shoved him out.

Justin knew the role he was meant to play. He climbed the steps and apologized to the driver. Z sat in an aisle seat, ten or fifteen rows down. He had headphones on and was looking at his phone. For the moment, Justin remained unseen. He could leave, tell the driver he'd gotten the wrong bus, and Z would never have to know.

"Do you all have tickets?" the driver asked.

Justin turned around to find Diana, and behind her Vivian and Errol. He couldn't believe they'd followed him onto the bus, and yet he'd been sure they would. He'd been certain of this, even as he didn't know what would happen with Z, or how he might mess it up. His friends kept pointing ahead, as if he didn't know that Z had noticed, as if their noisy, insistent company hadn't disrupted everyone on the bus. He was so frustrated and so glad. They would never leave him alone. They would be there whether he liked it or not.

Z had stood up. His mouth was slightly open. He took his headphones off. Justin glanced back at the group.

"Ask him if he's sure he needs to leave," Diana whispered.

"Tell him you're sorry," Vivian added.

"There's a new karaoke place around the corner." Maybe Errol had already lost interest. Or maybe he was a genius after all.

"We're going to karaoke." Justin faced Z again. "Do you want to come?"

Z looked confused. The other people on the bus grumbled. The driver stood up. "Hey now, people have places to go."

Then Diana said, "Z, you have to!"

She nudged Vivian, who chorused, "Please!"

Errol joined in. "Even I'm going."

The bus driver blinked at the sudden energy of the group. "My man, I think you have to." Somehow even he'd caught on. Justin felt painfully obvious, grinning as widely as he was.

"Okay." Z bent down to grab his bag, and when he stood up, his dimple winked.

They jogged off the bus and into the early evening light. The hours left in the day felt expansive, pushing Monday morning further off to the side. His friends debated what songs they would sing. Grace took out her phone and started recording. Justin covered his face with his hand and Z's.

"Say hello to your future selves," Grace said. She'd turned her phone around.

Under the glow of the setting sun, they saw themselves reflected in the screen, waving at whoever waited on the other side.

The New York Times

Grace Li, From Canceled to Copied

By Rachel Liao

SEPTEMBER 16, 2016

Type in MeMeReproductions.com and you might think you'd wandered into an alternate online world. From the familiar white-and-red color palette to the bubble letters and simple grid-like lines, the fan-created website is an exact replica of acclaimed YouTube creator Grace Li's channel, known by her handle MeMe Productions. The website was created soon after Ms. Li deleted her account two months ago on July 20, in the company of her original *Bad Asians* actors—Diana Zhang, Vivian Wang, Justin Yu, and Errol Chen—shocking her 1.5 million subscribers. Ms. Li, who is working on her first documentary feature, following her critically acclaimed short *A Strange Quirk of Human Nature,* told *The New York Times* that she had no idea how devoted her fans remained, especially after her controversial profile. She is dedicating her feature to these long-time viewers, who have often wondered how autobiographical her videos are. While she's secretive about the rest, she was willing to drop a tongue-in-cheek reference that no fan will miss.

"I'm calling the documentary *Bad Asian.*"

Ms. Li's channel's deletion has kicked off a startling trend of digital collectors . . .

You've reached your limit of free articles.
Already a subscriber? **Log in.**

ACKNOWLEDGMENTS

This book began on a walk around a man-made lake. Thank you to Elizabeth Fang for the inspiring conversation. Thank you also to my early readers: Gina Balibrera, Sumita Chakraborty, Alana DeRiggi, Phoebe Gloekner, Barbara Jones, Jennifer Metzker, Emily Nagin, Ali Shapiro, Robin Yang, and Angel Di Zhang, with special thanks to Julie Buntin, Lydi Conklin, Sam Krowchenko, Tim Trieu, and Maya West. To Yin Li, Hongying Wang, and Christopher Wang— your love and support make everything possible. To S.Y., who is too wonderful for words. And to S, my emotional support donkey; my kindest, smartest reader; and my best friend.

This book was enriched by multiple experts. Thank you to Constant Motion Productions, especially Tom Wille for sharing his experience as a filmmaker from the 2000s to today, and Ben Douma for letting me into the editing room. To Michelle Chua, Richard Gadsden, and Aislinn Toohey, who are all excellent law-yers. To Larry Shinagawa, for our conversation on racial identity in Montgomery County. And to Amanda Wang, for answering my questions about Asian sororities at the University of Maryland. Any and all errors are my own.

Sharing excerpts from this book throughout the years made it possible to keep going. Thank you to the generous in-person and online audiences of the Sewanee Writers' Conference, Lite-rati Bookstore, Mendocino Coast Writers' Conference, Kenyon

Review Winter Workshop, Rock and Roll Reading Series, Good Words Reading Series, Kansas State Visiting Writers Program, Hollins University Reading and Lecture Series, and Kundiman Writers Workshop. Special thanks to anyone who turned on their camera, and also to the Ann Arbor Book Crew for A/B testing the title.

Thank you to the brilliant Adam Eaglin, who read more drafts than I can count and always knew how to make the next one better, and Vivian Herzog for her sharp feedback. Retha Powers, Laura Macaulay, and Juliet Garcia, for believing in what this book was and could be, and giving me the runway to take that leap. And a huge thank you to Leela Gebo, for all her help. Thank you to the entire Holt team, including Janel Brown, Allegra Green, Sarah Bode, Catryn Silbersack, Carla Benton, Jason Reigal, Vi-An Nguyen, Nicolette Seeback Ruggiero, Amanda Hong, NaNá Stoelzle, Kayley Hoffman, and Meryl Levavi, with special thanks to Laura Hartman Maestro for the beautiful neighborhood map.

Finally, it is a pleasure to be able to share all the works that enriched mine and recommend them wholeheartedly:

Kids These Days by Malcolm Harris

The Overachievers by Alexandra Robbins

Driven to Distraction by Edward M. Hallowell and John J. Ratey

The Group by Mary McCarthy

Fire Shut Up in My Bones by Charles M. Blow

Bi Men: Coming Out Every Which Way edited by Ron Jackson Suresha and Pete Chvany

Robert Altman: The Oral Biography by Mitchell Zuckoff

Mike Nichols: A Life by Mark Harris

Alright, Alright, Alright: An Oral History of Richard Linklater's Dazed and Confused by Melissa Maerz

Every celebrity profile written by Taffy Brodesser-Akner

AVAILABLE AND COMING SOON FROM

ONE

AN IMPRINT OF PUSHKIN PRESS

ONE – an imprint of Pushkin Press – is the home of our English language publishing from around the world. The list is as varied as it is distinct, encompassing new voices and established names, fiction and non-fiction. Our stories range from dystopian tales to comic ones, prizewinning novels to memoirs. And what makes them ONE? Compelling writing, unique voices, great stories.

THE SECRET LIVES OF CHURCH LADIES
Deesha Philyaw

SMALL FIRES
Rebecca May Johnson

THE FAMILY CHAO
Lan Samantha Chang

DINNER PARTY SERVICE
Sarah Gilmartin

NATIONAL DISH
Anya von Bremzen

THE BATHYSPHERE BOOK
Brad Fox

FLATLANDS
Sue Hubbard

THE FISHERMEN
Chigozie Obioma

ALL YOU CAN EVER KNOW
Nicole Chung

HANGMAN
Maya Binyam

NUMBER ONE CHINESE RESTAURANT
Lillian Li

SHE WOULD BE KING
THE DRAGONS, THE GIANT, THE WOMEN
Wayétu Moore

ONLY KILLERS AND THIEVES
DUST OFF THE BONES
Paul Howarth

SYMPATHY
Olivia Sudjic

DINNER WITH EDWARD
Isabel Vincent

LITTLE GODS
Meng Jin

THE OTHER'S GOLD
Elizabeth Ames

MACHINE
Susan Steinberg

SHE COME BY IT NATURAL
Sarah Smarsh

IN THE HOUSE IN THE DARK OF THE WOODS
Laird Hunt

THE INLAND SEA
Madeleine Watts

THE EXTRA MAN
Jonathan Ames